"A FAVORITE OF
DISCERNING THRILLER FANS"
Publishers Weekly

AMBROSE USHER FINDS BEAUTIES AND A BEAST IN BOSTON.

GEORGE FLETCHER

Bluff, bossy, big . . . and very dangerous. His investments may topple Britain's shaky economy, especially if his cash comes from the KGB.

GLORIA

Wonderful, wacky, beautiful . . . and dead. She was Fletcher's first wife. Was she also his first victim?

ALYSS

Serene, sexy, raven-tressed . . . and available. Does this attractive art expert want Ambrose Usher as a sweetheart, or as an ally?

CLAIRE

Blonde, bonnie, bewitching . . . and scared. She is Fletcher's second bride, and she just found out what happened to his first.

"Devotees of Gervase Fen, Edmund Crispin's erudite and irrepressible Oxford don/detective, will warm to the biting wit and intelligence of Oxford philosopher Ambrose Usher."
Booklist

Avon Books are available at special quantity discounts for bulk purchases for sales promotions, premiums, fund raising or educational use. Special books, or book excerpts can also be created to fit specific needs.

For details write or telephone the office of the Director of Special Markets, Avon Books, 959 8th Avenue, New York, New York 10019, 212-262-3361.

A TREASURY ALARM

JOCELYN DAVEY

AVON
PUBLISHERS OF BARD, CAMELOT, DISCUS AND FLARE BOOKS

All the characters and events portrayed in this story
are fictitious.

AVON BOOKS
A division of
The Hearst Corporation
959 Eighth Avenue
New York, New York 10019

Copyright © 1976 by Jocelyn Davey
Published by arrangement with Walker and Company
Library of Congress Catalog Card Number: 80-52081
ISBN: 0-380-58917-6

All rights reserved, which includes the right to
reproduce this book or portions thereof in any form
whatsoever except as provided by the U. S. Copyright Law.
For information address Walker and Company,
720 Fifth Avenue, New York, New York, 10019

First Avon Printing, April, 1982

AVON TRADEMARK REG. U. S. PAT. OFF. AND IN
OTHER COUNTRIES, MARCA REGISTRADA, HECHO EN
U. S. A.

Printed in the U. S. A.

WFH 10 9 8 7 6 5 4 3 2 1

Qui non son conosciuto
Ne vo' farmi conoscere
Per questo ho le mie gran ragioni

(I am not known here
Nor do I wish to be
For which I have the best of reasons)

Rossini: *The Barber of Seville*

I

AMBROSE was being difficult. Normally, when the Foreign Office pried him out of Oxford to lend a hand on some little problem overseas, he went along willingly enough, even if he launched first into a token display of reluctance for the sake of good form. But this time he had begun the head-shaking almost from the word go, and in a style which seemed to indicate that he really meant it. The Treasury had been mentioned as an interested party, and it was this, apparently, that stimulated a mood of dissent. "No, no, cannot be done, impossible, grown out of these frolics, too many duties at Harvard, and a different view now, no, no, all over. . . ."

"But Ambrose, you always seemed to enjoy. . . ."

"No, no, forsake my cage, my rope of sands, shake hands forever, cancel all our vows. . . ."

Hepworth had taken him to lunch at the Travellers'. It was a ritual that Ambrose accepted: and at least this part worked as usual. From the moment he climbed the steps to enter the modest-looking doorway, the word seemed to go round — "Ambrose Usher's here," and the diplomats young and old were buzzing around him. After all, he had tutored half of them at Oxford, and in the other half, bereft in youth, had made up for it in service, especially in the United States, where most of them got a post sooner or later, and where Ambrose constantly dropped in. They all had their own stories of him and did their own imitations of the bubbling torrent that was his conversation, with its inexhaustible anecdotage in a tone that was both affectionate and dismissive — fireworks that never just trailed away in smoke but set off bangs and sparkles endlessly from all who stood by. Everyone, it was assumed, loved it equally — the

Queen, Brezhnev, Agatha Christie, Dr. Kissinger: perhaps they all did their own imitations afterwards like everybody else. Was the Travellers' always as cheerful as this? Probably not. At the bar, at Ambrose's table, people stopped by to say hello in the lively style that he somehow instigated. At this stage Ambrose simply sailed on, gathering gossip while he might, multiplying it all, as it was provided, with a wild kind of allusiveness. In this mood the world, after all, might be something to smile over. The idiots, poseurs and bunglers were grist to the laughter mill.

The joy of having Ambrose around was not that he fitted in but that he stood out. In the midst of these bright young men, for the most part fair and elegant, he was a change — a squat, dark-haired, rather untidy figure, a high domed forehead saying one thing, large brown eyes, unspectacled and clearly romantic, saying another. Against the drawling English that they all exuded, whether by birth or affectation, he rattled off his comments with a faint trace of accent that they all assumed was Serbian. He had, in fact, arrived in England from his native Uscze — whence his family name — at the age of three: but Europe was there in the background. It made the F.O. jobs seem natural, even if he always made a fuss at agreeing to do them.

It was over coffee, in a quiet corner, that Hepworth had started to explain: and if anyone could jolly Ambrose along it was surely he, coming as he did not so much from the Foreign Office as from "the Terrace," that limbo world of Intelligence — or was it Counter-Intelligence? — where things undefined — indefinable — carried with them a certain appeal to the romantic in Ambrose. No one was quite sure how Hepworth could be both in the Foreign Office publicly — his name was in the List — and privately at the Terrace, halfway, as it were, between Hell and Purgatory. "Art thou truly that Virgil?" Ambrose felt like saying to him when Hepworth took him by the hand on one of those conducted jaunts.

Yet this time it wasn't working, and Hepworth was genuinely puzzled — knocked off his stride — by the swift reaction.

"It's because I mentioned the Treasury, isn't it?" he said. "But surely. . . ."

"Simply a catalyst of rejection," Ambrose said. "It's like somebody switching on the light at dusk. All the fantasies go pouf."

"I still don't understand," Hepworth persisted. "You never seemed reluctant when it was just for the Office — or the Terrace. You mean the Treasury is less important?"

8

Ambrose looked at him in sheer disbelief at the words he had heard. "*Less important?* Oh, my holy Aunt, not to mention my sisters and my cousins! You've never understood. I wouldn't have guessed. You surely never thought I did these Foreign Office things because they were *important*."

"Well, bodies have been found, countries go to war. . . ."

"Oh yes, *that's* important, but that's not how the Foreign Office — or the Terrace — spend their time. They're in the middle of a lovely game that doesn't affect anything, and sometimes I've joined in. Of course it's *entertaining*. But the Treasury is rather different."

"Don't know why you think they're more serious. They're certainly inefficient. They always get things wrong."

"Indeed: I am not defending it, just explaining it. I have never in fact been through its portals. Where is it? Whitehall?"

"Great George Street — corner of Whitehall, opposite the House of Commons."

"Ah yes: just where you'd expect. Important spot. And they *are* important. What do we mean by important? The Treasury takes a decision — sixpence on the Income Tax or five shillings on a bottle of whiskey — and immediately millions of people are affected. Or they raise the rate of interest and suddenly unemployment is doubled — or halved: I can't remember which. But that's what I call important. Of course, it never works out the way the Treasury expects. That's what *you* mean by saying they're inefficient. I don't disagree. But it's important that people's lives can be invaded in this wholesale way by a Minister and a few officials. I'm not saying important in a deeper sense. Doesn't solve anyone's *moral* problems: the categorical imperative is still a mystery. But in terms of action and consequence, yes, I think we can say that the Treasury is important. *From Whitehall goeth forth the Law, and the word of the Chancellor from Great George Street.*"

"Well, if it's so important, why don't you want to join in?"

"Ah, dear Charles, you touch me on the raw. I simply have no taste — I confess it — for the mechanics of mass manipulation. It will all go on, happily or unhappily, without me. Buttons will be pressed, men and women will have more to spend, or less: presumably this is how the Treasury greybeards get their fun. Are they in fact grey-bearded? One rather assumes a great wagging of beards: *'tis merry in hall when beards wag all.* But perhaps they're as clean-shaven as curates. I daresay I had a lot of them through my hands, but I can hardly remember any of

9

them now. Except, of course, for that Assistant Secretary who skipped off to China — Primrose, Ernest Primrose."

"You heard about that? They put out a different story. We tried to keep it dark."

"Oh yes, indeed: we heard, we heard. He'd been at St. Hilary's, bright young man with a great gift for languages. So my friend Basruk told me. You know Basruk? He's the economics tutor at St. Hilary's. A Turk, you know. Indeed I think I can say a *terrible* Turk: *Peace shall go sleep with Turks and infidels.* He was fond of Primrose — taught him to read Turkish poetry. Basruk said he had a real gift for languages. I'm quite sure he only defected to learn Chinese — but I expect they took a different view at the Treasury. Basruk found it most amusing. I expect he put him up to it. That terrible Turk: he's as frivolous as I am."

"Ambrose: this act you're putting on. I don't believe a word of it. You *know* it matters very much if people walk off with secrets."

"I know it matters at the *Terrace,* because that's the game you people play there. It matters very much to the Arsenal when Leeds United scores a goal against them. But of course one knows that in due course the *Arsenal* will score a goal, not necessarily against Leeds — perhaps against Liverpool, who in turn . . . and so on. Goals go back and forth — highly enjoyable — lots of foul play — onlookers drawn in — riots — Governments make protests — but nothing has gone *wrong*. The game's being played according to rules mutually agreed. It would only go wrong if nobody ever scored goals. Same at the Terrace."

"You mean it would make no difference if we gave up all security, and. . . ."

"Oh, *no.*" Ambrose appeared horrified. "Of course not. You have to play at the game so that everybody can share the secrets round — through the agents, and then everybody can keep in step. If a country opted out, it wouldn't know where it stood. No: you have to have the system, and it's highly enjoyable for those who are playing it, with a special spice of danger — just a bit more than mountaineering — because agents *have* to get shot now and then, and that's sad, of course. But for most of the people, it's just an intellectual exercise — or a social exercise, plus the nice feeling of both having the friendship of your own club and the wider fellowship you share with the opposing clubs.

I'm told all the agents know each other, or most of them do: use the same informants and all that."

"It's never worked as mechanically as that for you, has it?" Hepworth said. "If you remember. . . ."

"Ah, yes, it's never been humdrum for me precisely because you've only brought me in to stir things up. I have this effect: that's why I like it, of course."

Hepworth groaned. "*That* part's true. I remember saying to you once: 'things don't happen to you: you happen to things.'"

"But not as an *operator,*" Ambrose insisted, "and that's why I'm blind to your Treasury blandishments. I never *do* anything. Things may re-arrange themselves around me just because I'm there — as a *punctum indifferens.* Yes, I think that's it. You throw me in, and everything in the circle reacts. But that's not because of anything I *do.* It's due to the fact that we all live — I really believe this — in a closed circle."

"I've read about it. Those philosophers. The Vienna Circle. Or is it the Ambrose circle?"

"It's also the Hepworth circle. We're all linked. By a certain stage in our lives — we're already there, you and me — we've gradually created a circle around us — the like-minded, the like-interested: we've pre-selected everybody we're likely to meet. We don't know them all — couldn't possibly, but they're all linked; so if one meets someone now, either one knows them in advance or at one or two stages removed. Bound to happen, even if I went on this Treasury frolic that you've hinted at. The center may not hold, but the circumference does."

"I haven't in fact told you anything about a Treasury frolic. I simply mentioned the word and you leapt in with both feet. As a matter of fact. . . ." Hepworth broke into a broad smile. "Yes, I think I have you, petarded and bombadiered by your own hand."

Ambrose looked at him in some alarm. "I thought I had extracted myself very decisively. I leapt back from Great George Street. . . ."

"Into my waiting arms. As you so decisively explained, you *do* like the Foreign Office jaunts, because they have no practical effect — they're unimportant, airy, pointless. . . ."

"Well. . . ."

"Well, this little frolic is not basically Treasury at all. It's a copper-bottomed F.O. exercise, as airy and fairy as you could wish for, with just a little stimulus from the Treasury. I only mentioned the Treasury first because I thought it would interest you: but now that I know, we can get things into their true proportion. I'm learning, I'm learning. Ambrose, you're becoming transparent in your old age."

"All right," Ambrose croaked in a voice of doom. "Spare me the hallelujahs. Let's hear what you're after. But if it ends up in the Treasury. . . ."

"It doesn't end there. It merely begins there, and with as daft a proposition as ever emerged from the Foreign Office. I can tell you this part in one sentence. Somebody in America — in Boston, in fact — is pouring dollars into England. The Treasury are saying: 'Heh, wait a minute. What's the idea?'"

"And I'm supposed to tell them the reason?"

"No, no. Much simpler. All they want you to do — or rather *we* want you to do — is to meet the source of all this bounty and tell us how he strikes you — or indeed *if* he strikes you."

"Ha-ha. I suppose you expect me to do this when I go over to Harvard?"

"Exactly. When are you going? Next week, isn't it? Right. I don't know how much lecturing you're doing, but I suppose you'll be living in Boston or Cambridge."

"Cambridge, at least as a base. I'm going down for one night to lecture at Princeton, and up to Toronto, but Cambridge most of the time."

"Yes: that's what we heard. And this character we're talking of lives in Boston, so you're bound to meet him. That's all. Tell us what you think."

It's too simple, Ambrose thought. Not at all the kind of thing Hepworth usually asks for. There must be some angle to it that he isn't revealing. Some character who's pouring in dollars? Just have a look at him?

"What on earth is *wrong* in shovelling dollars to England?" he asked. "Isn't that what we want?"

"This one's a bit funny. Might have overtones. The Treasury and the Bank of England have been watching him operating for a little while now, and it's developing an odd pattern. He's a very big operator — apparently unlimited funds, and he's acquiring a strong base in a number of very big companies here. Of course, full-scale takeovers are protected: it hasn't got to that stage yet. But it's the *pattern* that interests them — and us."

"And what *is* the pattern?"

Hepworth settled back. It had worked. Ambrose was hooked.

"These are all companies with a big potential in the Bulge. Oh, sorry. We've got into the habit of lumping the three south-eastern countries together — you know, Russia's soft-under-belly — Hungary, Rumania, Bulgaria, hence the Bulge."

"Surely Bulgaria's firmly in Russia's pocket."

"Not now. That's the new switch we're on to. Some of the old fuddy-duddies here want to play it cautiously, but there's a big chance that's worth exploring — a huge stake in engineering contracts as well as ordinary exports. It really started with that meeting of the three at Bucharest in 1971. You must have heard about that."

"Yes, but not what happened afterwards."

"It's been very startling. As you know, they set up what they called 'the Complex Programme' for their development. Involves buying western equipment, licenses and experience. But now it's moved into a higher gear. We've got wind of some exploration they're doing, vastly intriguing, mostly in two fields — oil and copper. It's always seemed odd that the oil's been limited mainly to Rumania. It *is* odd, isn't it? And copper: are they really on to it on a big scale? I needn't tell you what it would mean if we got access. Politically, of course, it would be quite interesting if this built up into a growing detachment from Mother Russia, with us as partners. That's looking ahead a bit: but the interim picture has its points, too. With our British companies helping on construction and exploration, it makes it a bit easier — to put it mildly — to have some of our people from the Terrace there, doing a good day's work. So you see why we have to be careful about takeover bids."

"You mean that this American character — or the group behind him — might be planning to take our companies over to get in first, so that all the profit would go to America?"

Hepworth looked at Ambrose quizzically. "That's one angle — the obvious one. But is it the only danger? I would have thought one might get a different picture if one stood on one's head for a minute."

It always took a little time, Ambrose thought, for Hepworth to emerge from his blandly innocent shell, but here it was. "Let me see," Ambrose murmured. "Stand on one's head? Yes, I see. This becomes interesting — really as daft as one could wish for. You mean that the whole anti-Russian ploy by the Bulge is really being organized by Russia."

"Always possible, isn't it?" Hepworth said. "If the Russians want to retain control, they've more chance of finding out what's going on through getting someone sympathetic to stir things up against them, especially if this character brings along a lot of cash. Let the Americans do all the work, pour in all the cash and technology, with the Satellites loving it all: and at the right moment. . . ."

"So you want me to look at this American — tell you if he's a genuine bloated capitalist or some sort of provocateur: where does his cash really come from: is he inner or outer-directed? A very nice problem. Do I know him?"

"I think you do," Hepworth said. How easy it is, he thought. For a moment he had the grace to feel slightly sick at what he was really up to. Perhaps something of this came through, for Ambrose — was it that sixth sense? — seemed to feel his hackles rise at this point.

"Someone I know?" He looked at Hepworth suspiciously. "Is this what you've been leading up to? Back to the Vienna Circle?"

Hepworth waved his hand airily. "*You're* the circle man, not me. But of course, it's true enough: small world. You may have to look at people you know with a sceptical eye."

"You make it sound so grubby," Ambrose said, "but I suppose that's what you're up to all the time at the Terrace, plotting to see which of you is going to come out on top, like the In-and-Out Club in Piccadilly. Who's in, who's out? For all I know, you'll be after *me* next."

It seemed to Ambrose that Hepworth looked a little startled. Probably imaginary. Nothing could startle Hepworth.

"We'll try to restrain our natural curiosity," he was saying easily. "Let's stick to this American for the moment. I didn't want to tell you who it was until you agreed to come in. Might as well stick to the need-to-know basis. But I think you're about ready now. Or do you think it's all too grubby?"

"I can get used to it," Ambrose said. "There's a sense in which one *has* to know. Not because it will affect the fate of nations, but to know who one's talking to. I suppose that's why you spend such a lot of time sniffing round each other at the Terrace. There's an intellectual satisfaction in it. I can see that. Like defining the terms in an argument before you start."

"Leaving no dark corners?"

"Oh, I don't know about that. One keeps some things reserved. Not everything lends itself to definition. '*Whereof one cannot speak, thereof one remains silent.*' At least *I* do. But not our American friend. Poor chap. The veil stands ready to be

14

torn off him. My oldest friend, apparently. Or just a casual acquaintance?"

"Well, *you* tell *me*," Hepworth said. "I'm sure you must have known him when he lived in Washington. See if you can remember his name. Englishman by origin — huge construction business — wife was American, very young, very fond of parties. . . ."

"You mean George Fletcher," Ambrose cried. "Of course I remember him. Wee Georgie Fletcher, they called him. He's about six foot six. And now he's in Boston?"

"Yes, he's head of a lot of businesses there, especially the Trans-Commonwealth Corporation — TCC they call it. Started in Canada, but now very heavily in England."

Ambrose was sitting muttering to himself. "George Fletcher. Well I'm damned." Pulling himself together, he turned to Hepworth. "You can't be serious. Of course, he's rich and ambitious, but he couldn't fit your bill as a schemer, still less a coverman for some deep Russian interest. Ardent Catholic for one thing. It doesn't make any sense. He's not the type."

"You don't think he's tough enough?"

"Oh, he's tough, and I would say ruthless. He's a hard liver, very Anglo-Saxon in the bad sense — very bluff, very bossy. But he wasn't really so rich in those days. Rich enough, but. . . ."

"Well, he's rich now, or at least TCC is. The figures the Treasury have been given of his involvements in England are staggering, and all rather suddenly. They're very diversified too. But it's the Bulge angle that bothers us most."

"Anything to show where the money is coming from? Any possible Russian source?"

"Money from Russia wouldn't be deployed this way, in company finance. It would be kept handy for other uses. We have a few hints on this, but nothing firm. It would help us to get more. Naturally, we're giving him a little attention by our own people over there, and we've got quite a bit from our American opposite numbers. But who knows? You may spot something different in your own peculiar way."

"And how will I meet him? Same old society frolics?"

"Oh, you can leave all that to the Boston Consul-General. I don't know if you know him — Donald Upjohn. He's quite a lively chap: Up John and at 'em. He's in the picture. You can count on him. You'll hear from him when you get there. No problem."

There were some mixed thoughts in Ambrose's head. For the moment he let them pass. There was something puzzling in Hepworth's attitude, too. All the same. . . .

"Charles," he said finally. "Let's get this clear. I'm going to Harvard to give some lectures. I will accept a social invitation from the Consul-General. Right. I will keep my eyes and ears open. I will do everything you ask — *'make mad the guilty and appal the free'*. But one thing I have to know first. How serious is all this? Quite apart from your Terrace interests, is there going to be some big blow-up over it in the City? Are some of the British companies that Fletcher's after at breakpoint?"

"Ah, now we're really getting into it," Hepworth said. "On whether it's critical, the answer is yes: but I want you to get this straight from the Treasury itself." He looked at his watch. "Half-past two. Good. They've set up a meeting there at three. You recall that I asked you to keep yourself free to four-thirty. Well, that was why. You're to go over there to the meeting. O.K.? Then you can have a sleep until your cocktail party at the Reform Club."

Ambrose looked at him in astonishment. "Cocktail party? You mean that publisher's party? How on earth. . . ."

"Did you accept? Doesn't really matter. You'll be welcome. I told Macdougalls to send you a card. I suppose you saw: it's a book they're publishing on international trade by a Harvard professor. I was sure you'd be interested after today's affairs."

"Charles," Ambrose said, "you are a dull and muddy-mettled rascal. I should know better than to trust you, but in fact I do — or largely. Not entirely: just largely. I'll see how I feel. But I suppose the Treasury is a must. Are you coming too?"

"No, I'm going straight back to the Terrace, so I can't give you a lift. It's healthier for you, anyhow, to have that nice walk through the Park. Just go to the main door in Great George Street and announce yourself. Sir Olaf McConnochie, you will say, is expecting you. He's taking the meeting: he's head of the Finance Sector. Do you know him? Probably not. He wasn't even at Cambridge. Oslo and St. Andrews, I believe."

"There you are. My circumference is breaking down. But I have in fact heard of him. He's said to be the best backgammon player in Great Britain. That must be significant, somehow. A huge Viking, I suppose."

"Not exactly," Hepworth said. "More like a troll. But a rather elegant one. You will see."

Ambrose put on a mock disconsolate face. "I feel that I'm

16

getting out of my depth already: out of my circle, somehow. Do you think the Treasury is going to give me a new fulcrum — a new center for my circumference?"

"Perhaps even more startling than that," Hepworth said. "I remember something that Chesterton said about God that really applies to the Treasury: '*The nature of God is a circle of which the center is everywhere and the circumference is nowhere*'."

"Sounds more like Balliol," Ambrose said. "I think it was Empedocles, by the way, not Chesterton. But never mind. I'm beginning to get the idea."

At the door of the Travellers', a few minutes later, Hepworth got into a black Rover that was waiting with a patient driver, and Ambrose turned into the Park for the short walk to the Treasury. And as he began to walk, the real question had space at last to shape itself in his thought.

Why hadn't he mentioned Gloria? He had been waiting for this moment of being alone to let it all run through his mind. He hadn't debated the question with himself when Fletcher's name had been mentioned, but merely let the talk move on as if she hadn't existed. Of course, there were areas of oneself that one reserved, especially if one was aware of failure — perhaps even moral failure. But now Gloria was part of the picture. She had been Fletcher's wife — part of his background, and perhaps part of his motivation.

Around Ambrose, as he strolled past the tightly-packed flowerbeds, all glowing in the early September sun, the air seemed full of cheerful normality — no pressure, no suspicion, but merely a heritage of trust and order, with a dash of style to show you where you were. A young cavalry officer was striding haughtily, precisely, across the Horse Guards but with a distinct twinkle in his bearing, like a Haydn Trio: the towers of the Foreign Office ahead, massive but airborne, were as dreamy as a middle-aged romantic. The lake was a miniature Turner: the chrysanthemums offset it, sedate, earthbound. Here was a bed of carefree dahlias, tossing their heads in all directions: and he had a sudden picture of Gloria, so fair, so pretty, so absurd, half-baked, crackpot, so eager to give, to expand, to flow — so dotty in what it usually led to.

Was this why he hadn't mentioned her? He had always ignored this side. He had liked her, and responded without question. She was just more alive — more *gracefully* alive — than everyone else around. He didn't know anything about her

17

death except that it was a car crash. Somehow, that was right, too. After all that bursting idealism — the passion to learn, to love, to take off at will — one couldn't see her drifting down to middle-age, thickening, slowing-up. No: she had lived and died the same way.

Imagine trying to describe her to Hepworth, especially the daft way she had believed what all her cronies told her — some of them openly and intelligently left-wing, others phoney and transparently so with their orchestrated cliches. And of course she had liked the phonies best, because there was a strong dash of danger, fraud, disappointment, betrayal in these types, and she needed something of this to nourish her inner excitement.

Pinto: he was the worst really, or at least the one who had impinged on Ambrose most awkwardly. *Jacques* Pinto: utterly absurd. He came from Brooklyn, and his name was Jack, or Jacob, but it had to be Jacques. "Isn't it a lovely name?" Gloria had said. When she came to Ambrose that night asking if he would stand by her, he'd agreed without a moment's thought, only half-listening to her nonsense as she rambled on.

She was so breathless in her explanation. If Fletcher ever found out about Jacques, he could ruin him and *would* — deliberately, ruthlessly. It was horrible, when the marriage was dead anyhow. She so longed for a few days with Jacques, somewhere in the country, while Fletcher was in New York. If Fletcher asked where she'd been, when he got back, could she say she'd been at Ambrose's cottage on the Bay for a few days, alone? Of course she could: she could say anything. "Oh Ambrose!" — those big melting eyes. Quite sincere too: one knew it deeply. Had Fletcher, in fact, questioned her? Had she brought Ambrose into the picture? He never asked: and now, of course, it was too late.

He had been very casual, easy-going, in those days. It was wrong. He knew it now. One never knew where it led. Well, it was a long time ago. All over.

It was as he came out of the Park and turned into Great George Street, with the Parliament towers pinnacled against the sky, that a more involved question suddenly shot into his mind. Could Fletcher himself have had some left-wing involvement that Gloria knew of and kept to herself? Could this be the possible Russian link that Hepworth had hinted at? Oh God, he muttered. He was giving in too easily to Hepworth and the Terrace. He needed something to pull him together, something that sounded like Sir Olaf McConnochie.

He was in the doorway now, and giving the name. Two flunkeys were instantly at his disposal, one offering a Pass for signature, the other guiding him, once he had signed, along the corridors of power. He was in the Treasury.

At the Terrace, Hepworth took a few messages from his secretary as he went by, and asked her to get hold of Patrick Willis. While he waited, he buzzed to ask her to get Richard Harvey to join them. Willis and Harvey were both full-timers at the Terrace, and in his own role, half-in and half-out, he worked through them constantly. More accurately, he had been put into the Terrace specifically, by the distant figure behind it all, to re-establish an operational trio that had somehow fallen apart.

Douglas Freeman had been the third member before this. The three names were similar enough to have produced the nickname for them of England's happy triad of shoe-makers—*Freeman, Hardy and Willis*. But Freeman had disappeared one day. Nobody seemed to know how. Hepworth had been put in with a wide-ranging mission that took this in.

In odd moments, Hepworth asked himself if there wasn't a moral for him in the nickname. *Freeman, Hardy and Willis*. The shops were still there on every High Street, but one could be sure that they were now part of some large conglomerate. The three partriarchal shoemakers had disappeared. Anonymity had taken over. Their shoes were probably still excellent value, but who in fact was one talking to when one entered the shop?

Had something similar happened to the triad at the Terrace? It wasn't easy to see it in the remaining two. Both were real enough as human beings, if only because they were so different individually. Willis, of medium height and with a calm, well-modulated voice, had a rather prosperous look and sported a fine set of bristling whiskers to go with it. Harvey was tall and skinny, urgent and nervous, chain-smoking, untidy, with wild hair that was almost an Afro. Typically, Willis played golf and Harvey chess. One felt in the first glance that one knew everything about them. Hepworth, waiting in his room, may have been less certain. One didn't bank on anything in that atmosphere.

It was always a gamble in a place like the Terrace, where all full-timers seemed to have secret loyalties — the schoolboy friendships, the sexual overflows, the personal attachments of agents, double and treble, to whom each alone had — or thought he had — the key. Any link could snap: one knew it.

But one had to work, so one took a chance and simply tried to establish some contervailing check. One approached the same problem from different ends. One launched stories and waited for them to come back, the way a bookmaker lays off the money that flows in.

The thought led him to Ambrose, and his face grew rather serious. In his mind's eye, he had the picture of waving to him as the car took off from the Travellers'. It had been a good talk. One always felt stimulated after a lunch with Ambrose. It had been easy enough to sound carefree. And yet. . . .

Willis and Harvey came in together. "How did it go?" Willis asked as they sat down.

"To plan," Hepworth said. "He's launched."

"You know, I can't accept any of it," Harvey said. "How did he take Fletcher's name?"

"Blandly," Hepworth said. "In fact too blandly. Asked all the obvious questions. . . ."

"Well?" Harvey asked.

"All the questions about Fletcher himself," Hepworth said sadly. "Not a word about the beautiful Gloria. No mention, no recollection, no question. A bit odd, don't you think?"

II

TROLL was *le mot juste*, Ambrose thought, as Sir Olaf McConnochie came across the room to greet him. Elegant, too, and in a highly individual way. One registered instantly the superb tailoring of a suit of the finest worsted, a very subtle grey-green in color, standing out so happily from the dismal assortment of clothes — some of them variants of black coats and striped trousers, but including also sweaters and pullovers — that the colleagues around him seemed to be content with. To a man they were black-shoed, while Sir Olaf's tiny feet were shod in a rich, dark-brown leather that glowed and glistened with the mark of its care. His shirt was a gentle pink: his tie a soft coral in Siamese silk. To complete the picture there was a cambric handkerchief, with the most delicate lace border, peeping from his sleeve.

A dandy, straight out of a Restoration comedy. Sir Wilfull Witwoud, perhaps. At any moment he would be tapping a jewelled snuff-box, and the air would be full of "Gad, sir" and "Demme." But the idea vanished as soon as one saw his eyes. They were full of sparkle. He dressed this way merely for fun. And how right he was, given his minute height. To be austerely "correct," with the stature of a troll, would have looked absurd. Instead, he had transformed himself — pink cheeks, sandy hair and bright blue eyes — into a colorful miniature that Nicholas Hilliard would have loved to paint.

All the same, it was a shock, especially after the cold introduction that the first few moments in the Treasury had offered. The huge tasteless staircase, the endless curving corridors whose stone floors echoed so harshly to the feet, seemed to have been designed to accentuate the difference from the harmonious comfort that Ambrose was used to at the Foreign Office. Sir Olaf's room, on the second floor, seemed at first merely vast and opulent. However, as he moved forward, he saw some rather surprising paintings on the walls. One in particular looked like — well no, it just couldn't be.

"So glad to meet you at last," Sir Olaf was saying. "Strange we haven't met before." In conversation, the dandy seemed in abeyance. He had a crisp voice, with a slight echo of Scotland in it. "I do go up to Oxford," he said, "but it's mostly to dine with an economist at The House that I'm fond of — Eugen Ratikov. I expect you know him."

"Indeed I do. He comes over to dine at St. Mary's. We never talk about economics, though. Just Pushkin. Why hasn't he brought you? Must see to it. Ah, there's someone I know from the Foreign Office. Has he been translated?"

A fair young man had waved to Ambrose and was coming over. "No," Sir Olaf was saying, "he's one of their Russian experts. They've sent him to us to liaise on this particular question."

One could begin to believe in class types. Timothy Fosdyke was tall, lissom, expensive. He had been a King's Scholar at Eton and got a double First at St. Mary's. "How marvelous," he said, reaching Ambrose. "Are you going to give us all a collective tutorial?"

"You see me *in subjectione,*" Ambrose murmured, "out of my depth. I'm not even numerate, as the Abominable Snowman keeps telling us we must be. Are *you?*"

"Of course not," Timothy said. "Might have to be at the Board of Trade, but totally unnecessary here." His voice descended to a mock conspiratorial level. "Deal with something far more important than arithmetic," he whispered. "*Power.*"

"*'The sumless treasuries',*" Ambrose whispered back approvingly, as they took their seats around a long table that ran along the length of a wall. "That's where they keep the valuables, I suppose: at the bottom of the sea. Or *here,*" he exclaimed suddenly, having raised his eyes to the wall he now faced. "My goodness! It *is* a Vermeer. How *can* it be?"

"I'll tell you afterwards," Fosdyke whispered back, as Sir Olaf brought the meeting to order. "May I introduce Mr. Usher?" he was saying, waving a hand toward where Ambrose was sitting. "Some of you will know him, I daresay, from Oxford. He's off to Boston next week, to lecture at Harvard. The Foreign Office have roped him in to see if he can turn up something useful over there about TCC. The Consulate-General in Boston will be his base for this."

The casual manner had completely disappeared. Business was at hand. There were ten in all around the table, and Sir Olaf ran quickly through their names for Ambrose's benefit, ending with a tousle-headed young man, with a distinctly rough-hewn face, whom he introduced as Prescott. "Perhaps we can start with you, Bert," he said to him, turning at the same time, with a word of explanation, to Ambrose. "A working party under Prescott has been doing an analysis in depth of TCC holdings and finances. We've all had the report." Fosdyke, sitting next to Ambrose, had fished a copy out of his briefcase and was putting it in front of him.

Bert, Ambrose thought. Was that how one addressed the ordinary Treasury man these days? *Burke,* maybe, or even *Dirk:* but "Bert" had a deliberately aggressive tone, like "Alf." Was the Treasury basically a no-nonsense outfit now, with Bert as the symbol?

One expected change: but the Foreign Office had managed to hold on. Abroad, a Foreign Office man would still play polo with the Shah of Iran. At home, he would dawdle over lunch at the Travellers'. Where did a modern Treasury man eat lunch? Probably at a cafeteria.

Cafeteria! Of course. There *was* a cafeteria. He had been told about it. In a little turning off Whitehall there was, it seemed, a crummy little eating-room serving sausages and mash, and restricted exclusively to current or former Treasury and Cabinet Office bigwigs. Some of them, by now, had taken over the commanding heights in other Departments, but this was where they foregathered, to murmur for a while informally and allusively about what was going on — a clearing-house for those in the know. How else could things run smoothly? From time to time they might have to make a sortie to the Athenaeum — and Sir Olaf would then stroll on to see his tailor in Savile Row: but for the most part they kept to themselves — the innerest of inner circles — guarding the fort against the inborn follies of everybody else.

Ambrose felt his spirits sink. How on earth would he be able to follow their arguments? The thick report that Fosdyke had passed over looked as forbidding as a medieval tractate on angelology. He would just have to let the talk run through his ears, in the hope that the themes would emerge later from his subconscious when he was relaxed — say, when he was shaving.

Sir Olaf, it was clear, was not troubled by any density of the language. "I must say, Bert" — he was turning over the pages lying before him on the table — "I thought your report was fascinating. Leaves us looking pretty helpless: but at least we can learn about their methods, and perhaps apply them — or *frustrate* them. Would you like to say a word about your conclusions?"

Bert, a rough diamond from Yorkshire, was eloquent and penetrating in the most rasping of accents. "There's something special about TCC," he said. "Everyone used to think that these multinational conglomerates win by sheer size, but it isn't true. Nor is it just their diversification. It's the special way they use it to give their cash-flow a tremendous momentum. Basically *our* conglomerates try to operate as single units; but with *them* you have to look at the utterly independent way the different divisions operate internationally. There's a lot of work been done on this by a man from the Manchester Business School. The art lies in tempo, as in bridge. There's no static plan, with everything moving one-dimensionally, gaining here, losing there. They treat each product-line as having its own growth and maturity rate so as to milk it at its peak to finance new research and product-lines."

Sir Olaf nodded. "Yes, it all comes out in the report. They follow up all the implications, don't they — closing lines and factories without warning, pushing on with new ones with no false delicacy? And they're ruthless in another way too: ignoring marginal money rates of return when the prime aim is to knock out local industry. *Our* people — or the banks — are far too timid, too conventional, on this. And it's not as if we're short of cash. On the Arab oil funds alone, the Governor thinks that out of about fifty-five billion dollars this year, at least six billion will be into sterling. And that's without Eurodollars and all the direct investment, like TCC."

"That's just what's wrong," Bert said morosely. "We've lost the link with genuine saving through the Stock Exchange. That's why we're at the mercy of this special money. Not much good to us if we lose control of the firms that are genuinely marked for large-scale expansion, especially those counting on direct participation in the Bulge countries."

Sir Olaf turned to an elderly man sitting opposite him. "How does this side of things look at the moment, Matthew?"

Sir Matthew Johnson now took over, sounding considerably

more traditional in tone than Bert, though equally trenchant in content.

"It's quite extraordinary how blind our people have been," he said in a slow measured voice. "The F.O. has simply played the Russian game, very polite over the Satellites — mustn't annoy Russia. Oh yes, a little trade promotion in Rumania and Poland, but hands off elsewhere, at a time when all the old categories have broken down. Nobody else is so hidebound. East Germany has diplomatic relations with Franco Spain — and even China, which must annoy Moscow even more. West Germany has a tremendous development program building up in Bulgaria, mostly through subsidiaries in Turkey. Certainly some of our companies have been burrowing away privately — and we've seen to it that they got special loans: I mean especially, of course, Tracton, and BFT, and Inter-Allied; but now, these are just the companies at risk from TCC. . . ."

The talk turned to takeover procedures, pressures on the City, the way they might have to advise the Chancellor to authorize further loans. Ambrose listened with half an ear to the jargon they were grinding out, especially when they moved on to talk of the draft for the Chancellor's speech to the International Monetary Fund meeting in Washington the following week. It was not easy for him to characterize the talk. Partly, of course, he was flummoxed by initials — like SDRs — and by the mysterious names they threw back and forth across the table — Ossola, Emminger, Polack, Witteveen, de Larosiere: it sounded like a kind of Zurich gnome-dropping that would have brought the blood of the *Daily Express* rushing to its chauvinistic head. Only one of these unknown foreigners had a quasi-romantic appeal — a woman they all referred to as "Rosa," who had just been over from the United States and whom they all seemed to like very much.

Even more bewildering, at first, was the way they threw *theory* around while apparently concerned with the most practical of aims. They couldn't even be simple about a thing like the balance of payments. Wasn't this something even a child could understand? You either earned enough to pay your overseas bills or you didn't. Ah, yes: but how do you *know* if you're plus or minus? What *figures* do you use? Rosa — that clever girl — had tried to convince them on her recent visit that the figures as traditionally presented were totally misleading. They treated capital flows and governmental transfers merely as

25

"residuals," ignoring their dynamism. Well, even Ambrose could see that that was wrong. And what about "the induced saving effect" of Foreign Aid? One had to understand this properly, as someone whose name sounded like Brian Hopkins had shown in the *Economic Journal*.

But theory, after all, had its attractions for Ambrose. In some ways, it began to feel like a meeting of the Aristotelian Society at Oxford. For two pins he might have tried to join in, but he'd left it too late.

Sir Olaf was looking at his watch. It was obviously close to the end. Any other business? There was a short mention of "swaps" publicized and secret. And then someone got back to the first subject — TCC finance.

"Where are they getting the money from?" he wanted to know. "It's all very well for Bert to show how they maximize liquidity, but the original flow of cash seems so limitless."

Bert was as bluff as ever. "I have a theory about that. It's not capital: I mean the money that tips the scale isn't orthodox money. It's *consumer* money." He saw them looking puzzled. "What's the organization in America that has a limitless flow of consumer money — ready cash — that it can tap at will and that it has to find a home for, no questions asked, once it has been laundered?" He turned to Ambrose. "I'm sure *you* can guess."

Ambrose, somewhat startled to be brought in, rose nevertheless to the occasion. "The Mafia?" he suggested ironically.

Bert turned back to the table. "That's exactly what *I* think," he said. "The Mafia. I don't know the mechanism, but that's where the trail leads."

"Oh, come on, Bert." There was general amusement. The meeting came to an end.

As chairs were pushed back and there was a general stretching of legs, Ambrose gave the picture facing him on the wall his close attention. He had felt its presence throughout the meeting. Surely a Vermeer — a woman sewing in great tranquillity, a man with a black hat standing in loving closeness, the light streaming in on them from an open window. It was perfect. Turning, he saw on the wall, at the other end of the room, a huge luscious composition in totally different style — Venus and Adonis, nymphs and shepherds frolicking in the background, Mercury in naughty attendance: it had to be a Rubens. Fosdyke, standing beside him, was watching his surprise with amusement.

26

"Yes," he said. "They're the real thing. They've been in his family for generations. His mother's family were Flemish and moved to Norway in the 18th century, I think. They say he owns half Norway — in the mountains to the North — as well as the pictures. Quite a character. . . ."

He moved away. Ambrose, still gazing with rapture at the Vermeer, found Sir Olaf at his side, looking at him rather puckishly. He had drawn the cambric handkerchief from his sleeve, and touched his nose with it gently before slipping it back. "Nice picture, isn't it?" he said easily. "A bit better than the stuff the Ministry of Works provides. Cheers the place up, I think. They were my mother's — the civilized side of the family. My father's family in Scotland were all Philistines, I regret to say. All they bought looks like *The Monarch of the Glen*. Oh yes, they did get hold of a George Stubbs — a rather good one. I keep it at home."

On one of the other walls, between two bookcases, was a head — square, masterly — that could have been a Cranach: but Ambrose had no chance to ask. Sir Olaf wanted to have a private word.

"I shall be over in America myself while you're there," he said. "After the IMF meeting, I'm staying on for a little break. I'll keep in touch in case anything blows up. I'll be in New York for a day or so for the Opera, and then I'm going to Colorado for two or three days to play a little backgammon. Do you play?"

It seemed a casual question, except that nothing could be as casual as the air which this tiny mandarin projected. Besides, to *Colorado* — for *backgammon*.

"I must learn the rules," Ambrose said gravely. "It has become the fashion, I hear. I remember being told that you're a Grand Master — Dean of the Dice. Is it skill or chance?"

"Well, one doesn't become a Grand Master by chance," Sir Olaf said, "but I like it because it's a very special kind of gamble. I like playing for real stakes — win or lose all, not, of course, on the turn of a wheel or the deal of a card, like poor Dostoevsky, but with one's whole mind, or rather . . ." — he groped for the right word — "with a part of one that never otherwise finds expression. Not easy to put into words. I suppose it's hard for a philosopher to understand. *You* weigh everything up. We gamblers have to plunge. . . ."

"So off to the Carlsbad Casino when you should be home writing *The Brothers Karamazov*."

Sir Olaf smiled. "Yes, it comes down to that at the end,

27

except, of course, that I never play in a casino. One has to be with people one understands — and with the same kind of resources. We alternate. They fly over to play in Scotland, and, when I can, I drop in at their place near Aspen. It's going to be a good game, but if you want to get hold of me while I'm there, they'll know at the Embassy how to reach me, and I'll get them to tell the Boston Consulate. I'll go back via Boston. I'll want to hear what you've been up to."

He spoke with the greatest casualness but with a distinct twinkle, fully aware that Ambrose was finding this both *épatant* and peculiar. They were near the half-open door now, with Ambrose ready to leave, when a dark, indeed swarthy man put his head in, apparently hoping to catch Sir Olaf. Ambrose looked at him in total astonishment.

"Basruk!" he exclaimed. "You terrible Turk! What are *you* doing here?"

"I work here," Basruk said, in the heavy accents of Asia Minor which he still affected, with devastating charm to the ladies. "I've just become an economic adviser to the Chancellor. Only part-time, of course. But it's the other way round: what are *you* doing here, you over-ripe Socrates?"

One never gave Basruk a straight answer. He never expected it. He was always on the move — infectiously, noisily, happily. They said he was a good economist, but as far as Ambrose knew he seemed to spend all his time with the girls, and indeed had once snared away a nice Yugoslav girl, Beba, who had swum into Ambrose's ken. He now had a word with Sir Olaf, and then went to one of the junior staff — perhaps Sir Olaf's private secretary — to ask for a set of papers, which he was given. With a raucous cry to Ambrose — one never knew whether these characteristic shouts were Turkish or just high spirits — he was off again.

Ambrose found himself walking down the corridor with Fosdyke, who had wandered back to him during the exchanges with Sir Olaf. "You see what I mean," he said. "He *is* a character our Olaf, is he not?"

"I haven't really recovered from that Vermeer," Ambrose murmured. "Tell me more about him. I don't know if you heard: he's off to Colorado after the IMF — just feels like some all-night backgammon. Is he free to do all this?"

"Well, he's unique, and he plays things his own way: but you know, the system's a bit funny, much kinder to civil servants than to Ministers. Ministers are restricted from absolutely anything private when they're in office — have to freeze their shares, everything. But civil servants, as long as they don't peddle their influence or use anything they learn for their own profit, are perfectly free to be rich, to play around, to gamble if they want to, to have a good time. Of course, most of them don't. They have no capital, they work terribly long hours, and they're just inhibited: they really *like* routine and formality: they see virtue in it: that's why they *became* civil servants. . . ."

"But the odd one can have a really wild private life?"

"Perhaps precisely because he's a cypher in his *public* life."

"Is there a Lady Olaf?"

"There was. She died about three years ago. He was terribly knocked out. That's when he went into backgammon in a big way. I suppose he needed it."

Ambrose was still dazed. "I must say: this is a new way of looking at civil service life. Unexpected attractions."

"Well, you have to choose your ancestors carefully or you won't have the wherewithal. But if someone like Olaf happens to be very rich and wants to enjoy himself, there's nothing whatever to stop him."

"No need to be Caesar's wife, I mean in life-style?"

Fosdyke gave Ambrose a cheerful look. "Who can be above suspicion these days? After all the cases, it's begun to work backwards. The more suspicious you look, the less suspected you are. We've been through all that and come out at the other end. I think Olaf's not really *above* suspicion: he's in a different category. His life-style starts where other people's leave off."

"And yet in his work here?"

"Oh, a whiz. Prescott and the others swear by him."

Ambrose was shaking his head wonderingly. "*Blest with each talent and each art to please,*" he murmured. "Fabulous."

They had walked down by a smaller staircase than the prestigious one in Great George Street, and come out into a great courtyard, with a gate leading into King Charles Street and the Foreign Office yard. "I'll walk with you," Ambrose said. "I'm going across the Park to the London Library."

One was on holy ground, taking this route. Had it all been designed consciously to echo the majesty of the ancient Temple at Jerusalem — the exterior courtyards of the multitude (Parliament Square), the interior courtyards of the priesthood (Treasury and Foreign Office), and finally the Holy of Holies, No. 10? As they looked through the Foreign Office gate into Downing Street, they saw a large crowd standing mutely before

29

the sacred shrine, and in the foreground three men, bearded and solemn, actually on their knees, praying for guidance or just for help. . . .

"I've never seen this before," Ambrose said. "It's very moving, isn't it? Just like the scene at the opening of *Boris Godunov,* with the crowd on their knees — *'Have pity, boyar, little father'.* . . ."

Fosdyke, in a delightful high voice, began to sing the words quietly: "*Smiluisa, boyarin batyushka.* . . ."

Ambrose joined in, in a rather crumbly kind of baritone: "*Otyetz nash, ti kormiletz, boyarin, smiluisa.* . . ."

It was a cheerful send-off for his walk through the Park. "Woe to Russia, woe without end," he sang to himself in the autumn sunshine. "*Pechal na Rusi, pechal beziskhodnaya.* . . ."

At the foot of the Duke of York's Steps, a policeman looked at him rather suspiciously. One was not supposed to be as happy as this. But then not everybody knew how stimulating the Treasury could be. No wonder the Prime Minister clung to his ancient title — First Lord of the Treasury. Unseen, but no doubt inspiring it all, he deserved a special greeting. "Hail, live and flourish, our father Tsar," Ambrose sang, climbing the steps. "*Slava! Zhivi i zdravstvui, tsar nash batyushka.*" Those Russian basses! He could hear them in the air around.

The curfew had long been tolling at the London Library, but even so they had to root him out of *Literature: English: Criticism* on the third floor before he was prepared to emerge. As always, the chase had gathered its own momentum. At the back of his mind was a new book by Gertrude Himmelfarb on John Stuart Mill that had just been sent to him from New York. He expected to be drawing on this in his Harvard lectures, not so much for the new light on Mill and Harriet Taylor (fascinating though that was) as for Mill on the distillation of tradition — the Coleridge connection, as one might say. There was a passage in one of the Coleridge Notebooks, if he could find it. . . . Surely in the all-embracing mercy of the London Library. . . . He found it, and looked up Kathleen Coburn's commentary on it, which took him much further. He would ask her about it when he went up to Toronto: but in the meantime he stood reading, already four thousand miles from Hepworth and his world.

With the caretaker shooing him out politely but firmly, the thought of Hepworth began to drift back. The cocktail party at the Reform Club across the road? Why not, even if it did seem rather distasteful to exploit an august establishment this way?

After all, Mill had been a member of the Reform: but could one imagine a party there to publicize *On Liberty*? Disgusting, he thought, as he entered the large room on the ground floor and saw a huge mob of people surging round. Rather pleasant, he conceded, as he took his first sip from the glass of champagne that had been pressed into his hand.

The first sip is always clarifying. Where before there was an anonymous crowd, Ambrose, looking round now, saw a number of familiar faces, a friendly intercourse of give-and-take, though with elements also (it had to be said) of watch-out-and-avoid. A young man, peacock-shirted in a style that bore the unmistakeable stamp of public relations, was bearing down on him in evident recognition. But in front was a man of older grace — Anthony Reeves, who had once published a little volume by Ambrose called *"Memory,"* now largely forgotten.

"How can Macdougall afford this?" Ambrose asked. "I don't recall you giving me a party for *my* book. Does it pay off?"

"Oh, Macdougall doesn't pay for it," Reeves said. "It's the author. He's fabulously rich and he's an Overseas member of the Club. Do you know him? Jefferson Cohen? He wrote a book on the new mathematics that's become standard in every college and university in the world. They say it's already made him five million dollars."

"I thought he was an economist."

"Yes, that's his real interest now. The economic journalists are very fond of him here, so he throws these parties, just to say hello and perhaps get some reviews. Very nice chap. Come and meet him."

This was clearly the aim, also, of peacock-shirt. They moved over towards Professor Cohen, a tall bald-headed figure, obviously having a very good time surrounded by his friends.

"I hope you'll come and have lunch with me when you get to Harvard," he said to Ambrose, when introductions had been effected. "I know I'll meet you at cocktail parties, but we'll never get a chance to talk that way, will we?" He waved his hand towards the crowd around him to draw the parallel.

"There are other compensations," Ambrose said cheerfully, taking another sip of champagne.

"You mean like Olga?" the professor growled in mock-Groucho style. He had put an arm around the shoulders of a dark, pretty woman next to him. "You certainly know Olga, the toast of Threadneedle Street."

The clue worked. "I know Nicholas," Ambrose said. Nicholas

Davenport, a very special kind of financial sage, was often at Oxford High Tables, and Ambrose had heard that his wife Olga was a good painter and very attractive. But no one had talked of the merry look in her eyes. It was always the same. People missed the most important things.

"You've solved a mystery for me," he said to her, as Cohen turned to greet another guest. "Economics is supposed to be the dismal science, yet Nicholas is always so good-humored. I can see why, now." He raised his glass to her.

She laughed. "You've been an ogre to me. Everyone says you're so brilliant. When I heard them introduce you, I thought I'd have to think of something terribly clever to say. But I have an idea that you're really quite human."

"Just a *facade*," Ambrose said somberly. "I'm probably quite horrible underneath. People can be the opposite of what they look. It must be the same in Threadneedle Street, where they're always toasting you. The pictures one sees of City men in the newspapers make them all look like monsters — *'the men whose heads do grow beneath their shoulders'* — but I expect they're as gentle as lambs really. . . ."

"Whereas you, who look like a lamb. . . ."

"Oh, I *have* to be ruthless privately, because I'm a professional philosopher. We're not allowed to fudge things. We have to understand what we're saying and act on it. The one thing we can't say is: 'Oh I didn't really mean it.'"

"How uncomfortable!" Olga cried. "Suppose you made a moral judgment on somebody and decided that the world would be a better place without him. Can you see yourself taking steps. . . ."

"We debate it all the time," Ambrose said. "We go even further. We ask ourselves whether we are really debating. We have only to go back to Hume. How can we believe in the veracity of our senses?"

"Well, *do* you?"

"I do, I do — but not, I fear, conventionally. I am not, therefore, what I seem."

"You are very nice," Olga said. "You don't frighten me a bit. Ah, *there's* a man who *really* frightens me. . . ."

Over Ambrose's shoulder, she was waving at someone without much evidence of genuine terror. Ambrose, turning, saw a familiar figure — dark, virile — bearing down on them, accompanied by a tall dazzling blonde. Of course: Basruk was bound to be here.

The blonde notwithstanding, he was embracing Olga succulently within seconds of slapping Ambrose painfully on the back.

"You goddamed usurper," he croaked at him. "First, you take over the Treasury, and now you're after Olga, my personal painter. Well, I've prepared myself. Let me introduce you. Olga, Ambrose: this is Ingrid. And listen, Ambrose. She is grappled to my soul with hoops of steel, so keep off."

Ingrid, well-endowed, seemed to ripple all over as she laughed. "This is always Zilto's yoke," she said in Scandinavian sing-song, "because my father is President of Sweden Steel Corporation. Zilto does not love *me:* he loves my father. Is that not so?" She looked down at her swain with the most total devotion.

Basruk, giving her a squeeze, was still concentrating on Ambrose. "You're changing over into the right field, moving to economics. I did a research study for her father last year, and look at the reward. I expect that's what you're really after. Besides, it's more fun. You never see a party like this when Freddie Ayer publishes a slim volume of philosophic doubts."

It was true enough, Ambrose thought, looking round at the guests. It was a strange example of the power of the word. These people — Treasury officials, City men, economic journalists — didn't *do* anything any more than he did, but when *they* spoke, or wrote, things happened — money changed hands, factories opened or collapsed, men went on holiday or on the dole. They all knew each other — spoke each other's shorthand. At one level they played it all, as the Foreign Office did, like a game: but the prizes here were surely too substantial to be left to innocence. One didn't sense corruption in the air — certainly not in this good-natured sparkle — but could it be absent with so much manipulation on hand? Strange that Olga should have asked him about a moral judgment and where it might lead. He'd never had that kind of decision to take: but now, dragged into this world, he might find. . . .

Was that how Basruk operated? *Hoops of steel.* He was certainly frank about the money motive. What was one to make of his suddenly turning up at the Treasury? He led one on, somehow, to this kind of speculation. Probably did it on purpose.

"When is my next sitting?" he was saying to Olga. "She's painting me," he explained to Ambrose with something verging

33

on unctuousness. "Would tomorrow at eleven be a good time?"

Ambrose turned to say hello to an old friend — or rather a *young* friend, Marina Vaizey, who had joined them. Her husband John, Professor of Economics in London, had taught for a while at Oxford, where Ambrose had met them. Marina, now art critic for a Sunday paper, had a somewhat mischievous look, hearing of the painting.

"How are you doing him?" she said to Olga. "We all wonder what lies behind that mask. Are you going to give him the Graham Sutherland treatment?"

"You're just jealous," Basruk said. "Olga's never offered to paint *you.*"

"Not Graham Sutherland," Ambrose pronounced. "Bellini. And not Giovanni but his brother Gentile. There's a miniature head by him of a young Turk in the Gardner Museum at Boston. I'm sure you know it, Marina. Weren't you at Radcliffe? It's a lovely picture. He's wearing a sumptuous gown, and a huge white turban. He has a beautifully satisfied look on his face — as if he's just found the ideal girl to add to his harem. Of course, she couldn't be as beautiful as Ingrid, but there's the same satisfaction. And the white turban!"

"I'm beginning to be frightened of you after all," Olga said. "I mean *Gentile* rather than Giovanni. . . ."

"I don't believe a word of it," Basruk said. "He's just performing."

"Not at all," Ambrose said. "It just surfaced. You and your Turkish aura. I thought of you precisely when I happened to be reading Vasari the other day. He has a nice story of how the Grand Turk saw a portrait by Giovanni Bellini which some ambassador had brought with him. It was the first portrait he had ever seen — painting likenesses was forbidden to Mohammedans — and he was quite staggered by the realism. So he got in touch with the Senate in Venice and told them to send Bellini to him to do some portraits, which he proposed to enjoy secretly, sinfully, the way the Indians drink whisky. The Senate didn't want to send Giovanni: he was too important. So they sent his brother Gentile, who was a good painter anyhow: certainly good enough for an infidel Turk who would never know the difference. Hence the young man in a turban now in Boston. And I will make a special point of going to see him again when I go over next week."

"I like the idea of drinking in paintings secretly," Marina said.

"Perhaps that's the answer to what I'm always being asked: what happens to famous paintings that are stolen and obviously can't be shown publicly? I can, in fact, believe that someone might gloat over them. . . . Ah, there's John. Come and say hello. He's going over to America himself in a couple of weeks."

As they pushed through the guests, helping themselves to champagne, en route, from a hovering waiter, Ambrose saw Hepworth at the other end of the room, and, for a moment, felt his spirits flag. He had a peculiar distaste, this time, to getting involved with him and his "just-keep-an-eye-open" attitude. He was suspicious of it, though for no reason that he could identify. Or was it Gloria? For a long time he hadn't thought of her: now she was on his mind. How had she died? It was so sad, so confused.

Joining the group with Vaizey proved sobering in a different way. It was the Common Market they were talking about, not the gossip of politics, and not even tangible realities — say beef or sugar — but something that sounded like the theory of customs unions, as if one were back around Sir Olaf's table at the Treasury. In the swift introductions, one man they seemed to be cross-examining was apparently Professor Harry Johnson of the London School of Economics. A tall fair young man, jumping in as if he were activated by quicksilver, was the prime cross-examiner. Ambrose remembered him — Peter Jay — as a precociously bright undergraduate. Now, of course, he was a precociously bright economic journalist. Another man standing there looked vaguely familiar. He was very healthy looking, rather solid, and with a bristling set of whiskers. His name, which had sounded like Williams, didn't ring a bell, however.

Peter Jay, having seen the new arrival, was delighted. "Ambrose! Just the man we need," he exclaimed. " We're trying to pry a mystery out of Professor Johnson. Can trade diversion through a customs union ever be beneficial?"

"He's foreshortening a bit," Vaizey said apologetically. "It's one of those seminal arguments. Started with Jacob Viner twenty-five years ago. Everyone's got in on the act."

"A very simple question really," Johnson said. "I've got a note on it coming out in the *Economic Journal*. You have to balance the initial shift of trade to a higher cost location — which by itself is welfare-*decreasing* — against the *increase* in trade due to substitution, which is welfare-*increasing*. Read my note. It's a plea for common sense against semantics."

35

"And that's all that Viner meant?" Jay cried. "It's the mystery of the dog in the night."

"Sounds eminently reasonable to me," Ambrose said, "speaking, of course, as a total ignoramus. Anything expressed as a balance is like one of Wittgenstein's non-stateable propositions. It's nice to state things in meaningful propositions if you can: but some things are meaningful by being simply manifest — or conjectures."

The whiskers-man joined in with evident approval. He had a surprisingly mellifluous voice. "An Achilles question," he murmured. "Puzzling but not beyond all conjecture."

The party was beginning to break up, and Jefferson Cohen had drifted across to them. "Come and defend me, Jeff," Johnson said to him. "I thought I knew what I had been saying until Mr. Usher here brought up Wittgenstein."

"But that's exactly it," Ambrose exclaimed. "It's what you're *not* saying that matters. You remember Wittgenstein's awful remark: 'My work consists of two parts: the words I have put down, plus all the things I have *not* written; and it is the *second* part that is the important one.'"

"'*Impelled of invisible tides and fulfilled of unspeakable things*'." Whiskers seemed to have a quotation for everything. First Sir Thomas Browne; now Swinburne. He's worse than me, Ambrose thought.

Out of the corner of his eye, he saw Hepworth making his way across. Yes, it was time they had a word.

"How was the Treasury meeting?" Hepworth asked quietly as they stood together alone. "Helpful?"

"There were moments. Yes, there were moments. I can see that there's a big issue unfolding. I heard a lot. I think I can say that I *learnt* a lot. But where I shall fit in, I know not. It's like listening to these characters here. I expect they're serious, but they have a way of making it sound like a word-game. I expect to be even more baffled at the American end."

"You should see Jefferson Cohen when you're there," Hepworth said. "I'll get them to send you his new book. He seems to understand international trade very well: and he has a great gift for simple explanation. He's written a text-book which has earned him millions."

"So I hear. But aren't we going beyond my brief? I thought I was simply going to see your friend there and tell you what I thought of him — or what's behind him."

"Isn't that what you're supposed to be good at, *Appearance and Reality?*"

"Might have been fun trying that at the Treasury today. What a set of characters! They seemed to be trooping on and off the stage as if they were performing for my benefit."

"Starting with Sir Olaf?"

"Sir Olaf indeed. But there were others too. Bert, I think, was my favorite: Bert Prescott, the Yorkshire terrier. Then Basruk erupted on the scene. And we mustn't forget Timothy Fosdyke, your own golden boy. We sang *Boris Godunov* together on the steps of No. 10. His Russian is superb."

The whiskers-man passed them at that moment with a slight wave. "Ah, you know him," Ambrose said. "Who is he? He recites quotations in the most beautiful speaking voice, so perfect that I know he must be a foreigner. But I couldn't determine the national origin. His name sounded like Williams."

Hepworth laughed. "His name is Willis, and he works at the Terrace with me — very closely, in fact. So he's *echt* British. Now, with that as a clue, where does he come from?"

"Well," Ambrose said, "with that meticulous pronunciation, it has to be either Aberdeen or Galway. Probably Galway. Faint Irish lilt."

"Galway it is. I thought you might have run into him in the United States. He's been working there a lot."

"I did think at first that I'd seem him somewhere, either in person or in a painting. A *painting!*" He broke off. "Of course. That's it. The whiskers. That earthy face plus those bristling whiskers. It's Rembrandt's *Polish Nobleman* in the National Gallery in Washington. That really rich solid face and bristling whiskers. Only one thing is missing: there should be a large pearl earring hanging from his right ear. Does he ever wear one?"

"I'll ask him. But it's the whiskers, isn't it? You can't imagine his face without them. When he's on a tour of duty he just shaves them off and becomes totally anonymous."

Oh dear, Ambrose thought. Shaving off whiskers and what else in Hepworth's horrible world. "*And thus I clothe my naked villainy. . . .*" Well, he was not yet entirely embedded in that atmosphere. He thought of this as Olga Davenport came up to say goodnight, and extended her cheek for a friendly kiss. Just the day before, he had been reading a spy story in which the hero says farewell to a beautiful blonde. " *He kissed her: and as their lips met, she passed him, mouth-to-mouth, the tiny steel capsule of instructions, which he slid easily under his tongue.*" Now why didn't Hepworth recruit Olga? Surely *that* would add to the gaiety of nations.

He went back to Oxford on the last train. The next days flew by while he got ready for the journey.

The Jefferson Cohen book duly arrived and was indeed illuminating. Its tone seemed very simple and practical after all the Treasury theorizing. Where theory surfaced, it seemed to go out of its way to be rather sceptical of Keynes. Perhaps that was the new fashion. The central theme was the flexibility of international trade. One began to see where Fletcher and his TCC fitted in, and it wasn't too reassuring for an Englishman. The multinationals might have haloes round them in Chamber of Commerce literature. In Professor Johnson's term, they were clearly "welfare-increasing." But there seemed to be a mailed U.S. fist there behind the scene. And if the fist was not genuinely American but motivated elsewhere — as Hepworth thought possible — it was even worse. One had one's own idea of how peace and welfare might grow. Fletcher didn't quite belong.

But did people always have to belong? Did there have to be a *clerisy,* in Coleridge style, of welfare-increasers? Surely there were people who stood outside any known style. Sir Olaf, for example — art fancier and gambler extraordinary. It was the gambler side that seemed the more significant. What kind of gambler was he? Not a Dostoevsky type, desperate and small-time. No: the scene would have to be more fateful.

Some music began to float through Ambrose's head — an opera — *The Queen of Spades* — those awesome timpani strokes as Herman's fate is sealed. Was Sir Olaf a Herman, very confident that after Three and Seven he will draw the Ace, but faced unbelievingly with the Queen that is turned up, with death to follow? Ambrose could hear the music surging: "*Shto nasha zhizn? Igra!*" — "What is our life? a gamble!" As always with Tchaikovsky, there was a delicious frisson to go with it.

He had come into Hall — it was his last evening — rather pleased to be going, yet somehow uncertain. The visit would have been routine, but now, the talk with Hepworth and the visit to the Treasury had released all kinds of doubts. Was Hepworth really innocent as he pretended? Was Sir Olaf — *per contra* — less devilish than he sounded? And what, in sober fact, was the use of speculating? Sufficient unto the day are the rhetorical questions thereof, he murmured in S.J. Perelman's immortal words, as he slid into his seat at High Table.

At the Terrace, too, they went on routinely with their work. Four days after the Treasury meeting which Ambrose had attended, Willis — whiskers bristling as ever — came into Hepworth's room carrying a piece of paper whose message he now sought to communicate.

"Not very good," he said to Hepworth. "The story's come back from two of my street-cleaners, one in Odessa and the other in Ankara. But this may be just an internal repetition. I'll examine it. Anyhow, it's the Treasury meeting. A summary of Prescott's report and the financial steps that Sir Olaf summarized at the end — identical with what Timothy Fosdyke told us."

"More detailed than usual?"

"Yes, it seems so. It *was* a specially important meeting."

"And the links?"

"Well, you know as well as I do. The old ones plus the new ones."

"New ones?"

"Timothy says that there's a new Principal in Olaf's office. I suppose one has to note also that it was the first time that Basruk had been around."

"And, of course, Ambrose," Hepworth said wearily.

"As you say, Ambrose."

Hepworth sat silent for a moment, and then looked up. "There's one more question, Patrick. Have you ever thought of wearing a large pearl earring in your right ear?"

"Pearl earring?"

"You must try it," Hepworth said. "Ambrose recommends it."

III

IT never let you down. How many visits, each one more marvelous? Sitting now in the restaurant, waiting for his host to come back from the telephone, he had a faint sight, through the curtained window, of the Gardens, and beyond that of Boston Common. In this particular spot, the surrender to America had a sigh of contentment in it. It was a peculiar joy to sit in a little 18th century enclave, aware of the 20th century excitement that the rest of the city generated. But there was happiness too in the gargantuan world outside to which this was such a contrast. The Fathers had found this huge country and responded in kind, with imagination on a scale that renewed itself continuously. It was a mood that had not ended with the postwar disillusionment. One could talk of Italy — or even England — collapsing: with America, collapse was shakeout or stimulus, as when they knocked down vast areas of brick and stone, filled in marshes, diverted rivers with careless confidence that the new dams or skyscrapers were what they had been waiting for. Driving from the airport, he had been dazzled at the height of the new Harrigan Center and the spacious complex of buildings around it, merging poetically with the old harbor skyline. Two years before it had not existed: now it was a living experience, quickening the blood.

He had lost his sense of excitement momentarily that morning, entering the British Consulate-General for the talk with Mr. Upjohn that had been laid-on. The office was in the Prudential Building, high-up and with a splendid view across the Bay: yet as one went in, past the posters in the outer office advertising the charms of Brighton and Gleneagles, it was as if one's spirit was being pushed back into one of those stiff ugly brief-cases that British civil servants carry around with them. At

41

first, Upjohn seemed part of the same picture. Only when he began to talk of the subject that Hepworth had raised did one see a different man. He knew his job: and his job was to understand the sinews of big business in and around the forcing house of Boston. As he spoke, a picture emerged that was very different from the business world that Ambrose had known in Washington. The power came here, it seemed, not through a labyrinthine exploitation of Government connections, but directly through money — or rather money and society: and society was a broader concept than the world of the Brahmin New England families. The Irish, the Italians, the Jews, the Greeks — one had to follow all the connections, all the influences, to see where they might lead. Mr. Upjohn seemed to know it all. No one could have expounded it better, admired it more, understood the detail more thoroughly.

But from the outside. And this, Ambrose realized, was where the difference lay for himself. His own fervor was not simply a dazzled reaction to the sight of these vast parkways and high buildings. Coming back here was to offer *himself* for transformation. Rationally, it was absurd. He knew, coming down the steps of the plane, that he would behave the same way, meet the same friends with the same interests. He had seen it all before. But he also knew that these old things would shake themselves into something new, injected with excitement that sprang from the air itself.

Oddly enough, one went through it in order to enjoy England all the more. He'd had a brief reminder of this coming into Boston from the airport and suddenly seeing a huge, scarlet London bus moving along the road comfortably, calmly, almost in disdain of the traffic confusion around it. Boston, it seemed, was having a British Trade Week, and the appearance of a London bus was *de rigueur* on such occasions. How happily it brought everything back — the human scale of London, its quiet pride, the heart-tugging outline of a London bus rolling — almost floating — over Westminster Bridge towards the pinnacles of the House of Commons. How awful, being here, if one didn't have that waiting quietly for one's return.

But in the meantime one had to break out of the accustomed grooves. Being in America was like some gigantic shaking of the dice, a game being played all through the night, with stakes doubled and re-doubled as excitement mounted — the way Sir Olaf played backgammon, no doubt. Yes: *there* was someone who obviously responded to America the same way. He, too, seemed to feel that if one gave oneself, something with the intensity of America came back. Intensity, size, power — perhaps in the end this *was* enough to explain it. Everything, good and bad, was bigger here — villainy, generosity, ruthlessness, imagination: and most peculiar of all, there were men who rose to all these qualities at once. One didn't have to approve: one responded. One knew on every visit that something startling would happen, without knowing how. Even here, in the Ritz-Carlton? Well, perhaps not. In this haven of luxury and soft lights, one simply recouped one's spirit — after a visit to the British Consulate-General — with the frostiest of martinis.

He had found a note from Jefferson Cohen awaiting his arrival at his hotel in Cambridge — the Mayflower. The Consul-General had already sent out invitations to the cocktail party for him, which was for the next day. Cohen, tracking down his lair, had proposed a lunch "before you're swamped," nominating the Ritz-Carlton in Boston as "the only place to eat when all is said and done." So here he was, and Cohen — he would surely be calling him Jeff before many hours had passed — was on his way back from the phone.

It was nice how everything was spacing itself out, as if there were a pattern ready to fall into. A quiet lunch at the Ritz to start with — two people from different worlds exploring each other. In the evening there was the party that Bill Rafferty was giving, which would be considerably more raucous. In the interval? Perhaps he'd go round the Museum of Fine Arts just to charge his batteries.

The restaurant was half-full, the waiters moving swiftly and silently against only the faintest tinkle of glasses and a soft murmur of voices. Between Ambrose and the doorway, a table had just been taken by a pleasant-looking couple, the man youngish, handsome in an Italian kind of way — clean-cut features, gray-streaked hair — the woman rather plain at first sight, black hair parted in the middle and pulled back to a large bun at her neck, in a style reminiscent of those eminently highborn Victorian ladies. No, he decided: more human and alive than that: more like Willa Cather or the young Mary McCarthy. Cohen, seeing them as he came towards Ambrose, stopped and raised his arms in the warmest of greetings. A brief word, with a glance towards Ambrose, and he was on his way back to him.

"Old friends," he said. "I suggested we might have coffee

43

together. You'll like them. Well, at least you'll like *her*. *He's* an acquired taste — or so it seems," he added glumly.

"Economists?" Ambrose asked.

"No, different world altogether. They're both in art history. He's an Italian — you can see it, can't you? Domenico Franzoni: he's on the Faculty. She's on her own: hard to describe. She's written some technical studies of Renaissance painting — very slender volumes, I think; but she also seems to be an adviser to museums and collectors."

It was clear enough that the professor's interest was far less casual than this all sounded. Her name, it seemed, was Alice Summers.

"She spells it Alyss," Cohen said, spelling it out, "Alyss Desmoines Summers."

"Ah, that's better," Ambrose said. "American women pundits always have to have those three-barrelled names, like Frances Parkinson Keyes or — "

"I like Alyss," Cohen said, "with or without all those names. She looks very quiet, doesn't she, very prim and proper? In fact, she's got something terrific building up. I don't know what it is, but there's a kind of excitement in her as if she were on the track of something. I wish she hadn't taken up with that Franzoni character. I suppose he's helping her, but I don't trust him. I don't know why. Probably because he's too good-looking."

The waiter had come up and they ordered. The range — the quality — it was all obviously perfect. If Cohen had shown irritation it soon vanished, especially when he heard that Ambrose had been reading his book.

"Hope it made sense to you," he said. "Of course, I'm not supposed to care about individual reader reaction. All that my publishers want to know is whether it has that "x" quality that will make it a must for college courses."

"You've done that already with another book, I gather," Ambrose said.

"Yes, on the new math teaching methods. But it's in economics where the prize lies. Samuelson's had it too much to himself, and I've got to knock him off. Besides, I think the Keynesians are all old-hat — macro-economic measures and all that. There isn't a natural market any more, or so I argue. Did you in fact find it clear?"

"Extremely so — especially on international matters, and for a reason that you could never have anticipated. I happened to

44

hear some Treasury folk gossiping on the day of your party in London about a mysterious American woman financier they all adored called 'Rosa,' whom I now see is only a mere male called 'Mr. Roosa': and I find that SDRs, which baffled me, are Special Drawing Rights and are as good as gold. Is that right?"

"Well, almost. Let's say as good as the IMF currency-basket."

"Ah, yes. I read about that in the *Financial Times*. I read it now, you know: I mean the *financial* part: I used only to read the Arts page — Andrew Porter and all that, best in England: but now I begin to follow the jargon in the other part. I can just about follow it, now that I've read your book. But you've left me very puzzled about one thing — liquidity. The supply of international reserves seems to have increased enormously with SDRs and all that. I think you said that they're now close to 200 billion dollars — much more if gold were counted in at the market price. What I can't understand is why should everyone be afraid of an impending shortage of liquidity. With all those reserves and floating exchange rates, shouldn't the system hold up indefinitely?"

"Indeed it should. But individual countries don't play the game in this spirit. They all want to be free to defend their chosen exchange-rates in their own way. No use counting on them to work according to floating-rate theory. They just want to be liquid by their own standards. They believe in it, like free will."

"I see," Ambrose said. "It reminds me of that poem by Rupert Brooke on the theological speculations of fish — you know, fish in a pond:

> '*And sure the reverent eye must see*
> *A purpose in liquidity.*'

We're all little fish, aren't we, especially poor old England, kidding ourselves that we're swimming around freely, but really being manipulated. For example, we have huge inflows of money at present, don't we — oil money and lots of speculative investment. Why can't we just sit on it and adapt it to our purpose?"

Cohen laughed. "You don't do too badly. Luckily for you, the Sheikhs of Araby still trust you with the money, especially as it offers a high rate of interest. But it's also your girls. It just happens that the Sheikhs adore English girls. I think it's the chubby kind they go for. You can offer them French girls or Italian girls, or even Swedes: but nothing ever gets them like these chubby English girls. It's your secret weapon. What these girls will do for King and Country is unbelievable. From what I've been told, the Bank of England sets them up afterwards in a little house in Cheltenham or Bournemouth and they're perfectly happy."

"And what's the *American* secret weapon?"

"Originality, it seems to me. Power, yes: but expressed in some original form. Security and a high rate of interest is quite satisfying. Now that the frontier is exhausted in America itself, we need the thrill of exploiting some great new frontier elsewhere — like China."

"What about Eastern Europe?"

"Oh, yes: that's where a lot of things can happen, and *are* happening: not Russia itself but the Satellites. It could be startling. The difficulty there is how to get in."

"I suppose the big corporations can channel their credits," Ambrose suggested.

They had reached the dessert stage in their lunch. A kind of *zabaglione* had arrived in a tall glass, with a biscuit in a saucer which Cohen picked up and crumbled slowly in his fingers.

"That's the *orthodox* way," he said. "I explained all that in my book. But, at the same time, a lot is going on in an *unorthodox* way which one can't pin down. Take the flow of money. Money isn't the same kind of thing everywhere, like water coming out of a tap. If it were, all you'd have to think about is money that comes through a bank. But cash — banknotes — gold itself: what's happened in European industry in the last ten years would be inexplicable without this element. It's been on a scale you can't believe."

"Where does it come from — or who does it come *through?* The Mafia?"

"A lot of it, yes. But it's so convenient for all the others to leave the legend with the *Italian* mafia. I wouldn't sniff at the *Greek* mafia — or the *Irish* one for that matter."

"The Kennedy complex?"

Cohen laughed. "It's really marvelous how the people who want to stay in the background manage to fob ideas off on the man-in-the-street. To you, Irish money means the Kennedys. But they're relatively small-fry, and they're also relatively clean. There's plenty that's Irish of the other kind, and far far bigger.

Did you see the Harrigan Center as you drove in from the airport?"

"I did. Immense. That's John P. Harrigan, isn't it? Said to be a recluse."

"John Patrick Harrigan. Complete recluse. No family. Never appears in public. Totally devout Catholic: and the lynchpin of every activity that you might call Irish mafia for the last fifty years."

"If he's a recluse, who runs his empire for him?"

"It's a double front. Openly, he works through some of the huge multinational corporations, but his hoods are everywhere behind the scenes, as bad as Chicago in the twenties. Everyone in Boston knows it. Perhaps I shouldn't compare it with Chicago. One has to allow for the local aura. In Chicago it had to be crude open butchery. It went with the place: they expected it. In Boston it's more discreet, more civilized, you might say."

"A corpse by any other name. . . ."

"No: I wouldn't write off the civilizing effect of Boston. I expect it's worked its way through to Harrigan in some form or other, whether we know it or not. I'm told he collects paintings, for one thing. We can ask Alyss: she's sure to know. I see that they want to join us."

As they got up to greet the pair from the other table, Ambrose realized that he had been right to see Alyss Summers in a Victorian picture-frame. But *late* Victorian — an oval face of great seriousness that one had seen in Burne-Jones, or in photographs of the great Fabian ladies. Was it this that generated the *living* quality, which came through in a kind of reassuring calm. She had a firm American voice, with some echoes, perhaps, of the Mid-West. She volunteered immediately that she'd "heard" of Ambrose's previous lectures and was "looking forward" to the new series. When was the first lecture? Tomorrow? She'd love to go if she could. They all professed to be interested. But all the same, Ambrose was rather pleased. This was the kind of audience he liked.

Cohen was fussing over her and rather ignoring the Italian, who seemed, if one was being objective, lively and attractive, even if he *was* too good-looking.

"We were talking about John P. Harrigan," Cohen said to Miss Summers. "Mr. Usher here — Ambrose — is obviously trying to find out all about Boston in one easy lesson. I said I'd heard somewhere that John P. collected pictures. Have you ever come across this side of him?"

"Yes, I have," she said. "I was telling Domenico about it. He seems to have begun collecting a few years ago. One gradually heard of pictures being bought for him at auctions. He likes Italian paintings with a Christian subject. He's paid some big prices."

"Have you seen them?" Ambrose asked.

"It's supposed to be very difficult," she said, "but I was lucky. I did a program on Renaissance painting about six months ago on Educational TV, and apparently he saw it and approved. Anyhow, I was invited to his house — it's a huge kind of fortress, with high walls and gates, about fifteen miles out, in the Beresford direction: and I saw his pictures — or some of them. Not very remarkable really, those I saw: mostly School of this and *Amico* of that. He himself is infinitely more unusual than his paintings."

"Jeff thinks" — Ambrose had decided that the time had come for Christian names — "that Boston culture may have softened up any earlier crudities."

"All I can say is that he terrified me," she said. "Not by anything he did, of course, but with his extraordinary intensity. He's very old now — well over 80, I suppose. He was a brawny Irishman once, but now he seems shrivelled up, almost like the pictures one sees of John D. Rockefeller the First. But there was something very peculiar about his intensity. It's the kind you might expect in a great scholar — or a saint: very pure. He's not so, by all accounts, in his business affairs."

"You were saying that he wanted to ask you about his Pinturicchio," Franzoni interjected.

"Yes. He wasn't very sure if it was authentic, and neither was I. It's a very dashing kind of painting — *St. John in the Wilderness* — rather like a fresco on the same subject in the cathedral at Siena. It seemed rather casual and gaudy to me. But then Pinturicchio is like that. Vasari has him pinned down perfectly. He praises some of the work as 'skillful' and then says: 'He did a lot of other works, but as they were not very excellent, I will pass over them in silence.'"

"I think Vasari could be just an old grouch," Ambrose said. "I was reading him by chance just the other day. It's true enough that Pinturicchio was a provincial kind of painter: it's all rather pretty. But he had a nice gentle feeling. I must say, I agree with

Berenson. He finds the Pinturicchio paintings in the Borgia apartments 'very charming.' Vasari just had a down on him." He broke off to laugh. "I love that story about the trunk that he tells."

She smiled. "Oh yes, do tell it."

"I think I've got it right," Ambrose said. "Wasn't it that he was commissioned to paint a fresco in a large empty room in a Siena monastery? There was a huge old trunk with heavy padlocks in the room, and he insisted on the monks taking it away before he would start painting. They said it was too heavy to move. He said: take it away or no fresco. When the monks finally got it outside, they decided they'd try to see what on earth made it so heavy. So they broke open the padlocks and found it full of gold ducats. Poor old Pinturicchio was terribly upset when he found out what his obstinacy had cost him. He couldn't stop talking about it. In fact he was so chagrined that he died."

"Just the kind of thing that might happen *chez* Harrigan," Cohen said. "I'll bet there are plenty of ducats stashed away there. He's the kind of man that has to keep it all in cash."

"And you say he has no family," Ambrose said. "No attachments? Has he any sense of continuity? What's his aim?"

"His aim," Alyss said, with a peculiar kind of seriousness, "is to go to Heaven. And *my* aim" — she changed her tone as she rose to her feet — "is to go to the Museum."

"By a strange coincidence," Ambrose said with mock solemnity, "that is *my* aim too. Always on my first day I begin the rounds, just for refreshment. I will accompany you: unless, that is. . . ."

"No, I would be delighted," she said. The other two had to go back to Cambridge, it seemed. Franzoni offered Cohen a lift. They were all on their way to the door when Alyss said unexpectedly to Ambrose: "I have something to do before the Museum. Suppose we meet there, say at four."

Ambrose nodded. "Let me make a private bet with myself. In what precise spot?"

She smiled. "Well, let's stick with the Renaissance. How about the panel by Benvenuto di Giovanni — '*Expulsion from Paradise*'? I call it the three Hippies — Adam, Eve and the Angel. Don't you think they look like hippies — so lean and wild-haired?"

When Ambrose was off on intellectual flirtation, he was impossible. Here he was, in full flight. "I have lost my bet," he said, looking into her eyes with great sincerity. "I was sure you would say in front of that huge painting of the Gay Quarters of Kyoto. Such a marvelous setting for a rendezvous."

She didn't seem to mind, responding in the same tone of solemn absurdity. "I might have chosen that," she said, "but it's on loan for an Oriental Art Exhibition at the Toronto Museum."

Franzoni burst into a great hoot of laughter. Cohen looked at Ambrose glumly. However, all was well as they parted at the doorway with many expressions of mutual esteem. Hurrying somewhat, Cohen and Franzoni set off towards the car. Ambrose, pausing while his topcoat was collected, waved to Alyss as she set off down the street.

He was still watching her, reflectively, as he slipped his arms into the sleeves of his coat. She was almost at the corner when he saw a man who had been standing in a doorway, close by the Ritz entrance, turn to follow her. There was nothing very hurried about it, but the intent was unmistakeable. She turned right at the corner, and so did he.

Ambrose stuck his hands into his topcoat pockets morosely. Some private detective, no doubt. Divorce or something. And if it *was* that, the odds were that she knew she was being followed. Was that why she'd preferred to go on alone? Could be.

There was a taxi waiting and he climbed into it to go to the Museum. As they rolled along, the scene was as cheerful as ever, but for the moment he was responding with less enthusiasm. To see someone being followed was disconcerting. A rather gruesome thought slipped into his head. He had assumed some petty marital involvement: but equally it might be some American Hepworth at work. The Hepworths of this world were busy everywhere. It was horrible.

A previous occupant of the taxi had left a newspaper on the seat. Ambrose picked it up: the *Boston Mail* — Rafferty's paper. He had read it that morning, but he held the paper in his hand for a moment, thinking of Rafferty. Somehow it was restorative. No need to worry about Hepworth with a man like Bill Rafferty around.

It would be a good party: bound to be. Why did one like Rafferty so much? Because he was so uncomplicated. He seemed to know everything and everybody, but was so relaxed about it. He just didn't give a damn.

Why was that admirable? One *should* give a damn: and to be accurate, Rafferty obviously did. But there were some journalists — and he was one — who could take in the horror without surprise, without alarm, just because, having seen everything, they had worked out a way of staying human through it all. He would be particularly good on Boston, Ambrose thought. It must be an open book to him — years on the *Globe*, and then, after Washington and Paris, to be back as editor of the *Mail*. No one was freer with information, especially after the whisky began to circulate. A pleasant thought. Ambrose sat back comforted.

He had located "*The Expulsion from Paradise*" when he arrived. Standing before it again for his four o'clock appointment, he tried to analyze the peculiar tortured quality that came through so clearly.

The painter, Benvenuto, was from Siena. Ambrose didn't see the three figures as hippies, though certainly it was a modern scene — Adam and Eve looking lost, for good reason, and even the Angel very unsure of himself. They were all three curiously flat and washed out. Was there something in the Siena landscape that stimulated despair? Think of the Massacio in the Carmine church in Florence on the same subject, where Adam and Eve are two beautifully rounded, elegant figures, a little unhappy, maybe, but still looking forward to a brave new world.

Alyss was there. He turned and saw her smiling. "I'm very fond of it," she said, "but then I respond to everything from Siena."

"Not so rich and creamy as Florence at the same time?"

"Something like that," she said. "Have you been round the Oriental part yet?"

"No, but is that what you want?"

"I'll follow you round. I owed myself a visit. Nothing special I have to see."

They wandered off, losing themselves in the huge empty "*Snowscape*" of Kino Sansetsu, and then to a succession of scrolls and screens, coming to rest at what was perhaps his favorite — it would certainly have been Hogarth's — "*The Chinese poet, Lipo, Intoxicated.*" In a seraphic mood of content, they sat down on a bench for a final chat, talking in an unforced way of many things. Of the man who had followed her, Ambrose said nothing. It was her private affair.

All very pleasant, except that he just didn't believe that her visit to the Museum was as casual as she had suggested. He had the strangest feeling — absurd as it sounded — that she had announced she was going precisely to see if he would go too. Why? Not for his *beaux yeux*, that was sure. It was rather as if she was feeling her way towards something and wanted to explore it further through Ambrose. She had seen that he was at home with painting, and thought of opening up some issue with him: but what? No hint in their talk of what it was: they had just wandered easily into a number of fields, all very casually, too casually. She was not a woman who wanted merely to pass the time agreeably. Too clever for that: and too purposeful. Uncomfortable in a way, but exciting. . . .

She was exciting to look at, too, the black hair drawn back to shape the oval of her face, large gray eyes — very cool — very alert. . . .

A woman curator came up to greet her and ask her advice about something. It was a signal for Ambrose to go. She asked casually where he was staying, and he told her. No talk of future meetings, simply politeness — "how nice . . . how pleasant." He took a cab back to the Mayflower, and got out his papers to prepare for his lecture next morning.

He had asked Bill Rafferty, when they talked on the telephone, why they had moved to Boston. He had always enjoyed their pleasantly ramshackle house in Cambridge. "Couldn't resist the apartment here," Bill had said. "So vast: so opulent. We could be gangsters. It's wonderful."

One had to remember that gangsters lived at different levels. The seedy desperadoes, stationed out in poolrooms or lonely diners beyond the city-line, lived off fear and fatigue, lightened only by a code they accepted: "Yeh, that's right. That's the way y'have to do it." For documentation, there was the marvelous "*Friends of Eddie Coyle*." Once you had met Eddie Coyle, you seemed to know every seedy Boston gangster who had ever lived.

The higher-ups, whom they rarely met, could live as solid citizens in New England Avenue, as Rafferty now did. The really top guys, for whom the hirelings worked at four or five degrees removed, lived in true baronial style like John P. Harrigan, safe from any intrusion except in the odd circumstances described by Alyss Summers.

A very stable picture, Ambrose thought, rolling along towards Rafferty's apartment at around nine o'clock. The feudalism made it so reliable. The day-to-day mechanisms were as securely fashioned as in the City of London. There were wild men here and there, but for the most part it worked through friendship, loyalty, an acceptance of one's place in the scheme of things. The vast business deals were beyond ordinary ken. At the human level, things were safely patterned.

The grace of Boston on a quiet autumn evening was part of this picture. Out of the window of the cab, he saw the floodlit dome of State House — splendor but on a human scale. At this season, the Common might be dry and dusty by day, but in the sweetness of the evening, with twinkling lamps dotting its mild slope, one responded to its ease and spaciousness. The trees rustled gently. The magnificence of New England Avenue stretched ahead proudly. They had just turned into it when they heard the first shots — two sharp sounds as from a revolver, followed by a rapid round of machine-gun fire which tore the air apart.

Ambrose felt a sudden swaying, almost as if he were bouncing on a bed, as the driver rammed on his brakes. Ahead, he saw people running.

"Think I'll keep out of this," the driver said. Ambrose fished hurriedly in his wallet and found a five dollar bill. The driver took his time to give change while Ambrose peered ahead impatiently, wondering what had happened. As he opened the door, a large black car raced past, and he had a sudden fear.

"Are we near the number I gave you?" he asked.

"Just down there — about a couple of hundred yards," the driver said nonchalantly, as he began to reverse and drive off in the opposite direction.

From the distance, Ambrose heard a faint wailing sound, and in a moment, it seemed, the police sirens had begun to ululate from all directions. He rushed down the street towards the crowd, panting with the sudden exertion, and trying desperately to decipher the numbers on the doorways as he ran.

With alarm, he saw that it was at the number of Rafferty's doorway that the action was centered. In front of the doorway stood a large white car; and on the road itself a body was spread-eagled, with the police closing in around it. His foreboding was so strong that he elbowed his way, almost with anger, to get through the police and see the body. It was of a fair-haired young man, in a kind of chauffeur's suit. Not Rafferty, he thought thankfully, as a policeman grabbed him roughly to ask what the hell he thought he was doing.

"I'm visiting this house," he said, and suddenly saw Rafferty. "Bill!" he shouted. "It's Mr. Rafferty," he told the policeman. "He's editor of the *Mail*."

The police circle, with men on the ground examining the body, now enclosed Ambrose. What he seemed to hear most were sirens and racing engines. Suddenly there were two floodlights beamed on the body and those around it. To the crowd, now being forced back, it must have been crystal clear that Ambrose was the killer, held tightly by the police.

Rafferty, still a little distance away, had apparently not heard Ambrose's shout above the clamor: but now, holding a police-card high over his head, he was working his way through. He was tall, with grizzly-gray hair and a face lined with experience. The police knew him instantly.

"Well," he said in a faintly Irish drawl to the officer holding Ambrose. "You've got him, eh? Good work."

"Bill!" Ambrose cried. "For Godsake. . . ."

"O.K.," Rafferty said, nodding at the policeman. "He's visiting me. Who's the boy? Oh, I know him. It's O'Connell's chauffeur. Is O'Connell here?"

"He's in the sergeant's car," the policeman said. "They just winged him and he's waiting for the ambulance. Here it is."

The confusion was growing — more floodlights, a constant flashing of night-cameras, and a mounting chorus of calls and police whistles. Rafferty turned firmly to the policeman standing now next to Ambrose. "Will you take him indoors to my apartment," he said. "It's Number 4F. I want to have a word with the sergeant about O'Connell."

To the crowd, with Ambrose now following the policeman as a free man, there was a sense of let-down. For Ambrose himself, the draining of excitement had left him totally limp. Kathleen Rafferty was standing in the hallway downstairs and led him to their apartment. Inside, the guests were standing watching at the window. Kathleen found him a Scotch, and he began to feel more like himself.

"Who's O'Connell?" he asked. "Apparently the young man was his chauffeur."

Kathleen was everything the name evoked in an Irish context — dark, pert, mischievous. The Raffertys had three daughters, two already qualified as doctors and the third with just a year to go. But Kathleen still had the young look of a colleen from Killarney.

"He has the penthouse," she said. "His name is James but

everybody calls him Sligo. We're good friends: not exactly *visiting* friends, but we get on. The people who run the house — it's what *he* says that matters. Everything runs smoothly. It has to, or else. . . ." She drew her finger lightly across her throat.

"And tonight's little upset?"

"We just heard the shots. I expect they were waiting for him at the door."

"An aggrieved party, no doubt," said a handsome woman introduced as Victoria. "Didn't you have it once before?"

"Yes," Kathleen said, "but the other way round. It was real Chicago stuff. A car drove up as Sligo was coming out of the door: but just as they got their guns out, a car behind swept past and mowed them down. Never saw the second car again. Perfect timing. Everyone took it that Sligo had staged it all beautifully. But he slipped up this time, obviously."

"You'll have to come back to live in Cambridge," said Victoria's husband, a tall lean man called George Bristow, who was, it seemed a professor of engineering at MIT. "You've picked a really dangerous spot here."

"Do you think so?" Kathleen drawled in her pleasant Irish lilt. "We feel rather protected here. Sligo takes care of his own. They practically treat Bill as an honorary member."

A smallish man with an incongruously long white beard wagged a finger at her. "You are ignoring the warnings of Holy Writ. '*Can a man take fire in his bosom, and his clothes not be burned?*'" He had been introduced as Dr. Arnold Beekman, a theologian from Tufts. Ambrose remembered a rather pro-communist article of his in the *New York Review*.

Through the open door, they could hear the tramping of feet up and down the staircase — policemen, working their way through the house. One of them came in to ask them routinely what they had seen, and then left. Rafferty, who had come in with him and then disappeared to phone his paper, now reappeared with a drink in his hand. Kathleen closed the door, and they gathered round him expectantly.

"The lieutenant I spoke to seems to think it's a pay-off from that big bank job in Leander last week," he said. "They picked up a little runt called Twill who gave them some names that were bound to spell trouble. The gang who did the job were in the wrong territory."

"Is this the way a pay-off would be settled?" Ambrose asked.

"No, it isn't," Rafferty said. "It's out of scale. At the wrong level. I think the police are on the wrong track. Or perhaps they're just not telling me. But we hear a lot, you know, and I've heard there's something going on right at the top. I suppose you could call it a dynastic struggle."

"Is it personal or on policy?"

"Both. On policy, the Irish lot here seem to have been pulling themselves up to a different kind of business."

"Like the Mafia?" someone asked.

"A bit different," Rafferty said. "The Mafia have been diversified for a long time now, on both respectable and non-respectable fronts. But the Irish — at the top — have always had a yen for real respectability — lace curtains and all that."

"Haven't done too well at it, have they?" Prof. Bristow said in his dry Yankee drawl. "I recall old Joe Kennedy saying rather proudly that he was the only member of the Knights of Malta who hadn't been indicted."

"That's a long time ago," Rafferty said. "They really have moved into respectability in business deals. They own big businesses openly — although everyone knows where the money came from — and not just domestic: international too. In fact they've become especially active on the international front, because that's where they can feed in their loose cash with less questions than they'd be asked at home."

"Why don't they do some good by giving credits to Russia?" Dr. Beekman asked. "Highly respectable, and also socially useful."

Victoria Bristow had little patience for *that* idea. "Because they know as well as we do what happens to money that goes to Russia," she snorted.

"As in the Russian proverb," said a familiar voice. "When the flea has bitten once, the master is awake."

Ambrose had turned to greet the speaker, an old professorial friend called Ezekiel Ball. "Ezekiel saw de wheel!" he cried happily. "Have you been here all the time?" They were quickly at it, exchanging news.

The talk became more general as the guests helped themselves to food. Latecomers were drifting in. Drink was available in several rooms of the huge apartment. Ambrose, taken round by Kathleen, found himself back near Professor Ball and sat down with a group there.

"You are all to go to Ambrose's lecture tomorrow," the professor was saying. "What are you lecturing on, by the way? I hope 'memory.' Do you know," he told the company, "Ambrose wrote a book on Memory and everyone instantly forgot it. It's

56

very brief and out-of-print: but I think it's the best book he has written by far."

"With no disrespect to Dr. Usher," Victoria Bristow said, "I would view that recommendation with some suspicion. Ezekiel makes a fetish of the out-of-print book, the obscure article, the unknown author, the silent poet."

"Ah, now I understand his enthusiasm for me," Ambrose exclaimed. "But you know, it's rather nice all the same. I would have described Ezekiel rather differently: the genius of the unexplored middle. When I talk to him, he is always four conclusions ahead without having bothered to express any of the connections."

The professor was quite unabashed. "Are you in fact lecturing on memory?"

"Alas, no," Ambrose said. "I've forgotten what I thought about memory. I've had to think up something new. I think I shall be dealing with permissiveness and Women's Lib."

"You have been reading Gertrude Himmelfarb's new book on John Stuart Mill," Ball anounced.

Ambrose looked at him with alarm. "Is nothing secret? He is totally right," he said to the others, "and that is exactly what I meant. The genius of the unexplored middle."

"Well, it was obvious," Ball said modestly. "For two reasons. First, the combination of these two subjects arises very positively in her book. Second, she told me that she had sent you a copy to see what you made of it."

"And what *did* you make of it?" Victoria Bristow wanted to know. "Mill was one of the founders of Women's Lib, wasn't he?"

"Indeed he was," Ambrose said. "However in one regard at least, if one accepts Miss Himmelfarb's analysis, one should look on him more like an argument of *Men's* Lib. After he had finally married Harriet Taylor he became very much a mouth-piece for her views, and her views could be pretty wild."

"Men's Lib! Here's to it!" Rafferty had walked across, raising his glass as he joined them. "We've got to organize. At the present rate, the women will soon be running even the Mafia."

Ambrose sat down to talk with him. The whisky fumes seemed to vanish at will.

"Yes," he said quietly, when Ambrose asked him about the shooting. "I think we may be in for a real top-level gangster war, totally Irish this time. The Italians are running their world separately. It's more and more Vegas and California for them."

"You were talking about some of the big corporations being manipulated by Irish money," Ambrose said. "Do any of these fishy ones operate in England?"

"Well, there are a lot of rumors about TCC," Rafferty said. "That's the Trans-Commonwealth Corporation. It's Canadian in origin, but is centered on Boston now. There's one very odd character at TCC who has a lot to do with the English operation, a fellow called George Fletcher. He is, in fact, English — very pukka sahib. One of those awful Englishmen who batten on American money and get more and more British in the process. But of course: you must know him. He used to be in Washington before he moved here. Surely you remember him from there — head of the Potomac Engineering Company. Had a very pretty young wife who used to give a lot of parties."

"Oh yes, I remember her," Ambrose said soberly. "Gloria. I heard she died in a motor accident."

"Yes, I heard that too," Rafferty said. "I don't know when it was, but he married again. Claire. Very nice: very young and pretty. I think she was an actress — a rather minor one — when he discovered her. Come to think of it, very much like his first wife. God knows what they see in him. To me, he's a real creep. No accounting for women's taste, I know, but still. . . ."

"Nothing more impressive than an impressive Englishman," Ambrose suggested.

"Not to an Irishman it ain't," Rafferty said. "That's one of the mysteries. Claire is Irish — well, Irish stock. I daresay it all looks different in bed."

"Perhaps Claire's his entrée to Irish society here: and when I say 'society'. . . ."

"Don't bother to spell it out. I know what you mean. It's certainly true that he's in the top flight of the new Boston money people, and that's ultimately gangster money, according to what one hears. What I've never discovered is: are *they* using *him* or vice versa? He's certainly very clever and madly ambitious. He's a real financial whiz. He *must* be. But as a human being . . . Well, I will say no more. Got to watch out for the laws of slander."

"I expect he's invited to the Consul-General's party for me tomorrow," Ambrose said innocently. "You'll have to put up with him."

"I'll talk to Claire. Slightly more pleasant. You know we Irish have this great sense of communion, like the Jews. Once an Irishman, always an. . . ."

"I never knew you had it so strong. You left when you were a child, didn't you?"

"I was fifteen. It's really Galway, so remote from the rest. I went to a wonderful school there, the famous one at Macluish. I can still remember everybody in my class. It's not just that they were talented. They were sort of eloquent. They had ideas — crazy, often as not, but stimulating: never soggy like the English public-school boys I've met."

A wild surmise came into Ambrose's head. "This was the outstanding school in Galway?" he asked.

"Oh, yes: all the best boys were sent there. Wonderful lot." He took a deep drink of his whisky.

"You didn't by chance know a boy there called Patrick Willis?"

Rafferty looked at Ambrose in astonishment. "Pat Willis? Of course I did. He was the brightest of the lot — and the craziest. He could recite poetry by the yard, but he was crazy. I really mean it. He was going to save the world. How the hell do *you*. . . . Oh, I know: at least I'll guess. He told me that he worked for the British Foreign Office after the war. His family were English nationals, and he kept his nationality. I suppose you met him at some Embassy or other."

"Not at all. I met him last week at a cocktail party in London. He started spouting Swinburne in such a beautifully modulated English accent that I asked someone where he came from, and they said Galway. But did you say he *told* you about working for the Foreign Office. Do you see him?"

"Sure I do," Rafferty said. "Quite a lot since I'm back here. He works now for a big British export company — travels a lot and often comes to Boston. He rings up and we have a good old booze. Saw him just a few months ago. Trust you to know him. Is there anyone you *don't* know?"

Some of the others had sat down near them at this point. Victoria Bristow was in the lead as ever. "You can't monopolize the guest of honor," she said sternly to Rafferty, "even if you *are* discussing affairs of state." How odd these social gatherings are, Ambrose thought. Everyone takes on a role as if they were cast for it. Mrs. Bristow was beginning to remind him increasingly of Margaret Dumont, the bewildered matron of the Marx Brothers movies.

"We were far from discussing affairs of state," he said gently to her. "We were engaged in a classification of types, or rather a typification of classes, with special reference, I may say, to the

Irish. It's one of the oldest of philosophical problems, full of insoluble paradoxes."

"Don't look so alarmed," Ezekiel Ball said to her. "It's easy. How to include and exclude yourself in the same act of definition." He turned to Ambrose. "The Bertrand Russell version of the paradox, I suppose?"

"Two cheers for intuition," Ambrose said. "I had in mind really the Barber of Seville version, but you're pretty good."

"Will you two stop it?" Kathleen Rafferty said. "What on earth is the Barber of Seville paradox?"

Ambrose looked at Ezekiel, who waved his hand. "*You* tell it."

Ambrose plunged in. "Start with a clear statement of the Barber of Seville's working rules: 'a man of Seville is shaved by the Barber of Seville if, and only if, the man does not shave himself. The question then is: does the Barber of Seville shave himself? If you say 'No,' then as he shaves all men who don't shave themselves, he shaves, himself. If you say 'Yes,' then as he shaves only those who don't shave themselves, he *doesn't* shave himself."

There was general approval, except from Mrs. Bristow. "What has this to do with the Irish?" she wanted to know.

"Can you be Irish and non-Irish?" Ambrose suggested. "More broadly, can you be yourself and not yourself?"

There was not much more leeway in this kind of absurdity, and the hour was late. But back in his hotel room half an hour later, it didn't seem quite so absurd. With Hepworth in the background, one felt everyone throwing up questions of identity. The thought of Gloria came into his mind. Was he himself the same person who had responded to her so easily, so casually?

And what of Fletcher? Fletcher seemed to be growing like a djinn from the ink-bottle, and a really gruesome kind of djinn. There he was, a totally respectable figure, a man of wealth and power and yet — to Bill Rafferty — clearly not what he seemed. He was like the Barber of Seville. Look at him one way, and he shaved himself: turn your head and he didn't. And both were true.

He found himself thinking of Alyss Summers. He wanted to see her again. Soon.

IV

THE two newspapers provided for breakfast next morning were both unreadable — deficient particularly in the crossword and obituary departments. Rafferty's *Mail* had huge headlines on the shooting, but nothing new to Ambrose in the stories to go with it, except for a picture of the earlier O'Connell shoot-out which had by now a Bonnie and Clyde character. The *New York Times,* not to be outdone by Boston in crime stories, had a brilliant *exposé*, running on for four pages, of the peculations of a Deputy Financial Controller in Staten Island. For light relief, Ambrose turned to the Financial Section, to see what was going on at the IMF meeting in Washington. Alas. All the report discussed was the speech of the Chancellor of the Exchequer, instead of tracking down the undoubtedly more arcane activities of Sir Olaf McConnochie — not to mention Basruk, if he was there too.

For a moment Ambrose felt rather baffled. Before a lecture, he needed something with the otherworldliness of the London *Times* to clear his mind. Fortunately there was a *New Yorker* on the table. Burying himself in a rather intriguing analysis of the psychology of TV advertising — but why were *New Yorker* articles so long? — he was ready for the fray.

The invitation to lecture had come, as in the past, from Orville, one of his oldest friends. The title they had worked out between them for the series of four lectures — "*The Individual: Variations on a Theme*" — was vague enough (but also stimulating enough) to cover anything Ambrose might want to say.

As on his earlier visits, they had allotted him the Samuel Adams Hall for his lectures. The stroll there through the autumn sunshine had been the pleasant interlude he needed to let his ideas fall into some sort of shape. Now, joining his host in the reception room outside the hall, the formality of the exercise began to settle on him, and not unpleasantly. Where else in the world had academic dignity on the Harvard scale survived? Certainly not in England, where dons were — as often as not — scruffy, uncouth, apologetic. Here, the man about to lead him in was tall, confident, handsome. As always, there was a truly resounding name to go with it: *James Orville Thoroughgood, Winthrop Neversett Professor of the History of Ideas.*

In ordinary conversation, luckily, he was more relaxed than all this sounded. "I told my students they had to come," he said, "if only to hear about Pastor Noelscher from the horse's mouth. I assume that he will be brought into the discussion somehow."

This heavy irony was permissible among friends. Ambrose had more or less adopted this hitherto obscure Swiss philosopher, having edited a translation of his "*Confessions*" (published originally in 1827), and written about him with some originality.

"If any words of Noelscher rise to my mind," he said with mock pomposity, "they will be quoted."

"Is that how it really works?" Orville said. "Spontaneous combustion? I suppose that's the only way to explain it. Seen you do it so often now. You stand there, without a note, floating around happily with no visible means of support — like a glider really — just saying what comes into your mind, enjoying yourself."

He said something like this introducing him briefly to the audience: and he was not wrong, Ambrose thought, with no immodesty. Something magic did happen as one stood up ready to talk, provided, of course, one was not hamstrung with a prepared text. To read out words written down in advance was to turn ideas into clichés. The written word was designed for its own kind of communion. The writer, essentially alone, had wrestled with his soul. What he then offered the reader had been sifted, winnowed, worked out precisely. But with a living audience, thought took wings. One reached out, wondering oneself what would emerge from the recesses of one's feelings.

Of course, one might focus on a single person in the audience. It helped, sometimes, to start one off. Alyss Summers, he saw with pleasure, was in the fourth row, looking quiet and receptive. Nice of her to come. He had rather counted on it. Almost immediately in front of her there was a pretty girl — a redhead with a bright green scarf at her neck (wonderful color combination) and with large round glasses on the end of her nose. He half smiled, seeing her eager look. It reminded him so much of Gloria.

The magic was working. He had always responded to the *décor* of this hall, built archaically in a jumble of styles to evoke culture, but somehow getting away with it. The flat wall surfaces, painted in cream, were interspersed with a series of tall pilasters, whose mouldings were picked out in gold. Above them, an elaborate frieze made its way round, revealing classic figures sporting, no doubt, in Elysium. The aim of it all was clear. Forget the daily round. Surrender to the Idea. He accepted the challenge. As he began to speak, all the practical problems at the back of his mind were unwound. Hepworth, Fletcher — they might never have existed.

Towed into air, possibly, by Miss Himmelfarb's book, he started off with John Stuart Mill. In his own lucubrations, he had been reaching out for a true assessment of motivation, taking into account its essential complexity. Could one ever surrender to the overriding priority of a single principle, as say, Jeremy Bentham had to Utilitarianism? Was even Liberty an absolute, as Mill (admittedly only when under pressure from the awful Harriet Taylor) had argued boldly in his Essay? Surely the *real* Mill was right to see that no principle could assume valid, living shape unless subjected first to an "opposing principle" by which it had to be qualified.

It was a theme he felt free to develop with a great deal of dash — *Allegro Assai,* in the spirit of the first movement of Mozart's *Piano Concerto in D.* The redhead, he saw, was totally absorbed. Now — perhaps losing her temporarily — he went somewhat deeper, digging first into Weber and then into Durkheim to see if the individualism that the heirs of the Enlightenment thought basic was as absolute as they assumed. Didn't society count on more solid, many-layered, tribal, familial, integrating bonds? Without them, wasn't twentieth-century man at the mercy of rootlessness, *anomie?* He spoke rather more slowly here — *Andante* — if only because he had never made up his own mind what weight to give to this. Every *Andante* is a troubled self-probing.

The redhead was beginning to look puzzled. Time for the *Scherzo,* on a theme which came happily into his mind from the *New Yorker* he had been reading over breakfast. In TV advertising, is the viewer won more effectively by a simple or a complex attack? The *New Yorker* writer had unearthed a paradox on this which no doubt would have pleased John Stuart Mill. Advertisers used to think, apparently, that TV advertising was most successful when it hit you with a sledgehammer. Now they know better. To achieve maximum effect, the viewer has to be presented with an "opposing principle" — queries, involutions, that ultimately yield a firmer base for faith. In Zen terms, the writer said, it is called "the doubt-sensation."

Is the individual, then, merely a bundle of complexity; Ambrose was now ready, with a roll of drums, to plunge into his *Finale*. A monist philosophy of experience was, admittedly, inadequate. However, a surrender to incommensurate complexity was also not valid. It ran counter to our recognition that there are simple, unifying ideas to be grasped. If one exposes one's mind to strongly contrasted outlooks — as Mill did to both Bentham's radicalism and Coleridge's respect for tradition — it is not to end up vaguely "in the middle," but as part of the process of forging a truly individual response. One has to be willing to test oneself against an opposing view: one has, in one's own experience, to go to the edge.

A bell sounded in the distance. Time was up — perhaps in more senses than one. Some of the abstract things he had been saying had begun to turn in his mind into the specific problems that Hepworth had generated for him. How far, he asked himself, does a man like Hepworth go to the edge? Is everything *he* does, or orders to be done, defined by the opposing principle? Can virtues like freedom and loyalty acquire full meaning for him only in a context of betrayal or death? The gangsters in action the previous evening had a rough-hewn philosophy which clearly accepted this. If morality meant working to established and respected principles, they were the most moral of men. What of their spiritual cousins, Hepworth's men at the Terrace? He heard himself finishing, and accepting the applause, without resolving his question.

In the general flurry after the lecture, a number of people came up — some old friends, others strangers keen to pursue a point or merely listen in. Alyss had waved to him and disappeared, but the pretty redhead, her spirits clearly restored by his *Scherzo,* had joined the throng, delighted, among other things, by his mention of Zen.

"That bit about going to the edge," she said. "It was great.

One of the Zen masters had a saying about it: '*Bravely let go / On the edge of the cliff / Throw yourself into Abyss / You only revive after death.*' That's what you meant, wasn't it?" Was it? He smiled at the girl to show his appreciation. Someone else came up at that moment to make another comment. Orville, talking to a colleague near the door, was waiting to take him to lunch.

In a few minutes, the gossipers had thinned out. Of the audience left, a young woman, Ambrose saw, was hanging back patiently, obviously waiting to have a word, yet clearly a private one. She was fair, and good-looking: but what stuck out immediately in that setting was that she was too carefully dressed to be an academic. Seeing him free at last, she moved towards him, and the impression strengthened. She was out of place and uncertain, looking round nervously. She seemed to be in her late thirties, handsome, elegant: but as she got near, it was clear that she was desperately troubled.

He took a step towards her, and they were alone.

"I'm Claire Fletcher," she said. "I've got to see you privately. It's very urgent."

Oh God, Ambrose thought. There was something awful here. Ordinary words of greeting were stifled. He just nodded.

"Some place where we can talk," she said. "But I've got to be careful. I thought the Fogg Museum, if that would suit you. This afternoon?"

"Yes," he said. "I could make it by three. Of course, later on. . . ."

She smiled faintly for the first time. "Yes, I'll be seeing you later on. We're going to the Consul-General's cocktail party for you at six. I want to see you before then. It's something you have to know. About Gloria."

Out of the corner of his eye, Ambrose saw Orville getting ready to move over and take him away. He waved to him to indicate that he was coming, and tried urgently to get a feeling of what it was all about. But all he could say to her was: "Gloria."

"Please be careful," she said. "I'll explain when I see you. Let's go to the Museum separately. I'll be there from quarter to three, so that we're not seen in the street together. I don't know the Museum very well. Where shall we meet?"

Automatically, Ambrose made a suggestion. "There's a big room — Old Masters, with the effigy of a Spanish knight on the floor in the center. Easy to find."

She nodded, turned and moved off, leaving a waft of scent in the air. Ambrose, feeling dazed, walked over to Orville and moved off with him to lunch.

With the first lecture over, the lunch, to a few selected spirits, was to have signaled relief. But now, behind the banter, he heard Claire's low voice and her mention of Gloria. "Be careful," she had said. What on earth. . . .

Would the reason surface in his mind during the lunch? Not likely, he thought, with Professor Morgan in the company. "Distinguished economist from Aberystwyth," Orville had said. More relevantly, he was one of those Welshmen who are constitutionally unable to let the talk simmer along peacefully. From the word go, he was as effusive as the rugby crowd at Cardiff Arms Park. He had been invited to the Consul-General's party. "Everyone will be there," he cried happily. His wife was looking forward to meeting Ambrose again. She had been a pupil of his at Oxford.

Well, this was how the visit to Harvard was *supposed* to be celebrated — cheerfully, nostalgically: except that for Ambrose the Consul-General's party meant Fletcher, to be seen now in a new dimension.

Hepworth was in this somewhere. At the back of his mind he heard Hepworth telling him to have a good look at Fletcher — to keep his ears open, to let things emerge. Faintly, a thought began to surface. Could it be the other way round? Fletcher was coming to the party. Was *he* pulling the strings? "Please be careful," she had said.

He shook himself free of speculation and joined in the talk. The waiter, at his request, had handed him a dry martini before lunch. In the manner of American academic luncheons, there would probably be no wine, only the preliminary cocktail. Ambrose, before sitting down, had made sure of getting a second martini, large and frosty enough to banish Hepworth, at least for the time being. As he sipped it, life began to reassert itself in less insidious form. Morgan, bursting with Welsh volubility, grabbed the conversation ball from the scrum remorselessly. Ambrose began to respond willy-nilly to the rhythmic sonority of Betts-Y-Coed.

There's a peculiar relish in the music of Welsh conversation, he thought, as if they're constantly smacking their lips with delight. Morgan was great at it.

"I hear that Zilto Basruk has joined the Treasury as an adviser," he sang. "Now things will really start to hum."

"I have never understood Basruk's attitude," Ambrose said. "He's supposed to be a brilliant economist, but one never thinks of him at work. One feels that he's either out with a blonde called Ingrid or doing some great deal on the Stock Exchange. Where does economics come in?"

"Ah, that's just it," Morgan cried, clearly a Basruk fan. "He plays at economic theory brilliantly just to show that in the end the conventional attitudes simply don't apply. So he doesn't bother to waste time over them."

"The fly is out of the bottle," Ambrose said. They looked puzzled. "Sorry: but one can never beat Wittgenstein at this. Show up all the paradoxes, and when that is done, the fly, he says, is out of the bottle. One no longer wishes to ask the questions, or if one asks, it no longer matters what answers are given. Believing in answers is like believing in Keynes, which I'm told is out of fashion."

Morgan gave a bellow — Fluellen to the life. "Look you, Keynes was all right," he cried. "It's the way they've interpreted him, you see, as if you can zig-zag — expand, contract — with fine touches to maintain equilibrium with full employment. Keynes didn't say that. He didn't even believe in Marshall's *partial, temporary* equilibrium."

"Is that what Basruk will be telling the Chancellor?"

"Ah, that's different." His tone now became rather canny. "You see, they have to provide the Chancellor with predictions on what will happen if he does this or that. Basruk will tell him that it's all right to make speeches about predictions as long as he doesn't believe them. Economics is the science of imprecision. That's what Keynes came to believe, according to Joan Robinson."

"Then why is Basruk always so cheerful?"

"Ah, that's because there's one field where precision or imprecision is not the issue. What you need there, you see, is flair, instinct, and a willingness to gamble on it. *Gamble!* That's what really intrigues old Basruk — international business, multinational corporations. He's done well at that. Got a finger in lots of pies — or rather he *had*. Of course, he's given it all up, now he's an adviser."

Well, Ambrose thought, he can still have a girl-friend whose father owns Swedish Steel and God knows what other conglomerates. Helps to keep his hand in, no doubt, until he can get back to business. Morgan's voice sang on until the time came to part.

With a little time to spare before his rendezvous with Claire Fletcher, Ambrose dropped into a bookshop at the bottom of Quincy Street, not so much to examine the books as to let his mind find its way back unhampered to the issues which might be coming up. It seemed to work: and as he began to stroll up Quincy Street towards the Fogg at five to three, he felt somehow ready, though for what, he knew not.

He loved the Fogg for its outward modesty, with everything in it so carefully selected and so precious. Forgetting all his problems, he felt his heart lift as he came to its quiet doorway. He had been aware of a car coming up the street slowly behind him, but thought nothing of it. But as he stopped, the car stopped too: and a fair-haired young man in a leather coat was at his side, pushing him oddly and muttering something which seemed quite incomprehensible.

"The Boss wants to see you," he was saying. "Come on." He had one hand in the pocket of his jacket, and was pointing something clearly intended to suggest a gun. With the other hand, he was pushing Ambrose roughly towards the open door of the car.

There were people passing by and paying no attention. Ambrose felt a great anger inside him and pushed the hand back. The young man now seized him with both hands and turned him bodily towards the car.

It all seemed to happen in a second — no chance to shout for help. Ambrose simply struggled. But suddenly the young man was sprawling. Someone had come down the steps of the Fogg, and, with a kind of twist, the young man had been up-ended into the gutter. He picked himself up and ran, catching up with the car, which had started to move, and jumping into it. It was a black car, and as it disappeared in a rush, Ambrose had a clear picture of the back view — the two heads, one fair, one dark, the number-plate — as if he had taken a photograph. What on earth was it all about?

He turned to look at his rescuer, a sprightly middle-aged man with a thin military-looking moustache, and dressed in what looked like English tweeds. "Are you all right?" the man said.

"I'm fine," Ambrose said. "Just totally bewildered. I don't know how to thank you."

."Delighted to help. Don't often get a chance to use the old commando routine. Is there anything you want to do about it? Police?"

Ambrose was coming to his senses. Surely it had something to do with Fletcher, or Claire, or both. He certainly didn't want the police in, not until he knew more, anyhow. His rescuer was clearly English. The best thing was to play it that way.

"No, no. Perfectly all right. Probably a mistake. Thanks awfully."

"Any old time," the man said. No need to say more. The English bond had been agreed. Mustn't be surprised at the odd things that can happen to you when you're traveling in a foreign country. He gave a cheerful wave of his hand and took off. Ambrose walked slowly up the steps of the Museum. The whole thing had taken five minutes. The clock said five past three as he came in through the door.

The sight of the clock — so coldly factual — gave him an idea. He paused for a second to recall the picture he had in his mind of the back of the disappearing car. Taking a bit of paper out of his pocket, he scribbled down a number.

He turned left, as he entered, towards the Warburg Hall, with its recumbent knight waiting for him. As he walked down the corridor, he made a bet with himself. If Claire Fletcher was connected with the car, she clearly wouldn't be waiting for him. He was betting that she *would* be, and she was, sitting on a long bench facing the effigy.

"Sorry I'm late," he said. "Got delayed slightly."

She smiled faintly in welcome, but for a moment said nothing, apparently at a loss how to begin.

He was glad of the silence. He needed it to recover. They were alone in the hall. Immediately in front of them lay Don Diego Garcia of Burgos, at peace with the world. On the wall opposite, St. Francis floated through the air, receiving the Stigmata. Was it a Giotto? The scholars argued about it. What did it matter? It was magical.

She sat there, enclosed within herself. Close to, her face had the greatest refinement, not just in features but with its inward depth. What she had to say was too hard to get out. One respected it. How could a woman like this have got involved with the Fletcher he remembered — coarse, hulking? Bill Rafferty had said that she was like Gloria. Of course, they were both blondes, but otherwise? Gloria was like a wild, bubbling spring. Claire had the serenity of a mountain lake.

"You wanted to tell me something about Gloria," he said gently.

"Yes: I have to tell you." She was ready now, and spoke quite calmly. "It's not just the past. It matters for the present. Very much. It's a horrible story, but I have to tell you." She paused. Ambrose was silent. She seemed to take a deep breath.

"It wasn't an accident," she said quietly. "It was murder, or as good as murder. My husband did it. And you were involved in it. Accidentally, one might say."

Had he known this? Had he felt it in some obscure way? He sat listening.

"I only found out about it recently," she said. "I'd heard of you. I knew you were one of Gloria's friends, but of course I had no idea. . . . And then a man came to see me: a man called Pinto. I expect you knew him. A rather horrible man, but he told me things I had to know. And I've recently found out some things about my husband from someone else. I'm not free to tell you who it is."

Her thoughts seemed to stray slightly as she said this. Her mind had gone off to this unknown person. But then she pulled herself together, and went on.

"I don't know how well you know my husband," she said. "He's a very complex character. It took *me* a long time to find out. Perhaps I should have understood when I first met him, but I didn't. I saw only one side of him. Then things began to emerge: and in the last couple of years, this side of him has taken over — it's become obsessive: his jealousy, his ambition. He's been so successful with the companies he's running that I think it's made him into a maniac. When he began, he was just being used by the big business interests. Now, he seems to want to take them all over himself. And it's echoed in his private life. To the outside world he's so genial, so easy. Inside him, he's tormented by ambition and possessiveness. That was why Gloria died."

She paused. Ambrose waited. Then he said: "And I was involved?"

"Yes. Accidentally. Or incidentally. We're all involved — the way I'm involved now. One never knows how a man like him will twist things. In your case, he got the idea that Gloria was running away from him to join you in England."

"To join *me!*"

"She *was* running away, and he found out. Her friend Pinto

had got a job in Paris. They made their plans. She bought a ticket to London and was going to go to France from there after a few days. She was driving to the airport in a Jaguar they had, and the steering failed. A total wreck, and she was killed. I've no doubt now, putting everything together, that he did it. He would know how to. He's an engineer, you know. But it's not just that. In the Army, during the War, he worked in the Long-Range Desert Group, sabotage, bombing and all that. He was brave. He had a good record. I think it gave him a taste for violence when he wants to use it. Of course, it was just taking a chance. She mightn't have been killed. And if she hadn't been, perhaps he would have tried something else later. But it worked."

"You told me to be careful."

"I have a feeling that he's never forgiven you. He may have something in mind. He's been very strange in the last month or so. He's obviously got something big that he's working on. I've assumed it's in his business, but you may be in it too. I was with him when he read in the newspaper that you were coming to give these lectures. He read it out aloud and he said: 'Oh yes, Usher was a very good friend of Gloria's.' It was very odd, the way he said it. I felt that I had to give you some idea of all this before you met him today. I don't know what good it will do, but. . . ."

"It's most helpful. I'm terribly grateful. It helps me to understand why I've got to be careful. And I will be. You too, I suppose."

"Yes, I'm careful. My eyes are open." She was silent for a second, and then spoke in a different tone, saying just: "I must go."

She opened her bag to look in a mirror and do something with a lipstick. He rose with her. "I'll go on by myself," she said.

As she was leaving, she stopped and said, "I'm glad I could speak to you. I just had to."

He stayed in the room after she had left, looking at the paintings abstractedly while he tried to come to terms with what he had heard. She thought that Fletcher was mad, as all men of ambition are self-obsessed to mania. On the wall facing him there was a painting of St. Dominic, a gentle preacher who had turned inquisitor. The Saint stared at him — a composition by Guido da Siena. The face was framed in a stone arch, the eyes wide open and hypnotic: the effect was one of total power. It was too close for comfort. He wandered into one of the Far Eastern rooms. Here passion was always purged. But as he left, his eye was caught by a massive stone head — "*Buddhist Guardian*" —

a great bullyhead of a Chinese gangster — a 7th century Fletcher. He had better get out.

On the steps, he looked at Quincy Street, expecting vaguely that a black car might drive up again. He had never felt this way before, full of fears. He crossed the road, wondering what was happening to him. He had blundered into a world he didn't belong to. What could he do now, even about Gloria? He must shake himself free, get back to something more natural to himself.

For no special reason he turned into Harvard Yard, wandering round aimlessly, looking at the parched grass, the trees, the buildings — assorted, higgledy-piggledy, but, in a way, friendly — comforting. As he strolled along, he found that his dejection had begun to lift. Within the Yard, the outside world was cut off, leaving only the faintest hum of traffic from outside. A group of students passed him, chattering away happily. The warm brick of the buildings, glowing in the September sun, was welcoming. Harvard itself was welcoming — mature, intelligent, humane. For a philosopher, *this* was the reality, which would long outlive the crudities of gangsters, or Fletcher, or the Terrace. It was this he had to hold on to: he'd almost let it be smothered. What a privilege it was to be here at this moment, greeted for what he was, happy in the echoes which came back from people who understood reality as *he* did. One didn't want to fight the world, to change the world, to change oneself. One wanted to *be* oneself. Isn't that what he'd been saying in his lecture? To be true to oneself, content with oneself, in a small world: *that* was happiness. It was Figaro's happiness as the *Barber* opens, an individual who is joyful to be what he is. Ambrose found himself humming the words as he walked, and then, in that wide open space, singing them aloud with delight and a kind of relief: "*Ah che bel vivere/che bel piacere/Per un barbiere/Di qualità.*"

It was a mood which sustained him for a while, but back in his hotel room he sat down at the telephone and rang Bill Rafferty. There was a lively welcome. Rafferty assumed, naturally enough, that Ambrose wanted the latest on the shooting. O'Connell, he said, was recovering well in hospital — under strong police protection, of course. He had managed to see him. Quite a few things had come up. "I'll tell you a bit more that we can't print yet when I see you this evening," he said. "We're going to the Consul-General's party."

"That's why I'm ringing," Ambrose said. "There's something I want to ask you that you can probably find out and tell me there. If I give you a Massachusetts car registration number, can you tell me who owns it? I assume you have access?"

"Nothing easier," Rafferty said. "But what the hell are you up to. Not chasing some blonde, I hope."

"Oddly enough that's exactly what I *am* doing," Ambrose said, though without much sparkle in his voice. "Wait a minute. I'll give you the number." He fished the bit of paper out of his pocket and read out the registration details. Rafferty took them down and promised results. "But this isn't right for you, Ambrose," he said. "You're getting too old to be chasing blondes."

An hour later, standing by the side of the Consul-General to be introduced to the guests, Ambrose had the feeling once again that he was getting the wrong message. With Fletcher due any minute, he was acutely aware of distaste and foreboding: yet there was also a smell of *Hepworth* about it which increasingly puzzled him. He tried switching his mind to other things, as he shook hands with the visitors and exchanged pleasantries.

His Princeton seminar was due the following afternoon, at five. He would leave for Princeton early in the morning and spend the night there. That, at least, would be an escape. The Toronto lecture was three days later, on Saturday. With luck, he might be able to have a long unhurried talk there with Kathleen Coburn about her latest "*Coleridge Notebook*." What could be pleasanter?

But this didn't solve things. It wasn't *escape* that he was groping for, but the right approach to what was taking place around him. With his mind centered on Fletcher, the balance seemed wrong. Too much else was going on in the complex world of Boston and Cambridge. His thoughts went back with a jump to his lunch the previous day with Jefferson Cohen, and the talk on painting when the others had joined their table. *That* was what seemed right. He had felt doors opening to wider questions, especially when Alyss got on to old man Harrigan and his pictures.

Alyss wasn't on the Consul-General's guest-list. He had asked. Pity. He would have liked to see her again. Why was she being followed? Jeff had said that she seemed preoccupied — on the track of something, perhaps. But someone, at the same time, was on *her* track. . . .

The opulence of the Consul-General's house was a comfort. England could at least be resplendent at one remove — on Beacon Hill. Where in London did one find a family home that was both a jewel of elegance and at the same time spacious, efficient and comfortable? But those poor diplomats! How did they adjust when they got back to Ealing or Streatham? Upjohn would soon be finding out, alas. Boston was what they called a "terminal" posting.

Ambrose and he were receiving alone: Upjohn's wife, Dulcie, had not yet got back from a summer visit to England. The guests seemed to be a judicious mixture of businessmen and academics, with a few political characters thrown in.

"You must get a bit bored with all these receptions," Ambrose said during a short lull in arrivals. "Sorry to have imposed another on you."

"Oh, not at all. This is a relief after British Trade Week. That was non-stop."

"It's over, is it? I saw a London bus the other day in the street."

"The hard part's over. The Guards are still around. The Scots Guards sent a band over. Great success. They've gone up to Canada for a few days. I'm rather sorry. Could have done with a few kilts here. Brighten things up."

On an impulse, Ambrose asked him, while they waited during another hiatus, if John P. Harrigan was on the list. Hadn't he said that Harrigan was the biggest power behind the Irish business scene?

"He is most certainly," Upjohn said, "and many other things besides — not so proper. I wish I *could* get him here, but I've never managed it. As I told you, he lives like a hermit. Very mysterious character. They say he has a great collection of paintings, but I've never seen them. It would be good to get him on our side, whatever he stands for, if one could only reach him. I've sometimes wondered if George Fletcher might help. Ah, talk of the devil. . . ."

For all his wish not to let Fletcher loom into the center of things, Ambrose felt a shiver of apprehension looking at the huge mountain of a man walking in. Claire at his side — blonde, slender, elegant — was totally relaxed, with no hint of anything.

Fletcher had thickened in the intervening years. He looked now more powerful, more threatening — or was it only because of what Claire had said? One was prepared to read anything into a debauched frame of this kind. One heard something sinister in his voice — very English still, a kind of whisky voice. . . .

He had taken Ambrose's hand — there was no escaping it — with a bellow of greeting.

"Ambrose is a very old friend," he said to his wife. "He was a very good friend of Gloria's. Takes one back, doesn't it?" He was looking at Ambrose as if he'd been rather waiting for this moment, and was enjoying it. "You heard about Gloria's death?" he said to him. "Terrible accident. Car crash."

"Yes, I heard," Ambrose said, "but only that she had died. I didn't know any of the details."

"It was dreadful," Fletcher said. Was there some sort of glint of triumph? Outwardly he spoke with a wheezy kind of sadness, drawing a deep sigh from his great frame. "One of those accidents you read about — think it couldn't happen to *you*, only to someone else. She was driving on a parkway near the airport, going at a good speed — we had a Jaguar — when suddenly the steering failed. Just crashed — killed instantly. It was terrible."

Claire was listening to this with a very abstracted look in her eyes: she had heard this public performance many times before. But Ambrose felt that even if he had come to the scene with no foreknowledge, he would have sensed the enormous difference between these two. For one thing, the age gap showed up most painfully. She was a good twenty years younger than Fletcher. How cool she looked — a puritan, one would say: so different from Gloria. She was waving at a woman she knew, and walked away to join her.

"Very like Gloria, don't you think?" Fletcher said. One could read a leer into every word this monster uttered.

"She's very beautiful," Ambrose said neutrally. "Have you been married long?"

"We married very soon after Gloria's death," Fletcher said somberly. "I was terribly lonely. I missed her so much."

So this was the act. Bereft husband. One remembered his total lack of communion with Gloria in Washington days, not to mention his coarse and non-stop wenching. But presumably he liked having a pretty wife for public reasons, and always, of course, a Catholic one. Gloria, daughter of a Polish coalminer from Western Pennsylvania, was one version: Claire, with her brown Killarney eyes, was another.

He stood there, towering over Ambrose. Horrible. By now the

75

party had moved into high gear. Waiters in white jackets were everywhere with their trays of drinks. Serving-wenches were following them with *bonnes bouches,* hot and cold. The guests had spilled out into the adjoining dining-room and the study. The receiving process was over: but Ambrose, melting into the company, still found Fletcher at his side.

Well, there were still the Hepworth questions to be asked. It was sickening, but he picked up the ball.

"I expect you get back to England a lot these days," he said to him. "The Consul-General tells me that you've left engineering and are running some multinational company."

"Yes, I'm in Europe a great deal," Fletcher said. "All over it — and in the Middle East. There's a lot going on there that needs financing" — he leaned over towards Ambrose, lowering his voice with a revolting kind of confidence — "and not just on our side of the Iron Curtain. I get to Turkey a lot, too. Very good listening-post. And some of those Turkish businessmen. . . ."

Now, it was another kind of act that he was putting on. Ambrose couldn't quite pin it down. It was almost as if Hepworth had told Fletcher how to talk to him.

"I'm surprised you've never got into this field yourself," he said to Ambrose. "With your knowledge of languages. . . . Of course, I know you're a philosopher, but you could get involved in broad ways — as an adviser, I mean. There's a lot of money in it. We could do with some English advisers: the East Europeans seem to like them. You know a lot about that area, don't you?"

Jefferson Cohen had pushed his way across, just as Fletcher was hauled off by somebody else. Ambrose heaved a sigh of relief. He could be himself again.

"I've been offered a job," he said to Cohen. "How do you think I would rate as an adviser to the Trans-Commonwealth Corporation? After all, I *have* read your book, so I know all about international trade. But apparently I should speak Turkish. According to Fletcher, that would really give me the *entrée.*"

"Is he a friend of yours?" Cohen asked.

"Talk freely," Ambrose said. "In fact, talk. Tell. I gather he's in the big time — TCC and all that."

The rooms were now so crowded that it was almost impossible to move. Ambrose and Cohen were pressed, drinks in hand, against a bookcase. The general din was so great that they could talk for the moment in complete isolation.

"Oh, yes," Cohen said, "TCC and a lot of other things. But

there's something fishy about it. He's like a front man. And the people behind him don't seem to operate according to the book."

"*Your* book?"

"Any book. There's a lot going on that isn't logical — the source of the funds, the judgments, the absence of a real market. Plus the fact that the whole planning and rationale of the multinationals has been knocked to bits by floating rates. That's the other book I'll have to write: '*The Alternative Capitalist Society.*'"

"You mean they've given up Adam Smith?"

"Exactly. The economists produce facts, analyze, extrapolate: but there are groups of what you can only call arch-capitalists who laugh at this kind of approach. They really do meet in secret places and take their own decisions. . . ."

"I'd regard you as a ranter, or worse," Ambrose said, "but I read an article about one of these groups in the *Financial Times*, not exactly a ranting source. They gave the group's name, though the story about them sounded quite libelous. They meet in remote hideouts. . . ."

"I read the piece," Cohen said. "According to the man who wrote it, that's why the U.S. gold auction was such a fiasco. He said that the market's response had the hallmarks of a carefully orchestrated stay-away. *Orchestrated!* Just think what that means."

"You think Fletcher works with some characters of this kind? Is he a capitalist hyena — fascist beast?"

"Well, it's something either very right or very left. Could be either, I suppose. They're both beyond the free market."

There was a cry from the Welsh mountains. Professor Morgan was upon them, with a dull-looking wife whom Ambrose faintly remembered from Oxford. Somehow he survived them, and a succession of guests who followed. People were beginning to leave. The extreme crush was over.

Out of the corner of his eye, Ambrose saw that Claire Fletcher was standing nearby, and alone. He moved across to her.

He had no thought of picking up the things they had talked about earlier. But there was a human contact between them now. She was very quiet, restrained, when she spoke.

"I should have told you how much I enjoyed your lecture," she said. "I thought it was going to be just academic — above my head. But I found it applied to me. It was very moving."

"I suppose I like talking freely. It's my style."

She was silent for a moment and then said: "You were a very close friend of Gloria's, weren't you? I mean you understood what she really felt."

She wanted something exact. It wasn't easy.

"Yes," he said. "I knew her very well. I liked her for her youth. I suppose she liked me for my age. I think she felt she could trust me completely. I didn't make any demands on her."

She sighed. "Friendship and marriage. What a difference. I had a feeling that that was it. So different from what he told me. I very much wanted to meet you."

She had a very appealing Irish softness in her voice. But there was no sparkle: just a great seriousness.

"Gloria wasn't a simple soul," Ambrose said. "She was pulled in all kinds of directions. I have a feeling you're very different." He was looking at her very directly as he spoke. "More" — he groped for the word — "more unified."

"We had one thing in common," she said. This time there was a faint smile. "We married the same man. But I think we are perhaps very different." She was silent, and then said quietly: "I shall protect myself."

Ambrose stood looking at her, wondering how to take it further. But Bill Rafferty came up at that moment, with the cheerful rollicking gait that arrived for him with the third or fourth whisky.

"Claire!" he cried, putting an arm comfortably around her shoulders. "I told you, Ambrose, didn't I? Isn't she a broth of a girl, as we Irish say?"

"I've never heard any Irishman say it except on the music-hall," Ambrose said.

"Well, that's what we say in Galway," Rafferty insisted. "Or perhaps I only heard it in '*Playboy of the Western World*.' You're not from Galway, though, are you?" he said to Claire, who had managed to disengage herself from the bearhug.

She shook her head smilingly. "I'm from Clare County. I should really spell my name that way, but I've always added the 'i.'"

Rafferty was surging on. "Now, Pat Willis, *there's* a fine Galway man. A real *devil* of a man. And how he could recite the poetry." He addressed Claire. "Have you seen him over here recently?"

She looked at him in total surprise. "Patrick?" It seemed as if she had said the name involuntarily.

If Rafferty noticed her surprise, he made nothing of it. "Yes, a *divil* of a man," he said, taking another deep drink. "He hasn't been to see me for months now. Busy with all those export deals, I suppose."

"Oh, there you are, Claire." Fletcher had come up to them. "I think we'll have to go." He turned to Ambrose. "We're dining with some friends."

There was something in his unctuous manner that made Ambrose feel murderous — the voice, and the built-in corruption in that heavy frame. Claire, standing beside him, looked cool again, after the momentary confusion that the mention of Willis seemed to have engendered.

"I've got to get back to the office," Rafferty said, as the Fletchers left. "The O'Connell story is breaking right open. They've picked up one of the boys who did the shooting, and I was right. It's nothing to do with the bank job at Leander. Much bigger stuff. O'Connell was in with the bunch who are going for the Master himself."

"You mean Harrigan?"

"Who else?"

"Do they have a chance to topple him?"

"They might if they were united. The prize for a takeover is pretty tempting — all the businesses he controls. The opposition have been afraid to move in so far, because if there's one thing Harrigan is good at it's elimination. But there's a man across the Bay who thinks he's ready — Sean McLuskey. He's quite a character too, and quite young. As I read it, old Sligo O'Connell has been seen in McLuskey's company, which is rather careless of him since he's supposed to be a Harrigan man."

"Bit awkward for *you*, isn't it? Kathleen told me you were under Sligo's personal protection in your apartment."

"I'll have to get the word through," Rafferty said. "I'll be loyal to Harrigan if it's the last thing I do. If I'm not, it *will* be the last thing I do."

"How did you piece it together?"

"The boy who did the shooting is just a low-level Harrigan caretaker. For him to go for Sligo makes it obvious."

"Did they find the car?"

"Not that I heard. Sure to have had false number-plates for a shoot-out. Ah, yes: the car. I nearly forgot. You asked me to track down a number. I don't know what you're up to, but it sounds rather peculiar to me. The car you asked about belongs to a man we call Fitz. George Fitzalan. A very solid citizen."

"How very odd," Ambrose murmured. "A solid citizen."

"Of course, you mustn't take that too literally," Rafferty said. "He has a very solid business, but he's not quite what he seems. You were asking about Harrigan. Fitz is the closest man there is to him. He's really like his adjutant from what I hear. Keeps the machine rolling very sweetly. Has a lot of boys to help him. In fact, if you ask me, I wouldn't be surprised if he hadn't had something to do with the shooting of poor old Sligo. Very loyal to Harrigan is old Fitz. But how the hell are *you* interested?"

"Oh, just another Barber of Seville," Ambrose said mildly. "You remember: we talked about it last night. Not dear old Figaro, of course, but the Barber in the paradox that I expounded. You don't know where you are with him. Solid citizen or gangster."

"But why the Barber of Seville?"

"Because of the paradox. You obviously weren't listening. Does the Barber of Seville shave himself? Look at it one way, he does. Turn your head, he doesn't. What's the truth?"

"I don't understand a word you're saying," Rafferty growled, "Kathleen!" His wife had come along, ready to leave. "Ambrose has gone stark raving mad. He's going to spend the rest of his stay here debating whether to shave himself or hire a barber from Seville."

"He's obviously searching for his soul," Kathleen said calmly. "I'm told that men go through a personality crisis every morning as they face the shaving mirror. That's the real difference between men and women. We poor females keep looking at ourselves every ten minutes of the day to see if our lipstick's right, but we never stop the world, as we gaze, long enough to let everything come to the surface."

"How right you are," Ambrose said. "Kathleen, you are marvelous. That long hard stare. It can never be a stare of self-satisfaction; one gets right out of oneself. Robert Graves wrote a poem about it:

> '*I pause with razor poised, scowling derision
> At the mirrored man whose beard needs my attention. . . .*'"

Bill was not persuaded that this questing attitude had any application outside the ranks of Oxford dons and poets. "I wonder what John P. Harrigan saw in the mirror this morning, thinking about what happened to poor old Sligo. Did *he* scowl derision at himself?"

"Perhaps he has a beard and doesn't shave himself every morning," Kathleen said.

"Or perhaps he brings over a barber from Seville," Ambrose suggested.

The Raffertys went off in fair humor. Ambrose was staying to dine privately with the Consul-General and a few people he had asked to stay on. It was pleasant enough, and offered a good gestation period for the decision he felt sure about as he prepared to undress, back in his hotel room soon after eleven.

He had made up his mind. He would send a cypher message to Hepworth next morning to say that he was not going on with any more of the Fletcher business. He had felt from the beginning that there was something fishy in Hepworth's attitude. Without being able to explain why, the suspicion seemed to have grown. And now, with what he'd heard from Claire. . . .

Being concerned with Fletcher was not to be borne. It was sickening to think of even seeing him again. Nothing could help Gloria now. If only one believed in retribution. . . .

There was danger around. "Be careful," Claire had said. Fletcher was still not even with him. He had "punished" Gloria. How would he punish *me,* Ambrose wondered.

The business outside the Fogg? He had thought at first that this might be Fletcher. But if "the Boss" who had sent out the young goon to bring him in was Fitzalan, where was the connection?

He pushed all these floating thoughts away and got back to the central issue. Hepworth. Yes, he would call it a day. He had been intrigued at first, starting off in the heady atmosphere of the Treasury, coming fresh to subjects he had hitherto only glanced at in the newspapers. But now, close to the ground in Boston, where money began to seem as grubby as it did in New York, he felt a growing distaste to being involved. The talk that evening with Jeff Cohen about the arch-capitalists, totally independent of the rules of the market, worried him still further. In this mood one could begin to suspect one's own friends. If the prizes were won in an open game — the way Sir Olaf played backgammon — it might be different: but with everything moving mysteriously, he didn't like it. He wanted out, as Americans put it. Yes, he would send a message to Hepworth the next morning.

Having taken the decision, he felt a great relief surging through him. He would leave for Princeton in the morning with no weight on his spirit. One whole day off and he would be restored. From Wednesday morning until his return to Boston on Thursday for his second lecture, time would stand still. Merely to think of it brought peace.

To reinforce his mood, he recited to himself the useful bedtime verse in the 4th Psalm: *"Stand in awe and sin not: commune with your own heart upon your bed and be silent."* He was silent. He slept.

But while he slept, the world went on turning, with Ambrose being touched on tangentially here and there.

In Washington, leading members of the U.K. Delegation to the IMF meeting had been attending a large dinner party given by the British Ambassador. The Chancellor, having delivered his speech to the meeting, had flown back to London for a Party gathering. It was always good to get the Chancellor safely out of the way, and the mood in the Embassy was cheerful. The IMF had more or less accepted the U.K. proposals on re-cycling the oil funds and revaluing SDRs. Generally, things looked better than before: and British hospitality, in the Embassy setting, always had a quality of its own for Washington society.

If Lutyens, in designing this handsome edifice, had ignored the practical advantage of placing the kitchens within easy walking distance of the dining-room, it was a factor that was of little moment to the guests, unaware of the resourceful strata-gems that served to keep the excellent food reasonably warm by the time it reached them. The wine, laid down cunningly in more spacious days, appealed adequately to the Americans and spoke even more winningly to some of the knowledgeable European visitors. By the time the port was circulating, England had asserted itself to the full. The men, a gaggle of dinner-jackets, sat long and happily round the table, safe, in British custom, from the accusation of being rude to the dismissed ladies. The token reunion later was in a drawing-room unequaled in splendor even by the French Embassy. Perhaps England was slipping elsewhere: but on Massachusetts Avenue, the British, with their quaint life-style, still had pride of place.

After the other guests had left, Sir Olaf McConnochie had stayed behind with the Governor of the Bank and three others (one of whom was the Chancellor's economic adviser, Zilto Basruk) to have a word about a message that had come through that evening from London. A British consortium had got to the advanced stage on the long-nurtured development project in Bulgaria, with a parallel though smaller one in Rumania. They were planning to allow financial participation to groups from two other countries, one certainly Swiss, the other perhaps Iranian. News had leaked that evening in London of a tempting takeover bid by the Trans-Commonwealth Corporation of America for the main British company involved. Someone from TCC was flying to London over-night. The Stock Exchange was planning to suspend dealing in the shares for a few days, pending clarification.

"Has anyone heard anything from Ambrose Usher?" Sir Olaf asked. "He's supposed to be finding out what he can about TCC. Would be helpful if we knew tomorrow whether he's turned up anything we don't know."

No one had heard from Ambrose, but Basruk had a suggestion. "I'll fly up to Boston tomorrow morning," he said. "I know a few people up there anyhow, and I'll talk to the Consul-General and Ambrose."

They went on discussing the basic issue on the takeover for a while, and then, leaving the Governor, who was being put up at the Embassy, drove back to their base at the Sheraton Park Hotel.

In Boston, Alyss Summers stood at the window of her apartment on the third floor of a large old-fashioned building behind Beacon Hill, looking down on a street scene of the most delicate, antique charm. The moon was in its last quarter: its mild beams blended happily with the warm glow of gaslight from the street-lamps below. Immediately opposite was a short terrace of exquisite old houses, discretion and harmony in every line. Opening off it at both ends were more narrow streets, all laid with cobble-stones that glinted faintly in the peaceful night. The world was at rest, except for the figure she saw lurking in the shadows across the road.

She was used to it by now, but it was tiresome all the same. She had expected that she might be followed this way if the word was passed along. One could live with it, unless it moved into a more intense form: and surely this was likely.

The conclusion was inescapable. She had to get on quickly with what she had set her mind to or give it up altogether. Hanging about from now on, waiting for a better chance, would be dangerous. She had better phone and get things confirmed.

Her phone, bright yellow, was on her desk nearby. But she picked up some dimes and nickels, turned off the lights, and went downstairs to a pay-phone behind the elevator.

She dialed a number and waited. She seemed very relaxed — almost nonchalant — except that she talked very quietly when she finally got through.

"Tim?" she said, "it's me. Still O.K. for Friday night?"

The response seemed to satisfy her. "That gives us three days," she said. "Plenty of time."

She listened to the phone again and laughed. "Yes, the third man. It sounds right, doesn't it? I can get him tomorrow — no, Thursday. I'm sure it will be all right. I'll ring you on Thursday when I know, or very early on Friday morning."

Back in her apartment, she went into her sitting-room, lit only by the glow from the street lamps, and stood pensively by the window for a moment. He might refuse, but she had a feeling he wouldn't. How lucky that she had found out in time about Domenico Franzoni and the bribe he had taken. Well, perhaps it wasn't a bribe — just the fee for "an expert opinion": but it was near enough. One wouldn't be able to sleep very easily with a chance of gentle blackmail in the air.

She would have been safe with Jeff Cohen, and he might have been game for it. What a nice man he was. She'd obviously hurt him by taking up with Franzoni, but it was a ploy she had had to pursue. One had to be tough when there was a lot at stake. She could have turned back to him now, but he knew nothing about painting and she would need a second opinion quickly.

No; it had to be Ambrose Usher. It was providential that she had met him. He was exactly right. Besides — she smiled at the thought — it would be enjoyable just to tell him the story. He'd enter into it in the spirit of his lecture. He'd want to follow it through wherever it might lead, just as she did.

She would let him get through his second lecture, on Thursday, and then ring him up.

In London it was now about five o'clock on Wednesday morning. Hepworth, who normally slept through the night without a qualm, had woken at four and been unable to get off again. His wife, a comfort on these occasions, was up in Scotland with her parents. The Hepworth house — a rambling old place in the Vale, Chelsea — seemed terribly empty without her and the children. Desperately, he battered his pillow into shape and laid his head down again.

Patrick Willis. Another Philby. And it had seemed so natural when he said he would go to Sofia to keep an eye on the Bulgarian negotiation. That frantic call to Heathrow after Fosdyke had come over from the Foreign Office — but the plane had left. Always on time when you didn't want it. Of course, one couldn't be sure how to interpret the peculiar information on Willis's past that Fosdyke had come across, but it looked sinister enough. Willis must have heard somehow that the past was catching up with him and slipped away to Sofia on purpose, with Moscow as the next stop . . . No use saying it couldn't happen when one thought one knew him so well. It just did happen.

It brought back — maddeningly — something that had been said when Freeman disappeared. Harvey had hinted — no more — that he wasn't entirely happy about Willis's role. But the evidence had been too vague. Or so it seemed. . . .

He'd had a quick word with Harvey after receiving Fosdyke's message. They'd got a message through to Sofia to be on the alert. But if Willis was still there, they'd have to give him a loose rein, even with the danger of him slipping away. Not easy.

Behind it all there was a distressing element at another level: Ambrose. Willis had been the channel. The crucial message had come through him. Was it a trick, with some other motivation? He beat the pillow into shape, and turned desperately on to his other side.

A very unlisted number rang in the basement of the august suburban mansion that George Fitzalan called home. It was a large untidy room, dominated by a bed, a refrigerator and a television set. A gas-cooker in one corner, and a small table near it, were covered in pans, glasses and dirty dishes. There was a smell of *pizza* in the air, beer-crates and a copious disarray of comics on the floor.

On one wall, a door fitted with heavy locks gave to a cellar in which a great deal of equipment was neatly stored. It might have been routine household equipment except for an unwonted accumulation of ropes and heavy bars on the shelves, and large piles of ammunition cases on the floor. A young man — fair-haired, leather-jacketed and extremely tough-looking — was in the cellar, putting something away, when the phone rang. He moved quickly to pick it up, and whined unpleasantly when he heard his caller's voice.

"O.K. — O.K.," he said impatiently. "You can lay off all that.

How was I to know that I'd run into a *karate* maniac. Yeh: that's what *I* think: must have been his bodyguard. If I see him again. . . ."

He listened for a minute and then laughed. "Just where you're wrong. The Boss wasn't sore at all. Matter of fact, he was pleased. Seems we got the wrong tip-off. This guy isn't in business with Fletcher. Nothing to do with him. He's a professor: he's giving some lectures or something. . . ."

There was a squawk from the other end and he broke in: "That's what I told the Boss. Must be if he had a bodyguard. The Boss said that side's none of our business."

There was a gabble, and he resumed. "O.K., I'll tell him you're sure about Fletcher. He doesn't want to believe it. Says Hooley isn't in with McLuskey."

He listened again. "It's no good, I tell you. Says he wants another check. Matter of fact, Fletcher's not here. The Big Boss has sent him across to London on some business deal. But he'll be back in a couple of days. . . ."

He broke in again. "Neh, I tell you the Boss says the professor's clean. Yeh, that party the British Counsel gave for him — yeh, Fletcher was there, but that's the way they do it. No connection. O.K. We can keep an eye on him. Wouldn't do any harm." He chortled. "Pretty funny, us looking after an Englishman. I can tell you, if I run into that wrestler again. . . ."

On this aggrieved note, he rang off.

At the Sheraton Park Hotel in Washington, the others had now gone to bed, but Sir Olaf, deducing from his watch that it was only ten o'clock in Colorado, picked up the phone and put in a call to his friend there.

What a relief it was going to be to put all the IMF routine out of his mind for a few days of joyful oblivion. Of course, Washington hadn't been as dreary as usual this time. That late night visit to the basement of the Mellon . . . a 'new' Pinturicchio? Absurd. The Director had been so cagey, but surely he didn't think. . . . All the same it had a nice look about it — and what a pleasant diversion for an autumn evening. . . .

His friend in Colorado was on the line. "All set," Olaf told him. "I'll take the morning plane on Thursday from New York and we can get going."

He listened to a complaining growl, and laughed. "Because I'm going to the opera in New York tomorrow night, that's why. We'll have plenty of time. Anyhow, I want to ask some people in

New York about the jump in Tri-State Mining in the last few days. I don't trust your neighbors out there. I suppose they're officially denying that they're getting to work on those old gold mines just to make people believe the opposite — that it's a new '49. It's an old game."

The squawk broke out again. "Come now, take it easy," Sir Olaf said. "You'll have your chance at the table. No, no: it's *got* to be Sunday. I have to stop off in Boston to see a friend there. No, no. Not backgammon. A philosopher. From Oxford University. Yes, I agree: it *is* all philosophy. I think he'd make a good player if he started. Maybe I'll persuade him."

In his book-encumbered home in Cambridge, Mass., Professor Ezekiel Ball had been typing a note to Gertrude Himmelfarb in New York, to accompany the offprint of an essay of his that he was sending her. With the formalities of the note completed, he went on with the usual kind of academic postscript.

"With Ambrose here," he wrote, "everything has suddenly become more lively, as always. I went to his first lecture this morning. It was great: a *tour de force*. He quoted your book, and with evident approval. He was less convincing when he got on to Weber. I don't think he really understands him. We must find a way of getting him back to Pastor Noelscher, where he is, of course, *sans pareil*.

"But there may be a greater issue ahead. You know how Harvard feeds on Ambrose from the moment he arrives. The rumor is now spreading with the speed of a prairie fire that he is spending all his time here prowling round assorted restaurants and museums in close attendance on an attractive brunette who is said to be an art historian of very dogmatic disposition. Is a new Harriet Taylor situation about to burst on us? If so, you, as the undoubted authority on this subject, may be called upon for advice. . . ."

He was about to pull the paper from the machine, but he paused for a moment and then added a few more words.

"Of course, Harriet wasn't really an ogre. You show in your book that she meant everything to Mill, but just pushed him too far sometimes — pushed him to the edge. Perhaps a Harriet would be good for Ambrose — stiffen the sinews, summon up the blood. Very odd that in his lecture today he talked about the need to go to the edge. We shall see. Further bulletins will follow. . . ."

V

THE world might still be spinning fitfully, but to Ambrose, with the decision taken, everything now seemed very peaceful. Wednesday at Princeton was exactly as hoped for. The seminar was stimulating, the dinner party in the evening *recherché* and amusing. In the early plane from Newark to Boston next morning, even the *New York Times* seemed more manageable. It may be prolix, he thought, but some of the stories have a lot of meat. He liked particularly a very long but beautifully clear account by one Edwin L. Dale of the real issues at the IMF meeting, now virtually over. For a brief moment he even felt slightly rueful at having now divorced himself from these fascinating topics. Well, at least he would understand them a little better in future, which was something.

The IMF story began on page one, and ended up in the depths of the Financial Section on page ninety-four. On the same page, Ambrose saw a short A.P. message from London reporting a rumor that an American corporation was about to launch a takeover bid for a very large British company in the next few days. TCC was mentioned as the possible bidder. Highly plausible, Ambrose thought, putting the paper down and beginning to think about his lecture. He was going to talk about Goethe. The seminar at Princeton had thrown up some ideas very relevant to what he thought he would be saying. He closed his eyes for a moment, letting the thoughts rumble in his head, as the plane came in to land.

Back at his hotel, with little time to spare, he rang the Registry at the Consulate-General to see if there were any messages for him. On the previous day he had stopped off *en route* to the airport to hand in his message for dispatch by cypher to Hepworth. There should be a reply by now. There was.

"I can read it to you on the telephone," the clerk said. "It's *en clair*. It's a bit funny, but I expect you'll understand it. Are you ready?"

Ambrose, with pen in hand, heard the clerk say: "Message begins. For Usher from Hepwroth. There's a long long trail awinding so be patient for a few days. Message ends. Do you want me to send you a copy?"

"No thank you," Ambrose said. "I have memorized it at a stroke. Are there any other messages for me? I expect they would be left with the Consul-General's secretary."

The call was switched through. "Yes," the girl said. "A Mr. Basruk was inquiring for you yesterday afternoon. He said you would recognize his name. He was sorry to hear you were away and said he would get in touch with you on your return."

"Did he mention the hotel he was staying in?" Ambrose asked.

"No," the girl said. "I had the impression that he might be staying privately, with friends."

The audience at the second lecture seemed even larger than before. Rather reassuring, Ambrose thought. In any case, having cleared the ground in the first lecture, he felt freer now to get into his stride.

In deciding to devote the second lecture to Goethe, he had thought to draw on him rather formally, in typical academic fashion, to illustrate the two conflicting forces — romanticism and order — that the individual reaches out to. He would trace the Goethe legacy in later German philosophers, analyze the underlying "conflict," and then work towards a synthesis. In the event, however, the lecture didn't quite go this way. For some reason, having launched himself along prepared lines, he found himself moving on to talk more of Goethe as lyric poet than philosopher. "*In allen Wipfeln/Spürest du/Kaum einem Hauch*." A few lines about silence in the tree-tops had more power to move us, somehow, than all the burgeoning ideas of *Faust, Part Two*. Was it the perfection of the words, or some state of mind that one is reaching for? Reason, feeling. . . . He got back to the academic groove, but felt quite exhausted when the lecture was over.

He had seen at the beginning that there was no Alyss in the fourth row this time, and felt a distinct let-down. At least the redhead proved loyal, as pretty and eager-looking as ever, and among the questioners who drifted over at the end. She was still on Zen, and having now become a regular, seemed to feel it polite to introduce herself this time. "I'm Lindsay Sonnieski," she said. "I'm a philosophy major at Radcliffe." Well, well, Ambrose thought. Major Sonnieski. Very nice too.

There was a lunch as usual — genial, but with nothing said one remembered afterwards. In fact, everything seemed to have slowed down in interest. The Boston papers were still running the gangster shooting story, but had no more revelations to offer. Glancing through the *Mail* in his hotel room after lunch, he saw only one item that was faintly interesting. The legendary John P. Harrigan was receiving an honorary degree — Doctor of Religious Law — at Notre Dame University on Saturday, in a special ceremony to take place on the football field just before the game. Apparently he had given Notre Dame — the Oxford of Irish Catholics — a vast sum to found a History of Art department. How about a History of Crime department, Ambrose thought rather grouchily, throwing the paper away. But perhaps the Italian Mafia had already taken care of this at the University of Chicago.

History of Art? Ah, yes. He was probably going to leave Notre Dame his pictures. Alyss Summers had said, rather surprisingly, that his picture collecting was basically religious: that he was a sort of shrivelled-up old saint, despite the less proper side of his life. Perhaps she was going along for the ceremony. Why hadn't she come to his lecture? He must ring her up.

No message from Basruk. One wondered what he was up to: perhaps getting involved in the TCC takeover which had been rumored in the *New York Times* that morning. Or perhaps just seeing a girl-friend. Much more likely.

He was feeling rather tired after the very early start at Princeton, and lay down for a snooze. Much refreshed when he woke up, he settled down to some reading. He had been summoned to dine "informally" — probably only about ten people — with the President of Harvard that night. It was to be an early meal, as usual here: but he still had a good hour and a half before he needed to get ready.

He picked up Ezekiel Ball's new book — "*Theology of the Post Industrial Society*," and had just read about ten pages when the phone rang.

Bound to be Basruk, he thought, reaching for the instrument. But it was a very different voice, rather mellifluous in tone: "Is

91

that Mr. Usher? Ah yes, good. Perhaps you will remember me, but please don't pronounce my name. '*Impelled of invisible tides and fulfilled of unspeakable things*'."

"Good God!" Ambrose cried. "Of course I remember you." No mistaking Swinburne in that lilting voice: Patrick Willis, Hepworth's man with the whiskers. No surprise really, even the odd approach. Rafferty had said that he often came over "on export business." Perfectly good cover. "How nice to hear from you. Are you going to give me all the gossip from home? Just when I feel like a nice cup of tea."

"Yes, I very much want to come and see you," Willis said. "I could be along in fifteen minutes. There's rather a lot I need to tell you. But can I count on you not to mention to anyone at all that I am here: and I mean no one?"

"Of course," Ambrose said cheerfully. "All instructions will be obeyed. And I will order tea and toast against your arrival."

At Willis's request, he told him his room number. The tea, having been ordered, arrived in fifteen minutes, and Ambrose gazed at the tray in happy anticipation. Just what he needed to banish the afternoon boredom. Ezekiel Ball's theology would have to wait. In any case, it was clear from the first ten pages that he didn't really understand Rousseau, whom he quoted at such length. Why didn't he stick to Weber, where he was really good?

It would be interesting to meet Willis properly after the talk with Rafferty about him. A *divil* of a man, Bill had called him. And Claire Fletcher. There must be something more personal behind those anonymous whiskers.

There was a knock at the door.

Perhaps he should have guessed this too. The man who came in had no whiskers, and indeed was totally unlike the comfortably plump figure, with a full head of hair, whom he had met spouting Swinburne at the cocktail party. The man facing Ambrose now was half-bald, with close-cut iron-gray hair: he was lean, roughhewn: real. It was clear instantly that the whiskers were only part of a disguise adopted for deliberate confusion.

What this man had, too, was great seriousness. It took away any joking reference Ambrose might have made to the whiskers. Something important had happened. Feeling this, Ambrose greeted him quietly and merely offered tea. Willis nodded, but before sitting down walked across to the window and looked through it from an angle. He accepted tea with milk and sugar, and a piece of toast. Then, pulling out a packet of cigarettes, and with Ambrose registering no objection, he lit one, dragged on it deeply, and sat back in his chair ready to talk.

"I've come over to get things straight with you." he said. "I've been very much involved with you without you knowing it. I've been working up to a decision which I put into effect two days ago. It's meant cutting myself off in every direction: and I don't feel any responsibility about it except in one respect — to you. I owe you an explanation. It's a debt. I'm taking a great chance in paying it off, because my being on this side of the Atlantic has got to remain absolutely secret. I'm not going to ask you to promise to keep it secret. I'm just assuming you will — if you like, in return for my paying off the debt. I'm taking a chance."

Ambrose looked at him mutely. He could instantly understand what this might mean in the context of a man from the Terrace: and in the same apperception he realized that he had been right in suspecting something odd in the attitude to himself at the Terrace. He had been used as a tool. But why? Why?

Willis had put his cigarette into an ash-tray and ground it out. It was as if he wanted to think a little before going on. He lit another cigarette slowly, and this seemed to bring things to a head for him.

"It's no use my just telling you about the last bit, which affected *you*," he said finally. "It makes no sense unless I go right back. I'll keep it brief. I think you can fill it out yourself from the outline. It's not a very nice story. Some of it is fairly familiar. A question of loyalty — going back a long way.

"I was brought up in Ireland — in Galway — though my parents were English nationals. I was pretty bright at school, and also pretty wild — not in a bad way, just dying for adventure. The Irish causes were stifling: too parochial. I wanted to save the world — not me personally, but the movement. I didn't join the Party. I was one of those they kept 'clean' for better things. And I did a lot of them — with total obedience. I don't have to spell this out. I did it all — whatever they asked. The lot. I'll leave it to you to imagine what that might include. Not very nice.

"I'd come over to the United States for the Party and was operating for a time as an American, under a different name, with all the papers to go with it. I rather liked the name they'd invented for me — Clive Nixon. I managed to get a small job for a time in the Irish Embassy, as a local recruit. It was a good place to work from. I used to read about you in their reports sometimes when you were over there, but my work was at too low a level to meet anyone socially. In any case, most of my time was spent on the real job — outside the Embassy.

"That's where I first got to know about George Fletcher. His wife Gloria went around with a lot of characters from the Left — well, *you* know that. Some of them were phonies, but some were colleagues of mine, you might say. I never met Fletcher myself, and I remember we weren't at all sure about him — how clever he was. He was close in with the FBI, and we wondered if he was just using Gloria as a come-on — a kind of flame for the moths. We had our own man in the FBI, of course. He told us that *you* were down on their list with a question-mark when you started spending time with Gloria."

Ambrose gave a sort of groan.

"Yes," Willis said. "It's a long time ago. It would all have dissolved in time, the way all those things did, except that Fletcher decided it wasn't going to. I'd gone back to England under my real name and worked my way into a government job — still under Party orders. The aim was to get me into the Terrace, and ultimately I managed it.

"In my Terrace job, they sent me over to Boston about six months ago to look into TCC, so I met Fletcher for the first time personally. I was supposed to be in the export business, and had plenty of genuine credentials. I should have realized that he might have known about me from Washington, through the links he had with the FBI: but I didn't. When I engineered a meeting with him — I thought I'd done it very skilfully — I soon realized that he'd been just waiting for me. I told you he's clever. He put it to me as coolly as you like. He wanted me to cooperate with him on a few things. Otherwise he was going to get a message through to the Terrace all about me and my past."

"Why didn't you go straight to Hepworth and tell him?" Ambrose wasn't reproving Willis. If anything he was on his side. He hated these turncoats and double-coats, but there was a man in front of him who had been through hell.

No: that was too sentimental. Willis, in this situation, was not so much a man as a case. In our own time, there had been a mutation in human conduct. In a horrible way, it was fascinating. One wanted to know everything about these characters who had turned up with a totally new approach to idealism, if that was what it was — the Philbys, the Blakes, and all the others, known and unknown. One had to try to understand how they had actually handled it. They had freed themselves from conventional caution. They had, as it were, gone to the edge. . . .

With a peculiar foresight that he was to recall very clearly later that evening, he tried to imagine whether he himself could ever agree to take part in something conventionally criminal for the sake of some so-called higher motive. Could it happen to anybody? After all, here was Willis, apparently "normal," and yet. . . .

"I couldn't go to Hepworth," he was saying, "because of one particular thing that would then have become obvious. A lot of things they would have tolerated, but not this one. A man had disappeared: I'll just use that word. It was a man who worked in the office: a chap called Freeman. The Party thought he was getting on to the truth about me, and one day he vanished. I never discovered what actually happened, but. . . ."

There was a pause. It was getting harder to ask the questions. But Willis had come here freely and was trusting him. "Yes, I can see," Ambrose said at last. "But in that case, why. . . ." His voice trailed off. The intent was obvious. Willis picked it up instantly.

"Why didn't I follow the trail to Moscow like the rest? Because after the Freeman business I had begun to hate the whole thing. It wasn't a question of saving my skin. I wanted to save my life in a different way — save my soul, I expect you could say." He smiled bitterly. "I can find an even cornier way of describing what I'd begun to feel. I wanted to do something that would straighten the record."

He himself paused now. Ambrose was silent, waiting for him to resume. A bizarre sense of communion had grown between the two men. The room had begun to darken towards the September twilight. As Willis struck a match for another cigarette, his face glowed in the flame, lean and intense.

"I'd decided before Fletcher started on me that I'd build something new out of myself — turn into a different man with no connection to the past, and do something decent that had the nature of an absolute. I thought, in fact, of becoming a monk, in a nursing order, where my origin would be sworn to secrecy. But then I met Fletcher's wife Claire, and I knew that I didn't want to give up the world. We were drawn to each other: I can't describe it. I wanted to find a way of setting her free."

"Free?" Ambrose was simply startled.

"Fletcher is a monster," Willis said. "Claire discovered it soon after they were married. She found out things about him — he even boasted about them — that she wouldn't even tell me. There was no longer any love between them, but he's madly possessive and jealous. He'd never let her go, and he's very clever. The only way she could get free would be if she could join me in some new existence — secretly. For that, I needed to create an entirely new set-up, with a fresh base, papers, money — the lot. Not too difficult" — he smiled wryly — "when you've had my kind of experience, first with the Party and then the Terrace. I needed a few months. So I decided to go along with everything that Fletcher wanted, for the meantime. And that's where *you* came in."

Here it is, Ambrose thought. But there was a preface to come.

"I'll tell you the kind of man we're talking about," Willis said. "I daresay you think of him as a top businessman — big figure in the TCC and all that. The fact is that he's become a total part of the Irish underworld — Harrigan's lot. I suppose you could call him special assistant to Harrigan. That's why he moved to Boston. Harrigan needed a front man for operations in Europe, and an Englishman was just right. And of course, he's a Catholic — very ardent — just as Harrigan is. Working in Europe as an obvious Englishman, he wouldn't attract the same attention that the Irish gangsters get automatically. One little job he did, I discovered, was to find a way of sewing up about three-quarters of the English gambling interests. The Italian lot — the Mafia — had tried it and got thrown out on their ear by the British authorities. Fletcher moved around in London with no difficulty, found out who could be bought, where to put the money — and that's the way the thing runs now. Did the same when it came to cashing in on the oil crisis. I expect you know that the American underworld made huge profits by getting oil from cheap sources invoiced as if it came from the high-cost places, so that the permitted mark-up netted them enormous sums — literally billions. It's because they've got all this free cash that they're so anxious to get into development in Eastern Europe."

"Very interesting," Ambrose said. "But where do *I* come in?"

"*You* came in when Fletcher read in the papers that you were going over to lecture at Harvard. Apparently, he's got it in for you in a big way. You seem to have done something terrible to him that he can't forgive. I suspect it's about his first wife, but I never found out. Whatever it is — and I don't know if it's real or imagined — it seems to be burning a hole in him. When he read about you coming over here, he got hold of me in London and told me that I had to do something for him — or else. He was totally open about the whole thing — seemed to be actually gloating. He'd worked out a means of going for you in a way that would really hurt — leave a trail of suspicion — even damage — that you'd never get rid of. He wanted to set you up in the minds of the Terrace and the Foreign Office as a secret agent for the other side. It was child's play for him, once he had me to help — and he *had* me, until I had all my plans functioning for me to get out."

Secret agent. Ambrose sat back in his chair with a faint air of satisfaction. After all, there has to be a first time for everything.

"All he needed from me," Willis said, "was to produce a couple of fake messages from the other side that seemed to point to you as a source. He himself started the ball rolling, in Boston. It was so simple. If people only knew how easy it is. . . .

"In your case, all he had to do was to have a confidential talk with the Consul-General here. I can imagine the conversation so easily. He'd heard a very strange story about you, he says, when he was in Eastern Europe on business. He wouldn't have believed it, but it reminded him of something of the past from Washington. Terribly sorry, you know — talking man-to-man — to drag it all up, but after all, security is security. It had reminded him that you used to see a great deal of his late wife in Washington, and she — he hated to say this, of course, but he *had* to — she'd had a lot of Leftie friends — very involved with them and all their views, some of them had been exposed, the famous ones. It was one of those things about his wife that he'd kept to himself, and since she was now dead there was no need. . . . But if Usher was really still at it, shouldn't the British authorities look into it — make a few inquiries. . . .

"Well, it got back to us at the Terrace. Hepworth said he couldn't believe it, but after all, one has to examine everything these days. As far as Hepworth was concerned, there were *two* questions: were *you* suspect, which he didn't want to believe, or was Fletcher putting this over to confuse us, as an agent for the other side? One had to ask if he'd been secretly in league in the old days with the people his wife used to see. The solution was to rope you in to have a look at Fletcher, without giving you the real reason. If you discovered that Fletcher was a secret Russian sympathizer, that would go a long way to clearing you, though it might still be a device, just to show how reliable you were. We'd have to check and double-check, to be sure. It was *you* we had to get clear about. Fletcher had got things going so that you were at least a *possible* suspect. All I had to do for him, to make it stick, was to get a few messages from contacts on the other side to show that things you had heard at secret meetings in London were leaking there. That was all I had to do, and I did it."

"Well, thank you very much," Ambrose said. "So now there's a trail of evidence about me that's going to be on a file forever. Very nice."

"No: that part's been taken care of," Willis said. "I flew out of London two days ago — Tuesday morning. I was supposed to be on my way to Sofia on Terrace business. In fact, I went somewhere else on a different plane. Then the next day I came on here. Hepworth knows now that I've run off. He has no idea I'm here, of course. He'll think I've gone to Russia — or perhaps China: I don't know. Anyhow, skipped. I posted a letter to him before I left, second-class post, to hold it up a bit: but I suppose even so it's arrived by now. I told him just one thing: that the messages I'd reported about you were faked. I explained how he could prove this, in case he thought you and I were in league. You're in the clear over there. But that wasn't enough. I wanted to tell you it all in person — part of the business of putting things straight. Just one part of it. I've got the rest planned."

Ambrose sat for a moment thinking. The damnedest thing that had ever happened to him — or at least that he knew about. Perhaps things like this had gone on over his head before, without his knowing it. What a game they played at the Terrace. On the surface, total trust: beneath it — one didn't want to know.

Well, he could live with it: but *Willis?* He thought he could put things straight for himself by some unequivocal act. Whittaker Chambers had thought this. Perhaps Philby thought it too.

Willis had risen to his feet, ready to go. He made no effort to shake hands, or even to frame some sort of apology. He simply raised a hand in mute gesture, and left.

It was just after six. Ambrose sat for a while in the gathering dusk, and then, switching on the light, moved into the bedroom to put on a clean shirt for dinner with the President.

Somehow or other he was looking for a sign that Providence had not really deserted him. And there, on the chest of drawers in his bedroom, he saw it. On the plane coming over, he had bought a small bottle of whisky, just to make sure of having it near him for an emergency. With a silent nod of acknowledgment to the Almighty, he poured a good measure, added a little water, and drank. Mercifully, the confusion began to lift. It was like waking from a nightmare. He was alive. He was himself. It was something to be going on with.

VI

ONCE again — and this time in its Holy of Holies — Harvard was ready with a special message. The last time, as he strolled through the Yard, it was Figaro in a rather passive mood who had come into his head. This time it was Figaro asserting himself more boldly.

One had to remember what Figaro was really saying. Anyone can be a barber: but *his* kind of barber — *un barbiere di qualità* — floats above everything humdrum in the daily round. The variety of work that comes his way is an engrossing celebration of life — the joy of having a special role in a world of fun and high drama. Surely, Ambrose thought, anyone willing to adopt the same attitude can reap the same reward — even a philosopher. One will find oneself moving at speed — as in the opera — from triumph to disaster, and vice versa. When there are shocks, they will be truly startling: by the same token, the quiet moments — as when one sits at dinner in the home of a President — will have a detached kind of richness.

Sitting here, he felt, was to catch his breath, ready at any moment for a delightful *aria* to float over his head. He had just had a peculiar example of life in the raw: but Providence never left things this way. There was a pattern that had a more satisfying shape when one took it all in. There would be echoes of it in conversation. If only Rossini were around, one would hear it in song.

For this to work, there had to be a common language, a frame of reference in which everything that had been happening could find the right expression. Perhaps it was even more than this. If one listened carefully, casual conversation in this kind of setting might pick out the central issue, the central character around whom everything was turning. Who, in fact, had been the axle in the last week? In one sense, Fletcher: yet everything said of Fletcher had led, somehow, to John P. Harrigan. It was no surprise, then, when Harrigan's name surfaced into the conversation.

It was a stag party, all academics, with everyone sharing a common relaxed free-masonry. At one point, the talk got round to honorary degrees. How had Oxford got into such a mess, they wanted to know, first offering President Bhutto of Pakistan an honorary degree and then withdrawing the offer? From this they went on to talk about the current price for honorary degrees given to financial benefactors, as distinct from those conferred on scholars and politicos. Was there a recognized scale in England, stretching from Oxbridge to Redbrick? It could never be as wide-ranging, of course, as in the U.S. scene with its vast proliferaton of colleges. . . .

"Surely the standing of the university is not the prime factor," one of the professors said. "It's more relevant to consider how clean the money is."

"You mean the more the dirtier," another said sardonically. "Which might be thought to apply to our own John P. Harrigan. Did you see that Notre Dame are giving him a degree on Saturday? Taking everything into account, what do you think he gave for it? Somewhere between five million and twenty-five, I suppose, but nearer which end?"

Somehow or other it stuck in his mind. He was thinking about it back in his hotel room at around eleven-fifteen. It was part of the winding-down process. He had decided to call it a day, and was just about to undress when the phone rang.

This time it *must* be Basruk, he thought. Those Turks never know the difference between night and day. Wonder what he's been up to. But there was no Basruk bellow at the other end of the line.

It was Alyss Summers. She sounded as if she were whispering, but he recognized her voice — that slight mid-western accent, dry and clear — even before she gave her name.

"I've got to ask you something first," she said. "I can't help it if you're annoyed. Are you alone?"

No point in being annoyed. It was, in fact, rather intriguing. "Alone and palely loitering," he said cheerfully.

"I rang earlier, but didn't leave my name," she said. But why was she whispering? "Something very unusual has cropped up. It would mean a great deal to me if I could talk to you tonight, but I can't tell you what it's about on the phone. It will have to be in person. Are you willing?"

"Of course. When can you get here?"

"I can't come to you, for a reason I'll explain later. You'll have to come to me. I know it's asking a lot, but it's important, and it's got to be tonight."

Despite the whisper, she didn't sound as if she were in some danger. There must be another reason. Must have something to do with the fact that she was being followed, which he had assumed had some marital connotation. But now, that didn't sound right either. She just had something important to discuss. The fact that it was nearly midnight was irrelevant.

"Yes, I'll come," Ambrose said. "Are you nearby? Can I walk round?"

"You'll have to take a taxi. I live in Boston. And there's a certain complication. When you get the taxi — I suppose you'll walk to Harvard Square — would you just ask the driver to take you to Freemont Square? There's a café open there with music on till about two, which will make it sound O.K. Go one block up Beacon Hill which will bring you to Bradford. You'll see the back of some large apartment buildings there, one of them painted white, with a red door. That door's the back of my building. I'll come down and open it at twelve-fifteen."

He found a cab and was at the door at exactly twelve-fifteen. As he arrived, it opened. A minute later they were in her apartment on the third floor. The light in her entrance hall was off, but the door of the living-room was open, with a faint light coming from the street. She put her fingers to her lips as she led him into her bedroom, where a reading lamp by her bed had been left switched on.

Until that moment it had all been tense. Now, as she closed the bedroom door, she looked at him directly and smiled.

"I decided to take a chance," she said in a normal voice for the first time. "I think it's going to work."

"I had to bring you in here," she said apologetically, "because my living-room's bugged. So is my phone. I called you from a payphone in the lobby. It's behind the elevator shaft so I couldn't be seen from outside the front door."

Well, all right, Ambrose thought. That's the mechanics. But after all. . . . He raised his hands in a kind of baffled acquiescence.

"I know, I know," she said. "It'll take me a few mintues to catch my breath, if you know what I mean. I have to tell you a long story. Terribly hard just to plunge in. Can I give you a drink? I need one myself desperately. Scotch?"

He agreed readily, shaking his head at the offered cigarette. She lit one herself, with her drink before her, and sat back contentedly.

"That's better," she said. "I think I can face it now. I know it seems odd, but it had to be tonight. There's a decision I have to take tomorrow. So if you're to be part of it, I had to talk to you tonight."

Ambrose waited. "Yes," she said. "Why should *you* be involved? I decided to gamble on it. And you came." She took another drag on her cigarette. "Thanks for coming."

She smiled brightly at him — too brightly, and then stabbed her cigarette out with a fierce action. "It's no good stalling. I've got to tell you a story. Yes, it's a gamble. I just thought. . . ."

Ambrose took a sip of his drink. It was beginning to feel very pleasant — almost normal — in the half-darkened room. The armchair he was sitting in was very comfortable. Alyss was settling down too. She might be able to talk more easily now, he thought.

"I know one's supposed to start at the beginning," she said, "but it's very hard. It's easier to start in the middle. Do you remember that when you said you'd go with me to the Museum I said O.K. at first, and then changed my mind and said I'd join you later. That was the moment at which I took the decision — at least tentatively. In case I went on with it, I didn't want anyone to connect us by seeing us walking along together. You see, I was being followed."

No point in Ambrose confirming it. He waited.

"It's the same with the bugging," she said. "My nephew checked it out a few days ago. It's rather comic. This nephew of mine — Tim — used to work for the CIA, and now he's madly anti-establishment but knows all the tricks. He found my living-room bugged, and the phone, but is quite sure they didn't do this room. He thinks they were probably interrupted — didn't have time. Perhaps they thought that I couldn't possibly have an intriguing conversation in my bedroom. What do *you* think?"

"I think you're narrowing the field of your pursuer's interest. No: you're broadening it. Perhaps we're going to talk about Renaissance painting."

She smiled faintly. "Funnily enough, we are. You must have an instinct. It's what I hoped. I felt it at lunch. And then in the Museum I began to make up my mind. I wrestled with it for a few hours, and then I decided there was no other way. It's such an odd bit of luck that you landed here at this moment and that you knew Jeff. I suppose things do fall into place by coincidence."

"Not coincidence," Ambrose said firmly. "It's Usher's iron law of mutual interest. However. . . ."

"It seemed coincidence to me," she said. "I desperately needed someone to confide in, someone who was outside everything and yet knew what it was àll about. And you showed up. I couldn't let the chance go. Besides" — and this time she smiled with the greatest naturalness, all her nervousness gone — "I think you'll be interested. I think it will amuse you, as you English always put it."

"Well, now at last I know why I'm here," Ambrose said indulgently. "To be amused. So be it."

"Yes, now I can really tell the story from the beginning," she said. "The funny thing is that it's not really so unusual if one presents the bare bones. The same kind of thing has happened before, I'm quite sure. It's just odd being followed, and bugged. I don't like that. But the rest is a challenge. The truth is that I wouldn't be involved if I weren't enjoying it."

She had settled down completely and was going to talk now without any more inhibitions. The shadows in the room seemed to match the mood of confidence. It was agreeable and oddly natural.

"I didn't think you'd get the theme so quickly," she said, "though I did give you a clue over lunch. All the same, it's a little more than just painting, as you can imagine. The real theme is old John P. Harrigan and his paintings. More precisely, perhaps, his sculpture and the other objects in his collection.

"I said at lunch that he'd invited me to his house after my TV program to see a Pinturicchio. It obviously meant a good deal to him to know if I thought it genuine. It didn't seem so to me, though it was very good. It wasn't in the catalogues, but paintings can turn up from the limbo. He didn't tell me where he'd got it. I thought I'd better be polite, so I said it really did have the look and feel.

"He showed me his other pictures in a huge kind of gallery on the ground floor of his house: but what came through most, as we talked, was a tremendously intimate feeling he had about the *subjects* of Renaissance art, and especially one subject — St. John the Baptist. And then I began to understand the reason. The fact that he's named for St. John is tremendously important

105

to him. It isn't just paintings or sculptures that he's interested in. It's the Baptist himself. He's totally absorbed in him. He feels that he's been under his protection. He worships him in an utterly literal sense. He's preparing to meet him in Heaven.

"I told you at lunch that his aim is to go to Heaven. If you think of his life, this can't be a *moral* question in the ordinary sense — the way he's earned a living, whether he's been good or sinful. These mundane things are irrelevant. What matters to him is his total identification with his personal saint. His way of going to Heaven is to live with the Baptist in the most intimate way: and he achieves this through art.

"I began to realize this when I saw how much he knew of all the great paintings and sculptures of the Baptist that emerged in the Renaissance and later. The strange thing is that he wasn't open about it. He was cautious, not giving much away. But the clues came out accidentally. I remember that I mentioned the Vienna Museum, and he began talking about a panel there — part of a triptych — of the Baptist just holding a lamb in his hand, a very poor shepherd, simple, inspired, believable. He mentioned what was to him the exact opposite — that famous Velasquez, *St. John in the Wilderness*, in the Art Institute in Chicago. You must know it — absolutely golden flesh, purple draperies, skin smooth, untouched by work or wind: he *hated* this. *His* Baptist was tortured, hungry, angular, agonized, inspired. There's a Baptism by Joachim de Patinier at Vienna with just this look. Jesus is in the water — pale, visionary, unearthly. John is attending him. He's in a brown shift, very human, a peasant who is working towards something he doesn't fully understand. This is what Harrigan responds to, not from the outside but from the inside. I felt it overpoweringly. Do you understand? Does it come through?"

"Perfectly," Ambrose said. Alyss herself seemed to have been carried away by Harrigan's emotion. It was riveting.

"At one level," she went on, "we were talking rationally: with enthusiasm, but rationally. And then it came to me that he was not rational on this, but mad. You might say: is a response to art — or religion — ever rational? Obviously not. When I say he was mad, I mean he was obsessed — capable of any acts by which he could fulfill the passion he had. He would be rational — even cunning — about acting this way, but the justification for it was not rational but obsessional. I saw it. I understood it. It clicked in my mind. And now I was on the *qui vive* myself. I felt my senses sharpened.

"I tried to think back to first base: the Pinturicchio. Why had he summoned me? It had to fit in somehow, but where? And then I had an inspiration. No, not an inspiration: I remembered something I had just been reading. It really *was* coincidence. You'll have to admit it this time."

"I'll never admit it," Ambrose said. "You remembered something you'd been looking for."

She shook her head. "Well, tell me when you've heard. I'd just been reading a very interesting article in *Apollo* on a quite separate subject: '*tarsia*' — you know, wood inlays. The point is that it was a meticulous description of a set of *tarsia* panels that had originally been in a chapel of the cathedral at Siena, though they were installed somewhere else later. It's a marvelous little chapel — every visitor to Siena knows it — right next to the Piccolomini Library — you must remember it."

"Of course," Ambrose said. "With the Pinturicchio frescoes. But why. . . ."

She smiled. "You've forgotten the subject. The chapel was built for St. John the Baptist. And that's what the frescoes are about. Scenes from his life. When I thought of it, I began to get a wild idea in my head."

Ambrose looked at her entranced. He took a sip of his whisky while she lit another cigarette. Her eyes were dancing with a remembered excitement.

"You can imagine how I felt," she said. "Here I was, with a man obsessed by the Baptist asking me about Pinturicchio: and *there* is a chapel with Pinturicchio going to town on the same subject. There *had* to be a connection."

"He wanted copies?"

"Well, that might be part of it, but there's something else — far more important. You'll see it as soon as I remind you." She broke off to take a sip of whisky herself. Ambrose sat watching her. He thought he'd never seen anyone so beautified by excitement.

"I'll give you the details and it will all come back," she said. "You remember the chapel: just a little protrusion from the cathedral wall — small, round, and very high, with a dome and lantern. The frescoes come later: it's the origin that matters. They built it around 1480 as a shrine for what they believe is a true relic of the Baptist himself — his right arm and hand."

"How did they get it?"

"Through Piccolomini — Pius II. It had been preserved in the East: and when it fell into his hands after the fall of

Constantinople, he gave it to Siena, his native city and they built the chapel for it — panels, frescoes, and then something in the middle."

"The Donatello! Of St. John!" It suddenly all came back to Ambrose.

"I knew you'd remember. It's the Donatello that's the real marvel there. It's amazing, isn't it — visionary, intense, almost like a gothic wood carving, though of course it's a bronze. What struck me, when I talked to Harrigan, was that this was *his* Baptist — a man in rags, so poor, even his skin seems to be falling off him."

"St. John in the Wilderness."

"That's it exactly. You can see why I began to think of it as I talked to him. I thought of the chapel: an expression of total devotion to the Baptist — the paintings, the statue, the relic. At that point I was just seeing a parallel: but even then I had a kind of instinct. We were in his huge gallery — almost like a Cathedral — high windows on one side, and at the bottom end, facing the entrance, a great tapestry covering the whole wall.

"Harrigan was walking round with me very slowly, talking, or rather croaking, when he suddenly stopped and pulled a bellrope. One of his servants — I suppose I should say one of his goons — came in immediately, with a wheel-chair. He just sat in it and said to me: 'Excuse me: I'll be back in a minute. Plenty to keep you busy', and the goon rolled him away.

"Of course, I guessed what it was. Old gentlemen have to be taken to the john at odd moments, and he is very old. The moment they'd gone, I had my inspiration. I knew they might be away only for a minute, so I walked over quickly to the other end to look at the tapestry. It seemed, somehow, out of key. I wondered if it had another function.

"I was right. It wasn't a fixed tapestry, but sort of two huge curtains, pulled together very tightly and joined in the middle. It was easy enough to separate them partly with my hands and look through. It wasn't a flat wall behind. There were two ornamental gates, opening into a round space, with frescoes on the walls and a statue immediately opposite. I only had a second to look. I rushed back to where I'd been, but I'd seen enough. There was no doubt. This was what explained his interest in Pinturicchio. He'd built a replica of the Siena chapel. It was all in character, but I just wondered what he'd actually installed there."

"My God!" Ambrose murmured. "I don't think I can take this

unaided. I need some more whisky." He walked over to help himself. She took a sip of her own glass while Ambrose busied himself silently.

Walking back, glass in hand, to his chair, he took a drink with a great sense of relief, and said: "I can make two guesses, both outrageous. But I can't bring myself to utter the words. It's much nicer just to listen."

It *was* nice. In the half-lit room, intimate by its nature, something more intimate was growing. There was a glow in Alyss as she told the story. He had had a lot of whisky. Was he just tipsy? He felt happy, relaxed.

Perhaps she felt something of this too. She was looking at him with the greatest affection. "Two guesses," she said. "You know, you are really marvelous. I knew it was going to be right to drag you into all this. *Two guesses: both outrageous.* Exactly what I felt myself."

He smiled back at her, raising his glass in salute. "I am limping behind you. You got there first through Pinturicchio. Unfair."

She laughed. "I know you won't admit the coincidence. Yes, it was really a deduction. Why did he want my view on his Pinturicchio? He was playing a game with me. He knew perfectly well that it wasn't authentic, but he wanted me to tell him if it was close enough to give the feeling of the original. And why? It was obvious as soon as I had looked behind the tapestry. He's had the eight frescoes done for his chapel, flanking the statue that he's put in. They've been done by the same man."

"He wanted an authentic setting for two outrageous suggestions."

"As authentic as possible. And then he could add something really authentic."

Ambrose felt a shiver. Had she actually established what was in both their minds? And suddenly he asked himself the question that had slipped away in the excitement. Why was she being followed — and bugged? Why had she summoned him in the middle of the night? What had she done?

"It was really obvious," she said, "once I'd caught a glimpse of the frescoes. The chapel's such a marvelous conception. Why hadn't he shown it to me himself? Because there may be other things in it that he doesn't want me to see. What could they be?"

Ambrose sat rigid. The shadows in the room seemed to engulf him.

"First I thought of the Donatello," she said, "and then my hackles really rose. *The relic.* What would this madman give to have the relic of his own saint in his own chapel? 'Give' is the wrong word. He couldn't buy it. What would he *do* to get it? The answer is he'd do anything."

"You do mean 'anything,'" Ambrose said soberly.

"Yes, I do. It would be an operation through his goons — through corruption or force — just like any operation over here to control a whole area or a whole product. What he wants, he takes."

"But you don't know if he has?"

She smiled a little grimly. "Haven't come to the moment of truth yet," she said, "but a lot's happened since that first moment of insight. If it weren't so, my telephone wouldn't be bugged and we wouldn't be sitting here in the moonlight."

"Which I find quite entrancing," Ambrose said.

"O.K. Entrancing. But its grim, too. And there's an angle to it which will appeal to your sense of irony, I think. If I'm at all right, he would hunger after the Donatello, but he would be impelled by something deeper to get the relic. Now *my* interest is the other way around. If he's stolen the relic, it's an extraordinary thing to have done: but if the *Donatello* has disappeared into his maw, this to me would be a sin against the Holy Ghost."

Ambrose nodded. No explanation needed. She was right.

"I couldn't just leave it in the air," she said. "But I couldn't do anything publicly. It was all a hunch — a feeling, at that point. I decided to approach it from the other end — Siena. I was due to go over to Europe within a month. I went to Siena and asked about the relic.

"You know they keep it high up on the wall in a niche above the Donatello. It's in a beautiful casket, though close to it's all rather grisly. What you can see through the glass is the Baptist's forearm, covered in mail chased with gold and precious stones, but with brown flesh emerging at the hand, *and with the thumb missing.* According to the story, his thumb was bitten off at some point and thrown into the mouth of a dragon to pacify it."

"Presumably it became a Christian on the spot."

She laughed. "Presumably. Well, it may be grisly, but it's a marvelous thing to see, except that on this visit it couldn't be seen. When I asked, they just fobbed me off with some story about cleaning the casket — has to be done at a certain temperature when they open it, and a lot more of this. It just wasn't available."

"Is it normally available all the time?"

"They always bring it down for the public on the day they observe as the Baptist's birthday — June 24th — which is when I was there. But this year they just didn't. In any case, they will always show an art treasure to an art historian. I produced my papers. They saw that I was qualified, but they said it wasn't available."

She paused, working obviously towards the real climax. "And the Donatello?" Ambrose asked.

"Yes, the Donatello. Oh, it was there all right. You look through the chapel opening and it faces you. Marvelous. I spent a long time looking at it. But I didn't really have to. I'm absolutely certain that it's not the original. He's done the oldest trick. When something is in the right place, most people don't look at it very closely. They take it for granted. But I *was* looking at it. I knew what I was looking for. And it wasn't there. I was looking at an imitation."

"Do you think the authorities there know and are just keeping it dark?"

"I don't know. You have to consider how it could happen. Was someone bought? If so, who? On the mechanics of it, there was something that I thought at first was just a coincidence. And then I thought — *some* coincidence! It was by design. The whole interior of the chapel was very fresh, and I asked about it. Yes, they said. It had been closed for several months during the spring for cleaning everything in it — the frescoes, and those wonderfully intricate pilasters that form the niches for sculptures. It all seemed clear to me. The people Harrigan was using over there knew all about this. The Donatello had been taken down to be cleaned at the same time. Everything had been covered in scaffolding and painting sheets. When it was all opened again, the substitute that Harrigan's people had got ready might look a bit new, though, of course, it would have been treated for age. But it would still have a different smell, so to speak: except that the whole chapel had this 'smell,' so no one need have noticed it."

"What has happened at this end?"

"That's why you're here. Nothing's happened yet, but it's going to: tomorrow. I need an ally, and you're it. After we'd met at lunch, and then gone round the Museum together, somehow you began to surface. Then I went to your first lecture, and it was extraordinary. Everything you said seemed to fit in directly. It all pointed the same way. You seemed the kind of person who would just possibly come in with me because you would understand what was involved."

Ambrose smiled at her. "Well, as you see, I'm here." He could guess what was coming: not the detail, but the general idea. Something had been planned that went beyond words: some act, and a dangerous one. She herself was quite relaxed now, as if she'd got the hard part over. Once the decision was taken and the alliance set up, the rest was easy.

Perhaps he *was* tipsy: but it seemed to him, at that moment, that to plunge with her into some kind of dangerous act on an issue of this importance was completely justified and desirable. Looking at her, he saw a transformation. At earlier meetings she had seemed reserved: but now that she had come to life in excitement, there was a radiance in her face. Her whole person expressed a kind of harmony. She was wearing black slacks with a deep red sweater, out of which peeped the top of a white blouse. Her black hair, drawn back, shaped the oval of her face with enormous appeal.

"I can see you've guessed it," she said. "We've got to get in there and have a look."

"Get in there?" Yes, he'd guessed it. But to hear it announced was different. He held on to his brave air, and took a sip of his whisky.

"I'll tell you about the mechanics first," she said briskly. "I couldn't have moved without Tim. He's been around Harrigan's house for the last three weeks at all hours, but especially at night, of course. He told me at the beginning of this week that he knows now how to get in, avoiding the goons and their dogs, not to mention the electronic business. Of course, we need more than this, and tomorrow we have it. Harrigan is going to South Bend, Indiana, tomorrow night to get an honorary degree the next day — Saturday — at the University of Notre Dame."

"Well, what do you know?" Ambrose said. "I had the clue and missed it. Bah!"

She thought he was expressing general disgust and tried to reassure him. "Oh, I know it's monstrous for a gangster to get an honorary degree, but it's really not so bad this time. I hear that he's given them ten million dollars to enlarge their History of Art department and start a collection. Obviously, he must have it in mind to pass on his own collection to them, or at least some of it. But at this moment, the real joy to me is that he's *going* there. Normally, he never moves from the house. I suppose he rules his gang from home with an iron hand. But getting an honorary degree means a lot, so he's going, and a whole lot of his goons are going with him. I was talking about it on the phone yesterday to someone I know at Notre Dame. He told me that Harrigan will be flying in his own plane. He'll have ten in his party — quite a bodyguard. Very nice for Notre Dame, and very nice for us. There'll be some guards left, but Tim thinks there's no problem. He says it's a piece of cake."

"I've heard the expression," Ambrose said. "In R.A.F. use it suggested scraping through an operation that by any standard was obviously suicidal."

"Oh, I don't know," Alyss said. "Tim says he got into much more difficult places for the CIA. You've just got to get timing right. He says we should be outside the house at 1:30 a.m. That's the time he feels is best. We don't go through the main gate but through an opening in the hedge — apparently it's as thick as a wall — that he's been loosening up last week and can be used now, he says, like an open door. We get into the house itself through a basement window that he's prepared likewise. Once we're in the main part of the house, we'll have fifteen minutes to explore what I call the chapel. Tim says this timing will be fine for the routine the goons have for going round the grounds with their dogs."

"Their *dogs!*" Ambrose gulped for a moment, but recovered in good order. "And if it's what we think, do we purloin. . . ."

"Oh, no. Just try to establish the facts — the casket, the Donatello, and the pictures I haven't had a chance to look at properly. But no purloining at this stage."

"I see. All prim and proper. Nothing criminal. Just breaking and entering."

"Well. . . ." She looked at him slowly as if she had never quite thought about it that way. "Well, yes. It's a bit unusual, perhaps. But after all, just think what we may find. Besides. . . ." She lost her momentary uncertainty and her eyes began to sparkle: "Don't you think it's going to be exciting? Are you game?"

"Don't have much choice, do I?" Ambrose said lightly. What was the point in being pompous? He had been ready from the word go.

"Oh, great!" She was sitting near him, and now she put her hand on his, just for a second, as if to seal things. The she jumped up. "I've got to get you back. My God! It's after three! I'm going to drive you back. The coast is clear now. My attendants have very precise hours. Come, I'll show you."

She led the way into her sitting-room and walked over to the window. "You see that little alley down there? The man that follows me in the late afternoon and evening always stands in there. He goes off at 1 a.m. The other one comes on duty at seven."

"You never explained that part. When did they start following you?"

"They must have got word back from Siena, from one of the people he uses there. I made a lot of inquiries, of course, and I suppose they must have thought it was a bit suspicious. Once my name came back here, he must have begun to wonder, since I'd been to his house. I was only aware of being followed in the last week. I got Tim in immediately to see if my apartment was being bugged. What's so nice about Tim is that he enjoys it all so much. He feels he's back in the CIA."

"*Oh, lucky Tim, how I envy him,*" Ambrose chanted, as they turned back from the window, ready to go. "The joys of being an expert. Which reminds me. Will I be up to it? After all, I'm not a professional. What about that nice Italian man you were lunching with the other day, to the infinite annoyance of Jeff Cohen?"

"Yes, I know." They were in the elevator now, descending. "I'd met Franzoni, and I did think. . . . But I found out something I didn't quite like, so I decided against it. Poor Jeff." She laughed. "He certainly *was* very miffed. I do like him. Ah, well. Perhaps he'll understand one day."

Her car, a little white Alfa-Romeo, was on the street in front of the house. A thought came to Ambrose as they settled in.

"No need to take me all the way to my hotel," he said. "Harvard Square will be fine."

He'd been off on a cloud: but now, some of his own problems were coming back. Willis had cleared up his own role, but there might be a lot of trails still to be unwound. He smiled to himself. Just what Hepworth had cabled: *there's a long long trail awinding.*

Yes, he'd better keep an eye open. Alyss had found someone following *her.* Someone may have been put on to *him,* too, and might still be under orders. Perhaps a clerk at the hotel. No need for Alyss to get involved in the reports they would be filing. . . .

"Do you like good jazz?" she asked, as they drove along.

"Very much," he said. "You're not suggesting we go some-where now. . . ."

"No, I'll let you off now. But tomorrow night — or rather

tonight. There's a rather noisy club in Harland Street just off Boylston called *The Cavern*. It's a huge place: was an underground garage before they converted it. They play very good jazz, real trad stuff. We could meet there, say at eleven-thirty. I'll get there without being followed. I'll get Tim to drive me there. He'll be driving us to Harrigan's in his own car and he can shake anybody off. So there we are. Unless I call you during the day, let's listen to jazz tonight, and take it from there."

At Harvard Square, as he climbed out of the car, she gave a wave of her hand and was off. Ambrose, feeling rather bewildered, made his way back to the hotel, shrouded now in dismal silence. He had kept his room-key and went straight upstairs. As he bent down to put the key in, it seemed to him that there was something white just visible below the door. For a second, his mind flashed to a letter-bomb. He opened the door with the most timid care. Yes, it *was* a letter, with only his name on it in a scrawled handwriting: *Mr. Usher*.

Gingerly, he picked it up. Did these things explode as you touched them? Surely not: only when you opened them. It was very thin. If it were a letter-bomb, wouldn't it have to have *some* thickness? Oh, the hell with it, he said to himself, tearing it open.

Inside was a single sheet of paper: the message scrawled on it had what one might call a Turkish vehemence: "*Where the hell have you been? I've spent the whole day saving the British Empire, and now when I want to report to you personally at midnight, you're not here, or so the hotel clerk says. I'll be along for breakfast at nine. Regards to you, by the way, from a beautiful redhead called Lindsay. She has been to your lectures and swears you are devoted to her. Basruk the Terrible.*"

VII

"NEVER mind the British Empire. How on earth did you meet my beautiful redhead?" It was obviously the first question as they sat down to breakfast.

"Well, I *could* say she's my cousin. In fact I *will* say she's my cousin." Basruk, picking up a large glass of orange juice, was perfectly happy to explain simple things like this to Ambrose.

"Your *cousin!* She's *Polish.* Sonnieski, or some name like that, she told me."

"My dear Ambrose: you are taking a very one-eyed stance. Too much influenced by one set of genes. Her father has a Polish name, certainly: and that's why she's a redhead. A great many glorious redheads in Poland. But what about her mother? As it happens, her mother's father was Armenian, and that's near enough to being a Turk."

"One of the Armenians you forgot to slaughter. All right, she's your cousin ten times removed. And you just happened to bump into her."

"You might say so," Basruk croaked. "In a strange town, I always sample the local delicacies. Doesn't everybody? *Sachertorte* in Vienna: lobster in Maine. I just happened to be taking coffee yesterday, in a place full of students, when this gorgeous creature walked in. Somehow or other we got talking. She told me about her grandfather coming from Turkey, and with a bond like that between us we felt we had to spend the whole evening together. In fact, if it hadn't been for her I would have come to see you earlier in the evening. I wish I'd caught you last night. So much to discuss. Where the hell were *you,* by the way? Having some long-winded philosophical argument, I suppose. That's what's wrong with you, Ambrose. You should try a little action instead of words."

117

Alyss would agree with that, Ambrose thought: but it still didn't make it right. In the sober light of day, the adventure due to start in a jazz club was beginning to look more questionable.

"Too much caution built-in," Basruk was saying, with his damned Turkish insight. Perhaps he was really a gypsy. "As a matter of fact, that's what I've got to discuss with you. You heard about the takeover bid by TCC. That's why I came up here. Our people at home are stymied. They want to oppose it, and I agree with them. It would be fatal. But they can't find rational grounds for objecting. In my view, we need a bit of strong-arm business." With symbolic relish, he addressed himself to the great mound of ham and eggs that the waiter had piled on to his plate.

"And who are we supposed to bump off?" Ambrose said cheerfully. Turning somewhat hungrily to his own plateful, he was surprised to find how fresh and full of appetite he felt despite his lack of sleep. Some of the previous night's zest was coming back. Breaking and entering — bumping off — yes, perhaps this was the pace one should aim at.

"Who's our villain?" Basruk asked querulously. "Why, it's obvious. George Fletcher. Really, Ambrose. I thought you were in the picture."

"I've had a few other things on my mind. Fill me in."

Basruk looked around to make quite sure they were not being overheard. "You know from the Treasury meeting how big the plans are for the British consortium. Literally billions of pounds' of orders, taking just the five years ahead, and certainly more to follow. Of course the credits have got to be very long. For this, they need a hell of a lot more finance, so they're going to bring in groups from two other countries. One will probably be Swiss, and the other could be a kind of joint Middle-Eastern, or perhaps just Iranian. In both these cases it will be just money: they won't interfere with the work itself being controlled and carried out entirely by the U.K. But if the central British company is taken over by the Americans, they'll just swamp the whole project and get their own allied firms into the work itself. And besides . . ." he lowered his voice, though their table was quite on its own — "there are some very cogent political dangers. I don't want to spell this out. We have a feeling, you know, that our American hero may not be on the up-and-up politically. He may have some Soviet links."

"Well, he may be a horror. He *is* a horror. But the idea of him being a Soviet stooge. . . ."

"I rather agree. Difficult to imagine, isn't it? But it's very hard to know what's his real game. They've become very suspicious of him at home. The trouble is that he has the *entrée* everywhere in the City, and I'd be surprised if he hasn't been spreading a lot of money around where it might help, quite apart from the takeover itself. What he seems to have in unlimited amount is cash. Where does it come from?"

"There's no real mystery about that," Ambrose said. "Have you see the Harrigan Center?"

"You mean Harrigan's behind it all? Well, I know he's powerful, but I thought he was basically just Boston-Irish, throwing his weight around through his paid-up supporters in City Hall. Isn't that how he operates?"

"Yes, it's still the basis, but it's a relatively small part of his operation. From what I see of the picture here, we've got to think of the Irish mafia the way we all think now about the Italian one. They're in the really big time, and it's all, ultimately, in Harrigan's hands. What they've got to do is to open up a channel so that all the loose cash can be laundered. I suppose that's why they're putting so much effort behind this bid. If it comes off, they're home and dry."

Basruk was adding it all up. "Seems to me to make it all the more important to get Fletcher out of the picture. I know what we'd do about it if this were a Turkish operation. Wouldn't be so namby-pamby about it as our City people or the Bank. We'd have a little action. You know, Ambrose, the scale of this thing is immense. I keep wishing we could just bring in the people who have cash and wouldn't interfere — the Middle-Eastern lot. We wouldn't have to tackle the Sheikhs directly. It all flows through the Lebanon. Just open up the channel in Beirut and we'd have everything we want. Seems such a damn shame to let everything get taken over and lose all the profit."

Ambrose, listening, felt a very unkind speculation beginning to surface in his mind. He tried to squash it but failed. He heard himself approaching it in a rather roundabout way.

"I expect you really feel sore because you're not in there operating yourself," he said. "Someone told me that you're one of those whiz-kid economics dons who actually play around in the market to good effect. Now that you're an official adviser you must be very inhibited. Don't you miss it?"

"Oh, God, no!" Basruk exclaimed. "What I'm doing now is much more fun. I just froze everything when I went down to the Treasury. Plenty of time to pick it up again later."

"But this particular occasion is passing you by."

"Ah, yes, but there are always my cousins. I expect my cousins are burning up the wires on this all over the place. We're quite a clan, you know. We've even got some of them in Beirut. Olaf is very funny about it. We were arguing about the takeover in Washington the other night. He doesn't seem entirely against the Americans getting in on what we're doing. 'I suppose you want to get your cousins there instead,' he said to me. He's a real card is Olaf. God knows what he's up to out in Colorado. I wouldn't be surprised if he's looking into those gold-mine rumors. He *said* he was going there just to play a little backgammon. Is one really supposed to believe that?"

"*I* believe it. I suppose I'm an innocent."

"*You* innocent? You can't be, by definition. You have more than one thing in your mind at once."

"Well, by that definition. . . ."

"Yes, I agree, I agree. We all show only one face at a time."

"And which face do we see when we look in the mirror? That's the real question, isn't it?" Ambrose sighed, as they got up ready to leave the breakfast table.

He came back to the question when they stood in the hotel lobby, about to separate, with Basruk on his way to the Consulate-General to see what messages on the takeover had come through from London.

"I phrased it wrongly," he said to Basruk. "The real question is how do we know what we look like when we're *not* looking into a mirror."

"Is this *Alice Through the Looking Glass*?"

"More like Wittgenstein through the looking-glass. It's the question that bothered him all the time. It bothers *me*. How sure are we of the external world? The old empiricists thought that the mind was a mirror reflecting it. *He* thought that *language* was the only mirror. We can't say anything about reality without using language. But what would things be like without the intermediary of language? He proves we can't know. But he's *dying* to know. Ernest Gellner — do you know his book *Words and Things*?"

"No."

"It would amuse you. He has a nice way of putting it. He says Wittgenstein is certain he can never know what he looks like when he's not looking in a mirror, but he keeps trying to peep all the same."

"Reporting what can't be reported."

"Just so."

It was as if Patrick Willis was in there chanting: "*Impelled of invisible tides and fulfilled of unspeakable things.*" Where was Willis now, Ambrose wondered. What face did *he* see, looking in the mirror?

"You are wanted on the phone, Mr. Usher," the man at the desk called out as Basruk went off. "You can take it in the booth over there."

Hepworth was on the line as clear as if he were round the corner. Perhaps he *was*! Ambrose had a moment of alarm. He didn't *want* Hepworth here. He didn't want him at all. With a great relief he heard him say: "How are things over there? I thought it would be nice if we had a word on the phone."

Poor old Hepworth. Had he caught up with Willis yet? One had to sympathize with the man. He must be going through hell. How does one cope with defection when it strikes? The Prime Minister. The Press. They would be on his neck once the story was out. One should be sorry for him. All the same, Ambrose felt sore.

"I just want to get you on the right track," Hepworth was saying. "Simpler on the phone."

"Below your usual cautionary standard, isn't it?"

"Oh, we can talk in riddles. '*And did those feet in ancient times walk upon England's mountain green*?' You will know of whom I speak?"

"Yes, I know," Ambrose said wearily. Those *Times* crossword games. One has simply to go on to the next verse: "*Bring me my bow of burning gold, bring me my arrows of desire.*" "Fletcher" means bowman, or more precisely arrow-man.

"I got your message," Hepworth said. "I didn't take it too seriously. You were tired of things momentarily. But it's moved into high gear now that he's come over here. You've heard what's going on? We weren't wrong, I think you will agree, to look into this character from all angles. As it happens, we've had some rather sudden developments over here. I know a good deal more than I knew when we spoke. Some things have come out which are quite revealing. That's what I meant with my message — '*there's a long long trail a-winding.*'"

"And roses are blooming in Picardy. Thank you very much. It's no longer of the least interest to me."

"Oh, but it is, Ambrose, it is. Besides, when one is inside a situation, one can't just opt out. Some of the terms may alter by new revelations — and there *have been* revelations. I'll tell you about it when we meet. On certain points my face is slightly red. But the structure is still there to be explored. Especially in your case."

"Why especially me?"

"By your own definition. You explained it to me so clearly: the Ambrose circle. We may have thought we were looking for *one* connection but in fact some quite different connection may emerge, something that may surprise even *you*. Has nothing unexpected come your way over there — something, perhaps, whose end you can't yet foretell?"

"Well, possibly. . . ."

"There you are. Let it go on. You can't tell where it will lead. '*I shot an arrow into the air.*'"

"You are impossible. And your jokes are getting worse by the minute."

"I wish I were just joking. In fact, there's one rather serious thing I have to say. At the moment everything seems under control over here, but if we've fallen down, as we often do, alas, it's just possible that you yourself might be in danger."

"*Me*? I am wrapped in cotton wool."

"Well, that may be. But if there's a sign of violence at your end, do take care. There's no reason why it should affect *you*, except that that's the kind of character you are. One expects you to get involved. You don't change."

"The mirror, I suppose."

"Mirror? What mirror?" For the first time, Hepworth seemed at a loss.

"I'm just conceding your point. You've solved a little philosophical problem that I was wrestling with just a few minutes ago. The image stays there whether one is looking in the mirror or not."

"I haven't the faintest idea what you're talking about," Hepworth said. "I've just been trying to remind you how you defined your own role. You're not an operator: things just happen because you are there."

Ambrose felt unable to deny this. He was perhaps Horace's whetstone, which makes steel sharp though it has no power itself to cut. "*Exsors ipsa secandi,*" he murmured to himself. Not a very creative role. Alyss had better not expect too much of him that evening.

* * *

Going up to his room, he decided to address himself to an immediately practical question. What he should be really worrying about was the lecture he had to deliver at the Toronto gathering the following evening. They had arranged it for the weekend, at his own request, to fit in with his timetable. From the details sent to him it was obviously very formal — *The Durham Lecture* — very prestigious, large fee, printed afterwards as a delectable brochure. Certainly not an occasion for just talking off the cuff. He had his notes ready, but he'd better start getting them into proper shape.

Unfortunately for his peace of mind, the announced title of his lecture was *Morality and Politics*. He was treating the subject academically — from Machiavelli to Marcuse, one might say. But how did one talk about morality with images of Hepworth and Willis flitting through one's mind — not to mention breaking and entering with Alyss Summers? The answer was: it was difficult, And when something was difficult, one tried to avoid coping with it.

He had taken the newspapers upstairs with him. That should keep thought away for a bit. The *New York Times* was usually good for half an hour if taken slowly. Alas: a few minutes were enough this time. Hopefully, he ferreted around in the Financial Section. The main article there was on uranium — some vast contract that was being formulated for the exploitation of the Rössing reserves in Namibia. Where the hell was Namibia? In South-West Africa it seemed. Now, if he were back in the Treasury this might have been interesting — the sort of thing Sir Olaf would talk about with his troll-like insight. But one couldn't milk it for much at this distance.

He turned to the *Boston Mail*. No further developments on the gangster shooting. Really, Boston had become very dull. The main headline was, in fact, on Hurricane Hilda. Hilda was cutting a swathe of destruction up the East coast, and was due in New England that evening. Danger signals were out in Block Island, it seemed. He looked out of the window to the bright autumnal sunshine. Yes, there were a few clouds, but nothing that could justify alarm.

There was nothing for it. He got out his notes and began working. At lunchtime, he went downstairs with a forbidding volume to read at table, aimed at discouraging would-be chatterers. In the wine-list, he saw a Californian *Cabernet* that someone had spoken of highly. He ordered it. They were right: it was excellent. Reading happily, and with an assiduous wine-waiter keeping his glass charged, he felt at peace with the world as he staggered upstairs after lunch. All would be well, he decided.

But he felt strangely tired. The late-late talk with Alyss — and perhaps the wine — had finally caught up with him. He lay down for a little snooze. A moment later — or so it seemed — he was awakened by the most fearsome banging and rattling. The room was dark. He lay there, unable to move.

It was the window. Something had come loose and was banging against it. Outside he heard what sounded like the wild hurling of huge girders against metal screens, accompanied by a rattle of kettledrums. The banging on the window went on. Summoning all his energy, he managed to get up from his bed and stagger across the room to see what had happened to the world he knew.

A strange gloom pervaded the air. The high trees in the square opposite were blowing in all directions, with strange creaking noises as if in agony. From the street he could hear rapid-fire noises like machine-gunning as garbage pails and anything else loose were thrown around in the wind. He looked at his watch. It was five o'clock. He had slept for two hours: and while he slept, Hurricane Hilda had arrived.

He sat down for a moment and then went into his bathroom to douse his head in cold water. Surely Hilda wouldn't tear up Boston itself. Hurricanes were supposed to move out to sea by the time they reached New England. He picked up the phone and rang Bill Rafferty at the *Mail*.

He was received rapturously. "Where have you been?" Rafferty wanted to know. "I was going to call you. Come over and have a drink. I've got to stay in the office for a while, but we can talk."

"How can I just come over for a drink? What's going on? It's like the plagues of Egypt."

"Oh, it's nothing," Rafferty told him. "The hurricane's moving out to sea, but we get the wind, and probably a lot of rain soon, as it passes us by. Often happens in September. I suppose it seems freaky to you, but it'll all be over in a few hours. Get a cab and come over. I've got a few things to tell you."

Somewhat comforted, Ambrose pulled himself together and got ready to go. A drink in company was what he needed. Perhaps they could dine together, and he would stay in Boston for his jazz club rendezvous. But the rain. He had a coat that would serve. No use trying to wear a hat in that wind.

As he came out of the hotel, the wind practically lifted him off his feet. Pulling his fluttering coat around him he put his head down and fought his way to Harvard Square. Gradually he began to feel exhilarated at the battle with the elements. When he finally found a cab, and settled back for the ride to Boston, he was exhausted but triumphant. There was a kind of omen in it. No more books. Action. This was it.

He had just got in through the door of the *Mail* office when the rain began. The skies opened and a solid sheet of water hit the ground with a tremendous slap and a force that swept everything else away. Ambrose stood in the doorway watching it in disbelief. America, he thought. Where else? Total power. If the skyscrapers around had just crumbled to dust in this primeval flood, it would have been no surprise.

Shaking his head, he made his way to the Editor's room. There, with a large scotch in his hand, everything seemed to have become normal again. "Yes," Rafferty said. "Pretty powerful. You can imagine what it's like when you're actually in the path of a thing like this: but a side-swipe, the way we get it, is O.K. We'll live."

How was Princeton, he wanted to know. What else was going on? They chatted for a few minutes, and then Rafferty got on to his news.

"I think you're going to see some action here," he said. "The cops are on their toes. I've been tipped off about it. I told you when the O'Connell thing happened that it seemed to me more than just paying off a debt. The gangs are watching each other. There's a feeling around that McLuskey is trying to move in and grab part of the area, or even take over. I don't think it's true. He couldn't take over the organization. It's too big — so much bigger than just running liquor and the usual things. The funds are all over the place — all over the world. McLuskey couldn't find his way in, unless, perhaps, he struck at the top. Anyhow, everyone's on the alert. And this afternoon, the police fished a body out of the Bay. One of Harrigan's men, but the police don't think he was bumped off by McLuskey's boys. They think he might have been seen talking to someone from the McLuskey lot, and that would be a death sentence. It's pretty grim."

He went on for a little in this vein, and then said, *en passant*: "There's a comic side to all this: perhaps ironic is a better word.

In the middle of it all, the Big Boss is getting an honorary degree tomorrow at Notre Dame. And do you know what degree it is? Doctor of Religious Law."

"Dr. Harrigan, I presume. Yes, I heard: but I decided that it may not be so out of place as it sounds. Someone who's met him told me that he's a deeply religious man: in his own fashion, of course."

"The way the Godfather was religious," Rafferty said, recharging Ambrose's glass. "Did you see the movie?"

"I never seemed to find the time," Ambrose said. "Doesn't it run for about four hours?"

"You ought to see it. It's on across the road as a revival. Why don't you see it now? Save you fighting your way through this rain. Are you free? I wish I could ask you to dine, but we're invited out."

"I might very well. I suppose there must be a restaurant nearby where I can get a steak beforehand, a really bloody one to get me in the mood. Yes, it might fit very well. But tell me: is Harland Street nearby?"

"Round the corner. Why?"

"I'm told there's an institution there where one can hear good jazz: *The Cavern,* it's called. I said I might meet some friends there later on."

"What a perfect evening! A steak, *The Godfather,* and jazz. It's a wonderful place — a vast cavern. Kathleen and I were there the other night. The food is good, too. Everyone goes there. Trust you to find the in-place. They've got a marvelous old trad band there at the moment — trombones and all that."

"Just what I love. Like Job: '*He saith Ha-Ha among the trumpets.*' And by that time, I suppose, the storm will be over, the morning stars will sing together, and all the sons of God will shout for joy."

He kept the cheering words in his mind as he forced himself into the storm a few minutes later, clammily drenched as he sat down for his steak. He had checked the times of the cinema showing as he passed the door. It fitted in comfortably. By the time he emerged from the restaurant, the wind had died down and the downpour had softened from a skyburst to a steady flood. *The Godfather* was perfect. Jazz with Alyss, regardless of what was to follow, promised a happy postscript.

No one had told him that a club offering late-night music had to be almost pitch-dark, with the light concentrated on the band in the remote distance, and, for the rest, offering only flickering candles. The contrast was all the greater after the well-lit lobby in which he had surrendered his sopping coat to a long-legged, eye-catching girl, virtually unbosomed at the top and wearing only a sort of *tutu* below. Peering into the gloom of the cavern, he began to thread his way through the tables, peering with apparent rudeness into the darkened faces of the guests to see if Alyss had arrived, and muttering apologies which were neither expected nor heard.

With no Alyss visible, he thought that he had better try for an empty table, and struggled round again. The leg of a protruding chair caught him, and he was down on the floor in a crash. A Good Samaritan helped him up, and he moved on. At the first step, he gave a groan. His left ankle had ceased to function. But a table had to be found. He limped on, groaning, and fortune at last smiled. A company of four were leaving a table backed to the wall and favored with a candle. He hobbled in, falling gratefully onto the banquette against the wall, and extending his leg in relief. A waiter, lynx-eyed, it seemed, was upon him in a second. He said he would wait for his guest, and turned his attention to the music.

Just the kind of jazz he most liked. His spirit warmed to the heavy stomp and the free-wheeling harmonies. He half-closed his eyes in pleasure. Opening them, he saw Alyss standing there, her face warm in the candlelight.

He struggled to his feet, but with an audible "Ouch" as a pain shot through his ankle.

"I tripped up," he said, "searching for you in the gloom — roaming in the gloaming. Not much of a hero, I fear: wounded before the battle."

"Is it very painful?"

"It will pass, I'm sure. I feel better already, seeing you."

She looked charming enough, though dressed with severity in a dark trouser-suit — perhaps to meet the practical problems ahead. The waiter arrived, and for a few minutes they busied themselves with the menu, plumping in the end for smoked salmon sandwiches and what seemed like a choice New York State champagne. They were sitting side-by-side on the banquette. The waiter moved off. They said nothing for the moment, just listening to the music.

"How do you feel about it all?" she said finally. "It's a funny kind of zero-hour, isn't it? It felt easy enough talking about it in the early hours, but now. . . ."

"I feel the same. A bit queasy. Any weakening of resolve?"

"Oh, no." Her old intensity was back immediately. "I only feel a bit queasy because I've never done anything like this before. But I'm not sure if I should have involved *you*."

"I'm here," he said. "My own free will."

"Ah, that makes me feel better. No: I wouldn't miss it for anything. I've been living with it for a long time, you know. I've just got to find out if I'm right, and if I am, what to do. The fact that it's got to be tonight, while he's away, makes it very exciting."

"I wondered earlier if the storm would make it impossible."

"Yes, I did too. We're lucky that it struck in the afternoon and not in the middle of the night. It was still pouring when I came here, but nothing like before."

"And Tim's still satisfied with the mechanics?"

"Completely. It was marvelous the way he dropped me here, avoiding any possible follower. Just whizzed around — reversed — all kinds of things. You'll see how he drives when he picks us up. We're to go out at twelve-thirty. He'll be waiting round the corner. He told me he was going off to get some false number-plates. He seems to be getting a tremendous kick out of it, which I can understand. It's CIA stuff, but for a good cause."

"Don't ask me if that makes it morally right."

"I won't. In my own mind, I'm quite sure it does. But there's something else in it for me. I've always specialized, as an art historian, in the Renaissance. I've really spent years living in that period — gangster Princes, private armies, murder, mayhem: and look what it produced in art. Well, it didn't *produce* it, but that was its legacy. I can't explain how it happened: they seemed to spend all their time cutting each other's throats — Guelphs and Ghibellines and all that. Perhaps that was symbolic: there was a cutting-edge to life. And what do we have now instead? Washing machines, packaged holidays, synthetic materials. It's a plastic world. I want to have one go at something elemental, where one doesn't count the cost." The champagne had arrived and was being poured. She lifted her glass. "To you! It's all through you, really. Meeting you somehow sharpened my will."

"Ambrose the Whetstone, at your service." He raised his glass in return and took a sip. It was excellent. The sandwiches were fresh and ample. The cavern seemed full of a bustling kind of happiness. In the background, trumpets and trombones were signing the vivid air with delight.

128

"It *is* odd that we met," she said. "Here we are, in the middle of all this, and I hardly know you. I've never yet even called you Ambrose, but I will now. Dear Ambrose." She raised her glass again.

"And what am I to call you? Alyss in Wonderland, I suppose." He stretched out for another sandwich, and as he moved felt a twinge again in his ankle. But it went when he found the right position for his foot.

She was frowning slightly, trying to clarify her thought, as she looked into her glass. "What I mean about meeting you," she said, "is that I can't imagine anyone else who would have known what it's all about and been willing to gamble on it. That's what makes it so extraordinary."

"Oh, *I* know someone you might have been happier with: knows much more about painting than I do, and infinitely more about gambling. On top of that, he bears the incredible name of Sir Olaf McConnochie."

"You've just made that up."

"No one could make Olaf up. If I throw in that he dresses like a dandy and is also our top financial wizard in England, you'll see what I mean. Oh, yes. He's also said to own half of Norway. I may be exaggerating slightly."

"I'm beginning to think you're right," she said. "What's his telephone number?"

"Colerado something or other. He's out there gambling: but not for paintings — at least I don't think so. All the same, I have the feeling that it's painting that matters to him most. He has the rare advantage of not just knowing about it but also owning a lot."

"Oh, I see. A collector."

"Well, I don't know if he collects himself, but he saw to it that his ancestors did. I wish I'd had the sense to arrange things that way."

"Don't we all?"

"At least we're making the best of what we have," he said, looking at her with some affection.

The music, the champagne, the bustle, the candlelight — it was all so beautifully private. Just the moment, of course, to be assaulted by an all-too-familiar Turkish croak: "So this is where you hide out at night."

Basruk was standing with a girl and an old gentleman in a black suit on the other side of their table. No surprise to see Lindsay with him, her long red hair cascading prettily over her shoulders: but the old gentleman. . . . He was rather short and very lean: his face looked scrubbed and bony. He was not just old, but gnarled and ancient: yet at the same time he seemed to be sparkling with vitality. He had a full head of gray hair and a fierce bristling mustache. Perhaps it was just the fierceness of the mustache: but there was something about the whole man, and the way he stood, that conveyed complete authority.

Ambrose was trying to make sense of it as he struggled painfully to his feet. But Basruk, clearly delighted at the surprise he had achieved, held for the moment the upper hand. These stray acquaintances, found sitting at a table, were to be made fully aware of the honor that had befallen them.

"Uncle Estovan," he said, turning to the old gentleman, "may I present Mr. Ambrose Usher, a philosopher from Oxford? Ambrose" — he raised his hand, ready now to play the master-card — "this is my grand-uncle, my grandfather's oldest brother, the head of our family — Basruk Pasha."

After that, anything that followed was an anti-climax. All the same, Basruk was eyeing Alyss with considerable interest. Ambrose presented her. Miss Lindsay Sonnieski, in turn, was identified to Miss Summers. A waiter, coming up behind them, was scurrying forward with chairs. In a moment, the five of them were at table.

Uncle Estovan had made it clear that he would sit on the banquette, to have the whole club in view. His eyes were darting everywhere, full of mischief. Ambrose had made to sit next to him on a chair, but the Pasha calmly took Lindsay by the hand and put her there. Ambrose, perforce, sat next to her. Basruk pulled his chair close to Alyss on the other side.

"My uncle is on his way to see some of my cousins in the Mid-West," Basruk explained. "Isn't it lucky that he could stop off here? I had a cable just after I left you this morning. We've had a splendid dinner at *The Bosphorus* — they gave us a really great *Kuzi Tandir* — and he said he'd like to go on to a nightclub. Lindsay said that this was everyone's favorite place. I might have guessed we'd find *you* here." He turned to the old gentleman. "It's not quite what you meant, is it, Uncle?"

Uncle had a light whispering kind of voice when he answered. Ambrose was reminded instantly of the Godfather. Of course! He *was* the Godfather, Turkish style. "I thought perhaps some dancing," he was saying. "The restaurant was good, but no music, no dancing. Very boring."

Ambrose was trying to do some mental arithmetic to work out his age. Grandfather's oldest brother. One could assume a large family, so the oldest brother. . . . He had to be well over ninety — perhaps a hundred. Of course, that was nothing in Turkey, especially near the border with Georgia.

The waiter was still standing by, ready for orders. "What will you drink?" Basruk asked his uncle. "I wonder if they have any raki." He turned to the waiter. "Do you keep it?"

"Sure. Raki, ouzo. We have some Greek customers who come here — musicians. Sometimes they play. All the raki you want. Shall I bring three glasses?"

"*Glasses?* Bring us a bottle, and some black olives. What about you, Lindsay?"

"Could I have a coke, please?"

Basruk raised his eyes to heaven in disbelief. Ambrose turned to her. "How about some champagne? I'm going to order a little more."

"Oh, yes." One up to Ambrose. "I was telling Zilto how much I enjoy your lectures. Champagne is just right." She giggled slightly and then turned to the old gentleman. "Mr. Usher was talking in his lectures about Zen Bhuddism. Do you have it in Turkey?"

The Pasha smiled at her patiently, as if he was well used to pretty young girls whose chatter was totally irrelevant to the business in hand. Lindsay, looking back at him, seemed eager, as always, for anything that might be expected of her. She had been respectful to Ambrose. She was clearly responsive to the young Basruk. But to the older version, response was submission. Perhaps he was simply the oldest *guru* she was ever likely to meet. Her eyes were wide open in devotion. He took her hand again and patted it gently.

Young Basruk, talking to Alyss but taking all this in, did not seem unduly surprised. *Surprised?* Ambrose suddenly realized with what love, *alla Turca,* the dinner *à trois* had been arranged. We were too used, after Mozart, to young girls *escaping* from the Seraglio: but if one loved one's grand-uncle, who was a Pasha. . . .

The drink was arriving. The waiter, depositing the raki and fussing with the champagne, addressed the old gentleman. "Excuse me, sir, I heard you say something about dancing. Sometimes, when the Greeks come, we clear the floor a little and they play during the band's interval. They're here tonight, so perhaps they'll dance."

131

The Pasha nodded. He seemed to take it for granted that things were arranged to meet his wishes. Lifting a full glass of raki, he downed it in one quick swallow, and sat back satisfied. He was having a good time. Ambrose saw that his left hand, which had been resting on Lindsay's, had now found its way to her leg, which he was stroking to her evident pleasure. She was sipping her champagne, her eyes half-closed. One would say that she was purring.

At the far end of the hall the band had stopped, and now a few plangent chords on the bazuki were heard. The Greeks! "Oh, this is marvelous," Basruk exclaimed. "If they're going to dance, Uncle will want to see it. I expect he'll join in. I'll go over and see."

"Isn't there a difference between Greek and Turkish dancing?" Alyss asked.

"Same thing basically. After all, we taught the Greeks when we ran the place."

"How long will you be in Boston?" Ambrose asked the old gentleman as Basruk went off.

"I'm leaving tomorrow morning on an early plane. I mean this morning, of course. I came in tonight from Turkey and broke my journey to see Zilto. I have a meeting in Denver with my nephew at noon. What is the time differential of Colorado from here?"

"Two hours," Alyss said. "But you'll still have to leave here very early to get there by noon, their time. Won't you be tired after all your traveling?"

"At my age one needs very little sleep," he said peacefully in his gentle whisper. He had stopped for the moment his casual caressing of Lindsay, and, turning to Alyss, seemed rather to like what he saw. "In Turkey I can dance all night, especially in the summer. Here the climate is not so good. We came through a very bad storm in the plane, and it was raining heavily when we landed. I need something to warm my old bones. Of course, this is a great help." His glass had been re-filled, and he tossed the drink down happily.

Basruk was back. "Yes, they're going to dance, and they've made room at their table for my uncle. Will you come?"

The Pasha rose. "You will see how we dance," he said to Lindsay. "It appeals to us more than Zen Bhuddism."

The younger Basruk looked at Ambrose and Alyss to see if they would go over too. Alyss had been looking at her watch and now said: "I'd love to watch, but I think it's time for us to go."

The old gentleman, despite his approval of Alyss, seemed pleased nevertheless to see her and Ambrose asserting themselves as a pair who wanted to go off on their own — obviously for the best of reasons. There was a distinct twinkle in his eye as he said goodnight to Alyss, raising her hand to kiss it gently in leave-taking. There but for the grace of a redhead of more tender years, Ambrose thought. . . .

"Let me settle them at the table, and I'll come back for a moment," Basruk said. "I want to ask Ambrose something."

The three of them went off towards the distant rostrum, with the waiter under instruction to transport the raki and glasses. Before this, he produced a bill for the champagne, which Ambrose dealt with. Alyss, he saw, had taken on a tense look again as she picked up her bag and got ready to leave. "Twelve-twenty," she said. "We've got to pick Tim up in ten minutes."

"Isn't he a marvelous old man?" Ambrose said. "I think I'm going to move to Turkey if we survive tonight."

"He *is* marvelous," she agreed, But her mind was clearly elsewhere, and she was fidgety. "I'll go and get my coat. You can meet me at the door."

As Ambrose waited for Basruk, he tested his ankle. It seemed all right now, as long as he didn't put any weight on it. No problem.

Basruk had hurried back. "I wanted to ask you if you'd heard from Olaf," he said. "He hasn't phoned the Consulate. Do you know when he's due here?"

"No idea," Ambrose said. "Presumably when he's cleaned out his Colorado friends. What a shame your uncle couldn't stay here longer. I would think Olaf would have loved to meet him. He's really fabulous. Behaves like the Godfather."

Basruk laughed. "Yes, he does. And that's how we treat him. But he's flying out on an early plane this morning to my cousin in Chicago."

"Oh, he's going to Chicago?" Ambrose asked innocently.

"He always goes there," Basruk said. "There's a whole Turkish community there. They make a great fuss of him. A real live Pasha. A personal friend of Attaturk. Not many of them left."

Ambrose waved, and joined Alyss at the door.

She had equipped herself with a rather heavy stormproof coat, though the rain was now very light. In the coat she seemed armed, ready for battle ahead. Ambrose, clutching his more attenuated raincoat, was still full of the Basruk encounter; but as they came out into the night, his pulse began to quicken too.

Tim, waiting round the corner in a rather scruffy-looking car, helped them in quickly and took off without delay. For a while, he drove very quickly and with many sudden turns. But finally, coming into a quiet street, he stopped the car and went over the plans.

In appearance he was the perfect all-American type: more correctly, the nice young man one sees in the *advertisements* of the all-American type — tall, fair, hair neatly trimmed, bland features in a friendly open face. Harvard or Harvard Business School one would say, to continue the typing — the ideal CIA recruit. But no real CIA man would smile so beguilingly.

"Equipment," he said cheerfully, handing his aunt a pair of heavy walking-shoes. "Your sensible shoes. You're always so sensible. And here are your gloves." She bent down to change her shoes, and he turned to Ambrose, "Here are some gloves for you. I forgot to get my aunt to warn you. No finger-prints. All very serious. That's my own little bag of tricks — on the seat beside you."

It was clearly just a lark for him. The discovery of a stolen Donatello or some other missing masterpiece was not for him the essence of the adventure. What mattered was the matching of wits, CIA style, against crooks prepared to do the same to you if you let them. Ambrose, trying to lift the bag by its handle, found it enormously heavy for its size. "What on earth have you got here?" he asked. "The Stone of Scone?"

"The weight? That's what lets us in. It's the very latest thing — post-Watergate. It's a little machine with a very heavy core: I expect they've refined it by now — lightened it. I got hold of it just before I left. When I've attached the leads to the right cables and arranged things, it diverts the juice before any kind of alarm can be triggered. We call it the Decoy. It's a pun. The man who invented it was a pal of mine called Donald Coy — D. Coy. Get it? It's a beaut."

"Well, that's a relief," Ambrose said. "I was afraid you were going to do a little dynamiting, in which case I would probably set it off before we got there, as I am inclined to be clumsy."

"Nothing to worry about," Tim said cheerfully. "Here's the timetable. I'm planning to get there at one-fifteen. I've got a little alley prepared where we'll leave the car. It's near a special entrance to the fence that I've fixed up. When we're inside the fence, it's five minutes to the house, and it will take me about ten or twelve minutes to get the Decoy set up and fool around with the locks. I timed myself three nights ago. When we're inside the house, we'll have fifteen minutes there. We've got to tidy things up and get back to our gap not later than two-fifteen. We stay in the car for ten or fifteen minutes because they have a patrol that goes round between two-fifteen and two thirty. Then we get going on our way home."

It sounded as if nothing could be easier. The rain had stopped, but it was a dark night, with heavy clouds and no visible moon. In a few minutes they were out of the built-up area and floating swiftly along empty roads, with tall trees everywhere to add to the eerie feeling that seemed to have been established.

From the point at which Tim had stopped, they were driving for about half an hour before anything developed. No one spoke as the car moved swiftly on. Ambrose, sitting in the back seat, looked behind him once or twice, but it was clear that no one was following them. Then Tim muttered: "Getting close," and switched off his lights.

He drove slowly and cautiously now. The sudden darkness had seemed at first impenetrable. Gradually a faint luminosity emerged above the black shapes around them. Tim seemed very sure of where he was. Suddenly he stopped and reversed the car into a little opening off the road. He backed down it for a few yards with great care, stopped, switched off the engine. Ambrose saw him look at the luminous dial of his watch. "On time," he said quietly. "Exact."

He wound down his window and listened for a full minute. There was no sound, and he seemed satisfied. Winding up the window, he gave the last instructions, still speaking quietly.

"I'll go first," he said, "then Aunt Alyss, then Ambrose. Stay very close to the fence when we get there. Your eyes will get used to the dark very quickly. When we're inside the grounds there's a good deal of cover from the trees. There's just one little danger-point that you must watch out for. Inside the fence there's a sort of irrigation ditch — almost like a moat: but it's no problem. Just look out for it. Climb down and out of it: but we'll have to go carefully."

Getting out of the car provided the first surprise, at least for Ambrose. The alley into which they had backed, being merely of grass, was now, after the storm, a quagmire of mud. Ambrose found it an enormous effort to lift his feet through it, even for the few yards they had to go. But in a moment he was used to it.

Tim was carrying his bag of tricks with no apparent effort. Ambrose had put on the gloves — large gauntlets which were somehow comforting. Silently they moved down the alley and then into the road. It was quite easy to see now. A tall fence was ahead, stretching a long way down the road. Keeping close to it, they followed Tim for a few yards until he suddenly stopped.

The fence was a tightly formed hedge — impenetrable, it seemed. Tim lifted some branches away and disclosed a narrow break. They scrambled through, and Tim carefully pulled the branches back and closed the break from the inside. They were there. The ground was soil again, swamped and squelchy from the rain, with one's feet sinking in deeply at every move.

Tim indicated that they should wait while he listened again. And now, with ears tuned to the silence, there were sounds. One heard the trees whispering and shaking, with an occasional spatter of rain from their branches. In the distance there were car sounds — a horn, even a faint screech of brakes. With eyes used to the dark, detail began to emerge. Ambrose saw the ditch ahead, and beyond it, a few hundred yards away, a great dark fortress of a house.

"I'll go first," Tim whispered. "Then Aunt Alyss, I'll give you a lift up. Stay absolutely still, and wait till I give you the sign."

Silently he moved forward, climbed down into the ditch and was up on the other side. He raised his hand and Alyss followed, scrambling up with no difficulty. Another sign from Tim and now Ambrose moved ahead, lifting his feet carefully through the deep mud.

He was just near the bottom of the ditch when his ankle gave way. He had forgotten it, but in the mud his weight had done the trick. With a cry of pain, he tumbled forward and lay prone in a pool of water, unable to move.

In a second, Tim was down beside him. "What the hell's happened?" he whispered.

"My ankle," Ambrose whispered back. "Give me a hand. I'll be all right."

Tim helped him to his feet and gave him a push from behind. Ambrose took one step and at the second gave another cry and fell back writhing in agony. Lying there, in water and mud, he could feel a searing pain in his ankle. "It's no good," he whispered. "It must be broken."

"For Christ sake," Tim muttered. Alyss had now clambered

down to join them. The mud seemed to be enveloping all three of them.

"Let's get him back to the car and we'll go in," Alyss whispered. "Will we have time?"

"Let's see how long it takes. Come on, give me a hand."
He put his bag down and began, with Alyss, to help Ambrose to get to the fence. By now, they could hardly move through the thickening mud. Ambrose, exerting every ounce of energy, was still a dead weight. Tim, pushing him on, suddenly stopped: "Listen."

They waited, breathing deeply, and the silence came back. "Thought I heard something," he whispered. "Let's go."

They were at the fence now. He opened the gap and pulled back the concealing branches. In horrible pain, Ambrose clambered through and they were on the road again, where he managed to limp along without complaint. Back in the alley they squelched through the mud to where the car was standing. Tim opened the door, and bundled Ambrose into the back. Then he looked at his watch.

"We've lost twelve minutes," he said to Alyss. "But it may be O.K. if we move fast. I left myself a little leeway. I'm game if you are."

Ambrose lay on the back seat, groaning internally — more at his clumsiness than his pain. Without a word to him, Alyss and Tim set off. At the end of the alley, still sheltered by the trees, they stopped. Coming down the road towards them was a glow of light, growing in a moment to a massive dazzle of headlamps. As the lights began to glare, they heard an increasing roar of engines, with the machine-gun sound of motor-cycles drowning everything.

A procession swept by. Two motor-cycles in the lead, followed by three huge motor-cars and two motor-cycles bringing up the rear — a white dazzle of light — a tornado of sound.

The procession swept up to the main gates further down the road. In a moment the gates must have opened, for the procession swept into the grounds — the headlamps lighting up the trees with an air of fantasy, the sound of engines growing fainter.

Suddenly the noise stopped and headlamps were switched off. And now they could see, over the top of the fence, a slowly growing halo in the sky as lights in the house were switched on,

137

one after another, with an utterly comforting cheerfulness. Normality had returned. John P. Harrigan was back in his home.

Alyss and Tim had watched it all, hidden in the trees at the end of the alley. Now they hurried back to the car, and got in beside the forlorn Ambrose. They looked at each other, their faces and clothes covered in mud, and for a second there was nothing to say. They began to laugh, and having started found themselves weeping with a hysterical kind of relief.

The need to whisper seemed over. Tim and Alyss were shrieking with uncontrollable laughter. Ambrose, sitting up, was still a picture of woebegone misery.

"Oh, Ambrose!" Alyss cried, leaning over to the back seat and throwing an arm around him, mud and all. "You darling! You saved us! Another five minutes. . . . I'm coming in beside you."

She scrambled in and now embraced him properly, with the tenderest of kisses. She was still weeping with laughter, the tears mingling with the mud. "You're a genius," she said. "I knew it from the beginning."

"What have I done?" Ambrose said mournfully. But her kiss on his lips was soft and loving. Gently, he returned it.

"How do you think it happened?" Tim, sober now, sat in the driver's seat scratching his head. "I saw him take off from the airport at eight o'clock with all his gang in their own plane. Why should they have come back? If it was engine trouble, he could have got another plane."

"Perhaps he was taken ill," Alyss suggested. "He's very old. He might have had a heart attack or a stroke." She had sat back now and was tidying herself abstractedly but in a feminine way, wiping the mud off her face, straightening her hair. To Ambrose beside her, it seemed as if, with all the strain gone, she had turned into a woman. Her voice had become gentler. He could still feel the sweetness of her lips on his.

"I have an idea," he said. "Maybe something quite different. He had to come back to direct operations." He realized, now, that the thought had been in his head vaguely since his talk with Rafferty earlier. Why hadn't he worked out what it might mean? Surely the Godfather movie should have suggested it. Jazz and Basruk had pushed it down. Perhaps the champagne had contributed.

"I was told tonight, by someone who knows about these things, that the police were expecting a big blow-up between

Harrigan's lads and someone else's who's been trying to take over. Suppose he got a message in the plane that they had launched it, with a killing or two. It would be a perfect time for them. They knew as well as we did that he'd be away in Indiana."

Tim was ready to buy this immediately. "Of course. He might have been there, ready to land. All he had to do was turn round and fly back. My God: if this is what has happened, there'll be blood in the old town tonight."

Alyss took Ambrose's hand in hers and squeezed it. "We would have been caught," she murmured. "I *said* you were a genius." What had happened to her? She seemed to have fallen in love with the man.

Tim was now pulling himself together on mechanics. "I've got to get my bag back and close the opening in the wall," he said. "Better not let them find it in the morning."

"Do be careful, Tim," Alyss said. "We've had one escape. Do you think it's safe to go back?"

"Got to." He opened the car door and went off quietly.

"We'll have to invent a new plan," Alyss said to Ambrose while they waited. "I'm not going to give up. I know you'll think of something. For some reason or other. I have total faith in you. My goodness!"

"What is it?"

"Your ankle! I completely forgot. How does it feel?"

Ambrose waggled it carefully. "It seems to have gone stiff. Probably swollen."

"I'll strap it up when we get back. You'll have to go to a doctor in the morning. I know a good orthopedist."

"Can't go to a doctor," Ambrose said. "I'm flying to Toronto first thing. I've got to give a lecture there tonight."

"Can't you cancel it?"

"Cancel the Durham Lecture? Cream of Toronto society?"

"But you'll be dead."

"Strange thing," Ambrose said, "I feel surprisingly alive. I think it's the Pasha. He's infected me. Can you imagine *him* being tired at this point? Probably just working up for a gay time with Lindsay?"

And then off to Colorado, he thought. Why had Basruk tried to fudge it with talk of Chicago? Olaf was in Colorado. What was going on in Basruk's head? He'd said something earlier about Olaf and Colorado. What was it?

The car door opened quietly. Tim was back, bag in hand. "All absolutely quiet," he said. "I think we'd better make a dash for it while we can. Hope to God we aren't stuck in the mud."

He started the engine but, as he had feared, they heard the back wheels spinning without being able to grip. Switching off the engine, he got out and picked up some of the branches blown off in the storm. With great care he arranged them against the rear wheels and got back to try again. With a bump they were off. Swiftly he turned the car into the road, without putting on the lights. And now he put on speed. There was nothing in sight. In a few minutes he switched on the lights and drove on happily. They were safe.

Despite his earlier liveliness, Ambrose now felt a great drowsiness coming over him. The quiet purr of the engine was part of it. Without quite realizing how it happened, he found Alyss's arm around him. It was comforting lying against her. He slept.

The engine had stopped. Opening his eyes, he saw that they were outside Alyss's apartment house. "What time is it?" he said.

"Two-forty," Tim said. "We'll let Alyss off and I'll drive you back to Cambridge."

"No," Alyss said. "I'm going to strap up Ambrose's ankle. You can leave us here and I'll drive him back myself."

"Fine," Tim said. "I've got the last item to finish. Change back my number-plates. What a night!"

He was quite cheerful about it. A very minor CIA operation, but enjoyable within limits. He joined Alyss in helping Ambrose out of the car, and with a wave of his hand took off.

Walking carefully, Ambrose was able to limp into the house, and in a few minutes they were in her apartment. They looked at each other, muddy and bedraggled, and laughed. Spontaneously, they put their arms round each other and kissed. "Come on," Alyss said. "Your ankle. Do you know what you'd better do. Have a hot bath first."

He undressed, and she spread out his clothes to dry. She had taken off her own muddy clothes and put on a heavy black silk kimono.

The hot steam — the whisky — it was bliss. Lying on her bed with a large towel around him, he felt her soothing hands strapping up his ankle.

"Does that feel right?" she asked.

"I feel wonderful." He stretched up his arms. She came and lay down beside him.

VIII

"ORDER is Heav'n's first law," said Alexander Pope — with Toronto in mind, Ambrose felt. The Toronto pace was gruelling — speeches, meals, galleries, sight-seeing: but it had a steadiness of purpose — a limitation of range, a beginning and an end — that seemed to restore his spirit after the perplexities of Boston.

His ankle held firm. God bless Alyss. Was it just the bandage she had put on so efficiently? There was more to it than that, as the Pasha understood so well. Energy restores itself in mysterious ways.

Perhaps it was just the change. Certainly he felt refreshed. Even the non-stop talking was not really exhausting. No sufferer from logorrhoea ever seems to mind it. It calls for and provides its own resources: one talks and acts with double intensity. Falstaff, the greatest prattler of all, established the point: *"I grant you I was down and out of breath, and so was he: but we rose both at an instant, and fought a long hour by Shrewsbury clock. . . ."*

For Shrewsbury, read Toronto. It was not even such a long hour. The time flitted by with little chance to worry about the practical problems in far-off Massachusetts. He might have put them out of his mind completely had it not been for the *Boston Mail* he had read on the plane to Toronto, with its gruesome confirmation of why John P. Harrigan had returned home so unexpectedly.

GANGLAND KILLINGS had been the tenor of the headlines. The story had started with the news Rafferty had given him — of a body fished out of the Bay on Friday afternoon. According to Rafferty, this execution — of a Harrigan man found guilty of fraternization — had been intended as an awful warning to the opposition. If so, it had failed. At ten o'clock that night, with Harrigan in the air over Indiana, McLuskey had struck in classical style. The club in downtown Boston used by Harrigan's top lieutenants had been surrounded and shot up, with four Harrigan men left wallowing in blood on its floors.

In the intervals of Toronto speechifying, Ambrose came back to it. What had been the follow-up, he wondered. One could try to reconstruct it *à la Godfather:* Harrigan had returned, held emergency parleys, given orders, and then, perhaps, taken off again for Notre Dame. He could just about have made it in time: and, after all, the degree meant a lot to him.

But if it was *The Godfather,* one blood-letting had to lead to another. In the early morning plane back to Boston, Ambrose scanned the *Toronto Globe,* but found nothing. Ah, well. Perhaps Harrigan was like that other Irishman, Field-Marshal Montgomery, gathering his forces together slowly and patiently before he gave the command to strike, with total effect, at El Alamein.

"*I gave commands: then all smiles stopped together.*" The line from Browning's poem came into his head by association. That was a Renaissance prince in operation, and Harrigan had this quality. "*My Last Duchess.*" One learnt it by heart at school because it was so dramatic — the Duke of Ferrara calmly bumping off his wife. One was supposed to admire this happy freedom to indulge in the arts and crime in one and the same spirit. Even Alyss had lingered on the idea.

How much grimmer it was in reality. His thought floated off to another man who had killed his wife. One tried to put Fletcher out of mind, but it never really worked. Nothing remotely princely here: just a sense of evil. The world would be cleaner without him.

Gloria. How could one forget what had happened? That lovely, silly girl. One owed her something, just because she had been so trusting. Browning had said it all:

> "... She had
> A heart ... how shall I say? ... to soon made glad,
> Too easily impressed: she liked whate'er
> She looked on, and her looks went everywhere. ..."

It was Gloria exactly: and that man. . . .

Hepworth had told him to hang on — to see where the trail

led, but to take care. Ambrose picked up his briefcase with a new kind of purpose in him. He was still aware of the feeling as the plane circled over Boston airport and came in to land.

Only two lectures still to come — Tuesday and Thursday — and the series would be over. For a time, on the plane, he had put his mind to them. He knew that once he had landed, things waiting in Boston would engulf him.

Some of them spelled horror: but life was always making up for its horrors, and usually without forewarning. He had telephoned Alyss several times from Toronto. They had not discussed anything about the next move on Harrigan. That was not for the telephone. She just seemed to think that Ambrose would come up with something. Really, she was a bad as Hepworth.

Poor Hepworth, with his long, long trail awinding. He must have known by then about Willis. The full story, with its nasty deceit, must be clear now. Was this why he had warned him to take care? Certainly there was violence in Fletcher's orbit. Whose would be the next body to be fished out of the Bay?

Driving from the airport, his mind turned to the more cheerful subject of Basruk. There would probably be a message at the hotel in vehement Turkish, except that one could never really count on Basruk. For all one knew, he might have flown off with the Pasha to Colorado. He had been keen enough to find out where Sir Olaf was, and what he was up to. But surely Olaf would be back in Boston by now, broke or triumphant. How seriously did one have to take him? What he was doing *must* be important, but it seemed to come out so oddly, as if one were hearing it in the wrong key, or the wrong language. . . .

At the hotel, the clerk, handing him his room-key, pulled out of the niche only one message, and not from Basruk. "*Miss Summers called. She will call again.*" He felt himself smiling.

The fact was that it was nice to be back in friendly old Boston, gangsters or no gangsters. At the newsstand, he picked up a copy of the *Mail* to see where the battle stood. The Godfather didn't seem to have got down to things yet. Plenty of black headlines on the Friday night massacre, but nothing in return. When would it all happen? Back in his room, he called Rafferty.

For once Rafferty was too busy to talk freely. "Just what you saw in the paper," he said. "We're in the middle of a meeting. I'll call you back later."

"Just one thing, Bill," Ambrose said. "Did Harrigan get his honorary degree at Notre Dame on Saturday?"

"Sure," Rafferty said. "It was on TV. Just before the football game."

The moment he had put the phone down, it rang. Alyss.

"I called earlier. Dying to see you. Such a lot to talk about."

"Are you phoning from your apartment? I seem to recall that you can't talk freely from there."

She laughed. "Free as a bird. It's all changed since Friday night."

"How?"

"I looked out of the window first thing on Saturday morning as usual, and my friend wasn't there. I went for a walk. He's deserted me. I guessed why, as soon as I'd read about the shootings."

"You mean all hands on deck *chez* Harrigan? No time to waste on art historians?"

"That's how I saw it. So I got Tim in and he de-bugged the phone and the sitting-room. I'm free again."

"They're tired of *you*, but are you tired of *them?*"

"Can you see me giving up? Just means a new approach. That's where *you* come in."

"Me? I'm still wallowing in mud."

"How's your ankle?"

"Oh, that's fine."

"Well, then, there's no problem. It's been a glorious weekend. Everything's dried out. This time, the ground will be firm under foot. You're not going to desert me now, are you?"

"Desert you? Never. I'm hooked. But not *firm* ground: *fresh* ground. New approach, as you say. I have a very faint glimmering. . . ."

"I knew it."

"Wait a minute. I said a glimmering, without knowing anything more. A very faint idea, but I don't know how. Give me time. It's a long long trail."

"As long as you like. And Ambrose. . . ."

She said something nice to him. He was feeling happy as he put down the phone. Somehow or other he was going to do it for her. The more difficult, the more he would enjoy it. One was still a sort of war-horse, saying Ha-Ha to the trumpets, smelling the battle afar off, the thunder of the captains, and the shouting. He rang the Consulate-General and asked for Mr. Basruk.

144

* * *

Mr. Basruk had gone back to England. It was the Consul-General's secretary who told him. Mr. Basruk had left a message with the Duty Officer on Saturday morning to say that he was going. The Duty Officer had asked if he wanted them to make the travel arrangements. He had said that he had his ticket and would manage it all himself. That was the last they had heard of him.

Had he, in fact, gone back to England? What was it about Basruk that made one wonder? If one was suspicious, it was because he wanted it that way. To be an open book, with everything spelled out, was a bore. To tease one's friends with conflicting moods — serious and comic — was a delight. And he *was* a delight — *Rondo alla Turca*. Why had Mozart called it this? Because in those days "*alla Turca*" meant switching back and forth all the time between major and minor, and that's what the piece did. The Turks hadn't changed.

"Oh, Mr. Usher," the girl was saying, "Sir Olaf McConnochie got into Boston late last night and left a message for you here this morning. He's going to be staying in the Consul-General's house for a few days. Unfortunately, the Consul-General is away at the moment in Washington for the Consular meetings, but Sir Olaf will be in his house. The message is: are you free to take lunch with him today?"

"Yes, delighted. Did he say where?"

"The Devon Club, at one. Do you know where it is? Very near the Ritz, facing the Gardens."

"The Devon Club? What kind of a club is it?"

She giggled. "Oh, it's very nice. Very special."

Well, of course, it had to be. Ordinary people could lunch at the Ritz. Not Olaf.

"Ambrose! I'm sure you don't mind if I address you in this familiar way. Two weeks in the U.S.A. and no one has a surname any more."

"How long will you be here?" Ambrose asked him.

"Just a few days. Pity, because it's a perfect set-up. All the comforts of the Consul-General's house without the Consul-General. And his Rolls too. My Treasury hackles rose when I heard of it, but I gather it's a very old one. I expect that when it gives up we'll make the Foreign Office replace it with an Austin Seven, but in the meantime what could be nicer? I always enjoy Boston anyhow, particularly this little club. Don't you like it?"

It was a club that might have been designed specially with Sir Olaf McConnochie in mind. If his clothes had seemed dandyish — *épate bourgeois* — in the Treasury scene, here they seemed natural to the man himself and in complete harmony with the warm elegance that the club spoke of. His suit evoked a soft heather feeling, responding happily to the living color of his sandy hair and bright blue eyes. The glow in his shoes was not fresh but old: years of patient polishing had brought out the fire in the ancient leather. The cambric handkerchief at his wrist was in perfect tune with the 18th century American furniture of the small hall in which they stood.

The Devon was indeed special, as if New England sobriety had been brushed over with French intimacy. Olaf, greeting him, had laughed as Ambrose took it all in with evident delight. "I think you'll like the food, too," he said. "It was always good but they've just achieved a *coup*. They've persuaded the chef from the Connaught to move here. The Connaught didn't mind too much because they'd heard that Labouchère of the *Aiglon* wanted to live in London for a while. So everyone's happy."

"Except the *Aiglon* clientèle."

"Let's not worry too much about *them*. I don't really know why we worry about the whole thing. If you knew what I've been eating happily in Colorado during the last few days. . . ."

They sat down, in what seemed like a little drawing-room, for a glass of *Chambery*.

"I hear your lectures are creating a great question-mark among the *cognoscenti*," Olaf said. "Almost a *scandale*."

"*Scandale?*"

"I had a drink with Orville Thoroughgood last night. Very deep, you know, our friend Orville. He tells me that the lectures are, of course, a sell-out — standing room only and all that. To the *hoi polloi*, it's the usual Ambrose fireworks — star-turn, just what they expect. But to the discerning, like Orville. . . . When did you give the last series here?"

"Six years ago."

"Ah, that may be it. Long enough for a change. Or maybe it's just age. Orville sees something very new. He says your performance used to be very smooth, very polished, very untroubled, but now there's a note of personal involvement, more daring, more penetrating. . . ."

"I suppose I ought to be flattered. It seems to me that I'm dealing with the same subjects."

"But don't the same subjects look different as one goes on? I know they do to me. One isn't content to take the received view. One pushes the thing further. One *wants* to be troubled by it. That's what I mean by *scandale*. A bigger question-mark."

"I suppose it comes through to someone like Orville."

"You say you're dealing with the same theme. Think how often the Renaissance painters and sculptors went back to the same subject but handled it with a shattering new depth. Take an extreme case: the two *Pietàs* by Michaelangelo. The early one at St. Peter's is smooth, 'perfect,' idealistic. But the *Rondini* — heavy, anguished, desperate."

"I'm not Michaelangelo."

"Well, for that matter I'm not Vasari. I'm not really as completely sold on Michaelangelo as *he* was. To me, he's so great that he's sometimes *too* great, too heavy, too solid, too expert. It's the High Renaissance, I suppose. In the earlier period, the artists were more on our scale, closer to us humanly. Take a sculptor like Donatello. . . ."

"Ah, yes, Donatello."

"One isn't in awe of him. When *he's* troubled, it's the way we are too. . . ." A waiter had come up and Olaf rose to lead the way into lunch. "How on earth did we get on to this?" he asked Ambrose plaintively. "This isn't what we came here to talk about. Far too important. What *we've* got to deal with are these totally ephemeral questions that we talked about that day at the Treasury. Poor old Chancellor. He's got to make it sound as if he knows the answers. That's the hardest part. It's so much easier for *us*. We don't know the answers either, but we don't have to make speeches about it."

"Things are getting worse?"

Olaf looked a little self-satisfied as he took his seat. "Not all of them. Got a few things through at the IMF, and subsequently. But I suppose he'll have to have an autumn Budget. Basruk left a message for me about it. I thought I would see him here, but he says he had to go back without delay."

For a few minutes they busied themselves with ordering their food. For all his alleged indifference, Olaf took great care in choosing the wine. With the waiters dispatched, they settled themselves for the real talk.

"Above and beyond anything else," Ambrose said, "I want to know one thing first."

"Backgammon?"

"Of course. Did they clean you out, or are you returning with your pockets lined with gold?"

Olaf looked at him quizzically. "Is that meant as a metaphor?"

"A rather hackneyed one, isn't it?"

Olaf was silent for a moment, and then said slowly: "They say you have second sight. I'm beginning to believe it. That's more or less what the Foreign Office said when they suggested we put you in the picture on the TCC business. You're supposed to stumble on things just by being around. I think I'm going to tell you the whole story." He smiled. "I *need* to tell someone. Too good to keep to myself. It will appeal to you. And you *have* got there on your own. Well, half there."

"You mean gold?"

"Yes, gold. I suppose I mustn't put it beyond you to have been reading the City pages in the last ten days even if you've been concentrating like a good boy on philosophy. So subconsciously you really knew of what you spoke. Gold has been bursting out all over."

"And especially in Colorado?"

"As you say. Ah, here's the wine." He had chosen a simple *Montrachet 1970* to go with the first course, a dozen clams. It was tasted, approved, and poured. Olaf raised his glass. "Let's be formal for once. Something marvelous happened out there. I need to tell someone, and you are it. To Colorado!"

"To you," Ambrose said, "I think that's what it really comes to." He sipped the wine anf felt the cold dry taste melt into fire.

"I can cut part of the story," Olaf said. The waiter had left them now with their clams. "You aren't a backgammon player, so you'll have to take that part without question. It was the most amazing game of my life. We played virtually non-stop for three days. At first I lost, and then I won. I suppose I played very well: but that's not where the excitement came from. It was the stake. We agreed on a stake, to depend on the net position at the end. Something more than money."

He took a clam and a sip of wine. Ambrose was beginning to feel light-headed, not so much with the wine as with the mood that had grown around them. It was "*The Queen of Spades,*" with Herman about to turn the fateful card.

"In the past," Olaf said, "we've always played for money quite normally, except that our stakes are very high, because otherwise it's boring. My friend out there — my opponent — is very rich: and, for that matter, so am I. We're never going to bankrupt each other, but it's still exciting. However, this time we had a better idea. There was a coincidence, so unusual that we agreed to exploit it.

"You may be able to guess one part of it. I expect you read in the papers a week ago about the sudden spurt in the shares of Tri-State Mining. The papers went to town on it, because gold always fascinates them. It was just before the IMF meeting, and the speculators had got the idea that the ultimate effect of what was going on would be a considerable rise in the price of gold. Tri-State own a vast area of old gold mines that had become derelict because the cost of production was prohibitive at the old gold price. But now it looked extremely feasible, and the shares shot up. Everyone wanted to get in on the act." Olaf broke off to laugh. "I tell you who was madly keen in a discreet kind of way. Our old friend Basruk. You know, his family in Turkey have a lot of mining interests. I think he assumed they would try to get a foot into Tri-State."

So the Pasha flies out to Colorado, and young Basruk, with Turkish caution, feels that it's none of Ambrose's business. Ambrose took another clam and a sip of wine. It was nice when things became clear.

Olaf was talking at a comfortable pace, without neglecting the food and drink that was before him.

"I think I had the idea in my head even then," he said, "of what special stake we might play for. I knew that my gambling friend in Colorado owned a large area of old gold mines privately. They had been in his family for two generations. I realized that he would be sitting pretty. And then I wondered. You see, something similar — not gold, but similar in other ways — had happened on the other side of the Atlantic. To me."

The waiter had come up to take away the clams and bring the *Boeuf St. Etienne* which they had both chosen. There was a *Mouton Rothschild '49* to go with it. Bliss rose to a new dimension. Olaf raised his glass again, in mock formality, as he resumed.

"My mother's ancestors left me a large area of land in Northern Norway, very wild, very beautiful, quite valueless as property because some old copper mines they had once exploited had become useless. But now, the Colorado story had happened there too. The price of copper had shot up and some new methods of mining had been developed. I had been wondering what to do — work the mines or sell them? The problem was tax. It was very hard to know what the Norwegian Government — and for that matter, the U.K. Government — would decide to do. And then I had my brainwave."

"The backgammon stake!" Ambrose burst out. What a man! All one needed now was Pushkin to write it up.

"Quite an interesting idea, don't you think?" Olaf said nonchalantly. For a moment he allowed the dandy to surface, as a counterfoil to Ambrose's excitement. But in a moment the memory of the game seemed to come back and infect him, too.

"I shall never forget it," he said. "Once I'd had the idea, it took over as if it had been planned for years. Just gripped us both. Over dinner, when I arrived, we exchanged information. There was no question of matching the properties in money terms. Neither of us could possibly put a price on what might happen. The whole thing was a gamble. And we were in a unique position to agree on it. We both owned the properties outright. Whoever won or lost — it would be marvelous, but it wouldn't make us or cripple us. We've quite enough without it. But what a stake!"

"And you won!"

"We decided to play for exactly forty-five hours by the clock. At the end of it, he rang up his lawyer who came over from Denver and drafted a letter which simply made me the owner. I have it in my pocket."

"So now England has gold in Colorado as well as oil in the North Sea."

"Not to mention copper in Norway." Olaf was smiling, but in an odd way, as if Ambrose was being disappointingly simple-minded about it. "Let's say that that's the first stage," he murmured, taking a sip of the wine contentedly. "Pity you don't play backgammon. The whole art is to get into a good position for what you may have in mind later. That's really what's involved here too. Would you like desert, or cheese? No? Well, let's go into the other room and have coffee there. I'll tell you about it."

Moving into the exquisite little salon for coffee broke the spell for the moment. "Mustn't spend all our time on fun and games," Olaf said, as they sat down. "I'm sure you want to know what's happening at home on the takeover bid. Basruk told me he was going to put you in the picture when he came up here. We wondered if, in your ineffable way, you'd discovered anything relevant about George Fletcher. You know he flew over to London when TCC put in the bid."

"What I discovered about George Fletcher is not ineffable. It's *effable:* and that's a double pun. This F-man is a horror, humanly and morally, in ways I won't go into just now. Just by chance, I was given the low-down on him while I've been here. It overlaps with his role in TCC, but dwarfs it."

"And what about TCC?"

"You probably know much more than I do, but I'll tell you how it looks to me. The person one really needs to understand on all this is John P. Harrigan. He keeps entirely in the background: the Consul-General's never even met him. But from what I hear, his financial empire is far more extensive than TCC and the other publicly known things. It all started, of course, with his gangster activities. That's where the endless flow of cash comes from."

"I heard that he's run into trouble on that front," Olaf said. "That massacre of his henchmen on Friday night. Do the rivals look like taking over, from what you have heard?"

"At this stage, I would say no. But I may know more about it later. I've a good source who lets me know things about half-an-hour before they appear in the newspapers."

"They know a lot about this at home," Olaf said. "That's one reason why they've been very reluctant to sanction the TCC bid."

"I gathered from Basruk that the argument at home is wider than just TCC. Isn't it also a question of which countries they'll let in to provide the major finance for the Bulgarian contract?"

Olaf smiled. "And Master Basruk argues strongly for a Near-Eastern consortium. Very clannish fellow is Basruk. As a matter of fact, he's perfectly right about this. It's a correct judgment, even though it happens to fit in with family feeling. He would never argue for it otherwise, of course."

"And what's the present position on the TCC bid?"

"That's really what I want to talk to you about. They're inclined to be a bit hasty at home. They don't like Fletcher any more than you do. But I'd like to see around it a little before we decide. One might make it part of some bigger arrangement. It's backgammon again. One has several approaches on the board. One moves in stages. One doesn't get rigid in one position too hurriedly."

Backgammon. Stages. Ambrose had a sudden intuition. "Don't tell me that the Colorado story is coming into the picture."

"It might. It might. It's all one big circle really. One moves round it. Sometimes things fall into place this way. Haven't you ever found that?"

"I think I may say I have," Ambrose murmured.

"I don't mean that things are set in a pre-determined way," Olaf said. "But if one's in the right place, one thing can lead to another. That's why I'm staying on here for a few days. I want to have a long private talk with John P. Harrigan. I expect you can arrange it. I hear he has a fine art collection. Well, I have some things too, as you know. Perhaps we can establish a bond this way. Do you think I could call on him?"

What was one to do with a man like Olaf? *Second* sight? He had *tenth* sight. He was ten jumps ahead. But what was one to do about the intervening stages?

It was business that Olaf wanted to talk about with Harrigan. He had some deal to propose — some private arrangement linked with Colorado. But art was also in the circle. Could Alyss be brought in? Wild ideas began to burgeon.

"I seem to have flummoxed you," Olaf said mildly, as Ambrose sat silent. "Have I said the wrong thing?"

"Oh no: you've said the right thing. Absolutely right. It's just that I haven't yet learned how to play backgammon. I think that if I had, I'd know just what to do at this point. Isn't it part of the game that the opponents can take turns in challenging each other to doubling the stakes?"

"Between them they can multiply *ad infinitum* if they want to."

"Well, that's just the position I've reached. I'm going to double, though I'm a bit shaky about it."

"You mean you know something about Harrigan that might enlarge the stake, and you're not sure how to make me a party to it. Take your time. You have to decide before you throw the dice."

"Let me think." Ambrose sat silent again, and then relaxed. "I expect you see the difficulty. It's not really my secret, but I'm sure it belongs here. I've got to learn how to gamble, so I'll start right here. Let me do a deal with you, Colorado style. You probably shouldn't tell me anything about the deal you want to work out with Harrigan — sworn to secrecy: and I'm party to a secret on the other side. But I'll gamble on it if you will."

"It's a deal. I'm beginning to have high hopes for you, Ambrose. You'll make a gambler yet."

"My side's easy," Olaf said. "I would have told you anyhow. I thought you might have guessed part of it, though not all. Gold mines in Colorado, copper mines in Norway. I've got them both at the moment: speculative, but they exist. Do I want them? Not really. I told you of the tax problem over the Norway mines. It would be the same with the Colorado ones — plus another little problem that I expect you can work out for yourself if I give you a hint. What would you say is the better bet for continued price increase — copper or gold?"

"I'd obviously say gold, and presumably I'd be wrong. You mean there's too much of it?"

"You're getting warm. Think of all the gold that's stashed away in official reserves — immobilized. If it starts coming out, what will happen to the price?"

"So you think the speculators have got it wrong?"

"Let's say they're taking a short view. They always do. In any case, gold is something I have to keep out of, given my position. It was an amusing stake for a gamble: but the real gamble I had in mind was to come afterwards. I felt that if I won both sets of mines, I would be able to use them as a powerful counter for a deal I might want to do. It worked — at least to this extent. While I was in Colorado, I discovered that there was something Harrigan has that I want to get hold of, not for myself but for England. That's why I want to see him. I want to propose a swap."

"Why should *he* want the mines?"

"I'm just guessing at the moment, but I think it might appeal. As an American, he's quite free to operate Colorado and Norway. Their tax system actually encourages it. And it might suit him because he keeps spreading his interests. I heard this, and you've confirmed it. So my idea is to ask him if he'd like to have both these outlets. And as a sweetener, I'm also prepared, if need be, to arrange for TCC to get approval for the takeover."

Ambrose looked at him in astonishment. "My God: you must want something pretty important in exchange."

"I do. I have to admit that it's the gamble that amuses me: but the stake this time is pretty decisive, too. It's not gold. Far more important. Uranium. The biggest uranium deposits so far undeveloped are in south-west Africa. You probably know — well you *may* know, as it's public — that Rio Tinto Zinc — RTZ — have a large concession in Namibia. But there's an area adjacent which might have much more but has been handled very secretly. What I found out in Colorado, from my friend there, is that a huge financial group in the USA have bribed their way into it and are about to get the concession."

"And Harrigan is involved?"

"They say he controls it. And now, here's the turn. I can't really operate Colorado and Norway because I'm an individual, but he could. The uranium is just the opposite. He'd have a hell of a job, with his reputation, to get the U.S. Government to let him operate the uranium. All Governments like to keep their citizens under a close watch on this. But if a U.K. Government body could sign the concession in Africa, there'd be no problem. So that's the switch. I'd have to feel him out, but I think it could work."

Ambrose was looking at him with a certain awe. "Have I got it right? You hand over your stuff just like that? No cash nexus?"

"Oh, really, Ambrose. I thought you'd understood. All my stuff, as you call it, is an embarrassment to me. How can you compare it with getting the concession for the U.K. Atomic Energy Authority? Now, come on. I've told you my side. What about yours?"

Ambrose gulped. How does one come down from these heights? It's in the circle, he reminded himself. The same circle. No problem.

"My side's a little more nebulous than yours," he said. "No cash nexus either. Very limited, though. Just one object — at least to start with. An Old Master, if one applies that term to sculpture. A Donatello, in fact."

Olaf sat up in his chair almost with a jump. "A Donatello! How? What do you mean?"

"I'll be very brief," Ambrose said. "I'll give you more detail if anything comes of all this later. But here's the gist of it. Harrigan, as you heard, collects works of art. But that doesn't really describe his motivation. What he's concerned with is St. John the Baptist. St. John is his patron saint. He set out to surround himself in his own home — which is huge — with the most noble evocations of the Baptist from the Renaissance period. This isn't a hobby. It's an absolutely fanatical drive — religious, devotional. I would say it far outweighs all his financial manipulations, and all his gangster stuff.

"I haven't met him myself, but what I'm telling you is at

firsthand, from a friend who is an art historian. I believe it completely. Harrigan's studied the subject deeply. What he's done to capture the Baptist is astonishing: and one of the things is a Donatello. He may have just lifted it."

Olaf had become so tense that he almost whispered. "A Donatello of St. John? You don't mean the one in the cathedral at Siena, the extraordinary bronze in the little chapel."

"Thank God I can talk about it to someone who understands. That's just what I do mean. He's built an imitation of the whole chapel: and facing you, as you look in, is the statue."

Olaf was still whispering. "You mean *stolen?*"

"Substituted. My friend has been back to Siena. She's sure that the statue that's now there is an imitation. And if so, the one in Harrigan's house may be the original. Someone's got to have a look at it. And you know who that someone's going to be."

"Wow!" Olaf had drawn the cambric handkerchief from his sleeve and was actually mopping his brow. And now he began to smile. "What a quest! How do we set about it?" He jumped up and pulled a bell-rope. "I need a brandy. Will you join me? My God, this dwarfs everything. I can understand you getting involved. You *have* been involved?"

"In a sort of mudlark."

"Mudlark? It'll need a bit more than that, won't it? What do you have in mind? How do we proceed?"

"I haven't the faintest idea," Ambrose said. "I just wanted to get it into the circle. There are other linked things, too, but I'll leave them for the moment."

"And who is this wonderful woman who's put you on to this? I take it that she *is* wonderful. She *must* be, to have got all this out."

"Her name is Alyss. There is a certain wondrous quality about her. I will agree."

The waiter, having been instructed, now arrived with two double brandies. Olaf raised his glass. "To Alyss!"

"Alyss.'"

It seemed as if they had not stopped drinking toasts all afternoon. Perhaps it was the old-fashioned atmosphere that encouraged it. Or just Olaf. A man to drink with.

Sipping his brandy happily, Olaf glanced at his watch and sighed. "Just when I'm enjoying myself. It's half-past three and I promised to phone London. I'll have to go to the Consulate. What time will it be in London? Eight-thirty or nine-thirty? I suppose they'll all have gone to bed."

Ambrose, feeling a little shaky on his feet, followed him to the door of the club, where the Consul-General's Rolls and chauffeur were waiting. "Would you like to be driven back to Cambridge?" Olaf said. "Come with me, and then you can have the car."

They were both silent as the car whispered its way through the traffic. It was as if the issues now opened up had to find some shape of their own. A few desultory words wouldn't help at this point.

It was as the car stopped, and Olaf prepared to descend, that Ambrose felt the need, for no conscious reason, to ask a question going back to the early part of their talk at lunch. "Is Fletcher still in London?" he said. "Is he still negotiating on the takeover?"

"I don't know," Olaf said. "I'll ask when I phone."

They parted with a wave of the hand, without any protestations of mutual esteem, gratitude or interest. The English way. Ambrose sat back and closed his eyes. Fifteen minutes later the chauffeur was opening the car door for him outside his hotel.

He picked up an afternoon paper at the desk and stood reading it for a few minutes to see if there was anything on the killings. Still a strange silence on Harrigan's side. The longer he was silent, the more ominous it seemed. No news meant more speculation. Ambrose worked his way through the inquest stories on the shot men, linked material, background, interviews with police. There was even a page of pictures of the ceremony at Notre Dame on Saturday afternoon. One wondered where the body-guards stood in that august scene. Had they been fitted out with academic gowns to help them melt into the background? Some of the berobed figures looked tough enough. . . .

He was just walking to the elevator, when the clerk called out his name. Phone call. He took it at the desk.

It was Olaf. "Is there a call-box near you?" he said. "Not through the switchboard. Ring me back." He gave the number.

Ambrose went to the pay-phone behind the elevator and was through immediately. "I've just spoken to London," Olaf said. "Something rather odd. Do you remember that you spoke of a very effable character — not *a*ffable, *e*ffable. You asked me to enquire if he was still over there?"

"I remember."

"Well, they were keeping an eye on him — a very special kind of eye: they love him so dearly. Apparently he checked out very hurriedly on Saturday to catch the two-thirty plane to Boston. He went through the gate, and a message was sent over here on a certain network to look out for his arrival. They were waiting for him here, but he just didn't arrive, so this was flashed back to London. On this kind of network they don't bother to mention these things locally, which is why I only heard about it from London."

"Very odd," Ambrose said.

"I thought you'd be interested. And Ambrose, on that other little matter you spoke of, which I called a quest. . . ."

"I am all ears."

"An idea has come into my head. Very vague at this stage, but it may help. The cue-word is 'homeless.' Does that ring a bell?"

"Absolutely not."

"No: I didn't think it would. I'll tell you when we meet, which should be very soon. On the visit I want to make to a certain art-collector. I suppose you want time to think for a bit and consult. Would you ring me tomorrow morning early — any time after eight? And think about the abominable F-man. If you have any good ideas, we ought to tell London."

There was no need to urge Ambrose to think about Fletcher. Now that his presence — or absence — had surfaced as an issue, it would be haunting.

He'd disappeared on Saturday, immediately after the gang-land killings. Surely it must be linked. He would be privy to a great deal, however respectable he was supposed to look. He would have had a phone call from Boston soon after the killings — say six or seven o'clock London time on Saturday morning. If he suspected that Harrigan was losing out, might he switch to the opposition? More likely that he would want to rush back to assert loyalty to his boss.

He'd rushed to the Boston plane all right, but it had shown up here without him. One had to assume that he'd either slipped away to stay in England, or had switched into a plane for some other destination than Boston. What would make the most sense? That he would want to be in or near Boston, keeping an eye on developments but without being seen. He might have taken a plane to New York or Montreal to throw off anyone following him, and then rented a car to bring him into the Boston area.

There was something sinister about it. He could be desperate — afraid of the outcome of the gang war. One knew that he was jealous, vengeful, nasty. If desperation was added, he was a man to be feared.

But was it the gang war? *Willis!* Of course! He might have phoned Willis in London and found that he was away. If he'd guessed, or discovered, that Willis was not just away but in flight, he would wonder immediately if Willis had come clean with the authorities and implicated him. They were following him in London: he might have spotted it. He would feel driven from all sides. . . .

Two days had passed. Where had he got to? If he was holed up in the Boston area, and desperate, one had to be on guard. He was a man who wanted to get even. He still has a score to settle with me, Ambrose thought. And Claire. Surely he knew how much she hated him. If he suspected her feeling for Willis. . . .

He was around, somewhere. One had an eerie feeling about it. Could one just sit back and wait? This was to let danger catch up on one. One had to be more prepared.

He thought for a minute and rang Alyss. They arranged a time and place for dinner and then he added: "Can you possibly reach Tim? If he's free tonight — say at ten — I have a little job for him that might appeal. If he's free, can he join us for coffee or a drink after dinner?"

With this laid on, he felt better. Fletcher might be around, but one was doing something about it.

IX

THERE are times when a hot bath is the only solvent. Ostensibly he wanted a little peace for a few minutes to think about his lecture the next day. The evening would be full of other things. In the morning, Olaf would be after him to see what he had thought up.

The lecture was at eleven. The subject planned was the individual in relation to the modern state: but as he lay in his bath, his thoughts kept drifting off to a more elemental paradigm — the quality of life in a Renaissance city, in which freedom could mean acceptance of dictatorial rule by a ducal family, as a safeguard against *external* domination. In the enfolding steam, he knew why his mind had turned this way. Alyss, poised for adventure, had felt that a world of naked power might be somehow conducive to artistic excellence. The Duke of Ferrara took this for granted when disposing of his Duchess. Perhaps Alyss had a yen to identify with one of the *female* d'Estes — Isabella or Beatrice. Well, which? Both were patrons on the grand scale. Beatrice had Leonardo at her side, Isabella Mantegna. It was one world: Harrigan and Donatello. Mantua and Milan, Boston and Ferrara. . . . Guelphs and Ghibellines. . . . The steam had taken over completely. He stirred himself with a mighty effort and rose dripping from the water.

He was feeling warm and relaxed, drying himself in one of those huge towels that American hotels provide, when he noticed an envelope on the floor near the door. Inside was a brief note.

It made sense as he read it, yet he would not have envisaged it. Willis was supposed to have disappeared. Perhaps he had. But whatever form he now assumed was solid enough to push a note under the door:

"You will remember me: impelled of invisible tides and all that. I may need to talk to you without going through the switchboard. There are two call-boxes a few yards from the hotel, at the corner of Wentworth Street. If I want to reach you, I'll ring you at the hotel just to alert you. I seem to have become Swinburne to you, so I'll simply say: This is Swinburne. Ten minutes later I'll ring the call-box nearest the hotel. If that's engaged, I'll ring the second one. I don't think I'll have to ring. It's just in case."

Ambrose tore the note up slowly. He felt somehow relieved to have a possible line of contact. One never knew what might happen with Fletcher. Willis had behaved atrociously, but at least he was now on the right side. One needed allies.

The phone rang. Rafferty. "Sorry I was tied up this morning. I'm free now. What are you doing? Come over for a drink."

"Love to. I'll be there in about half-an-hour."

Whether there was fresh news or not, everything made sense as one sat in Rafferty's office, drinking Irish whisky for a change. His door was wide open all the time, so that he seemed part of the endless clatter of the huge press-room. Far from this disturbing one, it created a satisfying sense of reality. One wasn't shut off — as Ambrose usually was himself — in a quiet room, trying to analyze a wildly irrational world outside. One was part of the confusion, living it out and therefore accepting its canons. Nothing human was alien to Rafferty. He joined in, keeping his fingers clean, but not with the superiority that academics generate. There was no tutt-tutting here. And that was why they all trusted him.

They had begun by talking generalities: but Rafferty, recharging Ambrose's glass, said, somewhat surprisingly: "Do you know why I asked you to come over? I'm worried about you. What are you up to here? And don't tell me you're giving some lectures. You've got something else cooking."

No point in trying to fool Rafferty. "You mean my interest in Harrigan and all that?"

"Plus tracking down car registration numbers. Put it this way. You may be on one of your secret service jaunts for all I know, but things can get dangerous here."

"Why do you assume secret service. . . ."

"Why do *I* assume? *Everybody* assumes it. We watch you

160

wandering round, having a good time, going to jazz clubs, shaving the Barber of Seville and all that, but we take it for granted that there's something else buzzing in that noodle of yours."

One had to warm to the man. "You're perfectly right, Bill, I *was* asked to keep my eyes open about something official. Funnily enough, that's become the least important thing. At the moment, I'm just letting one thing lead to another. All very virtuous, I assure you."

"I don't give a hoot about the virtue. It's the danger I'm worried about. You've been after me so intensely on Harrigan. You know, this isn't kid-glove stuff. I sometimes get the feeling that you're *looking* for danger."

Ambrose paused. "I sometimes wonder myself," he said slowly. "Perhaps it's the release from Oxford. When I'm *there*, I sit looking at words on paper. Here, I seem to want to get involved personally. In reality, I'm hopeless at action, awkward as they come: but here, I don't seem afraid of it."

"You'd feel very differently if you really got caught up in it."

"All too true. But I can reassure you. I owe it to you. I'll tell you something — on the usual terms." He looked through the open door. No one seemed within earshot. "You're right. I do have a special interest in Harrigan. But at the moment, it's not the gangster: it's Harrigan the art collector."

Rafferty was relieved. "Well, *that* should be safe enough. But you still want to know about the gang stuff."

"Fascinated. It's like being in the middle of a battle between the Guelphs and the Ghibellines. I'll pick Harrigan as a Guelph, because he's a good Papist, I believe. When is he going to launch his anti-Ghibelline counter-attack?"

"My guess is that it could all happen tomorrow," Rafferty said.

"It can't. I'm lecturing tomorrow."

"Well, after the lecture. Much more likely to happen at night, anyhow. So you pick Harrigan as a Guelph. Were they gangster capitalists, like the Medici? That would fit Harrigan all right. You remember my telling you about the range of his interests? I happened to hear yesterday that it's even wider than I thought. South America's the latest. I heard that he's into some very big mining interests there. He's getting so legitimate that he'll be going downtown in a top hat and striped pants any day now. *Very* respectable."

"Well, he *is* a Doctor of Religious Law."

"God, you should have seen that on TV. And Notre Dame went on to win the football game. Great day for the Irish."

Ambrose tried out an idea. "Do you know, I was wondering about one thing. When you published the names and pictures of the four men who were gunned down on Friday night, I didn't know who they were, of course, but it seems established that they were Harrigan men. Are you quite sure that they were shot up by the opposition? Couldn't it have been a preemptive strike by Harrigan himself against a group who were planning a *coup* against him? That's what happened to the man they fished out of the Bay, wasn't it?"

"Yes," Rafferty said. "Tag O'leary. He made a mistake. It was a straight execution for talking to the wrong people. I don't think that's what happened on Friday night. But you know," he paused reflectively, "you may be on to something. We're probably all conditioned by the traditional picture — Chicago, or *The Godfather,* and all that. They's why we expect bang-bang. But the under-lying picture's changed. It's on two levels now. Ordinary gambling, protection, drugs — that's probably still traditional: but when you get these huge financial interests that are so new in style, maybe they're fashioning new methods to get control. Take McLuskey. In some ways he's more like an urban guerilla type than a straight gangster. And there's one character that I'm never sure about — Fletcher."

"Where does *he* fit in?"

"Oh, at the top financial end. Of course he's the *respectable* side of Harrigan's empire: but when you talk about a *coup.* . . . Well, isn't that what top businessmen are always doing — waiting to pounce on each other?"

"You think Harrigan may be aware of this? Suspicious?"

"If he is, it may account for why he's lying low. He may be giving them a lot of rope, just to see how the opposition lines up."

"So there might be nothing happening for a few days. . . ."

"I suppose it's possible. And then it will be God help Fletcher if he's really on the other side. I tell you who I'm sorry for in all this, Claire. I'm really sorry for her."

"Yes, I'm sorry for her, too," Ambrose said. They went on gossiping for a while until Ambrose left to meet Alyss.

"I have news for you," Ambrose said as dinner was progressing. "I've betrayed your confidence. Twice, in fact: but only one of them mattered."

She looked at him smilingly. He was joking, obviously.

"No, I mean it. Except that the one which mattered was really under your instructions. Do you recall my telling you about a gambling art wizard called Sir Olaf McConnochie, upon which you asked me for his telephone number. He's appeared. I had lunch with him today. And I told him what you're up to."

"You don't mean about Tim and all that?" She was alarmed for a moment.

"I left that part out, but I did tell him everything else, at least the essentials. I hope you don't mind. I had to take a decision and I took it. I may say that at the time I was rather high, flown with wine: but I still think it's all right. We've been wondering how to get in there. You left it to me. I think we agree on no more mudlarks. This one's a different kind of approach. I can't tell how it will work out, but the elements are there, like a jig-saw puzzle. Things may fall into place."

She was smiling again. "I *said* you were a genius. I didn't think I could love a genius, but I'm beginning to change my mind."

Ambrose laid a hand on hers. "Ha: I should really stop right there. Forget the world, look into your eyes — just you and me — a flickering candle — a bottle of wine. . . ."

"I'm quite capable of braining you with a bottle of wine if you don't stop."

"It's just the atmosphere. It's gone to my head. It's so nice here." It was indeed. A small Italian restaurant, *Mario,* just off the Common, not too chic, rather rough and cheerful. The candles were sparkling, the waiters bustling around them with raucous cries announcing this dish and that, as if each one was special, delicious, magnificent, prepared as food had never been prepared before.

"Yes, it *is* nice," she said. "I thought you'd like a change after our jazz night. No Turks, of course. Wasn't the old Pasha marvelous? I wonder if he's taking Lindsay back to his harem."

"I'll know tomorrow. She's always shown up at my lectures, and if she doesn't show up tomorrow, it can mean only one thing."

"What about the Young Turk? Do you think he might object?"

"I think he'd do anything for Uncle. But wait a minute. You're right. He's gone back to England — or so they say. If she's not at the lecture, she may be with him. Ah, well. Not important for the moment. Let me tell you about the new approach, through Olaf."

"I still don't quite believe he's real."

"He's real enough. That's why it's very hard to tell you about the new approach. Has to do with his Treasury side — high finance, or rather high business. But I can tell you in broad terms, the way I told him about *your* secret without revealing details. He told me today that he needs most urgently to get in to see Harrigan to negotiate a big exchange of properties — a huge international deal that would help England. He's quite sure that if he could get in and talk to him privately they could do a deal, because it's an exchange that would also be of profit to Harrigan. The only thing is, how does he get in? Harrigan's kept our Consul-General at arm's length like everybody else. Now, how was it that he saw *you?*"

"Well, you *know*. Because of the paintings. He wanted my opinion of his Pinturicchio."

"Right. But basically, as you explained it to me, it's because of his passion for his patron saint. Could this be a link for Olaf? When I told you about him, I mentioned that he's inherited a lot of pictures himself: but when I talked to him today, I could see that he's not just an *inheritor* of works of art. He knows it all deeply. Can this get him in somehow?"

"You can't just ring Harrigan up and say you want to look at his pictures. A lot of people have tried. It doesn't work."

"Apart from everything else, if I may make a joke, I assume that his number's unlisted. Did he give it to you when you went there?"

"No. He telephoned himself and just told me when to visit him. But surely there's a much more serious factor at the moment. These gang killings. Everyone knows that the men shot were Harrigan's, and it's assumed there's going to be some revenge. He wouldn't see anyone from the outside just now, would he? He'd be far too busy."

Ambrose took a sip of wine, reflectively. "I wonder if you're right about that. Seems obvious, but I wonder. Things may not develop in such a hurry. Of course, he's got it all planned, but he may be sitting there like the Godfather, taking his time, and just looking at his pictures. So if at this moment another picture fancier asks to see him — why not? All in character. Perfect. Marlon Brando would take it in his stride."

"Well, that may be. But you haven't got the visit arranged yet. Or have you an idea?"

"None at all, but Olaf may be developing one himself. When

he spoke to me later today he hinted that he had something buzzing away in that little troll's head."

"Troll?"

"Oh, I didn't tell you. He's very small, and he's certainly a wizard in several dimensions, which makes him a troll. The main thing is that when I told him your feelings about the Donatello, he got terribly excited. He feels about it just the way you do. I had to give him your analysis — Harrigan's passion for the Baptist governing everything, and how that had led you to Siena to check. He said you must be a wonderful woman."

"And what was your comment?"

"I was quite neutral, of course."

"Well, he sounds pretty wonderful himself. What do you think he was hinting at when he said he had an idea?"

"He offered a clue which was completely meaningless to me. He said the key word was 'homeless.' Does that mean anything to you?"

"Homeless? Homeless?" She was trying it out, and suddenly her face lit up. "Homeless! I know just what he meant. My goodness. I wonder how it applies."

"Will you stop talking in riddles?"

"But you know the answer yourself. I'm sure you've used Berenson's '*Italian Paintings of the Renaissance*' — the big books, with all the pictures. Don't you remember? Under each painter, he lists where the works are to be found. And at the end of each list. . . ."

"I remember! If he's just got a photograph at *I Tatti* and no one knows where the original is, he lists it as 'homeless.' And Olaf may know about one of them — of the Baptist!"

"Exactly."

"My God! You can't recall anything that might be relevant?"

"No, I can't. But I have the books and I'll go through them when I get home. I should know in the morning, with luck."

"He'll tell me himself in the morning, I expect. I'm to ring him first thing to see what I've come up with."

"Has this anything to do with why you asked me to get hold of Tim?"

"No, no." Ambrose felt this liveliness evaporating. "Goodness I'd been forgetting about Tim. It was just an impulsive idea, about something quite different. Seems odd remembering it now."

"Well, he's coming. He was rather pleased about it. Should be here any minute."

Ambrose heaved a deep sigh. "I hate doing this, but I'd rather not tell you just now what it's all about. Almost certainly come to nothing. But as he doesn't mind playing CIA. . . ."

"He adores it. You saw that the other night. Don't worry about it." She put her hand on his. "Come on. Cheer up. You'll make *me* sorry if you pull such a long face."

Tim came into the restaurant a few minutes later and sat down to have a coffee with them.

"I take it you've put false number-plates on your car," Ambrose said by way of greeting. The sight of Tim's cheerful eager face was encouraging. It was probably a good idea to have got hold of him. Couldn't hurt, and one had to do *something* about Fletcher. . . .

It was just after ten when they got up to leave. "I'll tell you about it when we're in the car," Ambrose said to him. He nodded, and went ahead to bring the car to the door. Alyss had her own car. She kissed him gently as she left.

"Will you take me to Cambridge?" Ambrose said. "I'm at the Mayflower Hotel. Don't go to the front door. Park the car close by, round the corner. But can you stop at some quiet place near it so that I can tell you what it's all about?"

While he drove, Tim talked — though discreetly — about some of his CIA experiences. On the adventure side, it was clear that he missed it all. Coming into Cambridge, he found his way to a sidestreet near the hotel, where he switched off the engine and sat waiting.

"I've got a peculiar problem," Ambrose said. "The only way I could think of tackling it is CIA style, so naturally I thought of you. You can tell me if you think it will work. I expect you'll tell me that it's daft."

"I'll certainly tell you if I think so."

"I think it's daft myself by any normal standards, but I can't get it out of my head." He paused for a minute, impelled to drop the chatty tone he had started with. He went on more slowly when he started again.

"It has to do with violence," he said somberly. "There's an Englishman living here, a big businessman, who has a down on me. He hates my guts. He's partly justified, but not the way he thinks. It wouldn't worry me at all, except that he's a murderous character. And when I say murderous, I really mean it. There was someone I knew very well. She died in an accident. Only it wasn't an accident."

Away now from the chatter of the restaurant and the brightly lit main roads, Ambrose felt again his earlier sense of fear. The little street was itself dark and mysterious. There was no moon. The faint light from a quaint old street-lamp showed the huge elms as black masses in the sky. There was a glimpse of scattered little Cambridge houses with their odd bits of garden and picket-fence. Tim, sitting at his side, was shrouded in the dark. Only his handsome young face carried a touch of the reflected light.

"What has happened now," Ambrose said, "is that this character may have had his base shot from under him. He may be a desperate man, and want to get even with the people he hates. And I'm one of them.

"I wouldn't be telling you this except that he's disappeared. He was supposed to be on a plane to Boston from London and he didn't get here. I have a terrible feeling that he may have got here in some other way — through Montreal or New York. It's made me jumpy. If he's out looking for me — and he may be — I don't want to sit waiting for it. I want to smoke him out.

"That's where *you* come in. If he really is here and looking for me, I think he'd wait for me to come in to the hotel. He might try to get me into a car. I've had one experience of this already, and I didn't like it. But this time it's different. My idea is to *invite* it, wandering slowly up to the hotel, with you waiting as a back stop. I know it sounds crazy, but it really is important to know if he's here. It's not just *me* he may go for. There's somebody else — his wife, in fact, and we could warn her. I'm quite willing to be the decoy, as long as you're in the background."

"And you want to know what I think? I'll tell you. It's a routine ploy. I was trained for it. You could count on me for *my* part. I was quite good at it. It's *you* I'm thinking of. You aren't as agile as all that, you know. I seem to remember a certain muddy ditch. . . ."

"Tim, you're cheering me up, talking this way. The ditch proved to be quite lucky for all of us, didn't it? I have a hunch this could be the same. The whole thing is really a hunch. I've no evidence that he's here: but if he is, I do think there's a real chance that he'd be after me, and this would be a way to smoke him out."

"And what would be the next step? When we used to do this in the CIA, we knew what we were going to do with a man once we'd got him. What are you proposing to do with Mr. X, if he goes for you and I jump him?"

"Let him get away, deliberately, which will achieve two aims. The first is that it will establish that he's here. That's the most important. The second is that he will assume I have a regular bodyguard — he knows I'm close to the Government and could get it, so he won't try any rough stuff on me again. You see: it might work."

Tim sat thinking. "You don't want to tell me who this guy is? I mean, suppose he does get you into a car and I lose you. What am I going to tell my Aunt Alyss? She isn't going to like it."

"You mean the CIA could lose me? I thought it was a routine ploy."

Tim ran his hand through his hair perplexedly. "Ambrose, you're supposed to be a professor, aren't you? How the hell do you get mixed up in all this?"

"It's very simple. I *could* say that it's all due to an Englishman called Hepworth who's always leading me into trouble. But the real answer is that he only starts me off because he knows that I like it every now and then for a change — just to prove to myself that I'm still alive."

Tim bent forward to switch on the ignition. "Now you're talking. Mr. X, we're on our way! Watch out! By the way, what size guy is he? Can I take him, do you think?"

"Oh, I'm so sorry, Tim. I forgot to mention that he's huge — six foot six. But he's fat and paunchy now. You'll have no trouble."

The streets around the hotel were lined with cars, but Tim found a place into which he squeezed, just round the corner.

"I've got a little thing to give you," he said, switching off the engine. "You can never tell. If something goes wrong, it might help. Every woman carries one in New York, but this is a rather neat version."

He picked up his bag from the back seat, and, fishing into a little pocket inside, pulled out what looked like a rather thick ring. "Put this on your finger," he said. "It has a built-in whistle. Can you see where to blow? It you get stuck, it's not difficult to raise your hand to your mouth and then let go. It makes an absolutely terrifying noise. It's got a tiny transistor and loudspeaker. It'll frighten you as much as Mr. X."

"And where will *you* be?"

"I thought you weren't going to worry about *my* side. I'll be around. If you're just going to wander outside the hotel I can't really lose you. I'm still against it, but if you want to have a go, you can count on me."

Ambrose looked at his watch. It was just after eleven o'clock. "If he's here, I suppose he would have rung the hotel earlier — say at ten — to see if I was in. I was out, so he'd ring off without leaving a message. Then he would stand around waiting. Well, he's either there or he isn't. I'm off."

He got out, and walked slowly towards the front of the hotel. The street was empty. Apart from the warmly inviting hotel entrance, there was not much light. No one in sight. He walked into the hotel to take a quick look at the lobby. Empty too. He came out in a casual way, as if just taking a stroll for a breath of air. Turning left, he walked towards the street where Tim had parked. He had decided now that he was on a wild goose chase, and began to be quite at ease. Having gone about two hundred yards, he turned back towards the hotel, and sauntered beyond it in the other direction. At some distance behind him he heard a metallic kind of crash — obviously some car bumping into another — followed by the furious sounding of a car horn. There was a little shouting to go with it — city noises — all quite normal. At that moment, he had come to a small alley and took a step into it to have a look. Nothing. He turned back towards the road and felt his arm gripped from behind with a crushing force. The man holding him pulled him back into the alley with such power as practically to lift him off his feet. Where they stood was almost totally dark. Fletcher towered over him, breathing heavily. "You dirty little tyke," he muttered, and swung a fist at Ambrose with demonic fury.

It caught him on the jaw. He staggered, and Fletcher gripped him again by the arm for another swinging punch which struck him on the nose. The sudden pain was agonizing. He felt blood and tears at once. Fletcher stood before him. "You filthy scum," he muttered. "I've waited for this. I could have had you rubbed out, but I wanted to do it myself. You thought you could treat me as dirt — she did too — well I took care of her — now it's your turn" — he was holding him at the neck by his shirt and raised the other arm for a back-handed blow which struck with the force of a hammer. "No one's going to get the better of me" — and again he drove a fist into Ambrose's face.

Ambrose was dizzy with pain. Feebly he raised his hand to his nose to wipe away the blood. There was something hard on his finger. He felt it with his lips as his hand touched his nose. With no clear notion of what he was doing, he blew into it and heard a wild piercing whistle. Fletcher jumped and ran. All Ambrose could think of was the blood and the agonizing tenderness in his nose. He managed to get a handkerchief out and laid it gently against his nose for comfort. He heard a running of feet. A policeman was suddenly there, with Tim close behind.

"Are you O.K.?" the policeman asked.

Ambrose managed a nod.

"You people just ask for it." He was clearly not prepared to waste much sympathy on him. "Did he get your pocket-book? Can you describe him? Black, I suppose."

It was enough to pull Ambrose together. "He was white. Can't describe him. Doesn't matter. But he was white."

"Well, if you're O.K., we'll leave it. Keep off the street this time of night unless you're looking for trouble." He turned to Tim. "I've got all your particulars. I'll go back to the other guy. He's the fussy type." He slouched away.

"So it worked," Tim said wonderingly. "Your Mr. X, I suppose."

"Yes, it worked," Ambrose said. "And your whistle worked. But where was the CIA?"

Tim tried to speak, but a straight face was too much for him. He began to laugh, and speech was impossible. Finally, he managed to get out a few words. "Ambrose: let's make a deal. No more CIA outings for you and me." And laughter took over again.

Ambrose might have laughed with him, but his face muscles were too stiff and raw to move. "What happened this time?"

"Here, let me give you a hand back to the hotel." Tim was trying to keep a straight face, but it wasn't easy. "It's too crazy." And he was off laughing again. "I had a car accident. Can you beat it? I was standing keeping an eye on the road, and the guy in the car behind mine wanted to get out. I had you in sight, so I nipped into my car and went forward a foot to let the other guy out. But my foot slipped and I hit the car in front. *That* guy had just got into his car, and he let go with his car horn. There was a cop nearby — never there when you want them — so he came up. I tried to run off to see what had happened to you, but he wouldn't let me go without seeing my licence and taking particulars. The other guy was raving mad, saying it was a new car and all that. Then we heard your whistle. Are you really O.K.? He was beating you up real bad, wasn't he?"

170

"It wasn't good," Ambrose said. "I'm beginning to feel better. Well, he's shown up. I'm relieved. We know where he is. I think I may be safe now."

"You mean he's worked it out of his system?"

"In a way, yes. But *I'm* not the main thing. I'll have to think about what follows. After I've bathed my nose."

Tim looked at him out of the corner of his eye. "I suppose you don't want me to ring up my Aunt Alyss and get her over?"

"No, no. Let's keep this to ourselves." He looked at his blood-stained handkerchief and put it back to his nose to relieve the tenderness. "Amazing. I can bear it."

"He really worked you over."

"Yes, but now that it's happened, I'm glad. I'm terribly grateful to you, Tim. I wouldn't have launched myself in this unless you'd gone along."

"Oh, I was a great help."

"You were. That whistle. I must give it back to you."

"No: keep it as a souvenir. Besides, your Mr. X may be back."

Ambrose was suddenly struck by an idea. "What about your car accident? I must pay the cost."

"What cost?"

"Won't the man in front want paying for the damage?"

"He didn't have a scratch. Of course, he'll try to sue, but it won't be easy to track me down. It was a CIA job."

"But you aren't working for them now."

"No, I'm not. But old habits die hard, you know. I was carrying a somewhat misleading driving licence: and the car registration plates . . . well, you know about all that."

"I do, I do. I'll try to forget it."

Inside the hotel, all was peaceful. But when he stepped up to the desk to get his room-key, he found a message from Olaf: "Will Mr. Usher please telephone any time up to 1 a.m. Not later." Not later! Olaf must still be on Colorado time.

"Ah, yes," Olaf said casually, when Ambrose got through. "I'm having a little backgammon with one of the Consuls. He has the makings of an excellent player."

"I'm delighted to hear it. But I expect you wanted to tell me something else."

"Yes, about tomorrow. I asked you to telephone me in the morning, but I think it would be better if you could come over and have breakfast. I could send a car for you at eight-thirty. Would that be all right?"

"That would be fine. It had better not be too long a breakfast, though. I have to be at Harvard lecturing at eleven."

"No problem. We'll run you back. We need to have a personal word because something I was rather hoping for has worked. I've had a long telephone call to Scotland. All is well. I don't know if you've developed any ideas on the problem I posed, but if not, this may do the trick. Sorry to be so mysterious."

"Would I understand you better if I learned to play backgammon?"

"Possibly, possibly. By the way, do you think you could persuade your art historian friend to join us at breakfast? Not too late to telephone her, I hope? I fancy she might help us a lot with advice."

"I'm sure she'd love to come. I told her about you, including 'homeless.'"

'Ha. She understood, of course."

"She got the principle, but not the detail."

"Splendid. I'll keep it for tomorrow. The car had better come to you first, and you can direct the chauffeur where to call on her. I'm looking forward to making her acquaintance."

X

"I knew you'd get it once Ambrose mentioned 'homeless' to you," Olaf said. "If the subject was St. John the Baptist, what else could it mean?"

One more side of Olaf was now revealing itself. When he decided to exert his charm on a woman he was, it seemed, quite irresistible. Alyss was getting the treatment and loving it.

"I got the clue, but I didn't know which picture until I looked it up," she said modestly. "It was extraordinary that you could think of it."

"Not in the slightest. It's brought out and shown to me every time I go up there. And I knew old Robbie well enough to be sure he'd agree. The only question now is how to use it. I'm sure Ambrose will devise something."

Nice that I have *some* function, Ambrose thought. With these two doves cooing away at full blast, he was beginning to feel left out. Perhaps it was that his face still ached — especially his nose. However, the consular kippers were a great restorative. He took another mouthful and moved willingly towards the general amity.

As if anticipating Olaf's gallantries, Alyss had put on a beautifully-cut trouser suit of some dark purple material and done something special with her hair. She had looked stunning, and also very excited, when she joined Ambrose in the Rolls.

"I found out what it was just after you called last night," she said. "I nearly rang back but I thought it could wait. The homeless picture. I'm sure of it. Giovanni Bellini's picture of the Baptist — a very strange one. Berenson calls it '*The Preaching Baptist.*' It looks an astonishing painting from the illustration in the book — the Baptist high up in the foreground against a distant landscape, very distorted in scale, almost surrealistic, standing there with very bony elongated legs, head in the air to one side, agonized, immensely thin and long, like an El Greco. Obviously your Olaf must know where it is. Do you think he's got it hidden somewhere?"

"I put nothing beyond him, but he was a bit too speculative for that. Let's see what he says. At least you cracked the code. He will think highly of you for that."

And highly he did seem to think, treating her with a kind of sustained admiration suffused with courtesy. How convenient that the Consul-General was away, leaving them free to talk. Once they had helped themselves to food, Olaf got down to the business in hand without delay, addressing himself to Alyss as if her advice and approval were what really counted.

"What an extraordinary place Harrigan's house must be," he said to her. "The whole concept of identifying with the Baptist — astonishing. And, of course, if you're right about the Donatello, we'll just *have* to do something."

"I think it may be even more than the Donatello," she said. "There's what Siena calls 'a true relic' of the Baptist that seems to have disappeared. It may be there too."

Olaf sighed. "Things disappear into secret collections. I've seen some results of this. But this time, perhaps, we can put it to good purpose."

He got down to explaining. "When I realized there might be a chance of getting into Harrigan through his art side, I couldn't think at first how to work it, and then it came to me — something so familiar to me for years in Scotland that I couldn't link it, so to speak, to Boston. Once my mind had made the jump, it seemed obvious.

"My next-door-neighbor in Scotland is the Earl of Talloch. He's got about ten other titles — Viscount Craigie, Lord Pawkness — but Talloch is the simplest one. When I say we're neighbors, I suppose I should explain that his house is about ten miles from mine as the crow flies — about eighteen miles by road. I have about a thousand acres myself: he has about fifty thousand, and Talloch Castle is in the middle. Quite an old place, and lots of pictures, including Old Masters — bought, borrowed or lifted over a few centuries.

"His grandfather had a passion for it. He wasn't too choosy where he got the pictures. If it wasn't open and above board, he simply kept the picture in a private gallery, and didn't mention it to anyone, except close friends. Robbie Talloch, the present

Earl, is pretty aged himself now. We're good friends. One of the pictures he's got there is a strange painting of St. John the Baptist by Giovanni Bellini. Berenson has a picture of it in his book — says it's 'homeless.' Didn't know where it was. You guessed."

Alyss nodded. He accepted that she was deep in all this without needing to comment, and went straight on.

"The moment I thought of it, I put in a call and got Robbie on the phone. I said there was something he could do for the country, and he alone. I said I wasn't at all sure if I would need the picture, but I wanted to have it in reserve. If I needed it, would he lend the picture to Harrigan for life — and Harrigan is very old.

"Of course, he might have done this for me just for friendship, but I happen to know of something he wants passionately and which I can get for him as a kind of *quid pro quo*. I didn't mention it when we spoke, and he didn't either. You see," he said apologetically to Alyss, "if you want to do something a little close to the bone in our country — something that ordinary people aren't allowed to do — it's all right if you're a gentleman as long as you don't actually mention it. If you spell it out, it might be called bribery and corruption. But if you leave it unspoken, it's all right."

"I have a feeling that it isn't too awful in this case," she said.

"Well, I'll tell you. I feel like being indiscreet. The Earl of Talloch has innumerable titles and decorations. The one he's never been able to get is the really precious one: *Knight of the Thistle*. I expect you think I'm joking, but this is something the Queen gives with extreme rarity, and only to a Scot. He's dying for it. If I borrow his Bellini, I'll see that he gets it. He knows it: and he knows that I know that he knows. Not a word spoken. We're gentlemen."

Alyss laughed aloud. "How terribly couth! Knight of the Thistle. I think it's delicious."

Olaf showed himself delighted at her pleasure, leaping out of his chair to offer her more coffee and light her cigarette. He had known she would guess about the Bellini, but what now? Ambrose was to advise, and started thinking aloud.

"How to get invited into Schloss Harrigan? Well, let's see. You can't telephone. You can't send a message to say you want to talk business. From what I hear, he never appears personally on the big international business things. Leaves it to his nominees. So the Bellini is to be your calling-card. Right. But how to present it? We need a bit of luck. May I ask you a few questions?"

"As many as you like."

"The first. Are you by some lucky chance a Catholic?"

Olaf looked at him almost in disbelief at what he was being asked. "Of course I'm a Catholic. Surely everybody knows that the McConnochies are one of the oldest Catholic families in Scotland. Why do you think my poor mother had to leave her beloved Norway to live in those bleak Highlands? There wasn't a Catholic family in Norway good enough for her, according to my grandfather. She had to cross the water."

"Well, that's a good start. Next. Do you know the Cardinal here — even the Archbishop would do — on a really personal basis?"

"Afraid not," Olaf said. "Of course the Consul-General. . . ."

"No, we've got to find a really personal link. Ah: here's an idea. Do you by any chance know the head of the University of Notre Dame — the Rt. Rev. Monsignor President or whatever his title is?"

"Eddie Phelan? Old friend. I met him in Italy during the War when he was a chaplain and I was on liaison duty with the Americans. In fact, we both got our decorations from the Pope in the same ceremony."

"Knight of the Missile?" Alyss asked innocently.

"The papal equivalent," Olaf said. "Count of the Curia. You see, I was seconded from the Treasury after the Italian landings to keep an eye on the papal investments. They asked for someone from Britain: didn't think the Americans would be up to it, though I had to *work* with the Americans, of course. They put me into uniform as a Brigadier — well, you have to start somewhere. The Vatican was quite pleased with me, so I got this gong. Eddie got Commendatore, I think."

Ambrose turned to Alyss. "You see, Providence is on our side. I suppose I may now explain why Notre Dame is an important part of the calling-card."

"Not to mention the papal decoration," she said.

Ambrose addressed himself to Olaf. "Notre Dame just happens to have taken Harrigan over. They gave him an honorary degree last Saturday. All is now well. The elements are there: but the decisive factor will be style."

"Will you also deal with the time factor?" Olaf said. "I've got to get back to London very quickly."

"And that is the final favorable element," Ambrose said. "Let me set out a plan. First, you telephone the Monsignor at Notre Dame immediately after breakfast and ask if you can mention his name as an introduction to Harrigan. Second, you send for Alyss's Berenson and have the photograph of the Bellini copied and blown up to an impressive size. Then you write a letter."

"Just a letter?" Olaf was plainly skeptical.

"Not an ordinary letter: a knockout. First, it has to be on one of those huge stiff parchment sheets of crested writing-paper that the Consul-General will have, and in that absurdly large type that they dazzle you with in letters from No. 10 or the Palace. I expect the Consul-General's got one of those type-writers in his office to impress the natives. Above all, the letter has to be unfolded and therefore in a large parchment envelope, and with a great red seal at the back. This is what will get it through the front gates, especially as it will be presented by a Consul in formal attire — morning coat and top hat — driven there in the Rolls by a liveried chauffeur.

"Now for its contents. Starts right away with the Bellini. You are enclosing in a separate package a photograph of a painting of St. John the Baptist by Giovanni Bellini, because your old friend the Monsignor of Notre Dame has told you that this picture really belongs here, and not in the Scottish castle where it has been hidden for centuries. As he will see, it is a truly astonishing realization of the Baptist.

"You are the Government's chief financial adviser and must return to London tonight. Therefore the only chance you would have to discuss how this picture could come into his possession would be if you could visit him this afternoon. You could come any time between four and six o'clock. Your emissary will await a reply.

"Under your signature you will, of course, list a few honors, including your papal title. But you know what will really do the trick? The Mac in your name."

"Shouldn't I give him a bit more leeway in time? I'm wanted back in London, but I could stretch it out a bit here."

"Fatal. At this stage, you must appear to have only the most limited time. Of course, if something to negotiate on arises in your visit, you will delay your departure for one more day."

"Do British officials carry round their top-hats?" Alyss wanted to know. "Do *you?*" she asked Olaf. "Can I see you wearing it?"

"No problem at all," Ambrose said firmly. "Theatrical

costumiers, or the Boston Moss Bros." He looked at his watch. "I say, I really must start moving for my lecture."

Olaf turned to Alyss. "*You* don't have to go, do you? We could pick up your Berenson to photograph, and then perhaps you could come back here to watch the procession take off for Harrigan's house. I think it will be a memorable sight. We can probably mount it by one o'clock, and then we might go and have a little lunch. I expect Ambrose will be too busy to join us. He's much sought after, you know."

As it happened, Ambrose *was* engaged for lunch. Jefferson Cohen was giving a luncheon for John Vaizey, and he was invited. But surely there was no need to take it so for granted.

"If this all comes off," Olaf was saying to Alyss, "and I mean the business deal as well as the Donatello, it will be entirely due to you."

"Will I get the Order of the Cowslip, second class?" she asked.

"Your reward will be to come and see where the Bellini's been hidden, plus all the other things that Robbie's got. And I have a few myself. Yes, you must come over and see us *in situ*. I don't know if it makes us look less absurd or more. What do *you* think, Ambrose?"

Ambrose had given up on this particular front for the moment. Shades of the lecture-room were beginning to close upon the growing boy. He said he would telephone after lunch, and allowed himself to be driven off to Cambridge.

No Rolls this time. The Rolls was obviously being reserved to transport Alyss to her apartment to pick up the Berenson book. The alternative to the Rolls had turned out to be a Mini. It proved to be fairly comfortable once one had got in, but all the same it was a bit of a let-down. Presumably, once one gets used to riding in a Rolls. . . .

More seriously, he was aware, as the little car bumped along, of the conflict inside him. The talk with Olaf and Alyss had been on something open between the three of them. They could plan and act without holding anything back. But on Fletcher he had to keep his fears to himself. Even with Tim, he had felt it unwise to divulge Fletcher's name. Only with Willis could he have talked about Fletcher openly, and Willis was in a kind of limbo — unreachable. He had said he might phone. If only he *would*. . . .

It was not his own danger that he was thinking of. It was Claire. He wanted to alert her and didn't know how to.

He had found the telephone number of the Fletcher home in the Boston telephone book and rung it early in the morning. There was no danger of Fletcher himself being there. He had gone to some length to conceal his return to Boston, so clearly he wouldn't be at home. If Claire was there alone, he could warn her. But the phone had rung long and mournfully without reply. Perhaps they had a country cottage somewhere, and she was staying there. Bill Rafferty might know where it was, but it would provoke too many questions to ask.

He would have to wait. Recognizing this as inevitable, he put the issue firmly out of his mind and began thinking about his lecture. The individual and the state: not to express some abstract propositions, but rather to open up the social and cultural patterns in different settings. He could see now where it might lead.

The Italianate fantasies of his hot bath the previous evening had helped, but in an unexpected direction. If one thought of the Italian city-states, it was not to develop some romantic notion linking autocratic rule to artistic distinction. On the contrary, as Sismondi had shown clearly, it was the notion of individual liberty, based on natural law, which had generated the sustaining force. The citizens, unwitting ancestors of all our modern ideas about freedom under the law, had chosen powerful rulers, freely, to protect their status, and had flourished economically and culturally. When liberty evaporated, especially from the 15th century, Italy went into a decline.

As the Mini came into the Harvard complex, he had begun to think of parallels and contrasts: the Scottish Enlightenment (the individual *pur sang*), Germany (categorically imperative), Russia (with its blank on 'natural law'). . . . Launched into the lecture a few minutes later, he seemed to carry it through with no conscious effort.

Only one problem, that had surfaced at the beginning, remained still unsolved at the end. His glance had gone to the third row as he entered the hall. Lindsay was not there. Was she in Colorado, in Turkey, in London — or in her own room, a hundred yards away, in one of the Halls? One day, perhaps he would know.

Moving into lunch after the lecture, Ambrose tried to put out of his mind the undoubtedly more *intime* meal that Olaf and Alyss would now be enjoying. They had got on famously: well, that was fine. More to the point, they would both know by now whether the stratagem for getting Olaf into his meeting with Harrigan had worked. To have to sit through an academic luncheon, full no doubt of high talk, when one really just wanted to hear if Harrigan had said Yes or No, was frustrating in the extreme. However, there was nothing he could do about it. He would ring up Olaf as soon as the luncheon was over.

In the meantime, an academic lunch: and with a guest of honor as agreeable as John Vaizey it might develop some interest of its own.

The other guests were economists, and Vaizey was talking mainly about a new plan for economic stability that was being furthered in England by a Mr. L. St. Clare Grondona. The essence was that the Government had to guarantee purchases of basic commodities on an index that was only allowed to move gently, according to a subtle formula, instead of erratically. Ambrose, giving the discussion about half of his attention, wasn't quite sure at the end if Vaizey was for or against it. But he seemed to be expounding the scheme to general satisfaction.

On top of commodity prices, he also gave news proudly of a plan he had launched with a few other wild men to break through London's most sacred taboo — the exclusively male membership of the old clubs. He wanted his own club — the Reform — to take the lead in offering women not a partial begrudging presence at certain hours, but full and equal membership on the basis of individual merit. What better club to start this than one called 'Reform'? Some of the guests at the luncheon were, he knew, Overseas members. Would they write in to support him?

Ambrose, looking round the table, was amused to see a general air of embarrassment. "Look, John," Jefferson Cohen said finally. "we don't want to *change* the Reform. The whole attraction for us is that it's irrational and old-fashioned. If we want Women's Lib we can have it at home."

So the English are most acceptable in Rolls Royces, top hats and morning-coats. Had Harrigan felt the same? Back in his hotel room at three, Ambrose rang the Consul-General's house to find out. Olaf, at the phone, sounded jubilant.

"It worked like a charm," he said. "You should have seen the letter — and the seals — and the emissaries — when they took off. Alyss and I rolled over laughing. But it worked. I'm to call on him at four-thirty. He'll give me until six, when he has another appointment. It's all extremely formal, like negotiating with China."

180

"Child's play for you as a Treasury mandarin."

"I hope so. I'll tell you tonight. Come over at six-thirty. I've asked Alyss to come too. We'll have a good half-hour to talk. I've got to go out to dinner later on. The Federal Reserve of Boston are throwing a party for me. Alyss is coming along to hold my hand. She says she loves dressing up for a party. What a splendid woman she is. It's better than backgammon."

So it had worked. And perhaps Olaf would bring off something startling, with or without benefit of Bellini. One could expect anything of him. Yet Ambrose, putting the phone down, felt short of jubilation. Fletcher still dominated his thoughts. How to warn Claire? Perhaps she would phone. Might she not know that Fletcher was, as it were, on the run? She might be looking for help. . . .

Nothing to be done unless she phoned. He picked up a book he had brought with him from Oxford — the newly revised edition of Angsthofer's *Prolegomena* — and settled down for a long and difficult read. He would stay in his room for the next three hours just in case. Somehow he had a hunch. . . .

He had been reading for over an hour, getting increasingly sleepy over the mysteries of German romanticism, when the telephone rang. Not Claire: much better. What a relief to hear that mellifluous voice with its 'Swinburne' greeting. He had a feeling that things would now be taken care of. "O.K.," he said, putting the receiver down and dashing out to the assignation.

There was plenty of time. He was in the first call-box waiting for several minutes before it rang. "Usher," he said.

"Good. Glad we fixed this up. I need it earlier than I thought I would. Don't know if you've heard about our friend. He was in England but he's done a bunk. Had you heard?"

"Yes, I had. But how do you. . . ."

"Still got a few lines out. My guess is that he's around here somewhere, though I can't be sure. I suppose you don't happen to know. . . ."

"I do, as it happens. He *is* here and he's in a very ugly mood."

"Well, it's Claire I'm thinking of. She's out of town: I know where. I'm going out there and need some help. Are you free? Will you come?"

"Now?"

"Yes. Immediately. Have you enough money on you for a subway fare?"

"Well, yes. What do I do?"

"Take the train at Harvard Square. Change at Park Street for the Green Line. Get out at Kenmore. Round the corner you'll see Johnson Street. I'll be waiting there in a yellow Ford. O.K.?"

What a relief. "On my way," he said.

Half an hour later he was in the car with Willis.

"I thought I'd take a chance with you," Willis said, driving off without pause. "I don't expect you to forgive me for what I did to you, but I thought you'd do something for Claire. You're both in danger really." He smiled rather grimly. "Fellow victims, one might say."

Once again, Ambrose was struck by the transformation from the comfortable be-whiskered party-goer whom he had first seen at the Reform. It was not simply the physical changes — the trim iron-gray hair, the loss of whiskers and the clothes he wore — slacks and a loose kind of shooting-jacket: it was rather the feeling he gave now of a lean, tense alertness. He drove that way, with swift cool decision, moving at speed.

But more surprising still to Ambrose was the change in his own feeling. By any standard, this man had behaved to him monstrously. For his own reasons he had agreed to be a tool of nastiness. But with the story told, it seemed to have evaporated. The man was becoming positively likeable. Very odd. . . .

The car moved on. They were on what looked like a main road leading to the country. The buildings were getting more scattered.

"I guessed he would be here," Willis said. "Makes it all the more urgent. You said you knew. . . ."

"I ran into him last night," Ambrose said. "Or to be more precise, he ran into me. But I was looking for him. I wanted to find out." He went on to tell Willis what had happened.

"Took a bit of a risk, didn't you," Willis said. "You wanted it. Something direct. . . ."

"Yes. I realize that now. The story you told me — the feeling of hatred and guilt in the air — it's been hanging over me. I wanted to purge it somehow. . . ."

"Yes: I feel something like this too. And Claire, of course. We have to see her through it. God knows how it will turn out."

"What's the plan?"

Willis put his hand into a jacket pocket and produced a snub murderous-looking revolver. "This is what it's all about," he said. "I've got to get it to her. She's on her own till I can complete the arrangements I'm making. She needs protection."

182

"Will she know how to use it?"

"Oh, yes: she knows. I only hope to God she doesn't have to."

"Where do I come in?"

Willis, with the revolver stowed away again, gave the driving closer attention. He spoke with his eyes looking straight ahead, moving faster now as they came into something more like the country.

"The most urgent problem for me is staying out of sight. You can understand that. I've got to be alive elsewhere, if you know what I mean. But I've got to see to Claire as well. I know where she's gone to. The trouble is that Fletcher will know too. I daren't just drive there and hand her the gun. There may be people around. Fletcher has probably got a few goons on hand. What I'm counting on is that he won't want to let them in on this side of his life. But I can't count on it too certainly. And that's where you come in. Between the two of us we can find out. . . ."

"Case the joint, I believe the phrase is. I have to confess that I'm not the most agile of joint-casers. . . ."

Willis smiled. "It will be O.K. You'll be the lookout. I'll do the casing. . . ."

"Whatever the word means."

"We can discuss that on the return journey. Let me tell you the set-up. Claire has a cottage about thirty miles from Boston on the coast, not far from Weymouth. She inherited it from her mother. Often goes there on her own. I rang their Boston apartment a great many times and there was no reply, so I'm sure she's there now. It's an extremely primitive little place. There's no telephone. She shouldn't really be there on her own. If I can get to her now, I may persuade her to go off somewhere else until I'm ready for her: but she's pretty obstinate. If she won't move, at least she'll have a gun."

They were in more open country now — some farms, little villages, a happy radiant countryside, with a smell of the sea in the offing.

"Can I ask you something a little off the immediate track?" Ambrose said. "Why do you think Fletcher did a bunk like this? Do you know if it has anything to do with the gang-war business that's been going on in Boston?"

Willis turned his head momentarily to give Ambrose a sharp look. "Is this what you've turned up in the job Hepworth gave you? Yes, it could be true. He's consumed with ambition. I had a feeling, when I used to see him in London, that he had all kinds of private plans hatching to get his hands on the big money that's floating round. I wondered even if he might not have got in at the political level with some of those enormously rich businessmen — the kind we used to call fascists in the old days." He laughed. "*Fascist.* I don't think I've used the word seriously since those good old days. God! what a lot has happened since then. . . ."

If only one could just talk about these things, Ambrose thought. What a man to talk to. He'd shaken off the past, but could he talk freely? Could anyone really be free after the discipline he had absorbed? If one could talk, this would be the setting. A country drive. Bright sunshine. A few cows, now and then, munching contentedly in rich pastures. A glimpse of ponds here and there. High trees, getting denser, as the car moved on, to form cool inviting woods.

He had turned off the main road now, and was finding a way along narrower lanes, looking at the road signs rather carefully. "I know the ordinary way," he said, "but I'm trying to get near enough indirectly. There's a hill up there. If I can get up to it, we can keep the cottage in view without being seen."

Ambrose nodded. There was nothing more to say until they got closer. The car moved on quietly. A good half-hour passed. Ambrose had been looking back occasionally, and always very carefully at turnings or cross-roads, to see if anyone was showing an interest in them. There was no sign of it.

"We must be getting close now," Willis said finally. "The cottage is called Kilruish, the place her parents came from. It's a little place on the sea in County Clare. That's why they gave her the name. But she spells it with an 'i,' the French way. Seems to suit her, somehow."

Kilruish in County Clare. It made it all so much more personal. One could almost forget the horror.

The car slowed down. They turned off the lane into a small overhung path and got out. "Let's see where this path takes us," Willis said quietly. "I think it's quite near."

They went along the path through a small copse of trees, and coming out on the other side saw the sea. Below them, about a quarter of a mile away, and completely isolated, was a little bungalow with an untidy piece of land around it — unfenced, casual, but inviting.

Looking down, Ambrose could see how the cottage would be approached by car — a winding little road that came from a different direction than the one they had followed.

"Just what I hoped," Willis said. "If we skirt around the trees, we can keep out of sight. You take it from the left: I'll go to the right. The thing to look out for is a hut. If Fletcher has come down here, he might be holed up in something like that."

They moved away as he suggested. Ambrose saw nothing as he walked along. In a few minutes they had joined forces again in a little hollow overgrown with bushes, near the house.

"I've seen nothing," Willis said. "You neither? Well, there's nothing for it. I'm going up close to the back of the cottage to see if she's there, and alone. If she is, I'll go in."

"Where do I wait?"

"Back at the top of the hill. I'll give you a few minutes to get up there so that you can keep an eye on the road. You get a really long view up there. If you see any sign of a car, you'll have to come running down to warn me, if I'm still inside. Knock on the back window and get off back up the hill as fast as you can."

"What if Fletcher is inside without you spotting it?"

"That's a chance I have to take."

Ambrose started back. A few minutes later, puffing and exhausted, he was at the lookout, with the car road below winding away in the distance. Nothing to be seen. Willis was presumably now moving into the cottage.

He settled down to wait. After the strain of the climb, everything had become very peaceful. In the general silence he began to hear sounds to be identified. Was that a car, with the sound getting nearer? A crackling of feet in the undergrowth? The air was full of noises — sharp sounds, whisperings. He listened and waited. Time passed. He heard a car again: it faded away. A plane passed overhead. In the silence after its roar, the birdsong suddenly asserted itself.

How long had he waited? No sign of Willis. Something might have happened, once he was in the house. . . .

Surely it must be half an hour. He had not checked his watch when he had left Willis. He would check it now. Another five minutes and he would go down to the house himself to see what had happened.

The five minutes passed. Five more minutes, he told himself, and then he would go. As he made up his mind, standing on the alert and scanning the countryside below, he saw a tiny black spot on the road in the distance. He watched it for a second. Yes: it was a car going straight to the cottage. He began to run.

All the abstractedness had gone. The smell of danger was overpowering, as when Fletcher had suddenly gripped his arm in the alley the night before. No time now to find his way down quietly. He bumped his way down through the bushes. How long would a car take to get there? How could one tell? He ran on. And now he was down on a flat piece of grass behind the cottage with the back windows in front of him. He banged on the window and heard sudden movement in the house. Instantly he turned back and began to climb.

The ache in his legs was torturing. There was a searing pain in his knees. He drew breath deeply, almost with moaning sounds. Fear drove him on — up, up, pushing away the bushes and branches. And now he heard a sound behind him and turned to see Willis running up. In a minute they were at the top together. Panting, Ambrose pointed down at the road, where the car was now close to the cottage — almost within a few yards, it seemed.

As they watched, the car disappeared from view, blocked out by the cottage, and then, a second later, reappeared, moving along the road away from the house. Without a word, they saw it move on, slowly, steadily, until it had become a speck in the distance.

"Terribly sorry," Ambrose said apologetically. His breath had come back. The ache in his knees had become a rather pleasant tenderness. He felt a total idiot.

Willis laughed. "*Sorry?* It was marvelous. Perfect timing. I did everything I had to do. Come on: let's go."

They made their way back to the car, and for a few minutes, as they drove back along the small lanes, nothing was said. Finally they reached the main road: and now Willis sat back at ease, all the tension gone.

"What's the position there?" Ambrose asked.

"He showed up last night, very late, and behaved in his usual way — wild, threatening. She won't leave though. She says he's in the middle of some big thing. She's sure of it, but doesn't know what it is. He tried to make some plan with her — where to meet him if things go wrong and how to keep in touch. She only half listened. Hasn't the least intention of helping with any of his plans. But she thought she'd be safer if she just appeared to go along with what he wanted."

"Safer? She did feel in danger?"

"Oh, yes. She told me for the first time what had happened before — to his first wife, Gloria. I can see now how it all fits together, with you. But Claire's going to be different."

"Especially with a gun."

"Yes, it was a relief to have it. She felt he might snap, and the gun was a safeguard. Strange to say, she feels a great pity for him. She says it's the ambition that's got into him. Doesn't know where it might be leading."

They were getting closer to town. Clusters of houses and shops were more frequent. The traffic on the road was getting thicker. The engine purred happily, comfortingly. There was a sense of communion between the two men.

Nothing was said for a while. Would he really disappear, Ambrose wondered. Can one disappear, start afresh. . . . But one isn't starting afresh. One has all the memories. . . .

"I was thinking of Gloria," Willis said. "I was sad to hear how it happened. You must have liked her very much."

"Yes, I did." He sat back in the seat, closed his eyes drowsily.

There was silence for a time: then he bestirred himself and looked at his watch. It was seven-fifteen. By the time they were back it would be at least eight: too late to go to Olaf's. By this time he and Alyss would be on their way to the Boston Fed — assuming, of course, that Olaf had returned safely from the Harrigan fortress. One felt that he had, somehow, and with the right result.

Well, he could entertain himself for an evening alone. If he was bored there was always Angsthofer and his new edition.

Willis had spotted a taxi ahead of them. "Have you enough cash on you to get back?" he asked. "I'll go ahead of it and drop you."

Ambrose nodded: "Shall I hear from you?"

"From Swinburne. But only if I have to."

Had a barrier gone up again? There was a slight feeling of it. As Ambrose got out, Willis turned his car swiftly and disappeared.

But in the taxi, the good feeling surfaced again. Was it their brief word about Gloria? The lines he had remembered murmured in his head. "*She had a heart . . . how shall I say? Too soon made glad. . . .*" God, how sleepy he was. But by the time the cab completed the journey, he felt restored.

XI

AT the hotel there was a small pile of messages.

Olaf had rung. One might have assumed that he would be in high dudgeon that Ambrose hadn't shown up for the meeting at six-thirty, but his dudgeon didn't seem all that high. "Sorry to miss you," the message ran, in a rather casual tone. "Come to breakfast tomorrow. I will send a car at eight-thirty."

Mr. Rafferty had called. "Would Mr. Usher telephone when he returns?"

There were messages from two university people, each an invitation to lunch on Thursday, the day of his last lecture. Nice little problem to solve here. Should he accept A, or B, or neither, or get them to join forces?

He went up to his room to restore himself with a glass of whisky.

Angsthofer — *wieder ausgelegt und verbessert* — was nestling by the telephone, pleading to be picked up, but Ambrose ignored him and rang Rafferty at the *Mail*. He was not there but had left a message with one of his assistants. "Bill said that if you rang would you like to join them for dinner? They're going with some friends to a little Italian place called Mario's, just off the Common."

"I know the place," Ambrose said, somewhat primly. "I will join them."

No point in being irritated. Well, he *was* irritated. He had enjoyed it here with Alyss. He could have brought her here again. Why had she run off with Olaf to a party of boring bankers and their undoubtedly dreary wives. Why? Because Olaf had to put up with it in line of duty, and she was helping him out. That's all it was. No other significance. Groping his

189

way through the candlelit gloom, he was greeted by cries of welcome from the Rafferty table and settled down to enjoy himself.

The guests were an English husband and wife team from the University of Wessex on sabbatical leave for a year, supported by a large grant from an American Foundation, to write a book on the social anthropology of gangsters. Looking round for a subject, they had found, to their astonishment, that no one had ever done it before. The huge army of American academics had overlooked a glorious subject lying right under their noses, and were still scratching round for grants to deal with nineteenth-century Wesleyans or Australian aborigines. Thank God for British enterprise, Ambrose thought. We might have lost India, but the ancient British spirit of adventure was still alive.

Armed with an introduction to Rafferty from a mutual friend, they had just flown in hurriedly from Las Vegas, where their main operation had been centered. Friends had told them that a classic gangster exercise was under way in Boston, and they had decided to switch locales. Vegas was relatively dull. Now, if there were a straight nationality struggle — say Italian gangsters versus Irish, or Jews versus Greeks — there would be something to get hold of: but the picture was too murky for that.

Their eagerness to understand was praiseworthy, but Ambrose, listening to their questions to Rafferty, wondered at a certain brashness which he could not fail to detect. "Do you think the manager would mind if I asked him a few questions about what kind of protection racket they pay to?" the husband said. "After all, Boston is Irish and they're Italian."

"I'd like to set up some sessions with the hat-check girl," the wife said. "I wonder if there's a characteristic pattern of home influences."

Ambrose caught Kathleen Rafferty's eye giving him a friendly wink. Well, it was all in a good cause. He allowed his glass to be re-charged with a quite reasonable Valpolicella, and addressed himself to the *piccata alla Senese*. It had seemed the right dish to choose, in loyalty, as it were, to Alyss.

From time to time, stimulated by the wine, his mind strayed off to a thread in Angsthofer's argument that he had found absorbing. He was joining in the talk freely enough, but the fourth lecture was still to be faced. There was something rather dark in Angsthofer that had stimulated him.

It was at ten-twenty that a waiter came over to say that Mr. Rafferty was wanted on the telephone. He went off, and returned in a minute to say that he'd have to go, and perhaps they'd like to come back to the office too when they'd finished their dinner.

"The reports are just coming in" he said. "Tit for tat. Bodies in all directions."

"Four killings?" Ambrose asked.

"Three so far," Bill said, "but the night is young. See you later."

This was the way to enjoy the news: in a huge press room — with a ringing of bells, a clatter of teleprinters, a moving-around of reporters and messengers and typists, and above all a *smell*. What was it? Ink, coffee, sweat, detergent, pizza, hot-dogs, and smoke — the wreathing clouds of it from cigarettes, pipes and cigars. Yet there was a sense of order about it all. Everyone knew his job and went about it calmly, complicated though it all was.

Four nights earlier, it must have been less confusing, since there was one locale, in downtown Boston, and four bodies lying all together on the floor for consideration. This time the gangsters had let themselves loose on a State-wide scale. Not a single body in Boston itself. The first had shown up, at the witching hour of ten, in a night-club just out of Gloucester. A few minutes later, the second appeared in Springfield. The third man, closer in, had been dealt with at his home near Lexington. The news editor had been sending out reporters, photographers and cars in all directions. Not that he minded the effort. It was a long time since they had had such a marvelous story.

The English couple were on duty with great seriousness, running round from table to table, notebooks open to record red-hot sociological material. In the intervals they were pep-pering Rafferty with questions on backgrounds, precedents, parallels.

Rafferty, once he had heard the names, was quite definite on the victims. "All high-up McLuskey men," he said. "This is what we were expecting."

"But no McLuskey?" Ambrose asked.

"Not yet. In fact, it doesn't follow that he'll be included. For one thing he knows how to protect himself. And then there's often a kind of respect between the very top men. Our sociological friends will probably be able to explain it in due course."

"And only three so far?"

"Doesn't have to be four. But I agree. One might expect it. Still, there's time yet."

Ambrose sat around for more than an hour, drinking coffee and marveling at the steadiness of purpose that was getting the paper together. By eleven-thirty, he felt he had had enough. There was to be a car, early next morning, for breakfast with Olaf. He went back to his hotel for a good night's sleep.

On the radio next morning the number of victims was still three. No use speculating.

Emerging from the hotel at eight-thirty, he was gratified to see the Rolls waiting, but rather miffed to be told by the driver, on being asked, that they were not picking up Miss Summers. Of course: she already knew what had gone on at Harrigan's. She was being allowed to sleep in after a wild night with the Massachusetts Fed. All the same. . . .

The one place left in the world where kedgeree is still served for breakfast is (probably) the Consul-General's house in Boston. This was to be a very English day.

"I'm sorry I didn't show up last night," he said to Olaf. "I got carried away — literally — with something else I was engaged on."

"I was a bit surprised," Olaf said, "but I expect there are a lot of other things going on. You do seem abstracted from time to time. But tell me something. You've seen the papers about the gangster killings. What I can't understand is that this is all supposed to be Harrigan. You told me so yourself. Well, how could he have arranged this massacre for yesterday evening and sit talking to me just before, for an hour and a half, about Bellini and Donatello?"

"You talked as planned?"

"I've never in my life had such an experience. Come to think of it, I *do* see how he could have a few practical jobs arranged for later and spend the time before on his works of art. It's exactly how the Renaissance princes must have operated: and if there's one man who's a Renaissance prince it's Harrigan."

"How far did you get with him?"

"Just as far as I intended. I worked out the strategy in more detail after you left yesterday morning for your lecture. Why do you have to give these lectures? I assure you this is all much more fun. Still, I had Alyss to talk to. Splendid woman, is she not?"

"She is indeed."

"What was so helpful was that she had time to tell me the story in full detail."

"Including our adventure the other evening?"

"Everything." He burst into a roar of laughter. "What wouldn't I have given to see you in the ditch! And that saved everything. God, you really have the devil's own luck."

"'*The shot of accident could neither graze nor pierce . . .*'"

"Well, let's hope your luck holds, because we'll need it in large quantity if my little plan is going to work. I tell you who else I met yesterday: the electronic Tim. What a delightful young man. Really, Ambrose, you seem to bump into the nicest people."

"Well, that's why the abominable Hepworth roped me in. He said things would happen. . . ."

"The shot of accident. . . ."

"That's about it. But we're going too fast. What's the new strategy?"

"Yes, the new strategy. I hope you won't mind. You're in the middle of it. You're coming out with me to Schloss Harrigan today."

"*What?*"

"That's it. A little excursion. Don't tell me you've got to deliver a lecture."

"No. My lecture's tomorrow, and it's the last one, thank goodness."

"Well, that's fine. I've set things up to go back there today accompanied, if you please, by two experts, so-called. You're one: and the other is someone you probably don't know. He just happens to be here and he's exactly right. Alistair Scott, *Colonel* Alistair Scott, I should say, of the Scots Guards."

Ambrose looked at Olaf in some astonishment. "I know that the *band* of the Scots Guards have been here for British Trade Week. The Consul-General told me. Is he a *music* colonel?"

"I doubt if he could even play the triangle. No, he came along with the Band for the ride. The RAF flew them all over in a special plane. They're going back on Friday. I may go with them, in fact. Imagine being up there in the stratosphere with haggis and bagpipes. Wouldn't you like to come?"

Ambrose groaned. "Kedgeree today, haggis tomorrow. No, I'll spare myself. Could I tempt you to go back to a more elemental question? What am I supposed to be an expert on when I accompany you to Schloss Harrigan? And Colonel Scott for that matter. Surely not the paintings."

Olaf settled down. He had had his fun. "I suppose you want me to start at the beginning. Always a dreary process. Let me tell you, instead, about Alistair. He comes from my part of Scotland. I've known him since he was a young man, and I saw him in operation in Italy during the War. He's rather a legend in the Service. Very active, first, in Long-Range Desert Group — and that's his style. Commando stuff. Knows all about bombs and one-man raids. Very dashing. Great improviser. And on top of that" — he chuckled — "he happens to know quite a bit about painting. He stays with Robbie Tulloch when he goes back to Scotland, and knows all about the Bellini. I had to take him into our confidence, of course, on the project in general. Very excited about the whole thing. Wants to help."

"But we're not going along as painting experts?"

"No: as improvisers. You're both good at it in different ways. So I said I would bring along two experts with me, and Harrigan agreed."

"You mean he accepted all your proposals?"

"Oh, no. I'm not even sure yet how firmly I've got to first base. The odds are that he'll turn the whole thing down today. I'm just planning things now for the next phase if we find ourselves blocked. It's all a game of backgammon, really. Yesterday's visit was the opening phase. Now we're in the middle game. And that's where one has to think ahead. I'm setting things up for the final assault later. Let me tell you what happened."

Breakfast had been cleared away. They moved over to a couple of armchairs.

"The first thing, of course, was to make sure that Harrigan was going to accept me in the proper spirit. He did. We should have guessed. *The Bellini:* he knew all about it instantly! Alyss *said* he'd tried to see every painting of the Baptist. He'd seen the picture of this one in Berenson. When I appeared with the message that I knew where it was, I was accepted immediately. I was on his wave-length. He was desperate to know more."

"Yes, we should have guessed."

Olaf bent forward. "I must say: the way Alyss described his obsession is absolutely right. If I'd just met him, I doubt if I would have tumbled to it: but once she'd expounded it, it rang completely true. When you see him on the spot, you believe every word. The long tapestry at the end of his gallery: I could just visualize the chapel behind it — the Donatello, the relic — everything."

"But you didn't see into it?"

"Not at all. That's for today — if we're lucky. Yesterday, I just had to set things up: and we began, of course, with the Bellini. It was a very good idea of yours to have the little picture in Berenson enlarged. He was rivetted by it. And to know that I'd seen the original! He asked me every kind of question about the way it was painted, the color, and above all what you might call 'the meaning.' What did I think the Baptist was really like as a man? What happened between him and Jesus? And all in that faint whispering Irish voice. Marvelous."

"He showed you his own collection?"

"He showed me the Pinturicchio that he's consulted Alyss about, and a great many other things. I agree with her about the Pinturicchio: a fake. As it happens, I was shown a rather mysterious Pinturicchio by the Director of the Mellon Gallery when I was in Washington. I didn't think it rang true, and I don't think the Director did, either. It's better than Harrigan's, but they could be by the same man. These modern imitators are very good. I was polite about it. He just went on talking — on and on. I was looking very pointedly at the tapestry at the end of the gallery, but he made no reference to it. Just talked."

"Did he press you on how he could get the Bellini?"

"Not a bit: and that's how I knew I was dealing with a prince. Once he'd satisfied himself that it was genuine — and he got that out of studying me personally — he dropped the subject. He seemed to know that if he was going to get it, it was going to be part of a big proposition. He knew my position in the Treasury. He may have thought that my visit really had some reference to the TCC bid, but that wouldn't really have brought me there. So he waited for me to speak.

"He'd given me till six. Around five-thirty, I plunged in. I said I also had a business proposition to discuss. He nodded. He'd expected it. I told him about my gold mines in Colorado and the copper mines in Norway. Then I mentioned his uranium option. He just sat there listening, saying nothing."

"No questions about the mines — I mean business questions?"

"Hardly any. It was as if all that would be left to underlings — or experts. But he knew all about it, because he did ask one question, and in fact a very good one. I don't know if I told you that out in Colorado, about fifty miles from the old gold workings, there are also a lot of derelict *silver* mines. I knew about them because they belong to a cousin of my backgammon pal out there. I got the distinct impression that one of Harrigan's companies might have been scouting around out there and become interested in them. But he didn't press me when I said I didn't know much about them."

"And then time was up?"

"Exactly. I had told him what I had in mind. The Bellini was what gripped him. It was quite clear to him that I could deliver. He sat for a moment or two just thinking, saying nothing. That was the bad moment for me. If he just said no, it would be all over — no uranium mines, and no chance to open up the next phase of the backgammon board, on the Donatello. I waited. He looked at his watch and said: 'Come back tomorrow at seven o'clock.' Then he gave me a very dry look and added: 'Unless, of course, you have to leave for England.' I said: 'I'll be here tomorrow at seven'. Then I had an inspiration.

"*He'd given way:* and I realized that this was the moment to push him — to test him, as it were. I said: 'When I come tomorrow, I want to bring two experts with me on mining economics, one on gold, the other on copper. Perhaps you could have someone here on uranium'. It was a good ploy, and he bought it. Just nodded."

"And Scott and I are the two experts? A leap into the void. I'm beginning to understand why you won the backgammon match. Just a question of nerve. What about a Donatello expert, in the shape of Alyss?"

Olaf smiled. "She made the same suggestion when I told her all this. She's dying to get in there. But, of course, that's just what we can't do. He knows she's been asking questions in Siena, so it would tip him off. He doesn't know yet that we know all about that part of the story, and I've no idea how we're going to lead him into it. That's why I need a couple of improvisers with me this time. We've got to crack him on the chapel. Somehow or other we've got to get in there: and if we can't this time, we've got to be laying the ground for a different approach later. As far as Harrigan is concerned, though, you're mining economists."

"Can I choose between gold and copper, like the casket scene in *The Merchant of Venice*?"

"You're to be gold. Alistair is copper. And don't tell me you don't know the first thing about it. Alistair doesn't either. But there's no problem. All you need is some of the patter, in case he puts a question to you. I remembered yesterday evening that the *Financial Times* had one of those big supplements a couple of months ago on metal mining developments, dealing especially with the new factor of steeply rising prices. I got one of the consuls to dig it out from their newspaper files. The article on copper is very good, and I gave it to Alistair to study last night. The article on gold's in the study, waiting for *you*. I don't imagine for a moment that Harrigan will really ask any questions of you, but it's good to be prepared. So there we are. We assemble here for briefing at five-thirty. Alyss is coming too: and Tim. There will be champagne to get us into the right mood."

"Where does Tim fit into the strategy?"

Olaf took on a very pleased expression. "Ah, this is where improvisation is taken to a new dimension — via electronics. You know about Tim's expertize in this. Alistair is a whiz at it, too. These tiny radio devices. He knows all about them from the War. We may need to communicate outside, once we're in there. I'd like Tim to be waiting close by. I put Alistair in touch with Tim yesterday through Alyss, and they spent the evening together. Got on like a house on fire."

To communicate outside? What on earth was Olaf hatching? Ambrose looked at him, this elegant little troll with his bright blue eyes, sitting back in his chair happily. Surely they weren't going to repeat the same adventure. . . .

"You're a little ahead of me," he said cautiously. "I can't quite see why Tim. . . ."

Olaf seemed to become a little more serious. "I think you *do* see," he said, "and you don't like it. I don't like it either. I can't quite decide how it adds up morally if we're pushed into it. That's *your* department really. Can there be a balancing-out of moral judgments? How high do we rate obedience to the law? Does something absolutely desirable wash out a legal infringement?"

Ambrose sat there wondering where this was leading. "Is this a problem for tonight?" he finally ventured.

"Oh, no. There's no moral problem tonight. Just a little harmless deception. I'm thinking of what might have to follow. If we get nowhere tonight, are we going to let him hold on to the Donatello? No, we're not. It's absolutely wrong for him to have taken it away from where it belongs. It's a crime against history — sacrilege. I'm entirely with Alyss on this: and you are, too — you *must* be, or you wouldn't have got involved in the first place. Well, are we to go in there, somehow, and lift it? We could do it. It would be child's play for Alistair, with Tim to help him. But that's ruled out morally. However, what we *could* do, as a step towards what we want, is to stage a sort of demonstration, a kind of Dieppe raid. You remember Dieppe, the first major Commando raid. The aim wasn't to accomplish something decisive in itself — to establish a foothold on the Continent and hold on to it. It was to get the facts on the spot, to find out the real disposition of the enemy, and above all to score a *psychological* blow. Well, this is rather how I see our position now. With Alistair coming with me tonight, he'll have a great chance to find out how things stand. Tim will be hidden outside. At some point, Alistair may want Tim to come into the grounds — to start a diversion, or something like that, so that he can have a real look. If he wants this, he'll be able to communicate. Tim's fitting him out with the right kind of radio equipment. God knows how these things work, but luckily *they* know, too."

"How will this achieve a psychological blow?"

"The aim will be to work out a way of getting into the house later, *even with Harrigan in occupation*. If they go through with this, they could make it clear to Harrigan that they've been there, with a warning built-in. Suppose, for example, they took the Donatello from its niche in the chapel and put it in the main gallery, with a card in front of it saying that it must be sent back to its true home in Siena. Can you imagine the effect on Harrigan? He would almost be ready to believe that the Baptist himself was telling him to do it. Of course, he'd know that it had been done humanly, but he'd read more into it. And I think he'd act."

Ambrose gazed at Olaf with mounting awe. "I have one question only," he said. "Why can't you handle the pound with this kind of *panache?* We'd have a currency that would make the *Deutschmark* look an Argentine *peso*."

"Everything in its own style," Olaf said comfortably. "After all, I do have a Treasury interest in the main proceedings for tonight. You're not forgetting the uranium mines, I hope."

"I had rather forgotten it for the moment. Very remiss of me."

"It's the same thing really. One looks ahead. I sacrifice a couple of positions on the board — the copper and gold, highly speculative — for the sake of coming round into the home stretch with the ground ready for what I really want."

"The uranium option's a bit speculative too, isn't it?"

"Oh, yes: there's always a risk: but I've plonked for it."

"We really *are* back in the casket scene," Ambrose said. "You're like Bassanio, spurning gold and silver because he's

198

hooked on lead. '*But thou, thou meagre lead, thy plainness moves me more than eloquence.*'"

"It's a gamble. I like gambling."

"Yes, that's what the motto said on the lead casket: '*Who chooses me must give and hazard all he hath.*'"

"So I'm Bassanio. I rather like that."

"And we all know who Portia is," Ambrose said lightly, without considering the implications. "'*Let us all ring fancy's knell.*' Which reminds me: I must ring her up to see if she's free for lunch."

"Sound move," Olaf said with mock seriousness. "There's a phone in that study."

Ambrose felt a slight unease as he began to dial. Bassanio and Portia . . . '*Tell me where is fancy bred*' . . . But her cheerful hello, as she answered the phone, sounded reassuring. Of course, lunch. She had waited for it. She had counted on it, and this time it was *her* turn to be the host. He protested. He agreed.

There was a knock at the door. The car had come to take Olaf to the Consulate to deal with telegrams from London.

Ambrose, sitting back in his taxi, could still hear the *Merchant of Venice* song in the air. '*Or in the heart, or in the head*' . . . How was one to tell with a troll — or with a philosopher, for that matter?

He had been faintly aware, even before he had telephoned, that there was something unusual he would have to ask of her. The idea had probably begun to work its way into his mind as soon as it had been established that she would not be accompanying the party to Harrigan's. Now, as he looked at her across the table, it was clear to him that he should ask her and that she would do it.

When he had asked her where they were to meet, she had given him the address and said that it would include a surprise for him. It *was* a surprise, though not quite in the way she had envisaged. Having discovered that he was a Serb in origin, she had gone to some trouble to track down a restaurant that someone had told her was Yugoslav — *Rashka's*. It turned out to have been taken over, like everything else, and was now firmly Rumanian. But Ambrose was touched by her effort: and the Rumanian aura was near enough in tone. A glass of *tzuica* to start (only *slivovitz*, really), *miel be spanac* (any good peasant knows how to cook lamb on spinach), and a rough *cotnari* to wash it down. All was well. They might have been lunching at Split.

For most of the time they spoke of Olaf and his plans. He is so droll, she said: and yet he was taking it all forward with such clarity. Tim was delighted to be back in the picture, very pleased at the contact with Scott. She was going to find it very hard to sit at home waiting for the outcome. . . .

"I don't want you to sit at home," Ambrose said. "There's another angle to all this that I'm concerned with. It hasn't anything to do with the chapel or the Donatello, so I haven't spoken of it; but I'm worried about it and I need your help."

"Of course." Her eyes had been sparkling, but now she was immediately serious.

"There's a peculiar thing I've been involved in," he said. "It's grown up round me while I've been here, though it reaches back to something in my past. I won't bore you with the details, but the immediate point is that someone I know may be in danger. I was busy with this yesterday afternoon: in fact, that's why I didn't show up at Olaf's at six-thirty. I was out of town on this business with a man who's being very helpful. He told me that he may ring me up if something more is needed, and that's what's troubling me. He may ring while I'm out with the party at Harrigan's."

"One has no idea how long it will last."

"Exactly. Harrigan's given Olaf an evening appointment. He's letting him bring two allies. Maybe he plans to offer us food. One will have to sit it out. And in the meantime this man may telephone me — perhaps just to tell me what's going on. I wouldn't want to miss his call."

"You want me to wait in your hotel room?"

"Will you?"

"Of course."

Ambrose took a sip of *cotnari*. Now came the hard part.

"No great burden to answer the phone, is it?" He sighed. "Well, I'm afraid it's just a tiny bit more complicated. This is where my past is catching up with me. Have you ever heard — has the whisper of rumor ever reached you — that I've occasionally been mixed up in what I might call 'confidential' work?"

"*Rumor?*" She burst into laughter. "As far as Harvard is concerned it's the only firm thing people say about you. No: there are *two* things people know. I found out as soon as I started asking about you."

"*Asking about me?*"

She stretched a hand across the table to lay it on his,

affectionately. "Well, you surely don't believe I take you for granted now that we're friends. I want to know all about you. I think I know *some* things, but I want to know everything. What people say is part of the picture: but, of course" — she smiled, very tenderly — "only part."

Ambrose affected a grunt, but gave her hand an answering squeeze before she took it away. "O.K. Two things. What's the other?"

"I asked a friend. He said you were a mystery man. Only two things known. One was that behind the professorial front you were really a super-intellectual member of the British equivalent of the CIA. The other was that you had discovered a hitherto unknown Swiss philosopher called Pastor Noelscher about whom you never stopped talking. But the general view was that these two things were inter-related. No one was really quite sure if Noelscher had ever existed. The idea was that you might have invented him as part of the cover-story."

"My God. *I have lost my reputation, and what remains is bestial.* How can you bear me?"

"I can bear you. But, you see, I'm well prepared for mystery. What about the telephone call?"

"Yes. The telephone call." This time his groan was genuine. "I'm afraid you're going to believe all the stories when I tell you there's a code."

"A *code!* Marvelous! The caller will announce himself as Pastor Noelscher."

Ambrose looked at her with admiration. "I'm beginning to believe in woman's instinct. You're almost right. Not Noelscher. Swinburne."

She burst into a peal of laughter. "You mean Algernon Charles? '*When the hounds of spring are on winter's traces*'? Oh, Ambrose! I really love you. But how am I going to be able to keep up with you?"

"You seem to be managing well enough. I can see we'll have to recruit you. Well, I *am* recruiting you."

She had recovered. "Sorry. It *is* funny. But I know it's really serious. Tell me."

"Yes, it's very serious. This man is very much under cover. When he wants to talk to me, he rings me up and just says 'It's Swinburne.' By arrangement I then go out to two call-boxes just outside the hotel, and he rings me there — the nearest one first, and the second if the first is engaged. If he rings while you're there, you'll have to tell him immediately that you'll take a message at the agreed place, and go down to the call-boxes."

"May he not be suspicious?"

"Yes, he may. You'd better be ready to recite a line. Not '*the hounds of spring.*' Say: '*impelled of invisible tides.*' It's a line he's quoted to me. He'll know you're genuine."

She looked at him, her eyes dancing. "Is this supposed to be a labor? It's entrancing."

"Well, it may just be a great bore. You may have to sit there for hours, just waiting. You'd better take along something to read. The only thing I have in my room is a huge volume in German by a philosopher called Angsthofer."

"Not Noelscher?"

"I thought we'd agreed that Noelscher doesn't exist."

"Oh, that's just what your rivals say. Aren't you always surprised when you happen to hear what people say about you behind your back?"

"This time I'm delighted. What one wants to hear is total confusion. I'd be very worried if they stumbled on the real truth."

"So there *is* a mystery about you. Give me a clue."

"I've already given it. The other half of the code. '*Fulfilled of unspeakable things.*' Especially about you."

"Spell them out one day."

"I will."

The waiter was hovering over them. "Time to go," Ambrose said. "I've got to try and absorb the article on gold-mining that Olaf has foisted on me."

"You poor man. Well, my contribution is the lunch. No argument. The bill's for me. Champagne at Olaf's at five-thirty. And don't forget to bring the key of your hotel room."

Outside it was raining rather heavily. "Not another Hurricane Hilda, I hope," Ambrose said, looking up at the sky in some alarm. "Perhaps Providence doesn't approve of my visiting Schloss Harrigan."

"There'll be no falling into a ditch this time," Alyss said. "Something else equally funny. I have a hunch about it. Woman's instinct. Remember?"

He got into her car for a lift to Park Street, where he took the train back to Harvard. It was still raining. He didn't like it. It seemed like an omen.

By five-thirty, Providence had changed signals. The rain had cleared completely, though there was a spasmodic rumbling of thunder, and flashes of lightning, to give a little tone to the weather.

The mood in the Consul-General's house took its tone from Olaf. Starting off on the right foot, he had sent not the Mini but the Rolls to transport Ambrose to the rendezvous. Alyss and Tim were already there when he arrived, and the champagne was flowing freely. Alistair Scott was due any minute. "You will like him," Olaf said.

Ambrose had put on his most "respectable" suit to fit the occasion. Olaf, he saw with some amusement, had carried this a stage further. There was to be no attempt, as in the Treasury, to brighten up the Harrigan scene with subtle color. He wore a black suit, beautifully tailored, with a dazzlingly white shirt and a quiet gray tie. However, the effect was formal rather than funereal because of a thin silk piping that sealed his lapels. Perhaps it was a suit for calling at the White House during his Washington visit. It was certainly perfect for Harrigan. A carefully folded white handkerchief peeped from his breast-pocket — with nothing foppish at his wrist.

There was a ring at the door, and Scott came in. He looked at Ambrose and stopped, with an air of amused surprise. Ambrose looked at him — a trim figure, a suit of English tweed, a thin pencil of a military moustache — and could hardly get the words out in greeting. "My rescuer!" he finally said.

"You two know each other?" Olaf asked.

"Not by name," Ambrose said. "He merely saved me from a fate worse than death."

"How splendid to meet you," Scott said, shaking Ambrose warmly by the hand. "I wondered what all that business was about. Didn't seem like plain mugging. Fogg Museum: wrong place, somehow. Besides, the getaway car. . . ."

Olaf was looking on happily as if he was never really surprised to turn up two useful and compatible numbers when he threw his pair of backgammon dice. Ambrose tried a short explanation.

"I was set upon outside the Fogg Museum the other day by a thug of evil design. The Colonel emerged, threw the man over his head, and walked off flicking the dust from his sleeve. I can see now why. A little Commando exercise."

Alyss said rather wryly to Scott: "What a lucky coincidence that you were there."

Ambrose shook his head vigorously. "No coincidence. Usher's Law at work. Small world. Common interests. Took us both to the Fogg: brought us both here. Totally predictable, *sub specie aeternitatis.*"

Olaf seemed to agree. "Well, that rounds up everything very nicely. I think we ought to go. I take it that you two experts have boned up on your mining information. What do you know about gold, Ambrose?"

"I can recite a great array of figures, which I propose to forget by tomorrow morning. Privately, I'm sticking to *The Merchant:* '*All that glisters is not gold.*' Of course, I won't tell Harrigan that."

The Colonel took a different view of *his* role. "That article you gave me was fascinating," he said to Olaf. "As soon as this is all over, I'm going to go prospecting for copper in the Yukon. It's quite clear that that's where the next big strike is going to take place. You're quite right, by the way, to give up the Norway mines. I've only been an expert for twenty-four hours, but I can tell you that with the greatest assurance."

"And what have you worked out with Tim?"

"No need to bother you with the details. Tim and I have a few ideas. We'll play it by ear. And I've brought along a little present for Tim that I collected this morning at the Armory. We gave a little Military Tattoo there during British Trade Week. I remembered something we used. Perhaps I could ride out with Tim in his car and go over it all with him."

Outside, Alyss climbed into her little Alfa-Romeo. Ambrose leaned through the window to give her the key of his room. "I don't think he'll ring," he said, "but I do feel rather reassured with you there."

"Nothing to it. Delighted. I've got the new Iris Murdoch which I've been saving up to read. And if I find time hanging on my hands, look what else I've found."

She picked up a slim volume lying on the seat beside her. "I tracked it down in the Public Library this afternoon." The lettering on the cover was very sparse. "*Memory: Ambrose Usher.*" She turned the ignition key: the engine roared and she was off.

Ambrose stood watching for a second. '*Or in the heart, or in the head. . . .*' He felt rather pleased.

Tim and Alistair led the way. In the Rolls, Olaf told Ambrose about some of the pictures he owned and the family stories behind them. Ambrose spoke in turn about a visit he had paid once to Berenson at *I Tatti.* The talk was gentle, rambling, unforced — "*Anecdotes of Painting*" . . . As they drove, the light was fading, with promise of a fine sunset, though still with thunder in the air.

The windows were open to the special flavor of the evening — the hint of turbulence signaled by an occasional flash and a deep growl which followed. The built-up areas were now far behind. They were in quiet country roads, with no traffic.

Tim's car stopped. The Rolls drew up behind. Tim came over with Alistair for a final word.

"We're just a mile away," he said. "I'll let you go ahead now. I'll be outside once you're safely in. You remember where I'll be, Ambrose?"

"No mud: this time," Ambrose muttered.

"No mud: no mudlarks. I'll just be waiting."

With Alistair aboard, the Rolls moved on quietly. By the time they reached the high ornamental gates — firmly closed — it had become almost dark. The chauffeur sounded the horn. Two men emerged, came over to look into the car, and without a word went back to swing the gates open. As they drove through, Ambrose, looking back, saw the gates being firmly closed.

The driveway, winding through the sighing trees, was unexpectedly long. The house, looming up before him, looked huge and threatening as they got out. After the crunch of the gravel, and then the noise of car doors being closed, a deep silence was suddenly manifest.

The massive door swung open. Two more men stood there in the brightly-lit hall. The visitors moved in, following one of the men into a good-sized room, filled with pictures, where, it was clear, they were to wait.

"I didn't see this room," Olaf said. "Let's have a look."

The picture nearest them was very brown and rather dead in tone — a shepherd standing in a wild rocky landscape that might have been Palestine, with a mysterious aura of light surrounding his head. The signature was unknown to them — George Francis Watson. "School of Holman Hunt," Olaf murmured.

The man had reappeared to take them in. A short corridor, and they were in the gallery. Ambrose gasped. Despite all he had heard in advance, it was astonishing — the vast area, the height, the feeling of being in a great Renaissance *palazzo*. In the center, almost with an air of being spotlighted, was Harrigan, a small wizened figure in a wheel-chair. He had a shawl round his shoulders, and a goon towered over him in protection. Behind,

Ambrose saw in the distance the long tapestry-covered wall. The chapel. He felt its presence.

Olaf, advancing, was the soul of dignity and respect. These two tiny men. Was this their bond?

They took their seats. The audience began. Olaf murmured their names — Mr. Scott, Mr. Usher — in introduction. Harrigan nodded slightly. It was Olaf he was concerned with. When he spoke, it was in a faint wheezy voice, with a noticeable Irish tang.

"I am sorry to have to receive you this way," he said, gesturing to his chair. "I am not very well today. And I have been very busy with many tiring things. But what we have to discuss is more important. Let me deal with it directly."

Olaf nodded. Harrigan was silent for a moment. Then he said: "I will tell you immediately that your business proposition is unacceptable as it stands. We might proceed with a part of it — not on the terms you suggested. But this is not urgent. What I wish to talk of is the Bellini painting of St. John. I have a proposal which I want you to put to your friend when you return to England."

He seemed to need to pause to get his strength together. He was clearly in bad shape. Was it merely the gang-war or was he failing?

"I have spoken on the telephone today to a friend in Italy who is an expert in this field. I have satisfied myself that the picture is likely to be authentic. I wish to have it. I will buy it from your friend. I know there are difficulties in the export of such pictures. That will be no problem. We will arrange it privately. That will also dispose of the question of tax. I am thinking of death duty. Do you wish me to talk freely before your two friends here or would you rather we spoke alone?"

"My friends are entirely in my confidence," Olaf said. "Please tell me what you have in mind."

"Very well," Harrigan said. "The value I put on the painting is hard to fix, but I'm ready to pay a million dollars. I will make this sum available to your friend in cash anywhere he wants in the world, and in any currency. I will arrange for the picture to be brought here with no problem — and, of course, with no publicity. I will trust you completely as the agent."

Olaf replied slowly and softly, as if adjusting to the atmosphere. "I will be as direct as you," he said. "For a number of reasons, it is out of the question to sell the picture. What I am prepared to do is to have it sent to you on loan. But for this, I

206

need your agreement to my business proposals. Will you tell me why you are not interested in them?"

The goon stood silent and immobile, towering over the small figure in the invalid chair. Ambrose and Alistair were equally irrelevant. The two principals were all that mattered. It was as if they were circling each other in a ring, like Sumo wrestlers, moving slowly, warily, until one of them saw how he could pounce.

"Your business proposals are unacceptable because I am not a gambler. I need to know what I am buying or selling. I have made inquiries on this, too, during the day. Your experts here will know what I am saying. The old copper mines in Norway would be a pure gamble and a very bad one. The gold workings in Colorado are of *some* interest, although in fact" — he seemed to manage a faint smile — "there are some old silver workings about fifty miles away which have more possibilities. However, I might be interested in the gold workings as a straight purchase from you if we could also arrange another matter in which you have some influence. I mean the offer to take over one of your big engineering companies in England by a company I am interested in — TCC. You have perhaps been thinking of this too?"

"I have, yes. Your Mr. Fletcher has been over in England."

A faint shadow seemed to cross Harrigan's face. "He is no longer handling it. I am sending another representative over."

Olaf let this pass. "If I understand you," he said, "you want the TCC takeover as part of the arrangement. And your uranium option in South-west Africa? Are you suggesting that this, too, might be suitable for a straight purchase by us?"

"I might consider it. I see some difficulties in my companies receiving permission to work the uranium. You have perhaps had this in mind?"

"That was the basis of my overall proposal. An exchange, I suggested, would fit all our needs. I am prepared to consider the TCC aspect. But there can be no sale of the Bellini painting. It can only be lent. I can send it on loan with no delay at all."

Harrigan seemed to shrink back into his chair. "We are back where we started. The one central thing is that I must *own* the Bellini. I will buy it. If that is impossible, this discussion can end."

His voice was quiet, almost faint, but there was an absolute finality in it. Listening, Ambrose could sense the passion that made ownership the criterion for this man. The Baptist could not be *lent* to him: it must be part of him. Behind the tapestry there was the symbol of how far this could take him — *the Donatello*. It was eerie to be aware of this passion. Alyss had felt it intuitively.

Olaf clearly sensed the finality too. It was unmistakeable. He said nothing — apparently thinking — and then rose to his feet. Alistair and Ambrose stood up too. The goon put his hands on the back of Harrigan's wheelchair. There was silence for a moment, and then, shattering the silence, the sound of a shot.

The goon took his hands off the wheelchair and whipped out a revolver. From the hall outside they heard shouting and then three more shots, not as a fusillade but separately.

Harrigan's man had rushed to the door, his revolver at the ready. As he reached it, it was flung back, knocking the gun out of his hand. George Fletcher stood there, with three men behind him, all holding shot-guns — stubby, murderous.

One of them covered the servant. The other two came in behind Fletcher. Harrigan sat in his wheelchair immobile.

Fletcher seemed for the moment almost to ignore him. "Tie them all up," he said to one of the men. The servant was prodded into the center of the room next to Olaf and the others. One of the men had handed over his gun to a comrade and gone outside. He returned with a copious supply of rope. Two of the men began tying, leaving Fletcher and the other man to keep everyone covered.

Calmly, methodically, the roping began. Fletcher still said nothing — nothing to Harrigan, no comment on the visitors. It was a military operation: a job, with no explanation called for at this stage. Harrigan was tied up first, in his wheelchair. Then came the others, each in turn pushed into one of the heavy chairs, ideal for the purpose. Ambrose was the second to be tied. As the rope came round his arms and was knotted, he felt an excruciating pain, first in his arms and then his shoulders. When it came to tying up his feet, the sense of being frozen, immobile, was horrifying. Struggling to be free, he felt the pain grow fiercer as the rope was pulled and knotted with even greater callousness. The man moved on to Alistair, and Ambrose tested his own rope cautiously. There was not an inch of free movement. No one spoke. From the hall came the sound of voices, but inside Harrigan, shrunk silently in his chair, seemed to set the tone. They were to wait.

In a few minutes it was over. Fletcher went round each chair, testing it brutally, with total disdain. His huge bulk was obscene Sweating profusely as he came to Ambrose, he gave him a look full of anger. But it was when he came to Harrigan that the hate really burst out.

"You're washed up! You're dead!" The words came out with total venom. The English accent lingering in his voice made it somehow all the more evil — corrupt, bloated like his frame. "You were out to get me, weren't you: but you got it all wrong. You're washed up," he repeated. "You're dead. Who did you think you were dealing with?"

Harrigan said nothing. His silence was like a taunt, full of contempt. It seemed to goad Fletcher to fury.

"You thought you'd hang on. We all had to do what Harrigan said. Who do you think was behind McLusky? Who organized it? You're blind. You're senile. Couldn't hand it on, could you? Everyone was going to be loyal to Harrigan. He had the power. Oh, yes, he had the money. Everyone was loyal. Well, were they? What about your own men here? Pat O'Leary, Frank Gorley, Jim Stanton — oh yes, very loyal. How do you think I got in here?"

Harrigan sat in his chair, his eyes shrouded. Nothing was going to make him talk to this man. There were footsteps outside, and a husky man with black greasy hair walked in and drew Fletcher on one side to say something.

"There's another cellar at the back," Fletcher said to him. "Frank should know the one I mean. Get in there."

The man moved off. Ambrose again tried to move. The rope was cutting into his arms unbearably. The chair he was in faced Harrigan directly, but away from Olaf and Alistair. He desperately tried to turn to see the state they were in, but there was no way of shifting his chair, and he could hardly move his head.

Fletcher was back towering over his victim. "You know what we're after, don't you? The cash. Where have you got it hidden? You're going to tell us. Is it one million — is it ten million? We're going to take it."

Harrigan said nothing. Fletcher looked round, taking in the trussed-up visitors. "These crummy characters aren't going to help you much, are they? I know why they're here. You thought you'd shut me out and do the TCC deal direct with the Treasury.

209

A fat lot of good that'll do you now. You're going to talk. And if you don't, they'll go with you."

The silence from Harrigan seemed to goad him further. "I expect you're counting on Don Shaughnessy to get back from Boston. Well, don't count. He's back. He's on the floor out there. You trusted him, didn't you? Oh, he was loyal all right. He could probably have told us the combination of the safe. Well, he didn't want to. And now he can't, even if he wanted to. So you'd better tell us yourself."

The shots. And now the rest of Fletcher's gang trampling round the cellars. What chance was there?

Fletcher, standing over Harrigan, seemed to come to a decision. "All right, you won't tell me how to get hold of that cash. Rather die, wouldn't you? Do you think I'll let you? Much easier to get you to talk. Let's have a look at your chapel. Plenty there to make you talk."

He began walking deliberately towards the tapestried wall at the end of the gallery. Ambrose, looking at Harrigan, saw a flicker of deep pain cross his face. Fletcher was at the end of the gallery now, and tugging at the tapestry. It moved slightly, but held firm. Fletcher took hold of one half and pulled with all his strength. There was a rending sound and the tapestry fell away. Immediately, he turned to the second half and pulled. The frame and the curtains fell into a great mound on the floor. In the space now open, Ambrose saw what had been hidden.

Alyss had told him what to expect, but to find it confirmed so literally was startling. In the frame of the arch were ornamental gates, fully open. Facing, in a circle, were the wooden benches, panelled behind. Above them, a circle of glowing frescoes. Above the frescoes were niches for sculpture. In the center, facing him, was a dark, haggard sculpture — the Donatello. High above it, one saw the front of a small glass case. It had to be the relic — the Baptist's forearm. Harrigan, sensing what happened, had lowered his head in agony. He seemed to be weeping.

Fletcher was back in the center of the room, at Harrigan's side. "You want to see it, don't you," he said, turning the wheelchair round violently. "There you are; have a good look for the last time."

"You all want to see it, eh?" Ambrose heard a screeching on the wood floor. Fletcher had twisted another chair round. Another screeching, and Alistair came into view, facing the chapel. Presumably the first chair was Olaf's, still out of sight. If the man-servant was still in the room, tied-up, he too was out of sight.

Harrigan had lifted his head, gazing at his treasures, but still silent. No bargaining with this man. Fletcher stood in front of all of them.

"No use my talking to *him*," he growled, "but you'd better think of your *own* skins. You'd better try persuading him, because I'll tell you what I'm going to do. I'm going to blow the whole thing up. If I can't get the cash, the chapel's going to glory come, and you're all going with it. You see, I know about bombs. I learned the hard way, in the War."

For the first time, the silence against him was broken — not by Harrigan but Olaf. "You're mad. Fletcher. You couldn't get away. The police would be here. What good would blowing it up do you?"

Fletcher turned on him sardonically. "Treasury wise-guy, eh? I'm mad, am I? Think I'm going to sit around waiting for the police to arrive. It's going to be a time-bomb. I'll give myself fifteen minutes headstart. Besides: do you think he's going to let all this be blown up? Do you know what it means to him? He'll talk. You better persuade him. I mean business."

Olaf, out of Ambrose's sight, must have decided that he'd done enough. He made no reply. But then he did speak, to Harrigan.

"You have to give in to this madman," he said. "I know what that statue is. It's the Donatello of St. John from Siena. You can't let it be blown up."

There was a silence and then came the quiet voice of Harrigan. "Yes, it *is* the Donatello. Isn't it beautiful?"

"Will you save it?" Olaf asked.

"Did the Baptist yield to Herod's torture?" Harrigan said softly. "He is my saint, and I will go with him."

"You bloody idiot," Fletcher shouted. "Well, you've had it. You'll see if I mean it."

Ambrose heard footsteps behind him. The dark husky man was back and in a great hurry. This time he made no effort to talk to Fletcher secretly. "We've been all round," he said. "Can't find the entry to the safes. We shouldn't have let Don Shaughnessy have it. He would have known, and he would have talked. What are we going to do?"

"We're going to make him talk. He'll have to see it with his own eyes. He won't believe it otherwise. You stay here and look after them. I'm going to get the stuff from the cellar. If we can't use it down there, we'll use it here."

He hurried out of the room. The goon stood there, gun in hand.

"Are you near me, Olaf?" Ambrose asked.

"Just behind."

The goon was angry. "Keep your traps shut, you two."

"Let me talk to Harrigan," Olaf said to him. "Fletcher wants us to persuade him. Move our chairs nearer."

The goon, flustered, seemed to accept the logic of the request. There was a kind of authority in Olaf's voice. Ambrose heard a scraping of the chair on the floor and in a moment Olaf, now in view, was closer to Harrigan.

Alistair now spoke. "Bring me nearer, too," he said. "We'll both try to persuade him." The chair was pushed along, ending up very near to Ambrose.

Olaf spoke again to Harrigan. "Are you sure you shouldn't give way?"

Harrigan's voice came back wheezily. "Aren't the frescoes beautiful? They are by the man who did my other Pinturicchio."

"Quite beautiful," Olaf said in a loud voice. "They have the real spirit. . . ."

He went on. Why so loud? The answer came in a moment. Beneath the talk between Olaf and Harrigan, Ambrose heard Alistair whispering to him very quietly. "Can you jab my left arm with your elbow?" he murmured. "Can you reach?"

Surreptitiously, Ambrose tried to move his arm. The rope cut into it. But he felt a very slight movement. He tried again, twisting round in the chair to give himself a little more leeway.

"I can almost do it," he whispered. "What do you want?"

"I've got a signaler to Tim strapped on. Just above my left elbow. Keep trying."

Olaf was still talking. The goon was standing there, sweating with impatience for Fletcher's return. There were shouts and the noise of footsteps in various parts of the house. Ambrose was still struggling but unable to reach Alistair.

"Can't do it," he whispered faintly. "Wait. I've got an idea. I'm going to try and fall on you."

With a superhuman effort, he tried to lean sideways towards Alistair to overbalance the chair. It was too heavy. He squirmed and twisted from one side to the other, watching the goon to make sure that his gaze stayed on Harrigan. Olaf's mild sophisticated voice floated clearly through the air. "The wood carvings look excellent, too," he was saying. "The setting is superb, worthy of the Donatello."

"I am so glad to share it with you," Harrigan said. "I have been so happy since I built the chapel. . . ."

One more effort to squirm and the chair began to topple, but in the wrong direction, *away* from Alistair. Pulling in his breath, Ambrose put all his force into a movement to go the other way. The momentum did the trick. With a great crash the chair was over, at Alistair's feet. Roped to his chair, Ambrose lay on the floor groaning. His right arm seemed fractured, shooting with pain. The goon had rushed across with a bellow of anger. Fletcher's voice could be heard outside and this seemed to galvanize him to action. Quickly he pulled the chair back on to its legs, with Ambrose shifting around as if he were a sack. His whole posture in the chair had changed, and, marvelously, his right hand had worked free. With great effort he held it immobile for the moment, hoping for more freedom in the arm itself. But Fletcher was now back in the room, carrying what looked like a heavy case, and putting it down on the floor with great care in the area immediately in front of the chapel.

Olaf had stopped his talk with Harrigan. The sight of the case had thrown a horrifying silence on the room. Ambrose, sitting as still as he could, tried to move his arm without attracting attention. The overturning had loosened the hold of the ropes. Bit by bit, he began to strain towards the limit of his new freedom. Had he fractured his arm? It felt like it. But there was movement in his fingers. Alistair, close by him, watched, saying nothing.

Fletcher, crouched before his case, was absorbed in some intricate work with it. The goon stood in watch over Harrigan, turning his head from time to time towards the others, with a particularly furious look at Ambrose. Total silence in the room, except for an occasional metallic click from where Fletcher was working.

Surreptitiously, Ambrose tested the range of freedom in his arm. With an effort now, he could reach Alistair. In the silence, even a whisper would be heard. He blinked his eyes at Alistair, who blinked back. They were ready.

Fletcher had finished. He stood up now and walked towards Harrigan. When he spoke, the earlier leering tone of his voice had gone. He was precise, authoritative, powerful — like a soldier. He had been a good soldier — a good war record, Claire had said.

"This is your last chance," he said to Harrigan. "All you have to do is to tell me where is the entry to the room with your safes, and give me the keys and combination. I want the cash. If you won't talk, I'll set this bomb to go off fifteen minutes after I've left. It will blow the whole chapel to smithereens, and everything in it — and all of you too. I'll give you three minutes to decide."

Harrigan sat looking at him and said nothing. But Olaf joined in, as he had before. Somehow he seemed to sense that there had to be talk in the room to cover anything going on between Alistair and Ambrose.

"You must be stupid to think you'll get away," he said in a calm contemptuous voice. "The men you've killed here already. . . ."

Fletcher broke in, almost as if this were a military discussion. "You seem to forget that once Harrigan's blown up, his whole organization collapses. I've got three fast cars outside. We'll take everything with us. I've got a fall-back position with McLuskey. You'd do better to stop arguing with me and tell that old baboon to agree. I'm giving him three minutes, and then it all goes up."

While they were speaking, Alistair had been whispering to Ambrose. "Just above my left elbow," he murmured. "You'll feel a button. Press it. One long, two short. Then wait a second and give two short ones."

Ambrose nodded, stretching out his hand with the greatest caution. The pain in his arm made him bite his lips to stop him groaning. With the tip of his finger, he felt Alistair's elbow and worked his way towards something strapped above it. The button. He felt it. He pressed it — one long, two short — waited, and then the final two short presses. He drew his arm back, exhausted. Alistair nodded, smiling faintly.

Fletcher had gone back to the bomb and was standing beside it without a trace of expression in his face. With an almost casual air, he raised his arm to look at his watch. Three minutes of grace passed in total silence. "Right," he said, and bent down.

They saw him take some wire leads and screw them in. Calmly, he went over all the connections, touching the equipment with the greatest delicacy. The final act was to make a slow, careful adjustment to the hands of a dial. One last look at all the equipment, and he rose to his feet. In that second, the machine guns burst out.

It was a long burst, shattering to the ears, immediately outside the window. Fletcher and the other men ran to the door. There was shouting in the house itself, and then another terrifying rattle of machine-guns outside, exactly as before. From inside the house there were cries in all directions. Once again the machine guns were heard — a long burst of firing, and this time followed by a loud shouting of men, almost as if it were an old-fashioned charge of soldiers with shouts of *Ah-Ah.* . . .

Outside, there was the slamming of car doors and a roaring of engines. The noise was fearsome. Again they heard the machine-guns, and then the sound of the cars racing away. And now there was silence. They sat, roped in their chairs, facing the chapel and the bomb in front of it, waiting. . . .

Behind them they heard footsteps, and Tim was in the room. He rushed first to Alistair, with a knife in his hand which he flicked open. In a moment Alistair was freed. Olaf was next.

"Give me the knife," Olaf said to Tim. "Go and help Alistair."

The bomb. Alistair had rushed over and was inspecting it. Tim joined him. Olaf had freed Harrigan first, and then Ambrose. Again there was a running of feet into the room. The chauffeur was there. Presumably he had been tied up, too, and then released by Tim.

Ambrose nursed his arm. Was it broken? His legs seemed paralyzed. But nothing mattered. Only the bomb.

Alistair was crouched on the floor, Tim beside him.

Olaf turned to the chauffeur. "Take Mr. Harrigan outside," he said.

Harrigan was sitting slumped in his wheelchair. Had something happened to him? They heard his faint wheezy voice. "No," he said. "I will stay here."

Olaf had gone over to Alistair. "What does it look like?"

"It looks all set to go and linked to the clock. Can't tell how long. You'd better all go out. Tim too. Leave me here." He had taken his coat off, and begun work, using the tools that Fletcher had left on the floor.

"We've got to take the Donatello," Olaf cried. With Ambrose beside him, they ran to the chapel. It was riveted into the niche. No chance at all of moving it.

"Let's go," Olaf said. "All of us." They went back into the

215

gallery. Olaf took the wheelchair firmly and pushed it to the door. Harrigan was now silent.

"There's nothing for it," Olaf said. "Got to get outside the house."

At the door, he and the chauffeur lifted Harrigan out of the chair. In a moment they were all outside in the dark, about fifty yards from the house. Tim had wheeled the chair down, and Harrigan had been helped back into it.

Now that they were outside, they were aware that the summer storm had grown more dominant. Every few minutes, it seemed, the sky was lit up wildly with a searing flash of lightning, followed by crashing rolls of thunder. But there was no rain, and no people. The machine guns. The shouting. The charge of soldiers. Where were they? It was impossible to ask, even to speak. They waited, with one thought uppermost. . . .

Fifteen minutes. Surely the time had passed. It seemed an eternity. At any moment now a terrifying explosion. . . .

"Where are you all?" Alistair, standing in the lighted hallway, was calling out cheerfully, in the tone of "Anyone for tennis?"

"We're here," they shouted.

"All's well," he shouted back.

With a rush, they were in the doorway with him. They carried the chair up with Harrigan in it and wheeled him into the gallery. Before the chapel, the bomb still lay on the floor, but with various bits and pieces now separated from it.

"Not too difficult," Alistair said. "He'd set it up very professionally. Great help. One knew what to look for."

"I suppose it was a piece of cake," Ambrose said.

"You might say so," Alistair said.

They stood there looking, too excited to talk sensibly.

Harrigan had signaled to the chauffeur to wheel him into the chapel itself. He sat in his chair, looking at the Donatello silently.

Harrigan raised his hand for their attention. Olaf went into the chapel and wheeled him into the center of the gallery. They sat around him to listen. He was in command again.

For the moment there were no explanations, only orders. Tim and Alistair were to go round the house to check on everything. Ambrose was to ring a number in Boston and get hold of Mr. George Fitzalan. Mr. Fitzalan was to come out immediately with six people, whose names Ambrose took down. He was to be told to bring "equipment" with him. If Mr. Fitzalan was not reachable, Ambrose was to make the same arrangements through a Mr. Robert Hooley. There was a third name as fall-back. Ambrose wandered off into a kind of office, opening off the gallery.

Through the open door of the office, Ambrose saw that Harrigan was now sitting back in his chair, Olaf at his side, and had laid his hand on Olaf's. There was almost nothing to be said for the moment: talk would come later. What mattered was that he had taken Olaf as his equal. Tim, Alistair, Ambrose — they were subordinates. Olaf was a master, as *he* was. Occasionally he said something to him. Mostly he sat silent, resting.

Mr. Fitzalan was at home. Harrigan's instructions were accepted instantly. "There's been a big upset here," Ambrose said. "Mr. Harrigan is alone except for four of us who are his friends. You'll find out when you come." Mr. Fitzalan seemed to be prepared. He would be there within forty minutes.

With the telephone before him, Ambrose thought of Alyss, waiting in his room. Closing the door of the little office, he rang the hotel and was through in a minute.

"How has it gone?" She was very excited.

"The official description is a piece of cake."

"You mean he's agreed."

"Nothing's been agreed. But there's an understanding between him and Olaf that is beautiful to behold. Have you had a communication from Swinburne?"

"Not a word."

Ambrose became more serious. "I hope he rings. I'm so glad you're there. If he does ring, will you tell him you have a message from me, before he just rings off?"

"What's the message?"

"Tell him I said there was really great danger tonight. Something's happened that really makes it very urgent."

"I'll make sure to tell him. What happened? Are you all right? You sound as if you may have had some trouble."

"Oh, yes, we did have a little trouble. I've got a bruised elbow to show for it. We're all right now — all of us. But give him the message. He'll understand. I'll be back as soon as I can."

Putting the phone down, he went back into the gallery and told Harrigan that Mr. Fitzalan had everything in hand. Tim and Alistair were back, too, with nothing to report on their search. The house was empty. No one tied up. Not even corpses to report. They had been taken away to be dumped somewhere, no doubt. Tim had looked around outside. No cars seemed to be approaching. The firing had gone by without attracting attention. If it had been heard in the distance it would have been taken for thunder. *The firing!* Wasn't it time to find out about it?

Alistair explained with his usual nonchalance. "It was from the little Tattoo we staged at the Armory. We'd made tapes which we played as accompaniment to some of the exercises. One of them was an attack under fire, so we had to have machine-gunning as an accompaniment. Then we gave them a kind of old-fashioned Charge of the Light Brigade with all the men shouting in the mad way they used to. It was all on tape. I thought it would help to create a diversion if I needed it to have a look round, the way Olaf had planned it. I had a small walkie-talkie strapped to my chest: of course, I couldn't get to that. But there was this little radio buzzer that Tim provided. We worked out a series of signals." He turned to Tim. "You brought the loud speakers in early on?"

"I thought I'd better be ready," Tim said. "I've got them on both sides of the house. Child's play once I got the signal to charge. Which reminds me: I'd better go and collect my equipment."

He went off cheerfully. At Harrigan's suggestion, Alistair went into an adjoining room to produce some whisky. They sat drinking happily until Fitzalan arrived with a bunch of goons.

Olaf had been at Harrigan's side throughout. With the tension relaxed they had begun to talk together freely, and apparently to their mutual content. Harrigan was sitting up now — alert, serene. Olaf looked very happy as they set off to return to Boston.

"What a man!" Olaf said to Ambrose as the Rolls floated along. "What do you think he was telling me when we sat talking? He saw it all as a vindication of his faith in the Baptist, or rather of his identification with him. It was *his* version of the Baptist's agony — being cast into prison by Herod. He was quite ready for death. If he was spared, it was because Providence wanted it this way."

"How does he fit his wealth and power into John wandering naked in the wilderness?"

"This is Providence, too. He quotes John's saying in the Gospels: '*A man can receive nothing, except it be given him from heaven.*' Fits everything, doesn't it?"

"Well, it can be applied," Ambrose said cautiously. "I

suppose it wasn't appropriate to pursue business matters when you talked to him?"

"Didn't have to. Only in the broadest outline. We understand each other very well now. *He* knows what *I* want. *I* know how far he'll go. He won't do the simple swap. He just doesn't like the copper mines. That damned instinct of his, I suppose. But he'll buy the gold mines and sell us the uranium option. We're going to tackle the details tomorrow. And, of course, I'll get him the Bellini on loan. He's dropped the whole 'possession' business. He's had his agony."

"And the Donatello?"

"Oh, that goes back to Siena. The relic, too. When I asked him, he simply closed his eyes and murmured: 'I will see to it. It will be arranged.' If you ask me, he saw the whole agony as a kind of sign from heaven against his presumption. Didn't say so, but that's what I felt. He was fascinated by Alyss, by the way. He worked out that that was how I knew he had it. He'd had messages from Siena that she was ferreting around and realized that she must be on the track. He doesn't hold it against her now. On the contrary: he wants her to go out with me tomorrow and see it. We must tell her. I expect she's at home, waiting to hear about it all."

Ambrose had a little private agony. He had no desire to start explaining why he had installed Alyss next to his telephone. The less anyone knew of Willis, the better. Simpler to be vague about where Alyss was. . . .

"I telephoned her from Harrigan's," he said, "and told her we'd all survived."

Olaf gave him a quizzical look. "Good thinking, Ambrose," he said teasingly. "And, by the way, that fall from your chair was also good thinking. In fact, it was *very* good thinking. Did you hurt yourself?"

"Nothing more than a bad bruise, I think. At the time, it felt as if my arm had come off. If you can have me dropped at my hotel, a hot bath will put me right."

About half an hour later, he was knocking, not too noisily, on his own door and Alyss was there, first with an embrace and then holding him at a distance for examination. "No mud, I see. I knew it. What about the bruise? This arm?"

"Ouch! I thought it was better. Did he ring?"

"Not a tinkle. I never moved from the room."

"Well, it was just a precaution. And look what it's got me."

This time it was he who did the embracing. But in a moment, the evening's affairs caught up with him. "I'm starving. All I've had is a drink of whisky."

"No need to worry. I thought I might be in for a long siege. I brought bread, pâté, cheese, and a rather nice bottle of wine. Will that do?"

"Will it *do?*"

Over the food, he told her what had happened. At the moment of relief, with the bomb dismantled, she heaved a deep sigh. When she heard she was to go out there the next day at Harrigan's invitation, she gave a whoop of joy. Then she seemed to become rather dreamy.

"Let me have another look at your elbow," she said. "I can see I have to take care of you." She stayed for a long time, and then drove home.

He was very sleepy when she left. Drowsily, he thought of Fletcher. Had he gone to the cottage? Willis would take care. There was nothing anybody else could do. . . .

XII

"*AND the hunter home from the kill,*" he thought irreverently. Was that where true appetite came from? He was tackling his bacon, sausages and eggs with a consuming kind of passion. Somehow the adventure — all over now — seemed to call for this kind of gross satisfaction.

The last lecture. The last lunch. Downhill all the way. There was danger still, but it could be absorbed. Nothing in the *Mail* as yet. They had been lucky. When the rest of the story surfaced, the Harrigan locus might be kept out of it. All the same, the memory of that long wait in the grounds outside — the sighing trees, the lightning, the rumble of thunder, and then Alistair in the doorway . . . One had to talk of it before surrendering to the daily round. He rang Olaf.

"I should have asked you to breakfast," Olaf said. "So much to talk of. What was in your mind while we stood outside waiting? We none of us said anything. . . ."

"Just what I was thinking," Ambrose murmured.

"It was the sudden darkness, I suppose. Fate knocking at the door."

"'*And all that lamentation of the leaves.*'"

"Yes. It will look different today when I go there. I expect he's assembled a mighty band of men by now. Don't give Fletcher much of a chance, do you?"

"No. But he's resourceful. I don't underestimate him."

"Shall I see you today? What are you up to?"

"My last lecture, and then a lunch. And in the evening a little supper that Orville's giving for me to say goodbye to the Faculty. Back to the academic grind."

"Oh, what a pity you're busy tonight. I thought you might have joined us at the kyely."

"What on earth's that?"

"*Ceilidh*." He spelled it out. "Highland sing-song. Alistair's lads are putting it on at the Armory tonight for the Boston Scottish Farewell party: lots of Highland reels and all that. I must take Alyss. She'll love it. Did you tell her that Harrigan's invited her to go out there today?"

"I did, later in the evening. She was terribly pleased. So I may not see you now again on this side. When does your all-Scottish plane take off tomorrow?"

"In the morning. Are you sure you don't want to come? They've laid on haggis *ad libitum*."

"I was afraid of that. And all those scrannel pipes. No, I'll stick to dear old British Airways. I'm booked for the night plane."

The easy chat had blown the nightmare away, but not entirely, as he found when he sat down at his desk to work for a while on his lecture. The outline he had in mind was to bring the themes of the other lectures together, but other thoughts seemed to be crowding in. The direct experience of violence seemed to demand some sort of expression. He had a picture of Fletcher tearing off through the night — Claire alone in the cottage. . . . Would he stand up and lecture with nothing of this coming through?

Time was passing. He turned to the notes he had scribbled down. There was the Angsthofer quote that he wanted to bring in. He found a place for it. A good phrase relating to it came into his head. He made another note. In a few minutes he was back in the academic groove. He collected his notes, feeling more or less satisfied. This was where he was at home. In two days he would be putting his feet up at Oxford again.

Oxford. Would Basruk be showing up there, breaking away from his Whitehall chores? How many days was it — only four or five — since he's been cavorting on the Boston scene? Had he really gone back to London? One never knew with him. . . .

He had a slight pang, walking through the autumn sunshine to the lecture hall. The last lecture. He would miss it all. Harvard was so beautiful. His audience, when he came in, was so welcoming. They had attended so loyally, listened so attentively. He seemed to know them all by now.

His mind went back to the opening lecture, with Alyss in the fourth row and a redhead in the third, just in front of her. No Alyss today. She was obviously holding herself ready to go out to Harrigan's. No redhead either. Well, he had already decided that she might be anywhere from Colorado to Turkey.

He launched himself into his theme: "the individual in search of himself."

Thinking about it later, he never could decide if this last lecture, because of its rambling spontaneity, was the best he had given or, by the same token, without form and void. At least it had a satisfying epilogue.

He began, as he had intended, with an attempt to explore self-expression in two very contrasted forms — music and poetry. Both reach the inner core "illogically." In poetry, there is a sense in which it is not "the argument" which matters, as he had shown with Goethe. Music dispenses with words entirely, yet it conveys an "argument" — as in a late Beethoven quartette — which has an unmistakeably *moral* impact:

> *"O cry created as the bow of sin*
> *Is drawn across our trembling violin."*

In the air around him, he still felt the presence of the evil he had lived through. Was music an expiation or merely a solace? He came back to Auden as the lecture developed:

> *"You alone, alone, imaginary song,*
> *Are unable to say an existence is wrong."*

For a time, glancing at his notes, he picked up the more formal ideas he had sketched out, but felt drawn away. "*Where shall the word be found?*" Eliot had asked, and had answered: "in silence." There was not enough silence "*on the mainland, in the desert or the rain land*" for those who walked in darkness. Conrad, usually so lavish with words, had come to this too in *The Heart of Darkness*. Kurtz, dying in the jungle, is man at his most elemental, "civilization" drowned in power and greed. Ultimately he is beyond any explanation in words. "*The horror!*" is all he can cry out on his deathbed. The horror was what Ambrose felt as he worked his way to the close of his lecture.

He was about to end in this mood when he pulled himself up. This was his *private* agony. Did it really flow from what he had been saying in his earlier lectures?

"I have to thank you all for being so patient," he said to the audience as he gathered his papers together. "I am sorry if I seem to have ended on a rather bleak note. May I quote a poem by Day-Lewis which I always try to recall when the harvest seems blighted? Perhaps, he says, it's one's own high hopes that have made the wizened look tall:

> 'But it's useless to argue the why and wherefore.
>   When a crop is so thin,
> There's nothing to do but to set the teeth
>   And plough it in'."

It was still bleak, but more what he really felt. There was a short silence when he finished, and then a warm round of applause. He began to relax. It was all over. He had survived. Life would go on.

In a moment, the lecture atmosphere had evaporated, to be replaced by a cheerful bustle as people moved around to greet him or say goodbye. The problem of the lunch had been solved by a merger. His two hosts were close by, waiting impatiently to snatch him away.

The audience gradually thinned out, and he was just about to move off towards his hosts when, with a great rush, a beautiful young girl dashed in, her long red hair flowing behind her.

"Oh, Ambrose!" she cried. "I just couldn't make it to the lecture. I had to go and see another professor. It was the only time he could see me."

"Why, Lindsay, it doesn't matter at all. I'm just delighted to see you. I haven't seen you since we had that nice evening. I left you dancing with the old Pasha. What has happened since?"

"Isn't he marvelous? He invited me to go out to visit with him in Turkey over Christmas."

"And what did the younger Mr. Basruk think of that?"

"He told me to accept. He said I would have a lovely time. He himself has to go to spend Christmas in Sweden. It's just business. He can't get out of it. He has a friend there, a big industrialist, and he has to consult him."

"Yes, I heard about his Swedish friend. So you won't be seeing him."

"Oh yes, I might. He's coming out here in February to go skiing in Colorado. He asked me if I'd like to go with him for a week."

"How very nice. Skiing in Colorado. Isn't it a long way to come for a little skiing?"

"Oh, the skiing's fabulous there. I've been there before. It's wonderful. Besides, he's got some business to do there, so it will fit in nicely for him. He told me that his uncle had bought some silver mines out in Colorado and he wants to have a look at them. His uncle seems to be in the mining business. That's why he went out to Colorado last week: to do the deal."

"Well, isn't that interesting? You'll be doing a lot of traveling with the Basruks, it seems."

"Oh, I'm not sure if I'll go. But I may see him later, and that's really why I came to see you this morning. I just *had* to see you. I want to go to Oxford next year."

"To work with Basruk?"

"Oh no. I mean Zilto's very nice and all that, and very clever, and I like his uncle very much, but that's not what I'm interested in. It's *you* I'm interested in."

"*Me!*"

"Yes. I want to take a graduate course in philosophy in Oxford next year, and I want you to be my supervisor. *Will* you? *Please?*" She opened her big eyes, beseeching him. He was suddenly reminded of Gloria. The Glorias of this world. They were immortal.

"Write to me," he said. "If I can, I will, or I'll find somebody much better. But write to me. Write to me for Christmas."

His luncheon hosts were approaching him in tandem. Lindsay bent forward to give him a loving kiss, and off he went.

For once, it was an academic lunch with wine. He was feeling rather drowsy, back in his room, when Alyss rang. She was at Harrigan's.

"I seem to have a new admirer," she said. "I've had a long talk, I told him how I'd worked it all out and what I'd done. He seems fascinated. And he's asked me to organize the return of the Donatello and the relic — in a very discreet way, of course. I'll have to go out to Italy. He wants me to be his adviser on all these things. When he mentioned the retainer he had in mind, I nearly fainted."

"How is Olaf getting on with the business propositions?"

"Oh, that's very different. On the personal level, they're like brothers. But Olaf says that on the deal he's as tough as nails. They'll be at it all day, I think. I'm sorry I missed your last lecture. How did it go?"

"I can't really say. But there was a delightful bonus at the end. Lindsay turned up."

"She didn't go off with the Pasha?"

"It was a close-run thing. But she cleared up a few things for me about the Basruks, in her artless way. And *I* have a new admirer, too. She wants to come and sit at my feet at Oxford.

"Ha. I'm not too sure about that. I think I'll have to come over myself and protect you. I believe you're the susceptible type."

"You see right through me. Very uncomfortable. I think we're all susceptible, one unto the other. What about Olaf?"

"Now you're seeing through *me*. Isn't he marvelous? He's asked me to a Scottish party tonight — Highland reels and all that. Says you can't come. What a shame."

"I expect Olaf dances a very dainty reel. Ring me in the morning and give me a report. Shall we have lunch? Olaf will have flown off. You'll have to be content with me."

"Yes, isn't it awful? We'll have to save it all for lunch. I said I'd go out with them to the airport to see them off. Apparently there'll be a grand processional march with bagpipes. Sounds fun. I'll ring you as soon as it's over."

He put the phone down and thought he might try a little reading. But in the quiet of the room, his mind went back to things half-buried. Had anything surfaced yet? He rang Bill Rafferty and was greeted with a roar of welcome.

"How extraordinary! I was just going to ring you. I was hoping you hadn't left. Something surprising has turned up. You wouldn't want to miss it. A real sensation."

"The gangster front?"

"Right. In high gear. Something I've never known before. A real haul by the police."

"Who have they got?"

"They've got three very dead bodies, which is routine: but this time, they've got three nice little gangsters to go with them. All in two cars. Very handy. Do you want to come over?"

"Sure. I've finished my lectures. Gave the last one this morning. Time lies heavily on my hands. Just what I need."

So it was being wrapped up. It might be grim, but it had a satisfactory air of finality about it. He was on Harrigan's side now. One had only to recall the scene with Fletcher standing over him. He went downstairs, and took a taxi.

Fletcher had to be one of them: but he wasn't. Ambrose felt his spirits sink, getting the news in Rafferty's office.

Of course, there was always a comic side. How had the police managed it? Pure accident. Two black cars had been driving along the parkway about twenty miles out of Boston, not breaking the speed limit, just moving along swiftly. One of them had had a blowout and swerved. The other had come in behind to help them change the tire quickly. They had just finished when a police car had drifted up and stopped, more out of friendliness than anything else. With no great alarm, they noted that two of the men were familiar hoods. The policemen were walking round the cars in the flat curious way they adopt, just to have a look, when suddenly one of the hoods opened fire at the police and dashed off. The other followed. The police chased. Help came and they were caught. In the cars were three hoods and three corpses. Obviously they had been transporting the bodies for disposal somewhere. Rather bad luck.

"Who are the men? Do you know them?" Ambrose asked.

This is what Rafferty found so entrancing. "As far as I know, they're *all* Harrigan men. How does one explain it? Either McLuskey's lot did them in, and they were being given a decent disposal by their friends, or there's been some mighty blow-up *within* the Harrigan camp. Maybe a sizeable section of them were moving over. Harrigan wouldn't like that. But who's to tell?"

"Where's McLuskey in all this?"

"The word is that he's blown town — far off. Police are working on it, of course."

"Where is it all going to end?"

"This looks like it. Wholesale. My hunch is that it's finished. You can go back to Oxford. But I wanted you to be in at the last act."

"To be in at the kill?"

"You put it so elegantly. Is it too early for you to have a whisky?"

"It is not."

He sat around for a while watching the office at work. It never ceased to fascinate him. But nothing came in to change the picture.

He went back to Cambridge about an hour later and did a little reading in a perfunctory way. No call from Alyss before he went out to the supper party. Back around eleven, he went to bed.

XIII

It was at twelve minutes past nine the next morning that the story turned over. Rafferty was on the phone again, but this time without the wry detachment that the previous day's coup had generated.

"Very strange business," he said soberly. "They've found another body. Someone we know."

"George Fletcher?"

"How did you guess?"

"I've been involved in something that concerned him. Perhaps you guessed when we spoke. I was supposed to keep my eyes open."

"Yes, I had a hunch that it might be Fletcher. Very unpleasant character. It's Claire I'm thinking of. Not that she'll miss him too painfully."

"He was a horrible man. He had it coming," Ambrose heard himself say.

Rafferty was a little more tolerant. "Pretty grim all the same," he said. "I suppose he must have fallen foul of Harrigan's lot."

"You see it as a gangster shooting?"

"Oh, yes. It must have been. He must have been in deeper than I thought."

"Where did they find him?"

"His body was washed up on a little beach near Cedar Point."

"Whereabouts is that?"

"Do you know Weymouth, on the way to Norfolk? It's about ten miles beyond that."

Yes, Ambrose thought. Ten miles from Weymouth, which was about two miles from Claire's cottage.

"Have they any idea when it happened?" he asked.

"It's only a flash so far. I don't think they can tell when it actually happened once it's been in the sea for some time. They think a day or so. Probably begun to swell."

"Was he shot?"

"That's right. Several bullet wounds, according to the flash. I suppose someone let fly and didn't want to stop. Wanted to make sure. Or was just pretty angry."

"Thanks for letting me know. I'll drop in later."

He could have gone in a taxi, but he wanted to take it in slowly. He walked over to Harvard Square and rolled into Boston on the train. At Park Street, he walked down into the Gardens. It was a sunny day. He sat down on a bench facing the sun and half-closed his eyes.

Fletcher gone. He had thought the world would feel cleaner when this happened, and it did. An incubus of deceit and hate. All over.

His mind strayed off to Gloria. It was settled now. The memory had been a grief. Now it was assuaged.

He tried to think of it in terms of Providence asserting itself. There had been a human agent, but that was not to be thought about. Fletcher had died. There had been a balance to be restored.

The police would be less philosophic. They'd ask Claire a lot of questions. Surely it would all come out. Or would the gangster aspect dominate everything, as Rafferty automatically assumed?

Perhaps it was all coming out on Rafferty's tape right now. He sat on the bench in the sun, unwilling to move. He didn't want to know. With eyes half-closed, he felt beautifully drowsy. Un-resisting he dozed off, as if he were some old tramp on a park bench. Well, why not? They were people without pressure, who took whatever Providence offered.

When he opened his eyes a few minutes later, he realized what was wrong with the tramp philosophy. One got very stiff taking a nap on a park bench. He straightened himself out and began walking across the Common towards the *Mail* office.

On the way he saw a newsstand where he bought a copy of the *New York Times*. Nearby was another park bench, and he sat down for a careful read. He was quite aware of his motivation. He was trying to put off having to face any more facts about Fletcher's death that would be coming across the wire. Sooner or later he might have to face them, but for the moment he preferred not to.

It was nearly twelve when he finally got to the *Mail* office. Rafferty, shirt sleeves rolled up, had three newsmen in the room with him, and had clearly shed the personal concern that he had expressed earlier. A great news story was breaking. He checked a few things with the men, sent them on their way, and turned to Ambrose.

"This is really one for the book," he said. "We're just getting it on the wire. We all took it for granted that it must be part of the Harrigan business. Fletcher must have been caught out trading with the enemy, so he got it. But it isn't. Or if it is, it's still got a funny angle to it."

Ambrose had a sinking feeling. "What's the new development?"

"They found Fletcher's body washed up on the beach at about seven o'clock this morning. Several bullet wounds but no weapon. Well, they didn't expect one, but they had a good look round all the same. It's very deserted round there. Little lanes, lots of trees. About nine o'clock they came across a car hidden away very cleverly — blood on the front seat and all that. Obviously the body had been transported in it to throw it into the sea. They didn't say anything to the Press at that point: just checked the car registration. It belongs to a nice little Baptist minister in Boston. His car was stolen two days ago. Obviously it had been taken down there and kept hidden away for future use."

"Isn't that ordinary gangland procedure?"

"It could be if that were all. But it isn't. They started making a very thorough search all around, just in case the boys had dropped something, and they found the weapon. A revolver — a small one but very lethal. And the bullets fit. They rushed it back here for finger-prints and found some. They wired them to the FBI in Washington and they got their answer from the computer in about half an hour."

How would the FBI have Claire's prints? Surely she didn't have a criminal record. Perhaps she had worked for a government agency where they had to have it done. How had she got the car? Obviously Willis had helped. But why had they left her prints on the gun? Everyone knows you have to be careful to wipe them off?

"The cops are very pleased with themselves," Rafferty was saying. "They've just released the story. It's a communist killing. The FBI have identified the prints as those of a communist agent they were keeping track of a few years ago in Washington called Clive Nixon. Of course, they'd got his prints. At the time, they'd given him a little rope to see where he'd lead them to, and he'd disappeared. They thought he'd done a bunk to Russia, but here he is on the scene again."

"Clive Nixon." Ambrose had fallen into muttering to himself.

"Nice name, isn't it?" Rafferty said. "I don't suppose it's his real name, but what an alias! Of course, this guy could have turned from communism to a life of honest crime: he'd be well equipped. So he might be one of Harrigan's hoods just carrying out orders. Or maybe the Commies had some secret objection to Fletcher and this is how they settled things with him. After all, he was mixed up in international deals, and he certainly was a horrible specimen. I didn't like him and neither did you. Perhaps the Commies didn't either."

The wheels were buzzing round in Ambrose's head as he listened. *Clive Nixon.* Rafferty liked the name. Willis had liked it too. How idiotic of him to leave such an obvious lead of fingerprints on the gun. But was it idiotic? Was it?

He looked up at the big newsroom clock. Quarter to one. A hamburger was being suggested, but he wanted to be back in the hotel. Alyss would be phoning. Olaf's plane would have surely got off by now.

"I'd better go," he said. "I'm off tonight. Got to pack, and all that." He paused. "Glad I could see how it came out before I left."

Rafferty looked at him a little oddly. "Never quite know whether to believe you, Ambrose. You seem just a little too satisfied for my liking. Still, this does seem the end. Thank goodness you're going home in one piece. I was really quite alarmed for you at one stage. I think you should stay out of Boston for a while. We'll come over and see you instead. Much more peaceful. No gangsters in Oxford. . . ."

"Oh, I'm sure Boston will be completely peaceful once I've gone," Ambrose said. "I carry it all round with me. Isn't that the legend?"

He took a taxi back to his hotel. Alyss would be wondering where he'd got to. And Willis. Wasn't this just when Mr. Swinburne might be announcing himself?

* * *

There was no message from Alyss. He had a sandwich by himself, went up to his room, and began to pack. What a bore it was. Time dragged on. No word from Alyss, and nothing from Willis.

Reluctantly, almost miserably, he turned to the book he had left out for the plane. Would Angsthofer rise to the occasion? Strangely, he did. As Ambrose read, he saw with pleasure that a remark of his own on Noelscher was being quoted by Angsthofer with evident approval. Perhaps there was more: he read on. But it was no use. He threw the book down. Where had everybody got to? He seemed to have stopped the world and got off. He didn't like the feeling. The telephone rang.

"I have a call for Mr. Ambrose Usher from London," the girl said. There were clicks and buzzes, and Hepworth was on the line, sounding again as if he were just round the corner: "I was just wondering about your travel plans."

Ambrose had had enough. "My travel plans take me to Oxford tonight on a plane that will land in my college quadrangle from which I intend never to emerge."

"Will that be possible after such a success?"

"*Success?*"

"Oh, I take it for granted that the end of the arrow-man was an improvisation on your part. I've just had a message about it from the Consulate-General. Supposed to be some gangster killing according to the stories on the radio, they say. Of course, I don't believe that for a second."

"I see. And is all well at your end?"

"Extremely. I had a little local difficulty a few days ago, but we've managed to bury it. You haven't heard of any sensations from this end, have you? No rumors? Good. I'll tell you about it when you return. I had a little shock, but these things happen, and in a way it was all for the best. I'm really ringing to ask if you will bend your inflexible rule in order to have lunch with me next Wednesday at the Travellers'."

"I suppose you have a little problem."

"And, of course, you wouldn't dream of getting involved. However, don't dismiss it out of hand until you've heard the locale."

"Nothing would ever persuade me. . . ."

"But surely a visit to Rome in December, after term is over. . . ."

"Rome? Is this the Treasury again?"

"No, I thought you might have had enough of the Treasury. It's the National Gallery this time. They've asked us to look into something fishy that they say is going on, and I know how interested you are in painting."

"Charles, you are. . . ."

"Don't worry about it now. I'll tell you when I see you on Wednesday."

He put the phone down wonderingly. Well, Rome was different, especially if Alyss. . . . But where on earth was she?

A loud ring seemed to answer his question. But when he scooped up the receiver, he heard a very different voice. "This is Swinburne." He jumped to his feet and was downstairs at the call-box in a couple of minutes. A moment later Willis was on the line.

"I want to tell you a few things," he began. "I've read the stories in the afternoon papers. Slightly comic, I thought, the Clive Nixon angle. Appealed to my Irish sense of humor. Of course, they've got it wrong in one crucial way. I expect you worked it all out, but I want to tell you directly as I did before. It's part of putting things straight. I never really can, but I'm trying."

"Are you in fact round the corner or at the North Pole?"

"I'm exactly 280 miles away at the moment. I won't specify in which direction. I'm in a call-box with unlimited quarters. I like the idea of two call-boxes speaking to each other across the void."

"Deep calleth unto deep. . . ."

"Yes. Doesn't the verse go on: *'above the noise of thy water-pipes'*? That would be someone bugging us. Well, I don't think there'll be any water-pipes, but I'll talk anonymously all the same."

His voice had got back its relaxed Irish lilt. The tension seemed over.

"I'm sure you guessed it. The whole point was for her to be safe, at all costs. I've achieved that."

"That was what I thought. What actually happened?"

"He went out there on Wednesday night — not very late, about half-past ten. She says he was in an absolutely wild state. Quite desperate. Apparently there'd been some great showdown with his gangster friends and he had to go into hiding. He started trying to make her part of it, so that she could get money to him and all that. She refused absolutely. He became incoherent and threatening. She got so worked up herself that in the end she burst out that there was somebody else — me. This set him off completely. He said he'd see her dead first, picked up a poker and went for her. She has a great gash on her head. She got her hands on the little thing I'd left her. There was a terrible struggle, but at one point she got free and — well, you can guess.

"It was still only eleven o'clock. I'd told her that in an emergency she could telephone me. She drove to a call-box about three miles away and reached me. I was a long way off — I have to be. When I got her call I set off and drove through the night — five hours. Things looked pretty grim when I got there. I decided to shift the scene — and the person."

Yes, Ambrose thought. Why otherwise leave finger-prints which he knew could be identified?

"The first thing," Willis said, "was to distance things a bit. That wasn't difficult. I had a car hidden close by which I'd prepared just in case she had to leave in a hurry at any time without trace. The sea wasn't far off. I managed to do what had to be done. Then I drove another ten miles or so and left the car carefully hidden. What did you think when you heard it was found, with all the evidence?"

"I thought that if you'd wanted to hide everything you would have made a better job of it. But what if they hadn't found them?"

"I would have gone back and helped them a little. It had to be done this way. It had to point, without possibility of question, to the gentleman with the funny name. It's worked, so she's O.K."

"But the funny gentleman?"

"They can't track him down. The funny name came to a dead end years ago. That's why they've been led to it. True, there's always a risk of some link surfacing. It's a risk I'm prepared to take. But I think it will all stay put. The great thing is that the present view of what happened is making everybody happy. Nothing like having a ready-made bogey: and with a name like that, you can't lose."

"One will never see him again?"

"He's as undiscoverable as the person from Porlock. Someone else will take his place, no doubt. In fact, someone already has."

"So this is hail and farewell."

"Not quite. I have a favor to ask. I've no claim on your kindness, but, as you see, I've done my best to try and put things right. In any case, this is no burden."

"I'll do what I can."

"I imagine that in a few months she may take a holiday in your part of the universe. She may ring you or write to ask if you know where somebody is. That somebody may already have told you that he's in the same orbit, and where. So you may be able to pass it on. Not too difficult?"

"Not difficult at all. You sound as if you have everything under control."

"I hope so. In that sense, it's all over. Can I celebrate by reciting a bit of Swinburne, since that's how you will remember me?"

"Please do."

"It's amazing how one remembers poetry one learned at school without knowing when it will be just right to draw on it. And then it just comes into one's head:

> 'For winter's rains and ruins are over,
>   And all the season of snows and sins;
> The days dividing lover and lover,
>   The light that loses, the night that wins'."

"'And time remembered is grief forgotten,'" Ambrose said. "Goodbye. Good luck."

The phone was ringing as he reached his door. The key. The key. He fumbled, but somehow managed. And this time it was the right voice.

"Hi!" she said cheerfully. "I'm home at last. You've heard the news?"

"About Fletcher?"

"The chauffeur heard it on the radio and told us. This communist agent who killed him. It's unbelievable."

"Absolutely unbelievable."

"We must talk about it. You've probably got lots of theories. But I've got an insoluble problem that only you can solve. Do we eat out tonight or do I cook a steak right here?"

"Where have you been all day? I've been totally bereft."

"Ambrose: the day I believe you when you say you are bereft will be the day that I have lost my reason. You haven't answered my question."

"Nor you mine. Did Olaf get off all right?"

"Endless delays. He had to telephone Harrigan before he left to try and get something straightened out on their business.

236

Then he had to telephone London to get an answer on it and then telephone Harrigan again. It took till nearly one o'clock before it was all clear. Then the plane was delayed: something wrong with the engine. The horrible thing is that they never tell you when it's going to go off. I just sat and waited. Of course, I did have a marvelous talk with him while we waited. But you haven't answered *my* question."

"Eat in, of course. A steak. Imagine. My last steak. We starving English. . . ."

"Oh, good. Gives us much more time to talk. And with luck *your* plane will be delayed, too. I did enjoy the talk with Olaf. Isn't he wonderful?"

"I can't deny it."

"He's so relaxed and yet so full of authority. Is that the Treasury?"

"It could be. You find it admirable?"

"Within limits, of course. I'm rather drawn to what you were talking about in your first lecture — the opposing principle, the question-mark."

"Well, that's a relief."

"I must say: seeing the two of you together was fascinating. I never saw two people more different and more in tune."

Ambrose laughed. "You've hit it. Do you know how it struck me? I felt that we were in a kind of duo act, feeding each other with lines. And I know what it was: *The Barber of Seville.* I was Figaro and he was the Count.

"And he *is* a Count. Don't you remember? Count of the Curia."

"Of course. Of course. That establishes it perfectly. Just think of the opera. *There's* the Count, a real Count but always putting on a disguise — unknown lover, billeting officer, music teacher — just like Olaf. One never knows what he's really up to. And there am I, in full view of everybody, unchanging, role clearly defined: the factotum: *il factotum della città.* Are you sure you like me in the role?"

"I love you in it. Figaro's the hero. Why are you worried?"

"Because everybody keeps calling Figaro a scoundrel — '*Ah birbo!*'"

"Well, you can't win 'em all. But you've won a steak. When will you arrive?"

Mysteries in the Peerless British tradition from
Lionel Black
Featuring intrepid newspaper reporter, Kate Theobald and her barrister husband, Harry.

DEATH BY HOAX   41376 ... $1.75

In a small seaside town sweltering in an August heat wave, a prankster is calling out the fire brigade, emptying theatres, and stopping trains with phony threats. But his next hoax is explosively real . . .

A HEALTHY WAY TO DIE   43661 ... $1.95

Gorsedene is England's best known health farm, where the rich and famous pay to be starved and made fit. But suddenly, in this paradise of health, a man dies, and the Theobalds discover one patient after another with individual reasons for wishing that particular man dead . . .

THE PENNY MURDERS   48090 ... $1.95

When Kate and Henry arrive at the home of a distinguished numismatist to see his prized collection of rare coins, they are horrified to discover their host shot in the head. Their investigation into the world of coins leads them into deadly danger.

THE EVE OF THE WEDDING   55996 ... $2.25

It is the eve of an old-fashioned English wedding, where the bride's father has decided to throw a "polterabend"—a prankish abduction of the bride. But the bride is missed for a bit too long—and a mad search yields the bridegroom pulling a knife from his brother's body.

AV☤N Paperbacks

Available wherever paperbacks are sold, or directly from the publisher. Include 50¢ per copy for postage and handling: allow 6-8 weeks for delivery. Avon Books, Mail Order Dept., 224 West 57th St., N.Y., N.Y. 10019.

Black 12-81

A CHILLING DETECTIVE STORY OF MURDER AND MADNESS

AN EX-COP MUST FIND A CRAZED KILLER . . . BEFORE THE COPS CATCH UP WITH HIM!

THE DEATH OF THE DETECTIVE

MARK SMITH

This is a novel about murder, corruption, defilement and violence—every seamy reality you have ever read about in the daily papers . . .

The Detective is an ex-cop who left the force because he was too honest. Now, he must find an escaped mental patient with a terrible grudge who will kill anyone in his way. Here are two human beings, stalking each other in the American hell called Chicago, the city where people suffer and bleed; love and die. One is the pursuer, one the pursued; one the murderer, one the avenger; one the madman, one the detective.

"A COMPLETE SUCCESS . . . ABSOLUTELY WORTH READING . . ."   *The New York Times Book Review*

AVON 58016 $3.50

Available wherever paperbacks are sold, or directly from the publisher. Include 50¢ per copy for mailing; allow 6-8 weeks for delivery. Avon Books, Mail Order Dept., 224 West 57th Street, New York, N.Y. 10019.   DDet 4-82

Edgar Award-winning author
Tony Hillerman

"Hillerman is first-rate . . . one of the best new American voices . . . fresh, original and highly suspenseful . . ." *Los Angeles Times*

PEOPLE OF DARKNESS   57778 $2.25

The ancient culture of the Navajo Indian is mixed with contemporary suspense, as Sergeant Jim Chee stumbles onto a chain of superstition and deliberate deaths 30 years long. "Truly chilling . . . Top work from a top talent." *Kirus Reviews*

THE FLY ON THE WALL   44156 $1.95

John Cotton is a fly on the wall—the perfect reporter, seeing it all, hearing it all, but never being noticed . . . until he's caught in a nasty political cover-up while searching for a colleague's murderer. "Not merely thrilling but also a provocative ethical conundrum . . . stunning." *The New Yorker*

THE BLESSING WAY   39941 $1.75

Anthropologist Bergen McKee's summer expedition to a Navajo reservation to study tales of witchcraft turns into a grisly quest when a body is found on a desolate mesa . . . "Supense enough for anyone." *Saturday Review*

THE LISTENING WOMAN   53686 $2.25

The old Navajo died while the Listening Woman sprinkled yellow pollen over him. But Lt. Joe Leaphorn knows that an ancestral secret is still alive and dangerous. "Plenty of good, action-packed detective work . . . full of Indian lore and the feeling of the desert . . ." *The New York Times*

DANCE HALL OF THE DEAD   49494 $1.75

In this Edgar Award-winning "Best Mystery Novel of the Year," Joe Leaphorn tracks a suspected killer through the beautiful and savage American Southwest. "Much action and unusual dangers." *San Francisco Examiner-Chronicle*

Available wherever paperbacks are sold, or directly from the publisher. Include 50¢ per copy for postage and handling: allow 6-8 weeks for delivery. Avon Books, Mail Order Dept., 224 West 57h. St., N.Y., N.Y. 10019.

AVON Paperbacks   Hillerman 12-81